## CONTENT WARNING

This novel contains discussions about suicide and descriptions of graphic violence, psychiatric treatment, and self-harm that may be triggering to some readers.

# DEDICATION

I'd like to dedicate this novel to two important Geminis in my life. This novel, being the first I will publish, is especially important to me considering I've wanted to be a novelist since childhood. I undertook writing my first novel in sixth grade, and I have a huge stack of unfinished manuscripts. Life, as we all know, gets in the way of our dreams. My mother was the first to encourage me to write. She instilled in me the belief that I could be a writer. And so, this book is dedicated to her memory, to the boundless love she gave, and the lessons she taught. Miss you, Mom.

♦

I also dedicate it to Fran Friel, a Gemini like my mother, who is an amazing creative and old soul who has influenced me in ways she will never know. Her friendship, the intellectual discussions, the tools she introduced me to, and just the general light of her being have inspired me to finally follow through on that childhood dream. Thank you, Fran.

# INTRODUCTION

Briefly, I'd like to say a little something about mental illness. I use it in this book as a vehicle to carry the story, but I've attempted to do so with great respect toward those who deal with it in real life. It is not my intention to make light of it.

Mental illness can and does destroy lives. If you feel that you're ill, I encourage you to seek help.

I've included links to a few excellent organizations at the end of the book.

Sincerely, Angel…

◆

What is the Wyrdwood Project?
Learn more at WyrdwoodAngel.com/about/

# Stalking the Moon

## by Angel Leigh McCoy

**"Surrealism had a great effect on me because then I realized that the imagery in my mind wasn't insanity. Surrealism to me is reality."**

—John Lennon—

# CHAPTER 1

Driving my yellow Fiesta, singing at the top of my lungs with Pink, I cut through the city then turned off the highway onto the rural roads that would take me back to my workplace—the Vince Malum Residential Living Center, home of Peoria's non-violent socio- and psychopaths.

Once a week, I had an appointment with my psychiatrist—Dr. Richard Reuter. Richard was my head shrinker. I'd been seeing him regularly for twenty years. At times, it felt like we'd grown up together, although the age difference (more than fifteen years) made that a silly fantasy.

Richard kept an office in the Center's main building, where my mom, Gisèle Rose, had been a resident for more than twenty-five years. Mental illness was the Rose legacy. Being her daughter, I hadn't fallen far from the tree. In Mom's absence, I'd been raised by my grandfather, Abraham "Abram" Rose.

Along the field-lined road, the Center appeared in the

distance. The roof on the original Victorian stone house and the top two floors of the twin residential wings peeked over the treetops. A German immigrant named Vince Malum had built it for his schizophrenic wife in 1927 and named it the Morning Glory Institution, "a home for people in discord with the world."

Before long, there were more patients than rooms, so Malum built an addition at the back of the main house. Everyone called it the Tower. The patients lived in the Tower—men in the west wing, women in the east—and the doctors, such as Richard, had their offices in the main house. When Malum died, his grandchildren renamed the place in his honor.

I guided the car down the paved drive between the apple, cherry, and pear trees in Malum's Orchard. At harvest-time each year, when the trees were heavy with fruit, people came from all over and were free to pick as much as they wanted, so long as they gave ten percent of their harvest to the Center. The people got free fruit, and the Center got free pickers. Sometimes, whole families descended upon the orchard. They looked happy and normal with their ladders and baskets.

Abram and I had climbed up into those trees every summer, back when we were still trying to look happy and normal, back before I learned that my mother was locked away inside an institution. I remembered looking over at the Center's dark windows, glimpsing movement, and wondering who was inside. Sometimes a pane of glass would catch a ray of sunlight and reflect it with a wink. It chilled me even on the warmest summer days.

The main gate was an enormous iron monstrosity. People said Malum shipped it over from Germany and that it had once been the gate on a concentration camp, although no one had ever proved that.

The fence around the Center's land was not designed to keep anyone out—or even in. It was a mental blockade, intended primarily to discourage restless patients from wandering. An able-bodied patient determined to run away could scale the fence with relative ease. The Center relied instead on the vast acres of farmland surrounding it to keep escapees from succeeding, and it was rare that they had to send out search parties. Out there in the middle of nowhere, there wasn't much traffic and nowhere to go but into the corn fields.

I pulled up to the security box and swiped my employee badge across it. The gate opened, and I drove through the moment it was wide enough.

The main house had climbing ivy, gables, manicured shrubs, and a circular drive. It was a wannabe English manor. Some days, I appreciated the sight of it. Others, it repulsed me. As I approached, I found my feeling sentimental about the old place. It was, after all, my second home.

The staff entrance was on the women's wing, near the

employee parking lot. Out of habit, I entered there. Nurses, orderlies, and doctors all greeted me as I made my way to Richard's office.

Richard was seated at his desk. "Hey, Vivi. Come on in." He rebuttoned the collar of his white, custom-fitted dress shirt.

"Howdy." I shut the door behind me and went to the leather couch. It was overstuffed with a high back and deep seat. I felt small on it, but that was part of Richard's evil plot. Plus, it would have been impossible to fall off it while under hypnosis. It cradled me.

"What part of my psyche are we going to poke today?"

Richard folded his arms on the desk, a pen flapping in one hand as he looked me over. "I want to revisit your early days," he said. "I've been going through the transcripts of our sessions, compiling them, and there are a couple things I'd like to revisit."

"Let's get to it then."

The first time I met Richard, back in *the early days,* he was finishing his last year as a graduate student in the Psychology Department at the University of Illinois. He was in Peoria doing an internship at the counseling center, and Abram had dragged me there to get my head fixed—at the junior high principal's request.

Back then, Richard had a long ponytail and was every teenage girl's dream of the older college boy. I was only thirteen, and he was taller than me, though that changed when I had my growth spurt a few years later.

Thirteen-year-old Me had gone into his office with a chip on my shoulder, hating Abram, hating my illness, and hating Dr. Richard Reuter before I'd even met him.

He'd appeared in the waiting room and asked, "Viviane? Right? Would you come with me?"

"I don't got a choice."

Abram hissed, "Hey," at me, and said "Be nice."

"Yeah, sure."

I walked into the office and went straight to a chair, flopped there, and crossed my arms on my chest. The first thing I noticed that interested me was the plate of cookies on the coffee table. They were chocolate chip and appeared homemade. I pretended not to see them. I didn't want him to think I was going to stay all that long, and besides, my stomach didn't feel too good.

Richard sat in the chair opposite me and watched me for a full minute. Finally, he asked, "How old are you?"

"Fifteen." It was a bold-faced lie.

"I know you're lying."

I asked, "How old are you?"

"Twenty-nine."

"Are you a fag?" I said with vehemence, calculating his possible reactions.

He didn't even flinch. "Viviane, do you know why your grandfather brought you here?"

"Because he's a sociopath afraid of being noticed. I

draw attention to him, and he wants me to stop."

He smiled at that, and for the first time, but not the last, I thought how handsome he was.

In that first session, he didn't hypnotize me, though later, it became a regular part of our therapy sessions. Richard felt it was the best way to track down the source of my hallucinations. He would take me back to the time before my first hallucination, and we'd go over the events of a day or two in each session, gradually working forward through my memories. It was my own personal reality-TV show.

Twenty years later, I was thirty-three, and our regressions were catching up to the conscious flow of time. In the hypnosis sessions, he recorded my soul in bits and pieces, saved forever as audio recordings, transcribed to digital documents, and printed out on paper. He kept the files in his cabinets.

I'd often wondered what would happen when we finally caught up to the present moment. Maybe I'd die. Maybe he'd die. Maybe the entire world would end as the Ouroboros swallowed its own tail.

"All right." Richard got up from his desk. "I'm ready, if you are." He sat in the chair opposite me and leaned forward to turn on the metronome.

I said, "Take me to a happy day."

"You know the drill. Close your eyes, relax, and remember."

Not every tick and tock of the metronome sounded the

same. The differences were subtle, but they were there if I listened for them. It was a song without rhyme or reason.

It started small and distant: *tick.*

The cuckoo clock on the wall at Abram's house had to be wound. I loved pulling the chains that raised the heavy, metal pine cones. *Tock.* It had been my job, every morning, when I was a kid. My body rocked to the beat: *tick tock.* Time ebbed, and space flowed. My spine relaxed. *Tick.* Gravity released me. *Tock.* The metronome sang its song in my belly. *Tick tock.* I was energy, and I radiated.

"We're going to continue our journey back in time," Richard said. The waves of his voice rippled through me, and the present faded into the background.

I followed the metronome down into a trance. We had a signal. I raised a finger to indicate that I was ready to begin.

"Go back," Richard suggested, "to the moment when you first met Simon, when you were thirteen."

The scene formed around me, inside me, throughout me.

"Describe it to me."

*I'm home, and I'm taking a shower. There's blood running down my leg. It's swirling in the water and spinning down the drain. I know what it is. Lettie's had hers since last year, and she took me to buy the stuff I'd need. I'm really glad I didn't have to do that with my grandpa.*

*Lettie and me, we read the little instruction book that*

*came in the box and made fun of the pictures. She warned me how it would be, the cramps and mess, but it's worse when it's actually happening. It's scary and weird. I keep thinking that my blood is supposed to stay in my body.*

*So, I'm standing there in the shower, watching my blood drain away, and I'm trying not to cry, wondering if I'm going to die, and that's when I hear a man. He sounds like James Bond. "You're probably not going to die."*

*I scream and cover my private parts with my hands, but no one's there.*

*The voice says, "What I mean is, you are going to be just fine." But nobody's there. I'm freaking out. I jump out of the shower and run through the house. I'm screaming.*

*The voice is following me. "Oh, lass, it's okay."*

*I streak into the kitchen, and my grandpa is there, trying to calm me down.*

*I'm crying, naked and wet, shaking all over, blood staining my leg, and Grandpa thinks I'm upset because of my period, but that isn't it. It's the man talking to me right next to my ear, when there's nobody there.*

*He says his name is Simon.*

The metronome sang. *Tick. Tock.*

"When you return to your waking state," Richard said, "you'll remember all the events you described to me, clearly and in detail."

*Tick.*

"Feel the couch supporting you. It's solid and real. Feel

the air as it passes through your nostrils. You're here with me, now, in the present." *Tock.*

I opened my eyes and looked across at Richard's familiar face.

He turned off the metronome. "How do you feel?"

I answered with a nod. When I wake up and remember everything even more clearly than before, I'm reminded of my own life again, as if I've been looking through an album of old pictures.

"Are you hungry? Want to grab dinner?"

"Not tonight. I want to spend some time with Colin before I go see Mom. Rain check?"

"Yeah, some other time." Richard got up and went to his desk. "How's Colin doing?"

"Best fiancé ever."

"Great. See you next week."

I'd been dismissed.

◆

After my appointment, I went straight back home to our one-story, two-bedroom, three-mortgage house and found my grandfather cooking lunch in the kitchen.

"Want some eggs?" Dressed in jeans and a mustard-stained Chicago Cubs t-shirt, Abram loomed over the stove.

"Love some."

"Did you take your medicine?"

I sighed. "Jesus. Here we go again. Not yet. I'll take them with lunch."

"Good." Abram waved his hand at the coffee pot. "There's coffee." He served up the eggs. "So how's that crazy young man of yours?"

"Fantastic in bed."

Abram grunted. "It only gets worse from here, you know."

"Do we have to have this conversation again? It's as outdated as your flat-top. I love Colin, and that's the end of it."

Abram set a plate of eggs in front of me. "Okay. How was your session with Richard?"

"Fine." I dashed hot sauce onto my eggs. And that was the extent of the conversation. Most of them were some variation on that theme, the questions and answers in different orders. By then, Abram and I weren't exactly close.

◆◆◆

# CHAPTER 2

Several hours later, I got a call from Colin's doctor, Bella Rosenblum, asking me to come back to the Center. An orderly had found Colin out on the roof, a dangerous place for a man suffering from delusions and hallucinations. He'd been confined to his room and put on suicide watch.

I climbed to the Center's roof, four stories up, and looked out at the manicured lawn and down at the concrete patio. An eager wind blew from the northwest, sweeping in off the Illinois plains and pushing cumulus clouds ahead of it. It whipped my loose hair into a frenzied halo and dried my tears.

I wanted to understand—to see what he'd seen when he'd been standing there.

Two years earlier, I'd met Colin at the Center. We were in the garden, me with my mother and a book, and Colin with his ghosts. He'd been diagnosed with retrograde amnesia. He had forgotten his name and his history—everything from before he woke up in the hospital.

Our relationship started when my bookmark went

dancing across the lawn on a gust of wind, and Colin retrieved it for me. We started talking, and that led to walks, then picnics, and eventually we kissed beneath an old oak. We built dreams and plans around a future when his memories would return, when we could get married and have children.

As time had progressed, Colin's past remained elusive, haunting him. He presented with hallucinations and delusions that led the Center's doctors to believe he'd been ill even before the event that had caused his amnesia.

The grounds of Vince Malum Residential Living Center surrounded me on all sides. From my vantage point on the roof, it seemed so sane—the lush grass, the old oaks, and the paths with their strategically placed benches. In the distance, the employee parking lot was a patchwork of columns and rows, cars tidily arranged.

Inside the building, patients were tidily arranged as well, in rooms designed to suit their needs. Nurses and doctors went about their duties, distributing meds and accompanying patients to their sessions. *Tick. Tock.* By the clock, security guards patrolled the building on choreographed paths, their steps metered, their dialogue repetitive. This patina of order hid an inner world of chaos where no one and no thing was either predictable or reliable.

I turned away from the edge.

Doc Bella stood a few feet away. She'd been watching me. The wind disturbed her white coat, patterned skirt, and the short auburn curls heavily salted with gray. The staff called her Grandma Bella behind her back. She was in her seventies and still as sharp as a syringe.

"For a minute there," Bella said, "I thought *you* might jump."

I met her steady gaze. "And you weren't going to stop me?"

Bella smiled a psychiatrist's smile, non-committal. "Of course, you know that if you ever want to talk, I'm available for you."

My shoes crunched in the rooftop gravel as I crossed the distance between us.

"Thanks, Doc, but I'm fine. I just wanted to see—"

"—what might have been?" she finished for me.

"—how dangerous it really is up here."

"Colin has informed me, in no uncertain terms, that he's going to marry you."

I cringed inside. "Look—"

Bella interrupted me. "I'm not here to judge you. That's not my job. However. I feel it *is* my responsibility to give you fair warning." Her gaze was no-nonsense, as firm as that of a mother superior. "You're getting involved with a man who has no memory of his past. He could be anyone. I'm telling you this so you'll guard your heart. Save a bit back for your own good. When he remembers, you may not care for that person very much."

I nodded and said, "Okay," though she may as well

have been asking a rose to bloom only halfway.

Bella clasped her hands on her stomach and looked out at the scenery. "In order for him to be with you—once his memories return—he'll have to sacrifice that other life."

I had thought about that. Many times. What if his previous life had been beautiful? What if he had children? A wife who loved him? If so, I was the other woman and—even I had to admit—probably not worth the sacrifice.

I asked, "How is he?"

"That's what I came to tell you." Bella hooked her arm through mine and guided me toward the roof exit. "We've got him settled in bed. He says he *wasn't* trying to kill himself."

"What was he doing?"

"Trying to fly."

"Oh. Gee. That's a relief."

Bella chuckled. "A mixed blessing, yes."

When we reached the heavy security door, I tugged it open and held it for her. An emergency exit sign illuminated the concrete stairwell.

"Did you sedate him?"

"No."

"Restrain him?"

"For now."

As I started to follow Bella across the threshold, something made me look back over my shoulder and scan the roof, searching. We were on the roof of a four-story building, but it felt like we were being watched. It was the first of many such feelings, and it made my skin crawl. I rubbed the back of my neck and hurried to stay on Bella's heels.

When the door shut behind me, it cut off all daylight. Shadows swelled up from the floor and dropped down from the ceiling. One hand clutching the metal railing, I put the other in my pocket and found my straight pin. I placed the pad of my index finger against the point and pressed. The pin slid easily in. Pain helped me keep the panic at bay.

My footsteps echoed in counterpoint to Bella's. It took me a full flight of stairs to get up the nerve to ask my next question, afraid of the answer. "Do we have to cancel our plans?" For months, I'd been looking forward to a weekend in the countryside with Colin. I'd arranged a pass for him, contingent upon his good behavior.

"That won't be necessary," replied Bella. "We could all use some time away. Myself included. Unless something else happens between now and then, your trip is still approved."

"Even after…"

"You're his grounding wire, Viviane. What he did today was troublesome, but I think time alone with you will do him good. I trust you to watch out for him."

I released the breath I'd been holding.

"However," Bella said, "I want you to talk to him. Convince him he can't leap off buildings."

I admitted, "Sometimes it's hard to keep his feet on the

ground."

"Truer words were never spoken, my dear."

◆

I made my way through the Center to the Men's Wing and paused just outside Colin's room. My back against the wall there, I closed my eyes to focus on the breath going in and out of my body, deepening my inhalations and lengthening my exhalations. Gradually, the worried voices in my head quieted, and my body relaxed.

After I knocked, an orderly opened Colin's door. "Hey-dee ho, Viv."

"Hi there, Jimmy."

Jimmy had been a cannibal in a past life. He'd confided this strange secret to me on another evening when we were standing guard together over Colin. It had started with an innocent question for the sake of conversation.

"Jimmy, what made you decide to go into healthcare?"

The large man considered the question and his response, and finally, he said, "I was a cannibal in a past life. I have to make up for it in this one, by helping more people than I ate."

"I see."

"It's karmic balance, y'know? I was bad. Now, I try to be extra good so I can get a better life next time, maybe wealth or good looks. Y'know?"

I wanted to laugh, but he wasn't joking. "What makes you think you were a cannibal?"

Jimmy leaned toward me and lowered his voice. "I know because I remember it sometimes, at night, right before I fall asleep. I have flashes where I'm eating someone. It's a nightmare, except I'm awake." He paused, then whispered, "Sometimes, I can even taste it."

That was the thing about being public with your mental illness. People told you things they would never mention in polite society, assuming you wouldn't be freaked out by it.

After a brief, uncomfortable silence, Jimmy added, "You probably think that's crazy."

I shrugged. "Because you believe you were a cannibal in a past life? I've heard crazier. Truth is, I've never met anyone who was completely sane. Have you?"

He clapped me on the shoulder and gave a hardy, "No, ma'am, I sure have not."

Ever since that conversation, Jimmy had given me special consideration, as if we'd bonded over his secret.

I entered Colin's room. "You can take a break if you want, Jimmy. I'll stay with him for a while."

Jimmy made to leave. "I could use a piss and some coffee. After that, I'll wait outside for you. Just yell if you need me."

"Thanks."

I waited for the door to shut behind him, then pulled a

chair across the room. I placed it near the head of the bed and perched on the edge of it. "Hey, cutie. You awake?"

Colin lay on his back with his wrists buckled to the rails. A thick strap crossed his chest. It wasn't the first time I'd seen him restrained, but it never stopped bothering me. I undid the chest strap.

Colin resembled a child. His light reddish-brown hair had a wild, cow-licked quality, his tight curls a chaotic dance, and his face had the long-lashed, boyish features that would keep him handsome throughout his life, but there was more. He had innocence about him, as if he were seeing everything for the first time. That hadn't diminished over the years, though his delusions and hallucinations added a sense of whimsy.

Without opening his eyes or otherwise moving, Colin said, "I have to talk to you." His voice dropped so low that I had to lean forward to hear. "I saw her."

I unbuckled the nearest arm strap. "You saw who?"

"The hag. And I remember what she is."

"I don't understand."

"She's a scout—a tracking dog." Paranoia came with the territory of Colin's mental illness, but it unnerved me when he talked like that.

"Honey, why were you on the roof?"

"That's what I'm trying to tell you." He opened his eyes and looked at me. "She's looking for me. That's why I went to the roof. She nests there."

"Promise me you'll stay off the roof, okay? It's dangerous."

"Not for me," he said, so calmly, as if he were saying he had made a delicious ham and cheese omelet.

I almost believed him, but then he broke the spell.

"I can fly."

His confession triggered an explosion in my emotions—a dirty bomb at my core. It infected all of me.

"Don't say that!"

"It's true."

Through gritted teeth, I seethed at him. "It isn't true." I put my face in my hands and the image of him lying dead on the patio appeared in my brain. "Look. You can't fly. Okay? No one can fly. I need you to get better, Colin. I need you to be okay. Flying is not okay. Do you understand that?"

"But…"

"No buts!"

Lunacy ebbed and flowed. That was how it worked—the human condition. I'd never met anyone immune to those currents. Some people just worked harder than others to hide it, especially from themselves. So-called "stable" people pushed their emotions down deep. They had their methods—just as I did—for maintaining a façade of normalcy, but even the ones most in denial couldn't fully insulate themselves from the suspicion that they didn't quite fit the so-called norm.

Then there were those who gave up the fight for sanity. Keeping the tide at bay could be exhausting. When you had no strength left, it was far too easy to go with the flow. I knew this from experience. I called it "stalking the moon."

I found my pin and pricked my finger, then my thumb. I breathed. Finally, I said, "Honey, no matter what, you don't *have* to fly away."

"I might have to, to keep you safe."

"I can take care of myself."

"There's a chance that might be true."

I sighed. "Thanks for the vote of confidence."

# CHAPTER 3

By the time I left Colin's room, it was 8:45 p.m., and I was fifteen minutes late.

I threaded my way through the Center's halls to the Women's Wing. The atmosphere there differed from the Men's Wing. Security was tighter on the testosterone side. Men had a predictable tendency to express themselves through violence toward others. Women relied more on screaming, tears, and self-mutilation.

The nurses' station was a bubble of reinforced glass at the edge of an open recreation area. I waved to the worn-out, middle-aged nurse stationed there and received the same in return. Linda had been a fixture at the Center longer than I had. In her mid-fifties, she had no children, no husband, and only photos of her cats on her desk. Linda pushed a button and spoke into a microphone. Her voice came, tinny, out of speakers tucked high in the room's corners. "Good evening, Viviane."

I waved again but didn't pause. The recreation room was empty that late in the evening—lock-down was at 9:00. Lights-out came at 9:30. *Tick tock.*

The rec room had olive-colored, vinyl couches and armchairs facing a flat-screen television anchored high on the wall. Several round tables provided places to play games or draw pictures. One held a 1000-piece puzzle in progress. A picture of kittens in a flower garden graced the box. Years flowed onward, but nothing about the Center ever changed.

I headed down the hallway past a series of bedrooms. I used to glance right and left as I walked down the hall, peeking through open doors. Over the years, I'd seen enough private moments of despair, degradation, and self-indulgence, had met enough eyes staring back at me that I no longer looked. None of what I saw in those rooms surprised me anymore. After fifteen years of visiting and working at the Center, I'd seen almost everything—almost.

Voices called to me from the rooms or talked about me as I passed.

"Hey, Viviane."

"Hi, Viv."

"It's Gisèle's daughter."

"She's here again."

"Viviane's here."

I knew every patient on that floor by name and temperament. They suffered from a range of maladies—severe depression, bipolar disorder, PTSD, schizophrenia, phobias, and any number of other mental and mood conditions—so extreme they had either given up on blending into society or their loved ones had given up on them.

Vince Malum Residential Living Center rarely took the one-night or even the one-week stands. It housed patients for months, years, or even the rest of their lives. Sometimes, someone got well enough to reintegrate into the world, but it was rare. Most patients only left when they transferred to a different facility or went to live at home with relatives. Or they died.

My mom, Gisèle, stood behind the chair at the dressing table, brush in hand. She was ghostly in her white nightgown with billowy sleeves and eyelet lace, her face an expressionless blank, eyes gone distant. She was still beautiful, though her body had begun to soften and wrinkles had invaded the landscape around her eyes and mouth. She was the kind of woman who would always be lovely, classy, and graceful—no matter what.

She was brushing the hair of an imaginary child, a child who had long since grown up.

I took my seat in front of her, facing the dressing table, and watched her in the mirror. Her eyes were midnight blue, while mine were more like scratchy blue-gray wool. She had thick golden hair streaked with silver. I'd never grown out of my baby hair. Mine was thinner, curlier, had less gold and more mouse.

"Sorry I'm late, Mom." I felt safe there, in her sanctum—safer than anywhere else—and it was pleasant to be with her.

She pressed her belly against my shoulder—the most pleasant physical contact she and I ever shared—and brushed my hair as if it had been there all along, not missing a stroke.

Throughout most of my childhood, I'd believed my mom was dead. It wasn't until I turned eighteen, when a letter came from a law firm, that I realized the truth. In the time it took me to read the letter, my world had exploded. I learned that my mom wasn't dead and that my grandfather had been lying to me all those years. The news had hit me hard. I threw away all the acceptance letters I'd received from colleges and took a job at the Center in order to be near her, get to know her, and take care of her. Fifteen years later, I was still working at the Center and still visiting my mom five out of seven nights.

My mom spoke suddenly. "Kypris was young then—young and beautiful." My mother was a storyteller. Her stories were part and parcel of her delusion. Sometimes, they spilled from her verbally. Sometimes, she wrote them in her journals. The stories always involved a witch named Kypris and an elven prince named Chance.

Mom said, "Kypris had already been out of her head for a long time, but she'd only just understood what it meant. She took far too many risks, because she believed she had nothing to lose. And yet, it was her husband, Chance, who saved her life." She kept brushing, pulling the hair back from my temples and forehead, pausing only to work carefully through any knots she found. Her gaze remained fixed on a point perpendicular to my own reality.

"Winter will be here soon." Mom leaned over and set the brush on the mirrored dressing table.

"It's almost spring, Mom." I stood and went to the bed.

"When the cold comes, it gets in your bones and your brain. It eats you from the inside out."

"You'll be warm in your room."

Mom came to stand beside me. "When you go, take me with you in your heart."

"You're always in my heart." We had this kind of strange conversation from time to time. Though Richard, our shared psychiatrist, assured me that Mom was talking to an imaginary friend, I pretended we were actually connecting, and sometimes it seemed we were.

I pulled back the covers on the bed, and Mom crawled in and settled on her side. I leaned over to kiss her on the cheek, then drew the blankets up. "Good night. Sleep well."

Mom said, "And when you awake, I'll be near." She closed her eyes.

"I love you." I folded over the top edge of the blanket and smoothed it, then reached to switch off the bedside lamp.

Mom's hand wrapped around my wrist, tightly enough to startle me, and when she spoke, her voice hissed. Through clenched teeth, she said, "Watch out for the hag.

Do not drop your guard." Her eyes—now open and trained on me—reflected the glow of the night-light.

"You're hurting me." I pried at her fingers.

Her hand dropped to the bed. Relaxing back onto the pillow, she closed her eyes again.

I stood there, rubbing my arm until Nurse Linda stuck her head in to remind me it was time for lights-out.

"You okay?" Linda asked when she saw my face.

"Yeah," I replied. "It's just been a long day." And it was about to get longer. I headed for the Center's laundry facilities, where I worked the graveyard shift.

As I rounded the corner to the employee locker room, I heard a familiar voice say, "Thirteen."

Ajani Jones was seated on the bench, bent in half to untie his shoes. With his head down, the stealthy patch of smooth, dark skin peeked through at his crown.

"Thirteen years I been workin' this God-forsaken job."

I grabbed a clean uniform off the shelf. We washed, sterilized, and bagged them along with everything else. "You sure it's only been thirteen *years*?" I asked. "Feels closer to thirteen *lifetimes.* "

"Amen to that, sister," Ajani replied. He was speaking to the other woman in the room, a stranger to me. She had obviously worked the shift before ours. Ajani said, "I'd have quit long ago if I didn't have six kids eatin' me out of house and home."

*"Diós mio!"* The woman gave Ajani an exaggerated

look of surprise.

"I don't think God had a hand in it," I said. "It was definitely the Devil made him do it." My fingers knew the movements to open my locker's padlock, having performed them a million times.

Julio came into the locker room, his pace steady, and went straight to his locker. He was compact, only a little taller than me, with short dark hair, impressive eyebrows, and a smile that could light up a room—when he chose to share it.

Ajani told us, "This is Lucinda." He stood and removed his dress shirt, revealing a white tank top, muscled chest, and thick upper arms.

I offered Lucinda my hand. "Nice to meet you."

She accepted the handshake. "Thanks, Miss Rose."

"Call me Viviane. We don't do formality on the graveyard shift."

Ajani said, "Miss Viviane is the only white woman at the laundry, but don't let that fool you. She's the best damned floor supervisor we got."

I wagged a warning finger at him. "You better watch that racist shit. Around here, we're all just stains."

"True dat." Ajani laughed and nodded wisely. He took off his jeans and stood there in his boxers, turning his back to us.

"That's Julio," I told Lucinda. They gave each other a little wave.

I changed out of my street clothes. It was far too hot in the laundry to wear more than running shorts and a tank top under our uniforms, and some people wore less. I felt vulnerable without the added cloth between me and the laundry scrubs. It wasn't a question of modesty. Modesty wasn't necessary in the laundry—we all sweated together. No, it was about having an extra layer of protection against the three Ps, even if it was just psychological armor.

Scarlett "Lettie" Sorvino rushed into the break room, boobs bouncing and girly heels clattering on the concrete. She skidded to a halt in front of a locker, grabbed the waistband of her skirt, and shoved it down to her ankles revealing spandex bike shorts snugged tight to a curvaceous behind.

I said, "Cutting it close, aren't you, Lettie?"

"Sorry—had to break up with Nina tonight." She glanced at the clock as she kicked off the skirt and her shoes. Lettie had the kind of looks that could go in any direction, from slutty to Catholic schoolgirl, from dangerous to dazzling, and back again. She was a chameleon, but she called herself a mutt, and her African-Italian mix of genes showed in the color of her skin and hair, the prominence of her nose. I had always thought she was at her most beautiful without make-up, though she used quite a lot most of the time—even at the laundry.

"You broke up with Nina?"

"It was overdue. I'm fine."

I dropped it. "Ajani, you're on washers. Lettie, you're sorting. Julio's on dryers."

Lettie slid her jaw to one side and rolled her eyes. "I s'pose it's my turn." Nobody wanted to sort. That was where you ran into the three Ps.

Jaxon said, "Guess that leaves me ironing and folding?" Neither tall nor short, his body had a powerful, substantial mass. His trimmed beard and mustache joined sideburns and melded into a cap of hair, all the color of Turkish coffee.

"Yeah, Jax. You're the caboose tonight." I clapped my hands. "Time to go, people. This train is leavin' the station." *Tick. Tock.* The team spread out across the laundry facility, and we took over for the previous shift.

"Have a good shift," Lucinda called as we filed out.

◆

I still had three hours to go before we were done for the night and, I was steamy with sweat. After fifteen years on the job, I was used to it, but that didn't make it any less unpleasant. When you worked in the Center's laundry, you wore *sangfroid* as a shield. You had to, or you'd never make it. The laundry was no picnic. Far too often, you'd pull a sheet out of a bag and find one of the three Ps: piss, poop, or puke. It took time to get used to that. Whenever it happened to new employees, some gagged, some recoiled, and some quit—some on the first day, some a week or two into it. Those of us who stuck it out—who survived the heat, humidity, noise, mind-bending boredom, and constant contact with bio hazmat—were badass and proud of it.

Everything about the laundry dampened your senses, from the earplugs to the latex gloves. The washers went through their cycles, firing up, spinning down, and rattling away. The gargantuan laundry machines—three washers and three dryers—created a constant cacophony. Twenty-four hours a day—*boom, boom, boom*—the machines roared. Shifts came and went. *Tick. Tock.* The faces changed, but the machines never stopped because the three Ps never stopped.

Someone with a morbid sense of poetry once scratched a saying into the paint on one of the dryers. It became the laundry's motto: "Today, you're pain. Tomorrow, a stain."

I could tell by the tone of a washer's hum that it needed repairing, and I could hear a solid object knocking about before anyone else. It was a gift. The laundry facility was the one place where I was in control—of my world and of my mind. I'd worked my way up through the ranks to manager, and I ran a tight team.

My cell phone vibrated in my pocket.

*U coming 2 see me?* A text message from my fiancé Colin.

I typed: *Maybe.*

*Tease.*

I went back to inventorying supplies with a lighter step. As I counted, Jaxon Bellonescu peeled away from the ironing machine and crossed toward me. Even in a baby-blue laundry smock and pants, he could have been a desert nomad, skin tanned by a harsh sun, mouth hardened by a harsh life. "That load's done." he said. "You want me to start the next one?" His Turkish accent rolled the words roundly in his mouth.

"Yeah." I checked off another load on the big board. That made ten for the night. Right on schedule for another Productivity Award.

A scream sounded above the din.

All heads turned to Lettie as she stumbled back from the table where she'd been prepping dirty laundry for the washers.

"Kill it!" she cried. "Kill it!"

Everyone in the room dropped what they were doing and headed toward her, including me. She started cursing a blue streak, and as I got closer, I saw why. A snake lay on top of the pile of sheets, aprons, and towels. Not a big one, but a snake nevertheless.

"Somebody kill it!" Lettie shouted again, cringing away so she didn't have to look at it, then peeking, afraid to turn her back on it.

Julio M.F. Quinones worked the dryers. M.F. stood for Marcos Fernandez, despite what he told everyone. He walked right up to the snake and dropped a plastic storage bowl over it, relaxed as you please. A wave of relief rippled around the room.

"It's only a garden snake. You don't kill them," Julio said. "They work hard for you. Hand me that clipboard over there."

I stepped up, nabbing the empty clipboard and handing it to him.

Julio slid the board under the bowl with surprising gentleness. He picked the whole package up and carried it to the exit, where he paused. "Señorita Rose," Julio shouted, "Can I grab a smoke while I'm out there?"

The clock told me he was once again ignoring the 15-30-15 break schedule, but I nodded my approval anyway. How could I not, after that heroic display.

Earlier that night, Julio'd had us in stitches, telling us how his *gringa* girlfriend had dumped him to join a community of vegan hippies. He said it was his own fault. He should have stuck with Latinas as his mother had advised. "Latinas don't go vegan," he'd said, "and they don't leave a boyfriend—especially an employed one—to join a tits-free commune." Then, he'd spat into one of the garbage cans and walked away. That was how he was.

Maybe I sensed that his humor hid very real pain at the break-up. Maybe the thought of a bummed smoke called to me. Whatever the reason, I gave him a few minutes to release the snake outside, then followed after him.

As soon as the laundry's fire door closed behind me, the noise level dropped significantly, and I pulled the earplugs from my ears. I walked down the concrete-block corridor. No windows. No nothing. Cool air dried my sweat and left a pleasant chill on my skin. My footsteps echoed in the emptiness. I hit the door to the back stairwell with one smooth, practiced move. The stairwell was the best place to smoke. No one ever came down that way, so the likelihood of getting caught was slim.

"Hey, Julio," I said. "It's me. Gimme a…"

I froze in place.

Julio was sliding slowly down the wall. His arms twitched, hands like spiders riding their webs. Rolling upward, the whites of his eyeballs glowed in the fluorescent lighting, and his pupils eclipsed his brown irises. His mouth gaped, revealing a convulsing tongue and the entrance to his cavernous throat.

The door slammed shut behind me, breaking me out of my stunned inaction. I ran to him.

"Julio!" I cried, shaking his shoulder. He didn't respond—just crumpled to the floor and slumped to one side. "Julio!" I pulled out my cell phone and dialed the Center's security desk. Nothing. No bars. I stumbled up the stairs until I got a signal, then dialed again.

Esteban, the night watchman, answered.

"I need a doctor or an ambulance. Julio's having some kind of seizure, in the back stairwell, basement level. This is Viviane Rose. Please, hurry."

"I'll get—" Our connection broke as I raced back down the stairs.

Julio wasn't breathing. He had no pulse. What was next? Why hadn't I taken that CPR refresher last year? Whatever memories I had of the required training from years ago jumbled in my head.

I grabbed him by the shoulders of his smock, pulled him down the stairs toward the concrete landing. He was heavy, and as soon as gravity overtook him, it nearly dragged me down with him.

My version of cardiopulmonary resuscitation was inelegant at best, but I was determined to keep Julio alive. The air was going in and coming back out, but his heart had stopped. As the minutes passed and my back began to ache, I grew less confident that I'd have the strength to see it through.

Finally, Nurse Andrea, the overnight nurse from the women's wing, arrived.

"What happened?"

"I don't know," I told her between chest pumps. "There was…a snake. He was…taking it out. Went on break…and I was…looking for him…when I found him…he was having…some kind of fit…maybe the snake bit him…don't know."

Andrea checked his pulse. "I'll take over the heart massage. You breathe for him. I'll tell you when."

"Okay." Tears crawled up into my nose and sinuses. I sniffled. I couldn't afford to lose my shit. I *had* to keep it together. I felt for the straight pin I kept in my pocket. It was my anchor, my lifeline to sanity. I pushed it through my clothes and into my thigh. The pain brought everything back into focus, cleared my vision, and quieted my mind. In the space of a second, I was fine again. I positioned Julio's head, opened his mouth, and pinched off his nose.

Andrea counted. "Twenty-eight. Twenty-nine. Thirty. Now. Breathe." She paused long enough to watch me give Julio the kiss of life. We repeated it more times than I could count.

When the paramedics finally arrived, led by the night watchman, they brought equipment, a defibrillator. It took two shocks, but Julio came back. He sucked in air as if he had a black hole inside him. Andrea and I both gasped with him.

Julio began to talk, rambling in Spanish. "Ella se eno-ja. Coatlicue se enoja. Se enoja."

*She's angry. Coatlicue is angry. She's angry.*

The paramedics lifted him onto a stretcher. As they strapped him down, he hissed my name, "Señorita Rose. Ella se enoja," he croaked. He rolled frightened-animal eyes toward me.

"It's okay, Julio," I told him. "Nobody's angry. It's okay."

Around seven a.m., as I filed the paperwork requesting

a temporary replacement for Julio, I thought about calling Richard, but eventually decided against it. I didn't need my psychiatrist as much as I needed a good stiff drink

What I got was bacon and eggs. Abram had breakfast waiting for me when I walked in the door—as he usually did.

# CHAPTER 4

The next evening, I crossed the barrier into the Men's Wing and knocked on Colin's door. They had taken him off suicide watch, and I could visit him as I usually did.

"Come in."

I entered, shut the door behind me, and would have locked it, if it had a lock. We met in the middle of the room and went straight into an embrace, our bodies crushed together, hungry mouths seeking each other. He was taller than me, strong and masculine. The bit of reddish stubble on his cheeks scratched my face.

I thrust my fingers through his auburn curls, melding my palms to his head, and held his mouth against mine. It had been days that had felt like weeks, months even, since the last time I'd felt his arms around me.

He backed me against his desk, hands pulling my skirt up, tugging my panties down, and all the while, our tongues danced. The edge of the desk was hard against my ass, but I didn't mind. It added to the urgency of our lovemaking.

We were both ready when he slid into me, erect and

wet, and I bit his shoulder to keep from crying out. I locked my ankles behind his back, being careful—mostly—not to dig the heels of my boots into him.

He rocked me hard. I came. He came, and he held me so tightly that we were one body. I clung to him, hid my face in the crook of his neck, and breathed in his smell, trembling.

"One day," he whispered, "you'll be my queen."

"One day," I said, "we're going to get caught, and I'll lose my job." I licked up his neck to his mouth, and we kissed until he withdrew from me and pulled me to the bed where we rested together, letting our heartbeats slow. I was back in high school, hiding my boyfriend from Abram, making out in risky places.

"I want to find your lost memories," I said. "Hypnotize you the way Richard does me."

Colin sighed heavily. "We've talked about this, Viv. It sounds dangerous." He lay on his back, and I curled in against him, one hand on his bare chest.

"It's not, and if it can break through your amnesia—"

"If it could break through my amnesia, then Doc Bella would've tried it already."

I grunted in frustration and raised up on one elbow to glare down at him. "Sometimes I think you don't want a normal life."

"Viv…c'mon."

"Seriously. I think you're afraid to get well. Honey, the

sooner you remember, the sooner we can get on with our life together."

"Maybe I don't want to know."

"Not knowing is…more dangerous than knowing."

After a pause, he said, "Let's give it a try, but if it doesn't work, you let it go. For good."

I nodded enthusiastically and sat up. "Promise."

*Tick. Tock.*

He trusted me. I was the pillar against which he leaned, the crutch that held him upright. I had a touch of worry that I might not be able to handle what came up out of his subconscious, but I pushed it aside. We had to do something. I was impatient for Colin to be whole, to know what demons from his past we would have to overcome. Together, I told myself, we could handle anything.

I counted him down. For the first time, I understood how Richard must have felt whenever he and I were in session. With my role reversed, I had immense power, and it filled me with a calm elation—and hope.

When I was sure he was under, I said, "You're standing in front of a mirror. The mirror is foggy, so you can't see yourself. If you want, you can pick up a towel and wipe away the fog."

"I see the mirror. The towel is around my waist. If I take it off, I'll be naked."

"It's okay to be naked here," I said. "Nobody can see

you but you."

"Okay. I'm wiping off the fog. I see myself."

"Describe what you know about yourself."

"I'm very far from home."

"Where's home?"

"Gehenna."

"Do you know your name?"

"Yes."

"What is it?"

"You may hate me when you find out."

"I could never hate you."

Much to my surprise, tears flowed out of the corners of his eyes. His hands remained at his sides, still and relaxed. "I can never go back," he said. "They'll kill me." His face grew sharp, features taking on a more angular edge. That frightened me more than the tears. "I remember."

He remembered. Excitement and fear coursed through me simultaneously. I tugged at a hangnail with my teeth. The flap of skin pulled away with a sharp pain followed by a welling of blood. I sucked on it.

When I woke him, Colin's face relaxed, and the frightening mask fell away. He opened his eyes and stared up at the ceiling as if processing, then he turned his eyes to meet mine.

"What do you remember?" I asked him with more than a little trepidation.

He smiled. "Nothing significant."

"You said you were from a place called Gehenna. You said, 'I can never go back. They'll kill me.'"

"I did?"

"We can go again. Close your eyes."

"No." Colin took one of my hands. "I have the naughtiest urge to make love to you all night long," he said. "Did you put some sort of post-hypnotic suggestion in me?"

I laughed, and it broke the tension. I let it go—for the moment.

We went to dinner in the men's cafeteria, taking a corner table with our mashed potatoes, breaded pork tenderloins, chocolate pudding, and milk. The room buzzed with quiet conversations, the vibe different somehow, as if the patients were afraid to talk above a whisper.

"What's going on?"

Colin surveyed the room, then went back to his meal. "One of the guys died last night."

"Oh no. Which one? Did I know him?"

"Danny MacIntyr." The name rang a small bell, and I envisioned his face—quirky and mischievous.

"He was so young," I said.

"Twenty-two."

I put the fork down without taking the bite and rested my hand on his arm. "Were you guys close?"

"He was my friend."

"Why didn't you say something before?"

Colin put his hand on my cheek and looked me in the

eyes. "And what? Spoil our time together? No way." He kissed me on the forehead. "People die. Life goes on. I'll miss him, but not enough to stop grabbing every second with you. Or grabbing you every second I can. Or grabbing you for seconds, if I can."

I laughed. "Stop, stop. You had me at 'grab.'"

"Seriously, though. You never know how much time we have left."

Tears of love filled my eyes. "You're right."

"You have to be careful, okay? Promise me." Colin's tone went from casual serious to dead serious.

"I'm always careful."

"No. You have to be extra careful. She's watching us."

A cathedral of alarm bells sounded in my head. "Who's watching us?"

Colin lowered his voice. "The hag. The one who killed Danny."

I had a sudden memory of Julio's wild eyes, spitting out the words, "She's angry!" It shook me, so I resorted to platitudes and diversion. "It's okay. Finish your dinner. We're safe."

He rubbed my cheek with his thumb, then returned his attention to his food.

◆

"Girl, you need some down time," Lettie said in the

laundry break room the next morning, at the end of another exhausting shift. "I'm just sayin'." She had a motherly streak as wide as the Illinois River, though her methods of mothering weren't always by the book. "Why don't you and I go out tonight? Have a few drinks, dance, and watch the pretty people. It'll do you good, blow the stink off you."

"I dunno."

"I'm not taking no for an answer. You need a reminder that there's a real world out there, with real people. You been cooped up in this nut tin for too fuckin' long." She had a point, and something about the idea actually did appeal to me. I wasn't much of a partier—never had been—but it was nice sometimes to pretend I was normal.

There was one problem, though. "I don't have anything to wear."

"You don't know by now that I got you covered? Come by my place. We'll eat and play dress-up."

"Indian take-out?"

"*Chana masala,* yes, please."

Five hours later, we were at the Midnight Saloon in Peoria, drinking lemon drops. I wore my own tight boot-cut jeans and a tank top embroidered with red roses that Lettie had loaned me. I wished Colin could see me. I looked better than was good for me.

Lettie thought so too. She was plucking at my curls with one hand. "You're hot. I'm telling you. The boys—and girls—are gonna be all over you any minute now."

I said, "God, I hope not," but I was laughing.

"You should wear make-up more often. I didn't realize you had eyelashes."

"Smart ass."

A laser beam disappeared into Lettie's black hair. She asked, "Wanna dance?"

I enjoyed the sassy beat of the music, but I had no idea what to do with it. The country line dancers had taken over the floor and were kicking out. Although I periodically jerked around my own living room like a Devo puppet, I never felt comfortable dancing in front of others.

"I haven't had enough to drink," I answered.

"Mind if I go? This song is the best."

I didn't mind. Lettie slithered through the crowd, all hip-swingy and sexy, into a spot next to a group of cow-girls. Her skin soaked up the light, its natural tan pulling in all the color and flash. Her short dress and red cowboy boots reminded me of Dorothy from *The Wizard of Oz*. She'd put sparkles in her hair, and they glimmered from across the room.

A man sat down in Lettie's chair.

"Tell me," he said, raising his voice to be heard. "What's the first thing you notice about me?"

He watched the dancers, his face in profile to me. He had an enormous nose. And his hair looked like he ran his fingers through it, instead of using a comb. Other than that, there wasn't much about him that was remarkable, except maybe his eyelashes. They swept out and up, long for a man.

He turned and caught me looking at him. I felt the blush rising even before it hit my cheeks, and I looked quickly away without answering his question.

"I know you," he said.

The music bounced so heavily on his words that I wasn't sure I'd heard him right. "Excuse me?"

He repeated, "I know you," and that time, there was no mistaking.

"Have we met?"

"No. But I know a lot of things about you—how you see things sometimes—things nobody else sees."

I scooted away, and he put his hand on my arm. He wore a large, gold ring with a symbol stamped into it—a coat of arms for a college or secret society. A roaming beam of light hit it and ricocheted into my eyes. For a moment, it blinded me, and I cringed.

He leaned in. "I know what it's like. Always wondering what's real and what's not. You're probably even wondering whether I'm real." He squeezed my arm. "I am."

If I had a nickel for every time a hallucination said that to me... I pulled away, but I didn't leave. "What do you want?"

"I want you to be careful. You're mixed up in something bigger than you can imagine."

"I have a very active imagination, but I think you've

got the wrong person."

"You're Viviane Rose, and you live with your grandfather. You're engaged to marry Colin Aubrey, a patient at Malum Center. You work in the laundry room there."

"Now you're freaking me out." I edged away from him.

He shouted to be heard over the music and the distance growing between us. "I'm a psychologist. I can help you."

I got to my feet. He stood too and seemed ready to follow me. I escaped toward the dance floor. I could see Lettie there, through the bodies. They didn't part for me like they had for her, and I was a pinball, bouncing off the dancers. I sent my apologies on ahead.

"Sorry. Sorry. Excuse me. Sorry, excuse me."

The distance between Lettie and me got longer, not smaller. I couldn't seem to reach her, and the farther away she was, the more I wanted to be near her. That old, familiar paranoia made my head feel thick. Was everyone looking at me? Talking about the strange girl? Saying I didn't belong there. Laughing at me. Pointing.

*Watch out, psycho bitch comin' through.*

Then Lettie had her arms around me. "Hey. I thought you didn't want to dance?"

Her eyes welcomed me, and a feeling of safety enveloped me. The fog lifted, the voices in my head shut up, and I could breathe again. I searched the crowd as the paranoia receded. No one was talking about me or to me. No one had even noticed me.

"I recognize that look," Lettie said. "Are you freaking out?"

"There was a creepy guy talking to me."

Lettie craned her neck to scan the area around our table, but he had disappeared. "What guy?"

"I don't know. Maybe I imagined him."

# CHAPTER 5

The Friday before my mini-vacation with Colin wasn't as uneventful as I'd have wished. It began with my usual session with Richard. Smooth sailing—until the end.

He sat across from me in his office, one ankle over the opposite knee. Shadows sculpted him into a devil intent on mischief, eye sockets darkened and mouth hard between his black mustache and trim goatee. He would have been mortified if he'd known how the dim lighting warped his features. Everything else about him was calculated to convey a sense of professionalism, competence, and caring. He asked, "Are you still going out to the lake with Colin this weekend?"

"Doc Bella says it's okay. She thinks it might even do him some good."

"You've been taking your medication?"

"Every day."

"Any hallucinations?"

"None." It was a small enough lie, and one I was practiced at telling. I had learned early in life that it did me no good to be totally honest about what I saw, not even with

Richard.

He leaned toward me abruptly, his gaze fixed on mine and said, with attention to each syllable, "You know, you don't have to stay with him out of a sense of guilt or responsibility."

I recoiled and put a hand up between us. "I'm not talking about that again."

Richard closed his leather-bound notebook using the fancy pen I'd given him for his fortieth birthday as a bookmark. He set them both aside and reached for the glass of vita-shake on the table beside him. "Then I suppose we're done for the day. I'll see you next week."

◆

From there, my day got worse. Heading to work, I found the back stairwell empty, as always, a utilitarian tower lit with shabby fluorescent bulbs that flickered from time to time. I didn't dawdle. I rushed down the stairs so quickly, I almost didn't hear the noise.

I was thinking about the paperwork I'd have to do the following Monday. Payroll and inventory reports. I wasn't looking forward to it.

And then I heard a shuffling—a whisper. I froze, and my shadow froze too. Other shadows didn't. They continued to expand, stretching long down the wall.

"Hello? Is someone there?" I shook my head, squeezed

my eyes shut, then reopened them. The shadows grew. They moved like a storm front across the wall. "Who's there? Look, I don't care who you are or what you're smoking, but you're scaring me, so just say something." I went for my straight pin and drove it into the pad of my middle finger. The pain was real, even if the rest wasn't.

Another hint of a sound that I wasn't entirely sure I'd heard came from above. I strained to listen, and when the first tendrils of fog came rolling down the stairs, my body took over where my mind left off. It pumped adrenalin into my blood. My heartbeat increased, and the approaching choice—fight or flight—stirred in my limbs. My ears rang, the sound amplifying in gradual increments.

"Not real," I told myself.

Then, from behind me, someone grabbed my wrist.

I jumped and screamed.

Colin, in his pajamas, a step or two below me, as edgy as a cat on the verge of a fight, said, "You're not supposed to be here." He looked crazed. His curly hair stood out in all directions, blue eyes large and over-bright.

"Neither are you," I said. "How did you get through the security doors?"

He grabbed me by the wrist and pulled me after him. "C'mon!" I had no choice but to follow down the stairs, focusing on my feet so as not to stumble or miss a step.

He said, "Maybe the hag knows you're my weakness."

"Colin." I tried to sound calm, although I didn't succeed. More loudly, I said, "Stop!"

But he didn't stop. He kept racing downward, his bare feet slapping on the concrete. Talking to me or himself, he said, "Maybe she's just a spiteful cunt."

At the bottom landing, Colin input the security code on the keypad. He shoved me through the doorway ahead of him and looked back over his shoulder.

"How did you get that code?" I asked.

"Stay back, bitch," he growled. "I won't let you touch her." He pulled the door shut behind us. He grabbed my wrist again and tugged me down the deserted corridor. The giant laundry machines thrummed in the distance.

"You're hurting me!"

He stopped and swung me around him until I slammed against the wall. My head reverberated against the concrete blocks. He turned me to face him, pressed his body against mine, and closed his hand over my mouth. I bit the inside of my cheek and tasted blood.

"Shhh," he hissed. "Shhhh. If she hears us, she'll kill you." His eyes were frenzied—terrified, he looked everywhere but at me. The aroma of his sweat was pungent in my nostrils. Colin watched over his shoulder toward the door. His hand slid upward, closing off my nostrils as well as my mouth.

I couldn't breathe. I pulled on his arm, but the harder I fought him, the more firmly he pressed himself against me, all the while, saying, "Shhhh. Hush. Shhhhh. Stop."

I kneed him in the groin.

It took a second, but then Colin released me and fell to the floor with a loud groan.

I dropped my hands to my knees, breathing in gasps, trying not to puke or cry.

Ajani came out of the laundry room door. When he saw us, he sprinted the length of the hall and knelt beside Colin, though his concerned face lifted to me. "Are you all right?"

I nodded.

"What happened? Did he hurt you?"

I shook my head.

Colin sat up and told Ajani, "It was *her.* She came after us."

Ajani said, "It was her? Are you sure?"

Colin cocked his head to one side, listening. "She's gone now."

I sat back on my heels. "Please…don't encourage him."

◆

Ajani took Colin back to his room, and I continued on to the laundry. Shaken, I had a hard time focusing. I regretted letting Ajani leave with Colin. He might report the incident, and I didn't want Bella to cancel our weekend. After all, no one would have believed he'd been trying to protect me from my own hallucination.

I took Ajani's station until he returned, pulling hot loads of laundry out of dryers and putting in wet loads. It didn't take him long to get back, and he came straight over to where I was. We put our heads close together so we wouldn't have to yell over the machines, tall Ajani bending down to me.

I asked, "Did you have any trouble?"

Ajani shook his head, though his expression still held concern.

I needed to know. "Did you tell anyone?"

"No." He looked me over with his black-gold eyes. "You sure you're okay?"

My lip was swollen, but not in any visible way, thank goodness. The bump on my forehead—there wasn't any blood or broken skin—was already bruising, but I'd survive. "Positive. Is he?"

"He'll be fine. What happened?"

I waved the question off. "It was my fault. I imagined a noise in the stairwell, and it freaked me out a little. I mentioned it to Colin, and it got him worked up too. We both overreacted. That's all."

Ajani's eyes narrowed more instead of less.

I added, "We've been under a lot of stress lately." I wasn't lying. Stress comes with the territory of mental illness. It's rough when you can never relax your guard. I put my hand on his arm. "Thank you. I'd give you a raise, if I could."

Ajani laughed, and his whole body relaxed, tension draining from him as if someone had pulled a plug. He made a silly face to make me smile.

It worked.

The next day, I visited Colin in his room, and we wallowed together in tearful regret for having hurt each other. I apologized. He apologized, and we agreed to never mention it to anyone, especially not Doc Bella. He made me promise to stay out of the back hallway. I humored him.

◆◆◆

# CHAPTER 6

The morning of our trip finally arrived. On my way to the Center, in my little yellow Fiesta, I sang with Heart's "Crazy on You." The sun radiated happiness, a new warmth that promised spring flowers and an eventual harvest. Tractors streamed along tracts of land, turning the soil. Signs of renewal lined either side of the road, across the Illinois plains, barns being painted and the first few calves of the season. Crows gathered, waiting for their chance to pluck the seeds that didn't get buried deeply enough.

I sang at the top of my lungs.

Colin and I had taken short vacations before. Six months earlier, he'd proposed to me during one of them.

When his more serious symptoms had presented, Doc Bella had resisted letting him leave the Center. I'd finally talked her into it. I'd reserved us a room at the Cozy Comfort Bed and Breakfast, right on the shore of Clinton Lake where Colin had proposed to me. I filled a basket with chocolate, fruit, cookies, and nuts, and I bought him a new shirt, new jeans, and a toiletry kit. Living with Abram,

I didn't have many expenses, and it made me happy to spoil Colin.

I parked in a visitor's spot on the circle drive and walked around to the side of the building. Second-class citizens, patients, and employees didn't use the front entrance. I entered on the Women's Wing side—out of habit—and used the code to get through the locked door.

Jared Barker was on duty in the Receiving office. He looked up when I came in and gave his trademark nod, slow and low. "Morning."

"Hi, Jared. How's it going?"

"Quiet. Got no deliveries until later. I'm reading baseball blogs." He pointed at the computer screen. "No surfing porn at work. This is next best." Jared was younger than me, a brawny farm boy who'd been badly injured in a combine accident. He walked with a limp, and the arm they had reattached was forever bent, the muscles shortened and tight. His mind worked differently too, since the accident, all his etiquette barriers having fallen. "You're in early. You switch shifts?"

I leaned on the counter. "No. I'm not working this weekend. My fiancé and I are going out to Clinton Lake. We've got reservations at a little B-n-B, and we're going to relax for a couple days."

Jared's eyebrows went up. "Are you going to have sex?"

I winked. "God, I hope so."

He buzzed me through the interior door. "You get tired of him, I'm available. My dick works, even if the rest of me don't!"

"Thanks. I'll keep that in mind."

The Men's Wing seemed deserted, but that was an illusion. The distant rumble from the dining room signaled breakfast, the busiest time of the day for the patients, orderlies, and nurses. Everyone was there—everyone but Colin. I found him seated on his bed, reading. He stood and I went to him and slipped into his arms. "Good morning. Are you ready for an adventure?"

"I'm so ready." He kissed me on top of my head, and I rubbed my face against his chest.

"Perfect. Car's all packed, and I checked the list twice: lingerie, bubble bath, massage oil, a special playlist on my cellphone—R&B for those quiet moments. Did I mention I got a mani-pedi?"

He laughed. "You had me at lingerie."

I squeezed him. "Did you pack your toothbrush? That's the one thing I always forget."

"All packed. No halitosis monkeys allowed."

I didn't recognize his suitcase. "You got a new bag?"

"Doc Bella loaned it to me. I outgrew the other one. It's amazing how much stuff a person can accumulate."

Two years earlier, when Colin had first arrived at the Center, he'd only had the clothes on his back. He didn't even have a name, because he couldn't remember it. He chose "Colin Aubrey" for himself and said that having amnesia was like being born a second time, including the pain of the birth canal. Everything he'd known about himself had been gone, and he'd been left feeling broken and vulnerable.

A city hospital had transferred him to Malum Center because no one had shown up looking for him. The state paid for his care, feeding, and sessions with Doc Bella. The police had given up trying to find his identity, though Colin never had. He sat for hours browsing social media and scanning local news sites, studying faces, wondering if any of them—any single one of them—might know who he was and where he came from. He wanted to know his parents, whether he had brothers or sisters, and how they might have damaged him.

Doc Bella appeared in the doorway of Colin's bedroom. An invisible draft rippled her skirt. It followed her everywhere, but I was the only one who ever noticed it. It was just another of my many hallucinations—a trick played on me by mischievous electrical impulses in my head.

"Ready to go then?" As always, Bella's presence brought an instant seriousness to the occasion.

"We're ready." I stepped out of Colin's embrace. "I filed the paperwork. Contact information for the inn is there, and I documented our route, too."

"Good. Has Richard left yet?"

"He left this morning to go see family. He'll be back

on Tuesday."

"You didn't forget your toothbrushes, did you?"

Colin and I both said, "No."

"Get on with it then. The sooner you leave, the sooner your trip begins."

Colin asked, teasing, "Anxious to be rid of us?"

"Maybe I need a rest, too." Bella winked at him.

Colin put his arm around her shoulders and gave her a gentle squeeze. "Absence makes the heart grow fonder, Doc. Have a great time in Boston."

"I will, thanks. I'm looking forward to a change of pace."

Bella accompanied us to the car, her hand tucked in the crook of Colin's arm as we walked.

I asked, "How long will you be gone?"

"Three to six months. It depends on how long it takes to turn the patient around."

I said, "It's a compliment that they called you in to consult, isn't it?"

"The man's challenges fall within my area of exper-tise."

Colin said, "It's a job for Doc's famous chocolate chip cookies," and we all laughed.

When we got to the car, I caught an odd expression on Bella's face. Despite her encouragement, in that moment, when she didn't know I was looking, she frowned. I was eavesdropping on secret thoughts. While Colin loaded his suitcase in the trunk, I went to her and said quietly, "Don't worry. We'll be fine."

Her face transformed. She smiled at me—a confident smile, a psychiatrist's smile—and said, "Of course, you will. I'm just jealous. I can't remember the last time I had a romantic weekend."

"Maybe you'll meet someone in Boston."

"At my age? Nonsense."

We said our good-byes. Bella stood at the curb while we got into the car, waved as we pulled away, and didn't leave until after we'd turned the corner and gone out of sight.

◆

We'd been driving down I-74 for about an hour when Colin said, "Pull over for a minute."

I looked at him to see if he was sick. "What's the matter?"

"Nothing. Just pull over."

"Do you have to tinkle? I swear, you have the smallest bladder of anyone I know."

"I don't tinkle, woman. I'm a grown man. I take a piss, use the head, or drain the snake. I don't tinkle."

Once I'd pulled over and turned off the engine, he took my face in his hands. He kissed me with clarity, looking directly into my eyes. His mouth moved love across mine.

Tender and sentimental, the kiss stoked my heart rather than my belly.

"No matter what happens," he said, "you will always be mine. Never forget that."

I said, "Never," and for the first time in a long time, I felt hopeful that we could live a normal, happy life together.

Colin's eyes crinkled at the corners. "So mote it be."

I touched my fingertips to those crinkles. "Who talks like that?"

He grabbed my hand and kissed it. "Let's go. I want to get there."

"Hey, you're the one who wanted to stop."

"So I am."

♦

Back on the road, we came to the lake and began to make our way around it. A long bridge crossed the water at one of its narrowest points. Traversing it was amazing, as if we were driving directly on the water. The lake's surface gleamed in the sunshine. With the windows down, the moist, fishy scent of it filled the car.

I spotted a crane and pointed it out to Colin.

He leaned forward to watch it take off and fly away.

On my left, an encroaching darkness cut back the sunshine. It started as a movement at the corner of my eye.

I swung my gaze toward it, made out a figure, a person, climbing onto the guardrail at the edge of the road.

It was a man, dressed all in black, and he was crouched, a spring ready to be sprung. Before I understood what he was doing, the man leapt onto the road, in front of the car, his arms and legs flailing. I had no time to do anything but react, and I jerked the wheel to one side.

My eyes captured him, his face, and its intense expression, then we hit the guardrail going forty miles an hour.

# CHAPTER 7

The impact with the guard rail caused the airbags to explode in our faces.

Time turned surreal, *ticky-tocky.*

My mind scrambled to understand.

There are no accidents.

*Tick.*

Oh God.

*Tock.*

With a splash and a jolt, the car nose-dived into the water. I flew forward, arm slamming hard into the dashboard. White powder from the air bags made me cough.

I cried, "Colin!"

He was unconscious, blood on his forehead.

"Wake up!" I shook him, and pain shot up my arm.

Frigid water gushed in through the vents. It was happening so fast. I couldn't keep up.

I thought, *We're going to die.* I was staring into the lake's ominous murk, and my death stared back.

I fumbled with my seatbelt. When it released, it dropped me onto the steering wheel. I reach for Colin's seatbelt.

When I released him, he fell forward, dead weight.

"Fuck!" I reached for him, but I couldn't orient my body to get leverage.

The surface of the lake came level with the open windows and poured into the car. It hit me in the face. I flailed.

Our descent accelerated.

Cold water swirled around me.

I took one last deep breath as the water level pushed my chin up, and then we were fully submerged. I half-crawled/half-swam out through the window. My lungs burned already.

Though the lake surrounded me, I was free. I saw sunlight shimmering on the surface above, beckoning me, but instead I swam across the roof toward Colin's window.

His arm floated out through the window. I latched onto it and pulled him toward me, me toward him.

He wasn't coming out of the car, and the car kept sinking.

I reached in to get a better grip.

My lungs spasmed, clenching with the need for breath.

And then a man floated in front of me, nose to nose with me. I couldn't make out his features. I absorbed his face as a single whole. He was a Rorschach blot that I would never forget as long as I lived.

He took my shoulders and turned me away from him, leaving me no time to resist. He wrapped a strong arm across my chest and swam me upward.

I had no control, no air left in my lungs. My body did what it had been created to do—I inhaled. But, instead of air, the freezing water entered my lungs.

It was a losing battle. The more my body rejected the water, the more it let in.

As blackness closed in at the edges of my vision, I stopped blinking. The car was there, caught in my sight. I streamed backwards, away from it, dragged by the man swimming me to the surface. My hair flowed around my face, wretched seaweed reaching for the car, for Colin. Then nothing.

♦

The awakening was far worse than the drowning. With the first inhalation of air, my body convulsed, rejecting the water in my lungs.

Someone rolled me onto my side.

I retched, coughed, and inhaled—all in quick succession and repetitively. My lungs cramped. I vomited. Lake water spewed up from deep in my gut. I heard splashing and the rasp of my own breath.

A woman said, "She's coming around."

"Where'd you learn to do that?" a man asked.

The woman replied, "Lifeguard training."

A chime rang out, and the man said, "Aw shit. That raven bastard is close."

"Okay, we need to move. Get ready. When he comes back up, sleep him."

My eyes were blurry and sore. I couldn't stop shivering.

The man said, "We should take her with us."

"Can't," the woman replied. "She's normal."

I couldn't understand. Everything felt dreamlike, and I was sure I was hearing them wrong. The words didn't fit with one another—oil and water. Slippery.

A fit of coughing wracked my body, and I curled into a ball. I was so cold.

Someone put a hand on my shoulder. Heat spread outward from the touch, warming me. I wanted to melt into it.

"Here he comes," the woman said. "Do it."

There was a crackle of static and the smell of burned vanilla. I heard a cry of surprise and then another bigger splash.

"Good. Now her."

A man whispered near my ear, "You're going to be okay."

I grabbed at him, but he deflected my hands.

An aromatic wave of vanilla filled my lungs, soothing them, and I slipped into unconsciousness.

◆◆◆

# CHAPTER 8

I awoke in a bed. Something wasn't right, but I had no proof. Bright light cut through my closed eyelids, and I pulled the covers over my head to block it out.

"Good morning, sunshine." Simon's Scottish accent was pronounced.

Simon. I hadn't heard that voice in years, and my stomach lurched. I clutched at the blanket and shoved it against my ears.

"Come now. That's no way to greet an old friend."

I said, "Shut the fuck up," but it came out closer to "Shulla fucka." My brain was full of stinging bees.

"Oh, all right," Simon said. "I can see you need a moment to get your bearings."

"I'm hallucinating. I'm hallucinating." I hated Simon for being the only recognizable element in my nightmare.

I took a deep breath. The aroma of Eau de Hospital clung to the bed, unmistakable. I thought I must be at the Center. I must have snuck in to sleep with Colin. I reached out for him, my fingers spreading as they delved through the linens, but he wasn't there. "Colin?"

"Oh, bloody hell," said Simon.

"Colin?" My throat was raw. I sat up abruptly and threw back the covers.

I slid out of bed, but my legs wouldn't hold me. I collapsed to the floor, and something landed on top of me.

Simon said, "That a girl! Carpe diem."

A sharp pain lit up my arm. An I.V. needle—still—was causing it. Blood oozed from around the needle. It was angled wrong and pushing up my skin. I focused on that pain. Needles, I knew. I kicked up through the confusion and surfaced.

The floor was covered with linoleum, white squares made to mimic marble, a swishing pattern of gray. The swoon went from my head to my stomach, and I hovered on the verge of vomiting.

Hands touched me, pushed the hair out of my face, and lifted my chin. A pinprick of light shined into my eyes, and I turned my face away.

"Help me get her back into bed," said a man, and then raised his voice to add, "Miss Rose, let's get you back into bed," as if I were hard of hearing.

They picked me up. Fingers dug into my armpits.

I wiggled to get away, but they held on tighter.

"Watch the I.V."

The bed caught me. The pillow came up under my head, and I sank into it.

"Miss Rose, your grandfather said he'll be here as soon

as he can." The rails on the bed came up one at a time: *cuh-chunk, cuh-chunk.* It was Frankenstein's cell closing.

My eyes shut of their own accord.

◆

Much later, I awoke in the same bed. I remembered the accident, and I lay there for a long time—turning it over and over in my mind. Some of the shock had worn off.

I'd been untethered from the I.V.—no more needles, no more pain. Anxiety lurked at the edge of my consciousness, and I wished for a straight pin. I pushed my thumbnail against the tip of my middle finger, as hard as I could, until pain opened into a bloom of energy that I could focus my mind upon. It kept the panic at bay.

Muffled bings, shuffles, and rumbled conversations came from beyond the closed door. I took another breath, and it felt monumental.

Simon said, "You're feeling better, hm?"

"You're not real." My throat still hurt.

"The police want to talk to you. Lettie's here too, and your grandfather."

"Where's Colin?"

Simon said, "I wish I could say."

"Hello?" I shouted at the world. "I need help in here." While I was searching for the call button, my grandfather entered the room. He had dark circles on his dark circles, and his jowls hung heavier than usual.

Lettie came in next. They flanked me, and Lettie asked, "Are you all in one piece?" She never minced words or shied away from difficult subjects. She was 100% protective earth mother.

I said, "I'm fine. Bruises on my chest."

Lettie leaned over me and pulled at my hospital gown to look. "From the seatbelt?"

"Yeah."

She kissed my forehead. "Jesus, girl. Jesus. I was scared to death. All they'd tell me was that your car went into Clinton Lake and someone brought you here."

Abram cleared his throat.

"I know you're there," Lettie said flatly to him. She was one of the few people in the world Abram Rose couldn't intimidate. She was practically part of the family.

"I didn't *know* anything else," Abram said.

Lettie smoothed the hair back from my face. "Were you driving?"

"Yeah." I studies his face, looking for the answer to my next question before I even dared ask it. It came out as a whisper. "And Colin?"

Abram's expression didn't change. "They're still searching for him."

I wasn't sure I'd heard him right, and yet, I knew I had. "Still searching for him?"

Abram took one of those deep breaths that signaled he

had bad news. "Now, don't go crazy on me. All I know is they dove on the car right away." He sounded defensive. "They didn't find him. They think he might've tried to swim out." He picked at a hangnail on his thumb. "They've got teams walking around the lake. And divers."

My mind took me back to the lake, to the car, to Colin, and us up to our necks in frigid water. His face, so pale and still.

Worry put pressure on my eyeballs.

"You're sure he was in the car with you?" Abram asked.

"What?"

Abram shifted on his feet and used his diplomatic cadence. "I'm just trying to figure out how this could've happened. You're not covering for him, are you, kiddo?"

The bed became unstable. I grabbed the handrail and hung on. "Are you asking if I helped him run away?" It was true that Colin had been committed for his own safety, but Doc Bella had seen progress. Despite the roof incident, she'd allowed our weekend trip.

"The idea's been suggested." Abram licked his lips. "Not by me. By the police."

It made no sense. "It never even occurred to me."

"Okay, settle down," said Abram. "No need to get upset."

I couldn't have disagreed more. I was imagining the searchers giving up because they thought Colin had run off. I pushed the covers off and started to get out of bed.

"Whoa!" said Lettie. "What are you doing?"

"I have to find him." My legs held me this time.

Lettie stepped in front of me. "Honey, that's not your job. The police will find him."

"Please." The pitch of my voice rose. I had no control over it.

Abram cringed visibly.

I softened my tone. "Please."

"I love you. No." Lettie put her hands on my shoulders, warm through the fabric of the hospital gown. "Think for a minute, Viv. What are you going to do? Go out there in the cold and stumble around the lake?"

My mind was racing.

Abram raised his hands. "Okay, okay. Let's calm down. Viviane, you're shivering."

"C'mon." Lettie guided me back onto the bed.

I didn't have the strength to fight her.

Abram broached a new subject. "I heard you had an episode this morning."

"It wasn't an episode," I told him. "I tried to get out of bed too soon. I was half asleep and disoriented."

Abram and I locked eyes for a moment, him trying to figure out if I was lying, and me daring him to suggest it.

A man in a white lab coat entered, interrupting us. "Excuse me. I need a few minutes with Viviane, if you wouldn't mind."

Lettie gave me hugs and kisses before leaving.

Abram squeezed my toes and asked gruffly, "Is there anything you need, kiddo?"

"My sewing kit."

♦

After the doctor left, another strange man came into my hospital room. He had too much beard and too many wrinkles in his khaki pants. His hair, brown and thinning, definitely needed a cut.

I started to ask if I could help him, but he cut me off. "My name's Detective Stace Hayward with the Peoria P.D. I'm here to take your statement about the accident, if you're feeling up to it."

"I guess."

Detective Hayward had a scuffed leather bag slung across his chest. He lifted it off and sat in the room's armchair.

I asked, "Did you find him?"

"You mean Colin Aubrey?"

"Who else?" And we were off to a bad start.

"Not yet." He balanced his bag on his lap. "Frankly, Miss Rose, it makes me nervous. We walked the entire shoreline, dragged out your car, and sent divers in, but we didn't find him." The detective folded his hands on the flat plane of his stomach. On someone else, the gesture would have made him seem relaxed, but for him, it didn't work. His foot gave him away, bobbing with nervous energy.

"You searched the woods?"

His tongue pushed out his bottom lip as if he had a wad of chewing tobacco in there. "Yeah. And we talked to all the residents within a five mile radius. We flew a copter over and put his picture on the TV. We haven't had a single bite. Nobody's seen him."

"People don't just disappear."

"That's the mystery, Miss Rose."

In my ear, Simon said, "Be careful what you say to this man."

I shook my head sharply, "Ssht."

"I beg your pardon?"

"Sorry, not you."

Detective Hayward raised an eyebrow and opened his bag, "Why don't you tell me what happened."

"I picked Colin up at the Center around nine." I described it as I remembered it, right down to the sunshine. As my retelling approached the lake, however, my words faltered. It wasn't that I didn't remember— it was that I didn't want to.

Detective Hayward prompted me. "What caused the accident?"

"There was a man—he ran out into the road. I had to swerve to avoid hitting him."

"Can you describe him?"

The man was a blur in my memory. "It happened so fast. I think he was wearing all black? Dark clothes."

"Was he young? Old? Black? White?"

"Young enough to climb over the guard rail and jump out in front of me, but he wasn't a kid or anything. He was an adult. White, I think. I'm pretty sure I didn't hit him."

Hayward looked up at me, and his eyes were the color of a foggy forest at twilight. "We found your tracks, but we didn't find anything to indicate you'd hit anyone, and nobody has confessed to running into the path of your vehicle. As a matter of fact, we can't find any witnesses at all—except you, of course."

"He was probably the one who got me out."

"Tell me about that."

"There was a woman and a man, maybe two men. It was definitely a man who swam down to the car and pulled me out."

"Except the paramedics found you lying on the shore all by yourself."

I shrugged.

Hayward scrutinized me. He stuck his tongue in his bottom lip, a gesture that seemed to indicate he was thinking. It made it easy to imagine how he must have been as a boy—serious and thoughtful. He said, "Okay. Two, maybe three people were there. They got you out, then instead of going back for Mr. Aubrey, they left—all three of them."

"I think they *did* go back for him."

"Really? Then, where is he?"

"I don't know. Who called the paramedics?"

"Anonymous. It seems they used an untraceable cell phone."

"That must have been them."

"Maybe." Hayward cocked his head to one side. "Tell you what. Let's talk about something else." It was a good idea, until he added, "I heard Colin tried to kill himself."

"He wasn't trying to kill himself," I insisted.

"Hm. I heard he wanted to throw himself off the roof."

"He was trying to fly."

Hayward raised his eyebrows. "Well. I'm glad to hear it wasn't suicide." He made no effort to mask the sarcasm.

"Look. Colin has a mental illness. That doesn't make him suicidal. Colin's not dead. I'd know if he were dead."

"Lady, if I had a laugh for every time I heard that, I'd be Jerry Seinfeld." Hayward leaned forward, his expression very un-funny. "It's unlikely that your fiancé survived without help. There aren't any houses out there—not for miles. Even if he made it to shore, he'd have been soaked to the skin, and temperatures dropped almost to freezing last night. Without help…well…"

I said, "I think you should go."

"Just one more question. People saw you packing up the car at Vince Malum. So, where did Colin's suitcase go?"

"What do you mean? He put it in the trunk."

"Can you explain then, why we found only *your* suitcase in the car?"

"Huh?"

"It's creepy, isn't it? How a man can disappear? Right out from under your nose. What do you think happened?"

I just stared at him, confused.

Eventually, the detective nodded with finality. "We'll keep patrolling the lake." He turned off the recorder and stowed it. With one smooth movement, he rose to his feet and draped the bag's long strap across his chest. "I hope you feel better soon, Miss Rose."

I had no voice.

At the door, the scruffy detective looked back one last time and then left.

I threw back the covers, ran to the bathroom, and was sick in the sink.

# CHAPTER 9

I cried myself to sleep after the detective left and was woken by Simon shouting in my ear. "Hide! You have to hide. Now!"

I rolled over and draped an arm on my ear.

Simon's voice moved to the other side of the bed, though I never heard footsteps or rustling fabric or any other sound. It was as if he floated, or maybe he didn't have a body. "I'm serious. You have to hide. They're coming for you."

I pretended I hadn't heard him, and—technically—I hadn't. Despite his protestations to the contrary, Simon was my most persistent hallucination. He'd been my constant companion since junior high and had gotten me into so much trouble—until I learned not to answer him out loud. People talked about kids having imaginary friends as if it were cute, but right about the time you hit puberty, it becomes a lot less adorable.

"Hide!" Simon hissed.

Then someone opened the door.

I rolled to see a man dressed like a TV mortician, complete with pocket watch and silver rose tie pin. He was tall, slim, and well-put-together. His black hair angled down next to one cheek, cut asymmetrically, and eyeliner rimmed his eyes.

"Everyone decent?" He asked in an Irish accent. "Ah yes, I see you are. Pity." The strange visitor crossed to the bed. "Are you Viviane Rose? *The* Viviane Rose?"

"Who wants to know?"

"You can call me Nathan. Most everybody does these days."

I said, "Um, hi?"

He smiled, his teeth extraordinarily straight and white, a contrast with his tanned skin. I wondered if he were an actor. He was certainly dramatic enough.

"So, do you admit to being Viviane Rose or not?" He sounded chipper.

"Yeah, I suppose."

His face changed as if a light had been turned off, and he looked at me with practiced sympathy and sadness. "Then it'll interest you to know that I'm Colin's brother."

I pushed up onto my elbows. "Really?"

"I've been searching for him ever since he disappeared. That would be two years ago now. Our father misses him. It's heart-wrenching to see the poor old man worrying for his eldest. I don't mind telling you, it's taken quite a toll on his health."

"Oh."

One corner of his mouth twitched. "After I saw his picture on the television, I talked to the police. They told me about you."

"Have they found him yet?"

"No, not yet, and it's a tragedy. *You* wouldn't happen to know where he is, would you?" Nathan leaned forward, body language eager.

"I wish I did."

He *tsked* and scanned me as if he might find a clue to Colin's location in the wrinkles of my bed sheets.

I added, "Sorry."

"Reality is never having to say you're sorry, girl. It is what it is." He stepped closer. "By the time I got to the lake, it was swarming with useless people all busy-busy and self-important." He moved in so close his nose nearly touched mine, and I leaned away from him. "I'll find him. It's inevitable." The scent of magnolia bloomed over me. Then, he turned and left without another word, his hard-heeled boots clicking on the linoleum.

He was stalking the moon, and it took me awhile to relax after he was gone.

◆

It was late. I was used to the graveyard shift, so I laid there awake, trying to ignore the burbling stream of my thoughts.

A chill leaked under the covers with me. I rolled onto my side and curled into a ball. It got colder. I tucked the blanket higher, up to my chin, and pulled it in against my back. The blanket slid to one side, uncovering my feet. I yanked it back into place and settled down again.

Finally, I must have dozed, because when I came awake, it was sudden. The room was freezing cold, and my feet were once again in the open air. I never slept without covering my feet, not even in the hottest weeks of summer. It was a habit I'd developed as a kid. As long as my feet remained covered, nothing nasty could crawl into bed with me.

I opened my eyes.

I was not alone.

A woman was lying on the bed beside me, looking back at me. Her gray hair was alive. She had one hand on my breast, her touch icy through the hospital gown.

I didn't react. I'd learned never to react. I just looked at her while my insides roiled with fear.

She dropped her jaw, revealing the blackened, toothless interior of her mouth.

I couldn't move.

Her hand slid upward until her frigid fingers touched the base of my throat, and her eyes—the pupils void, black holes, dark matter—they sucked in everything she looked at. They were sucking me in, and her hand crawled up the underside of my jaw and over my chin. She began to envelop me, wrapping a leg over mine and inserting her other hand under my neck. She cradled the back of my head. Wherever she touched me, she was solid, then not solid, tickling, as if made of feathery tendrils or tentacles that stretched and retracted. Her expression alternated between passion and dispassion. She wanted me, but she didn't give a damn.

Her hand covered my mouth, and she pressed her body against mine. All I could smell was crisp, cold air. I breathed her in involuntarily, her misty presence invading my nostrils, freezing them, expanding into my sinus cavities and violating my lungs.

I heard a sound in my mind, but not in my ears. It was the sound of metal tearing.

The hag closed off my nostrils.

I had no control over my own body. I couldn't get away or fight.

That terrible, high-pitched shriek didn't stop.

I went to a different time and place, to the Center's basement, to the long concrete hall. Colin had been there, shushing me.

I'd tried to shove him away.

"Stop it, Viv. Stop it. She'll hear us."

He crushed me, pushed his hand against my nostrils. "She'll kill you if she finds you."

My throat clenched. My diaphragm spasmed. And then, I was in my bed, in the hospital room.

"She's gone." Simon was right next to my ear, barely whispering.

I swam as hard as I could to the surface of my mind and sucked in a lungful of air.

The room was dark, my heart pounding. Several layers of blanket covered me and my feet. I pushed up on one elbow and turned on the bedside lamp. I needed to see every corner, every angle, every inch of the room.

"It's all right," Simon said. "She's gone."

I couldn't help it. It started as a sob and ended as a scream. I needed to scream, because I could and because I hadn't been able to while that creature had had me pinned and dying.

The people in white coats rushed in.

I remembered her touch, the tickle of her fingers as they crawled over my eyelids, insisting they shut, willing me to die, and I couldn't stop screaming.

They tried to give me a shot, but I fought them. They held me down and forced me to take it. Then, I fought sleep instead, and I was successful—for a while.

◆◆◆

# CHAPTER 10

Wake up, Vivi," Richard said, pulling up the window blinds with a rattle and a tidal wave of painful light.

I reached my hand out to him. "Where've you been?" It was the first time I'd seen him since the accident.

He sat on the edge of the bed, pushing me over with his hip. I scooched to give him room. He looked like the college kid he'd been when I'd first met him, unsure and curious, his tight frame enhanced by rich corduroy and lamb's wool.

"I'm sorry. I just got back into town this morning. I came as soon as I could. I was out in the middle of Lake Michigan when I got the call." He took my hand in both of his. "How do you feel?"

"Like crusty shit on an old shoe."

"Of course, you do." He paused, then added, "Do you want to talk about what's been happening?"

"Not really. Tell me about your trip."

He humored me, waxing poetic about the rejuvenating effects of the Great Lakes air, his parents' boat, the barbeque they'd had, and doing yoga at dawn on the pier. Richard had a gift. He could talk for hours and say absolutely nothing. Through all that, I learned nothing of substance about his family or his feelings toward them. He was a private man, and our sessions had always been about me.

"I brought you a fresh set of clothes. I'm here to get you. We're transferring you to a room at the Center."

"Why do I have to go there? I'm fine. I'll go home and take it easy for a few more days. All I have are bruises."

Richard patted my arm. "We want to keep you under observation for a little while longer."

"No. I want to go home."

"We think it's for the best. You need to be somewhere safe, surrounded by people who care about you and who are trained to deal with this sort of thing."

"This sort of thing? I'm upset and scared, not crazy."

"I know. I know. I know you're not."

I thought, *What we say three times must be true.*

He squeezed my hand. "Unexpected symptoms can bubble to the surface when we're under stress. If you're staying at the Center, it'll be easier to have daily sessions for a while."

The only bubbles I wanted were the ones in my bathtub at home, but part of me knew he was right. I'd already had plenty of evidence that my hold on reality was deteriorating.

I got ready to leave and signed the papers they put in

front of me.

Richard said, "I'll get the car." He took my pile of belongings with him.

A male nurse guided me into a wheelchair. He wasn't a talker, and I was glad. He rolled me through the tile-lined corridor. A crowd of spectators—patients and visitors—saw me go by, undoubtedly wondering what flavor of "broken" I was. I had survived where they or their loved ones might not.

The cool air of the parking garage felt good on my hot cheeks, and I was up out of the chair almost before my driver had set the brakes.

Richard pulled up in his red Mercedes. Once I was in, he took his time starting the engine and pulling out of the lot. He kept looking over at me and asking, "How are you doing?"

"Are you worried I'm going to freak out or something?"

He shook his head too quickly. "You're a bit flushed, that's all. Sometimes, after an accident, it can be frightening to get back in a car."

"I'm fine," I said, and I did my damnedest to mean it. It helped that I wasn't the one driving. "Did you tell Abram about me going to the Center today?"

"Yes, he and I talked about it."

"I don't suppose he's going to be there?"

Richard snorted slightly, the closest he had ever come

to expressing a derisive opinion about my grandfather. "No. I volunteered to settle you in."

I wasn't surprised. Abram avoided the Center with a passion that verged on phobia. He apparently thought mental illness was contagious.

From the backseat, Simon said, "Can you ask him to turn on the seat warmers?"

I glanced over my shoulder and muttered, "Some things never change."

"Excuse me?" asked Richard.

"Nothing. Just thinking aloud."

The city scrolled by, and soon we were zipping along between corn and bean fields.

I said, "I should be out by the lake, looking for Colin."

Richard turned toward me, put his hand on the back of my seat, and said, "I went out there. They've got dozens of officers and volunteers looking for him. He's in good hands. You need to take care of yourself right now."

I knew better than to argue, so I watched the farms and gas stations go by and thought back to a time when I was with Colin. The memory that came to mind wasn't necessarily a happy one, but I slipped into it as if putting on a well-worn nightgown.

The day Richard had first met Colin, we were already a couple. I'd known Richard wouldn't approve, so I'd kept it from him for as long as I could. Then one day, he caught us holding hands in the garden.

He stood over us, with the sun behind him, a vengeful angel come down to smite me for my insolence. He didn't say a word until I introduced them.

Colin made the first move, offering his hand. Social grace compelled Richard to respond in kind, but after that, Richard kept trying to get me to see the folly in dating Colin. In one of our sessions, he took a circuitous route and asked, "Do you remember how angry you were at your mother when you thought she'd died and left you?"

I remembered. Instead of sadness, anger had been the touchstone of my youth. I hadn't understood death. I'd felt abandoned.

"And, do you remember how angry you were when you learned that she *wasn't* dead?"

"*Abram* let me believe she was dead. He abandoned *her.*"

"And, by extension, *you* abandoned her as well. You feel guilty for all the angry thoughts you directed at her when you were a child."

"I should have done something."

"What could you have done? You didn't even know she wasn't dead."

"There were clues. Like how Abram never took me to her grave."

"Hind-sight is 20-20."

"I know, but…"

"You changed the entire direction of your life, Vivi,

just so you could make that up to her."

I shrugged. "You sound like Abram."

"Look, all I'm saying is that Colin is not your mother."

"No. He's my fiancé," I replied quietly. In my mind, that ended the argument. It was reason enough to suffer through with him.

Richard looked down at his hands and said, "Each of us has our own personal flavor of suffering that defines us. We cling to the people and situations we find painful because if we let go, we'll have to change and become a different person. We find ways to repeat and replicate the suffering we know—the suffering that we think makes us who we are."

I had replied, "Today, you're pain. Tomorrow, just a stain."

Richard pulled his car into the long two-lane drive that led to the Center. "Vince Malum Residential Living Center," I said. "Why does that sound so civilized and nice?"

Richard said, "It *is* civilized and nice."

"Only on the outside—on the inside, it's all messy."

That made Richard smile. "Life is messy. Humans are messy."

The orchard scrolled past us.

"What room are they putting me in?"

Richard pulled into his reserved parking spot at the front. "Just down the hall from your mother."

"Good."

We got out of the car. A sturdy wind whipped across the Illinois plains and tugged at my hair as we walked toward the building. Although it had been days, it seemed like I'd picked Colin up for our trip just that morning.

"It's a job for Doc's famous chocolate chip cookies," Colin had said. Doc Bella had looked sad. I'd wondered why.

A green County Hospital van drove up the road and stopped at the side entrance. Two men in blue scrubs emerged and opened the van's sliding side door. One climbed inside, and the screaming began.

Richard put a hand on my arm to stop me from getting closer. I looked over at him—he watched the van. He was an inch shorter than me, and I noticed for the first time that streaks of silver were invading his black hair. As I looked at him—really looked—lines formed at the corners of his eyes. They squirmed into place as if the magic concealing them was fading.

It had never occurred to me that while Richard had been documenting my life, he'd been aging as well. I still thought of him as that intern with a college student's earnestness, smooth skin, and nervous energy. But, the earnestness had become ambition, and the energy had turned to drive.

Maybe it was the light of day that broke the illusion so abruptly. I usually saw Richard in darker places like his office and rarely thought of him as a human being with a life of his own. We never talked about *his* troubles or *his* dreams, his feelings or his needs. He was an extension of me.

The men guided a woman out of the van, one on each of her arms. She struggled against them. Her trauma pierced the peaceful landscape and silenced the birds. She kicked, squirmed, and screamed.

Jared Baker came out of the side door and joined the other two. He captured the woman's legs, using his reattached arm with surprising strength and dexterity. They took her inside and closed the door behind them. The woman and her trauma disappeared into the Center as completely as a mouse swallowed by a snake.

Richard said, "Come on. Let's get you checked in."

The birds resumed their song.

We also went in through the deliveries entrance, easing into the building, alert for any sign of the new arrival. She was nowhere in sight, though. They'd taken her deeper into the nest of offices.

Richard rang the bell at the intake counter, and a few seconds later, Jared came out. I heard the woman beyond the inner door, shouting obscenities as if they could kill.

Jared leaned on the counter and gazed at me with unhappy eyes. "I heard about the wreck. Don't worry. You'd be surprised what you can recover from." He rubbed his reconstructed arm.

Much to my surprise, tears welled in my eyes at his

kindness. "Thank you."

Richard took over. "We need to get Viviane signed in. She's going to be staying here for a little while, for a rest."

"Are you nuts?" asked Jared. "You go to *Florida* for a rest. Not Malum."

"Input the record, please." Richard used his don't-give-me-no-shit voice—difficult to ignore.

Because I worked at the Center, Jared had all my insurance and personal information in the computer already. I signed on the dotted line, and I was in. I barely had time to feel embarrassed.

Richard and I walked, silent and solemn, to the Women's Wing. While he handed my paperwork to the head nurse, I waited in the recreation room, trying to stay invisible and failing miserably. I was rarely there during the day, so my presence stood out more than a lawyer in church. Several people turned to watch me.

I did my best to avoid their eyes.

The place looked different. Sunlight streamed in through the high windows, breaking the room into a patchwork of squares. I began to see everyone as a piece on a chess board.

The king, Dr. Min, looked over his clipboard. His queen, Nurse Jones, talked with Richard, the king's knight. And then, there were the pawns—the patients. I didn't know all of them. Most were shells of people—éclairs with the sweet filling sucked out of them.

Several I did know were scattered around the rec room. Calla, for example. Her sister was visiting again. They sat with their heads together, little girls conspiring over a jigsaw puzzle. Calla, named for the lily, was plain and stocky. Her depression sometimes broke and became manic giddiness.

Amazon Una was stuck in a corner, rocking from foot to foot and talking to herself. She glanced at me, then looked purposefully away. I heard her distinctly say to no one in particular, "Another angel has fallen off the edge of the earth." She tilted her head as if to better hear an invisible friend's response.

At one of the tables, pretty Nurse Bea, the queen's rook, was painting Dahlia's fingers with No-Chew to keep her from biting her nails. Dahlia was a Jewish-American princess who—instead of getting long, acrylic nails to match the other women from her neighborhood—bit hers to the quick, until they bled.

Eun Hee and Iraida watched Batman stalk the halls of Arkham Asylum on the wall-mounted television. They made a strange pair, laughing madly. Eun Hee, a middle-aged Korean woman, believed she had a man living inside her. She wasn't transgender, she was possessed. He sometimes took over, and he wasn't very nice. Iraida always wore the black veil and robe of an Islamic woman. She was a wraith, rocking and clapping her hands with glee in front of the television.

Mrs. Dufour came over to me with a box of cookies

in her hands. Her husband was Michael Dufour of Dufour Dairy—everybody in the Peoria area knew Daisy the Dufour dairy cow. The famous Dufour estate sat on a bluff overlooking the Illinois River. Though Mrs. Dufour's husband hardly ever came to see her, her daughter did.

Mrs. Dufour said, "Hello, my dear. Have you come to visit your momma?"

I shook my head. "No. I'll be staying here for a little while."

She patted me on the arm. "Checking you in, are they?"

I nodded.

She asked in her sweet, gentle voice, "Can I offer you a cookie?" She pulled one out of her pocket and held it in front of her body to shield it from the nurses. Her daughter brought her a few cookies every week. Mrs. Dufour told everyone that her daughter made them from scratch, though they looked suspiciously store-bought. No one ever corrected her, and the nurses pretended they didn't know.

"Oh, no. Thank you. I'm not hungry."

"Come now. You don't have to be a good girl all the time. Have one."

"No, really. Thank you, but I don't want one."

Mrs. Dufour's face collapsed. Her eyes filled with tears and her mouth dripped downward. "You don't want a cookie? But they're…they're—"

"Okay. I changed my mind." I took the cookie and slipped it surreptitiously into my jacket pocket.

She brightened immediately. "Just don't tell anyone

where you got it. It's contraband, you know? But I think you'll be needing it. This isn't the kind of place you move into without a cookie on hand."

"Thank you, Mrs. Dufour. Now I'm all set."

Her wrinkles rearranged across her cheeks, framing a gentle smile. "At least your momma's here. Now you can visit her all you want."

"That's right."

"If you ever need a cookie, you come find me. I always got cookies. I'm the cookie lady."

I gave her a weak smile. "I'll remember that. Thank you. I have to go now."

Richard was ready to walk me to my room.

The bedroom we entered had ruffled curtains and a golden bedspread. The furniture—plain and mismatched, probably bought at auction—included a dresser, a chair, a desk, and a tall metal cabinet. The queen's army had stripped away all personal items left by the previous occupant. One of Abram's old suitcases waited on the bed for me.

I stood in the middle of the room feeling as if I'd traded places with some other woman. I didn't belong in a mental ward, and I hated how quickly and easily I'd ended up there.

Richard sat in the armchair and crossed his legs at the knee. "It's only temporary."

I looked around at the blank, whitewashed walls. "Famous last words."

◆◆◆

# CHAPTER 11

My grandfather had stuffed my t-shirts and jeans into the suitcase. He'd packed every piece of underwear I owned. He must have just tipped the drawer out. There were socks as well, my girly sneakers, and my sheepskin slippers. He'd included a few paperbacks I'd been intending to read, and there, in the bottom of the suitcase, was my sewing kit. My fingers shook as I picked it up and cradled it to my chest.

"What's that?" asked Richard.

I may have looked at him a bit too quickly or answered a bit too slowly. "It's my sewing kit."

Richard stood and moved to stand beside me. He reached for the kit. "What do you need that for?"

"Just in case. You never know when you're going to bust a seam." I had never confessed my need for pain to Richard or anyone. It was the one piece of my puzzle that I kept for myself.

"These are against the rules. I can't let you keep this."

"What?"

Richard returned to the chair, taking the sewing kit

with him. "Patients aren't allowed to have sharp objects or needles." He put it in his jacket pocket.

"You've got to be fucking kidding me," I said. "Seriously? I'm only here to rest, remember? I'm not those other patients."

The pause before Richard spoke said more than his words. "It's not you I'm worried about. It's the others. If one of them got hold of this, they could hurt someone or themselves."

"I'll be extra careful. I'll keep it hidden."

"I'm sorry. What's the big deal, anyway? It's just a sewing kit."

"No big deal," I replied. The tip of my middle finger tingled, ached for the sharp prick of sanity. I dug my thumbnail into it and turned back to unpacking. I itched with anxiety, irritation growing. The thought of losing the needles triggered my anxiety, and in that moment, I hated Richard. He treated me as if I were an invalid. I didn't need him. I needed my pins.

To hide my reaction, I carried an armful of underwear across to the dresser and pulled open the top drawer. Inside, I found six boxes from Nordstrom, a welcome distraction. I opened one. It held a brand new set of pajamas in burgundy satin.

"Did you buy these for me?" I started to remove the burgundy set from its box.

"They told me you needed at least three pairs. I got you

six, just in case. There's a robe too."

The pajamas had paper in their folds and, as if in an-swer to my thoughts, straight pins keeping it neatly to-gether. I quickly replaced them in their box. I was saved. The nurses hadn't bothered to inspect the boxes, assuming Richard would know better.

Later, I'd take out all the pins and hide them around my room, pushed into the edge of the mattress or threaded into the hem of the curtains, tucked into the corner of a drawer, or the upholstery on the chair, where I'd always have them at my fingertips.

Richard would never know I had them. No one would.

"Thanks," I said. I loved Richard.

I put the suitcase in the cabinet, then stood with my hands on my hips, looking at my room. Institutional, it re-minded me of summer camp, when we'd all moved into strange rooms with shared facilities, and the only things that felt comfortable were the few objects we'd brought with us in our backpacks. I was already missing my pillow and wishing I'd thought to request it.

"Can I go see my mom?" Her room was, at least, famil-iar. It was filled with her things, many of which I'd given to her.

"I need to leave anyway." Richard stood. "I'll walk down that way with you."

"I've been coming here for fifteen years. I know where her room is."

He said, "I need the exercise," and he held the door for me.

The hallway stretched the entire length of the Women's Wing. The floor was covered with industrial linoleum, and the walls were scuffed, painted matte white from the floor to the chair bumper, then wallpapered with apple blossoms on a faded peach background from there to the ceiling. Long before I had first visited the Center, someone had decided to make the Women's Wing more homey. It hadn't changed since.

The same pictures of flowers and landscapes hung bolted to the walls. They had no glass in them, only heavy-duty plastic. Many had been keyed like SUVs. Some had initials carved into them, and still others had crude drawings. The erect penis was my favorite. It didn't matter that they changed the plastic every six months or so. Within weeks, the penis returned. It was a Center tradition. Some said it was a ghost that carved it each time, bemoaning the loss of male companionship.

Richard and I passed several bedroom doors, some open, some closed, some locked.

Voices called to me from the rooms or talked about me.

"Hey, Viviane."

"Hang in there, Viv."

"It's Gisèle's daughter. She's one of us now."

"What a tragedy."

"Viviane's here. Poor baby."

"Such a shame; such a good girl."

I ignored them all and kept walking. I wondered whether my team in the laundry knew about the accident. Lettie must have told them. Did they know I was a patient at the Center and that they'd be washing *my* linens? Had they promoted Ajani or moved a supervisor from another shift to replace me?

Richard asked, "What are you thinking about?"

"Nothing. Just impatient to see Mom."

"You can spend the whole evening with her, if you want. I'll have your dinner brought to you there."

"That'd be nice."

Two patients peeked out of a bedroom. They came right up to us, and we stopped. One was Polly, the willowy half of the pair. She put a fragile hand on my arm. The other was Corona, the pillowy half of the pair. She hovered just behind Polly, fingers fiddling with a button on her pajamas. The two were nearly inseparable.

Polly's parents had died in a fire when she was eight, and she hadn't aged mentally since that night. Physically, she was in her early forties without an ounce of fat on her. She had freckled skin that hung loose on her body, as if the glue between it and her bones was breaking down. Her little pig eyes drooped under the weight of long, thick lashes.

Polly said, "Lady Viviane," in a mournful tone.

Corona said, "It's terrible." She had to have been at least twenty-one (or she wouldn't have been a resident at the Center), but she barely looked old enough to drive. She was an inch shorter than me, and from the waist up, she had the figure of a 14-year-old gymnast. Below the waist, she had full hips and a rounded bottom. She reminded me of a sweet, soft pear.

Corona had an unruly haircut, chopped unevenly, and her eyes were the most interesting thing about her. They were enormous, huge and brown, flecked with bits of copper. She had thick lashes that would never need mascara. She didn't blink very often, and so she always looked surprised. Her eyes were those of a romantic heroine, although the dark circles and sallow indents of her cheeks gave the story a gothic slant. And she was a mouth-breather. That was what Lettie called people who walked around with their mouths hanging open.

I said, "It's okay." I didn't know why I said that, because it definitely wasn't.

Corona knew it wasn't. "It's terrible."

Polly lifted a slim finger. "Your mom ate her supper."

"She did?"

Polly's dry hair was naturally red and faded, kept short because she had a nervous habit of ripping it out if it grew too long. She had a burn scar that ran from her chin down to her elbow on one side. She still ate like a picky kid, and the gauntness of her face made her eyes look saggy in contrast. After the fire, she'd been passed through a series of foster homes that had scarred her even more. It had taken years, but finally someone had diagnosed her properly, and she'd come to live at the Center on the state's dime.

Polly squinted at me. "Lasagna, garlic bread, peas, and mineral water. Nurse Bea took the tray away empty."

"That's good to know. Thanks for watching out for her."

Polly puckered up her mouth. "That's what a lady's maid does. Your mama isn't very good at taking care of herself."

"I know."

Polly curled her fingers in my sleeve and gazed up at me with eyes far older than her mind.

I patted her hand.

Richard said, "We have to go, ladies." He urged me forward with a light touch to the middle of my back.

Corona and Polly peeled away, letting us pass. Corona said quietly, behind me, "It's terrible."

Polly said, "Stop saying that."

"There's something wrong with our world," Corona replied. "Can't you feel it? It's a scritch in the dark or a tickle up the back of your neck. Someone's always watching."

Polly asked, "Who's watching?"

Corona shushed her and lowered her voice, though we could still hear her. *"They* are. It's terrible."

It occurred to me then that I was one of them, one of the shadow-eyed patients. I'd always been separate from them, a sympathetic employee, a visiting relative, but no longer.

We passed a couple of nurses. They said hello and called me by my name. They knew me well after so many years of visiting Mom, but their demeanor had changed. Their kindness wasn't the kindness of equals, but of care-takers, tainted with concern and condescending awareness of my state.

At Mom's door, Richard put a hand on my arm. "I'll be back around bedtime to get you, okay?"

"God, Richard. I can get back to my room by myself. It's just down the hall."

"All right. But don't stay too long. You need to get some rest."

"Okay, *Dad.* Don't worry. I can't stay past lights-out."

"You'll have to be back in your room before that," he said. "Lights-out is when you need to be in bed."

"Oh yeah." I was a patient, not a visitor. The rules had changed.

Mom was seated at her desk, a pen held immobile in her hand. She didn't even look up. She rocked slightly, back and forth, *tick tock,* her face relaxed to the point of frowning.

The last time I'd seen my mom had been the night be-fore Colin and I left for the lake. I crossed to her and put my hand on her shoulder.

"Hi, Mom." Tears swelled in my throat. Being there with her, in the only place I felt truly safe, I couldn't hold it back any longer. "There was an accident." My throat closed, and tears blurred my vision.

She kept rocking, the pen in her hand poised to continue writing in her journal.

"Colin's missing."

She didn't react. She maintained her rhythm, as regular as the ocean lapping against the shore.

I went to my knees beside her, crossed my arms on her lap, and rested my head there. "I don't understand where he could have gone. I think he might be…dead."

Dark clouds gathered on my horizon. Misery expanded inside me. I felt her touch immediately, so gentle, brushing down the back of my head, smoothing my hair. Such a loving gesture made it impossible to contain the storm; her touch coaxed it out. My face went tight. My mouth grimaced. No breath, then too much breath, and my stomach convulsed with silent sobs.

I choked, and my hands shook, curling like dead bugs against my chest. I couldn't make a sound. I was trapped in my head and body, torn asunder from the inside out, and I begged God to make it all right again, begged with all my soul.

My body stopped knowing what to do, but Mom kept stroking my hair.

The tempest raged. It cut me off from escape and shook me hard. Lightning illuminated flashes of memories. Thoughts thundered. The waves crashed against rocks, slashing into the darkest nooks and crannies where black-eyed crabs and sea stars clung for dear life.

It had been three days since the accident. I'd reached my threshold of holding myself together. I was broken, and I couldn't help but think, *He left me.*

My mom slid out of her chair and crouched beside me, surprising me. The movement was so unusual for her that it nearly shocked me out of crying. She had a cotton handkerchief in her hand, and she wiped the tears and snot from my face as if I were a child again. She tucked my hair behind my ear and made soft, unintelligible cooing sounds.

Some time later, she pulled me to my feet and guided me to her bed. She helped me take off my outer clothes and get in under the covers, then she crawled in beside me and held me against her. I remembered how it felt to have her soft, motherly body against mine. I remembered her smell and her warmth. I was small again and frightened of the storm.

Mom banished it, but in its wake, it left water-logged dream homes, scattered memories, and toppled lives.

I closed my eyes, and I was in the lake, underwater, floating upright. Colin was there, facing me, his hands in mine. His face had a blue-gray tint and his hair danced around his head. We looked into each others' eyes, and we were dying, together.

The water soaked into my pores. It waterlogged me. It tried to get in through my nostrils and mouth, through my ears, but I kept it out. I knew I would die and lose Colin if I let it take me completely. I could hold my breath indefinitely. I was weightless, one with the water. Colin looked peaceful. I felt the same.

Then, something grabbed my spine, just behind my belly button, a hand around a handle, and it yanked me backward. My body bent in half at the hips, and my hands came free of Colin's.

His eyes widened, and his mouth opened. A bubble emerged from it and rippled upward. Another popped out of his nose and chased the first. He reached for me.

I heard his voice in my head, "Viviane!"

I reached for him too, but whatever had hold of me dragged me away. I opened my mouth to scream bubbles and inhaled cold lake water. It rushed into my lungs, making them full and heavy.

My captor dragged me backward, upward. Colin grew smaller, and the distance obscured my view of him until he was nothing more than a distorted shape in the swaying water.

His voice became an echo inside my mind. "Viviane. Viviane."

I breached the surface with a splash and continued rising, lifted into the air by whatever had hold of my spine. I was flying, ascending backward over the lake, water draining off me in fat streams. Then, it released me, and I fell, screaming.

◆◆◆

# CHAPTER 12

A nurse set a tray on Mom's desk. "Please try to eat something, Viviane. Gisèle is in the dining room. You could join her." She didn't wait for an answer but just left.

I lay there, unable and unwilling to move. A glance at the clock told me I'd slept for three hours. The sun was waning, and the light coming in the windows had no energy. It didn't shine in so much as drain in, dappled by the rain-splashed windows.

Though Mom was gone, Corona was there, a lady's maid dressed in men's pajamas, black with white piping, sitting in the overstuffed armchair, legs tucked up against her chest, watching me with her loreful eyes. She touched her finger to her lips. "Shhhh. You're safe. Go back to sleep. I'll wake you up when it's time to go back to your room."

I had so many decisions I could make—whether to go back to sleep or not, whether to get out of bed or not, whether to cry some more or not, whether to kill myself or not.

Colin haunted me, circling at the periphery of my mind. I pushed him away, as hard as I could, and watched the water run down the windows, rivulets branching and melding, pooling, and then releasing with a rush. Eventually, my eyes drifted shut.

◆

The next time I woke up, Mom was seated in the armchair, facing me. She was snug in her lacy white nightgown and a pink robe. Her bare feet rested flat on the floor, hands folded in her lap. Someone had braided her hair.

The clock read 20:50. I thought about the first time I met her. The letter had arrived on my eighteenth birthday, special delivery. I had to show my I.D. and sign to prove that I got it. That was my first clue that it was important.

Abram wasn't home when the letter arrived, and I realized later that was probably for the best. I don't know what he'd have done if he'd been there—maybe burned it so I couldn't read it.

The envelope was nice paper, fancy type, and a gold-embossed logo. That was my second clue that it was important.

The letter itself had an air of formality. At the top, it said, "CONFIDENTIAL ATTORNEY-CLIENT COMMUNICATION," all in capital letters. That was my third clue.

I began to think maybe I was in trouble.

The gold-stamped logo was on the stationery too, along with the name of the law firm (Bagley, Smart, and Cobb), and the letter started, "Dear Miss Viviane Lenore Rose."

I had to wipe my sweaty palms on my jeans.

"Enclosed with this letter, you will find copies of documents that have been held in trust for our client, Gisèle Brigid Rose, to be delivered directly to you on your 18th birthday. " It listed several things included in the envelope. "Please call me after you read the enclosures." And it was signed, "Divana Smart, Esq."

One of the items in the package was a hand-written note from my mother dated July 11, 1984—the day she had supposedly died.

It read:

> *My beloved daughter,*
>
> *I had hoped that my imagination was once again carrying me away, but I can no longer deny that I'm about to be taken from you. Thus, I prepare so that you will be safe and sound without me.*
>
> *Change always comes upon a precipice. Have you noticed that, my darling? I'm the Fool with the hound of reality nipping at my heels. You can see forever from a height such as this, allegorical though it may be. One of the joys of aging is that I can finally look back*

*and see the patterns emerging. I recognize the choices I made and the consequences I paid for them.*

*I see the faces of everyone who died before me—for me and for our world. It's not an unhappy sight. I know they're waiting for me to be reborn, and I'm filled with peace.*

*I hold on to the knowledge that I have loved and lived as fully as any awkward kid from Illinois could. I remember it all, and my greatest wish is that I could leave those memories with you. Sadly, I've waited too long, and now I only have time for one letter. I hope you don't find it too confusing and that it helps you to understand the mighty chaos that has been my world. I wish I could have told you everything in person.*

*I realize now, as I consider my impending death, that I have nothing of value to give but words carefully picked from the river of my thoughts and stored in origami cranes and silk-lined boxes.*

*You are henceforth the keeper of my legacy. Guard it well, and I will never truly leave you.*

*He's here. Please forgive him. He's only doing what his fate demands of him.*

*Yours with forever love, your mother.*

The envelope also contained "collected monthly updates on the condition of Gisèle B. Rose, beginning July 16, 1984"—three days *after* she supposedly died—"through the present."

That was how I found out that my mom was a patient at the Center and not dead, as my grandfather had led me to believe. I didn't go see her the day I received the packet. I was so mad at Abram and so upset that I would have spoiled everything. The day I did go, I was still furious, but not nearly as out of my mind with it.

Richard drove me to the Center. I had a license, and I could have taken Abram's old truck, but Richard was afraid I'd freak out on the way or be too upset to drive myself home. He wasn't far from wrong.

Fifteen years later, I tossed back the covers on my mom's bed and sat up, stiff and sore all over. I stood, stretched, and then went to the window. Outside, the building sat in a pool of electric light beyond which the trees in the orchard blended into darkness, swaying as one body.

Simon said, "Somebody's coming." His warnings never came early enough to actually heed them. I didn't even answer him—I just turned to look toward the door.

It opened. Richard paused on the threshold, his face pale and his expression grim.

Simon said, "Uh oh."

I asked, "What's the matter?"

Richard shut the door. He crossed to me, took my hand, and led me to the bed.

We sat down together.

He didn't let go. "Viviane. I'm so sorry," Richard said. "They found Colin."

The words collided in my ears. I felt stupid. I didn't speak the language. "What are you telling me?"

Richard looked down at my hand in his. "They found Colin's body in the lake."

The air vacated the room, creating a vacuum. Deaf and mute, I perched at the forefront of my thoughts, waiting for them to restart and explain what I was hearing. The river of my consciousness had been dammed. Time had abandoned me.

Someone made a heart-wrenching sound, a sob, and I barely registered that it had come from me. My vision swam, and convulsions stole my strength. I felt the needle's prick when Richard sedated me. He'd come prepared. Then, nothing.

# CHAPTER 13

My world shrank to a narrow corridor between my bed and the toilets. People came and went. I saw them and heard them, but they were like the view out the car window, streaming landscapes, there and gone, fleeting, insignificant, forgettable.

Richard was a regular visitor. He turned on the metronome—*tock tick*. He talked to me. He wrote on his clipboard, and Simon read it aloud to me over his shoulder.

"Patient not responding. It's been three days since she learned of fiancé's death. Hasn't spoken a word. Barely aware of external stimuli. I've been unable to draw her into a hypnotic state. Dosage increased in the hope that she will emerge enough to participate in therapeutic dialogue. Continuing suicide watch."

Simon came to the bed and whispered near my ear, "Are you hearing this? Suicide watch. They think you're suicidal. You're not." He paused a beat, then added, "Are you?"

I stared into nothingness, a safe nowhere where I was nobody. A cyclone raged in my head, thoughts dive-bomb-ing me from all directions. I made myself as small as possible and huddled at the heart of a battle I couldn't escape.

I was aware—I just didn't care. They had to make me take my pills, make me eat, make me go to the bathroom. They bathed me. They covered my body in clean pajamas and sheets. They put me in a chair and then back into bed. The only thing they didn't need to do for me was tell me to go to sleep. Of all things, sleep was not my enemy. It held me and let me forget—usually. Except when the nightmares came, and I was back in the car with Colin, floating in the cold, murky water, his skin blue, his eyes staring at me. Every nightmare began with the hope that I could save him and ended with my failure to do so. Whenever I woke up screaming, there was always someone there—a face, right there.

One time, it was Lettie. Tears streamed down her cheeks, and she told me over and over that everything would be all right. I didn't believe her.

Another time, it was Nathan, Colin's self-proclaimed brother. He whispered in my ear, "It's not over. We must find him before it's too late. If you know anything at all about where he is, you must tell me."

And then, it was Polly's forty-something face and eight-year-old voice. She petted my cheek and talked to me. "Are you scared?" When I didn't answer, she said, "I'll leave my protector with you, if you want. She'll keep you safe."

"Your protector?" They were the first words I'd spoken in days. My dry throat barely managed the effort.

Polly nodded. "She lives in my vagina and eats my period blood, but she can go for a whole month without eating anything. She sleeps a lot." Polly petted my cheek. "Don't worry. She won't hurt you. She knows you're my friend. She only hurts men…who try to rape me."

I said, "Oh."

"She is Athena, a warrior-goddess. She's got a hinged jaw, and she can change in size, get really small or really big, but she looks kind of like a hairless mouse."

I said, "You need her more than I do."

"You may be right."

I pretended to go back to sleep until I dozed off for real.

Most often, it was Richard's face there when I woke up. He came every day, talked to me, and tried to hypnotize me. He was desperate to pull me out of the water.

Gradually, I emerged for longer and longer lengths of time.

During a session with Richard, I said, "You're weaning me off the heavier meds, aren't you? I'm waking up with relatively normal brains. I've lost some time, though, and I don't know how much. A week, maybe? Has it been a week?"

Richard replied. "You've been out of it for awhile. Today's March 10th."

"More than a month?" I only remembered those passing weeks in bits and pieces. I asked, "Are we done for today?"

"There's something I want to talk to you about. You know, we haven't discussed Colin's death." Richard leaned forward. "Viviane, they've cremated him. Should we think about arranging a memorial service or maybe finding a place to scatter his ashes?"

Cremation—the reduction of the human body to bone fragments and gleanings that are then ground into dust. Cremains. I saw the flames in my mind and heard screaming to accompany them, but then the flames died, and all that remained was water. I was in a snow globe, standing on a car, with ashes drifting down around me, piling like sand at my feet.

"Viviane?"

"Who arranged the cremation?"

"Dr. Rosenblum did. I think it might be nice to have a memorial. What do you think?"

"Nice?"

"I just mean I think it would be good for everyone if we honored him somehow."

I wasn't sure what to think. "Did you talk to his brother? Nathan?" My voice felt flat and lifeless. "He came to the hospital."

"You didn't mention him. His name is Nathan?"

"I didn't hallucinate him."

"I didn't say you did."

"He said he saw Colin on TV, when we were looking for him. He said the police told him where to find me."

Richard patted my hand. "I'll talk to the police and see what I can find out."

"His family may want the ashes."

"I'll check into it."

The irony of Colin finally finding his family only on the occasion of his death was not lost on me. It was one last kick to the gut by a god with a twisted sense of humor.

Richard and I sat in silence for a moment, each lost in our own thoughts. I was the first to speak again. "I can't believe he's dead."

"I know."

"I loved him so much."

"I know."

"It was my fault."

Richard scooted closer and put his hand firmly on my shoulder. "It wasn't your fault. It wasn't anybody's fault. Sometimes, bad things happen to good people. God never gives us anything we can't carry."

"Don't patronize me."

"He loved you."

"Who? God?" I snorted.

"Colin. Colin loved you."

My mind told me he hadn't loved me enough to get out of the car and swim to shore. He hadn't loved me enough to fight for our life together. I said, "I want to see my mom."

"As soon as you've had a shower and put on clean pajamas."

I started to say, "I don't need—" but he interrupted me, "Yes. You do." He waited while a nurse accompanied me to the showers.

I stood in the hot water for a long time, letting it wash away the dried tears on my face. I soaped and scrubbed. For a short while, it gave me the illusion that I could rinse my troubles down the drain. I put on clean pajamas, hunter green, and my robe. When I got back to my room, Richard was seated at the desk. He closed his laptop.

"You didn't make my bed?" My voice came out deadpan.

Richard's mouth lifted at one side. "My job is to straighten your head, not your bed."

"Aren't you the witty one, Mr. Wilde."

"I'm a poet, and I don't even know it."

I replied that he was a dork with a spork, an old comeback from my high school days, though my sass had no steam.

He chuckled. "I think we're devolving, but I'm glad to see you're feeling better."

"Don't get too excited. This is just my manic phase. It won't last."

"All right, let's see if we can use this mania of yours to get a good meal in you. Everyone has gone to the dining room for lunch, including your mother. Shall we?"

"You can't come with me. That'd be like Abram coming on a date with me."

"Fine." Richard raised his hands in surrender. "I'll come back to check on you before I leave for the day." When he had walked down the hall, out of sight, I headed for the dining room. It opened off the recreation room and was locked except during mealtimes. The kitchen was directly below it. Food came up in a staff-only elevator, and kitchen workers distributed it to patients. The dining room always smelled of day-old meatloaf and overcooked beans. I found my mom seated at a long table with Corona, Polly, Mrs. Dufour, Calla, Dahlia, Eun Hee, and Iraida— each with an empty table-setting in front of them. When the ladies saw me, they scooted down, and I took a seat on the bench.

Corona and Polly both looked at me with sad eyes. Eun Hee merely bowed in my direction, her black cap of hair bobbing. Iraida dipped her chin to her chest in greeting, a gesture that made her look remarkably nun-like in her burka. Mrs. Dufour, pretty in that fragile way only elderly women can be, smiled at me, and it lit up her eyes. She leaned over toward my mother and said, "Gisèle, your daughter is as pretty as Glenda the Good Witch."

My mother didn't respond, but I warmed even more to Mrs. Dufour.

Calla waved at me without enthusiasm, revealing the cross-hatched scars on her wrist; and Dahlia looked down her prominent nose at me. "You're one of us now, hm? Like mother like daughter?" She handed me her plate and bundle of silverware.

"It's only temporary," I replied.

Several of them mumbled, "Famous last words."

One of the kitchen workers—a swollen, middle-aged woman—arrived with a cart. She set out two family-style bowls of salad and a plate of individually-wrapped hoagies.

Mrs. Dufour reached for a sandwich with a tremulous hand. "The *Wizard of Oz* is a classic, you know. It has the answers to all life's questions."

I watched as Corona, my mother's self-proclaimed lady's maid, opened a half-sandwich for my mother and grabbed a handful of salad that she transferred onto a plate for her.

Calla said, "That was my father's favorite movie. We watched it every year on his birthday. He'd make special finger-food—fish sticks, tater tots, and crackers with corn relish, and we'd sit in front of the television and sing all the songs. He's dead now."

The table became a chaotic dance of arms and hands reaching for salad, sandwiches, condiments, and spices.

"That movie," Corona commented, "scared the crap out of me when I was little. I had nightmares about the witch on the bicycle in the tornado." She dun-dud-dut-dun-dun-dunned the tune.

With a disgusted expression, Eun Hee asked, "Did you know that Auntie Em killed herself? She took an overdose of pills and put a plastic bag over her head."

As Polly reached for a helping of salad, she said, "Auntie Em wasn't the one on the bicycle."

"I didn't say she was."

Dahlia chimed in. "Judy Garland tried to gack herself several times but failed. They say she died of an *accidental* drug overdose. Whatever."

"And why does it matter?" Calla asked. "She's dead. Dead is dead. Don't matter how you got there."

"Sssst!" Polly made a face, indicating me with a roll of her eyes. "Maybe talk about something else?"

"Why?" Corona pointed her fork at me. "The Oracle died of diabetes. What's that about?"

"The Oracle?" Mrs. Dufour sounded confused. "You mean the Wizard, dear?"

Polly sighed in frustration. "She means the Oracle from *The Matrix*." She turned over the catsup bottle and squeezed a fat dollop onto her plate.

"Yeah." Pixie-faced Corona grabbed a handful of salad for herself. "Can you imagine knowing you're going to die before it happens? I don't think I'd want that."

"C'mon!" Eun Hee snorted. "The Oracle could see the future. The actress couldn't."

"How do you know she couldn't?" Corona challenged the other woman.

"Point taken."

My mother ate with mechanical movements, and I was certain she wasn't enjoying her food. Her gaze remained distant.

Calla said, "I suppose you could say *The Matrix* is *The Wizard of Oz* for our generation."

"I think they're both stupid." Dahlia looked around the table, waiting for anyone to disagree with her.

I couldn't keep up with them. They had a rhythm they'd developed over years of meals together. I ate in silence.

Iraida was the first to rise from the table. She stood, and conversation paused so everyone could look expectantly at her.

She said, "As-salaamu 'alaykum."

Several people at the table, replied, "Wa 'alaykum as-salaam," on a sliding scale of correctness, going from faking it with mumbles all the way up to nailing it. They all spoke respectfully. Iraida turned and left the cafeteria, a floating, sable-draped figure, a ghost in negative.

Polly leaned over the table toward me and whispered, "She said, 'Peace on you.' And we said, 'On you too.'" She grinned. "We say it after every meal, when she goes back to her room to pray."

I pulled the edge of Polly's sleeve away from the ketchup on her plate, just in the nick of time. "You'll have to teach me."

♦

After lunch, I took Mom back to her room. The drawn drapes cast the room in darkness. I went to one pair and pushed them aside so I could look out upon the circular drive and the orchard in the distance. The trees had budded, the leaves filling in between branches. The last time I'd noticed, they were bare. I'd time-traveled several weeks into the future, as unconscious as Sleeping Beauty upon my dais, waiting for Prince Charming to come and kiss me awake. But my prince wasn't coming. Ever.

A large black sedan, almost a limousine, pulled up and parked in front of the Center. It had tinted windows that made it impossible to see inside. Colin's brother Nathan emerged from inside it. He was again—or still—dressed all in black, blending with the sleek lines of the car, his coat long and lean on his body. He tipped his head up and met my eyes.

His gaze entrapped me, and a sense of danger put goosebumps on my arms. I quickly closed the drapes. Afterward, I chided myself for my overactive imagination.

Mom said, "Kypris knew her father would be angry when he found out, but fear of his rage wasn't enough to keep her away from her lover." Although she spoke in a monotone, occasionally I heard or imagined emotion leaking into and out of her tale. I curled up in the armchair to listen.

*Kypris had fallen as irretrievably in love with Chance as a cherry that's fallen from the tree. She would have followed him anywhere, but his descriptions of his home, of Apfallon, made her want to go there for reasons other than just to follow him.*

*Nevertheless, it came as a surprise when Chance suggested that she could travel between worlds in the blink of an eye. It seemed a ridiculous idea, and she mocked him gently, until he showed her just how insubstantial reality is.*

*He took her to Apfallon. The transition to the other place was immediate and startling. Kypris suddenly found herself on an emerald hillside, all blinking forgotten. It was Chance's turn to laugh, and so he did.*

*He made Kypris his wife, and they took up residence in an enormous castle overlooking an apple orchard. From her window, Kypris could watch fairies chase one another around the tree trunks. The tiny creatures slept draped upon their branches and left apples on her windowsill. Kypris, barely out of childhood, was delighted with her new playground.*

*Chance pampered her, even going so far as to acquire a miniature golden dragon for her. She named her dragon "Simon."*

Simon. I'd often wondered about the significance of the name. I'd looked it up once. In the second century

A.D., Simon the Sorcerer had died at the Roman Coliseum while levitating in front of Nero to prove his magical powers were real. Many people thought he was a demon— others thought he was an incarnation of Merlin.

Saint Simeon the Holy Fool (same name, archaic spelling) lived in the sixth century A.D. His method of ministering to the people was to act completely bonkers while performing miracles in secret. He tripped people for no reason, dragged himself around on his butt like a dog, danced wildly with no music, and talked to invisible friends. He'd have fit right in at the Center. It wasn't until after his death that historical records implied that he'd been faking it the whole time.

Maybe Saint Simeon had been stalking the moon. Maybe his mission on Earth had been to make people feel and think, to teach that life is visceral—it's the smell of shit and the taste of mold. It's the feel of a loving kiss and the sound of the words, "You will always be mine."

I rocked myself—stalking the moon.

Simon asked, "Viv, are you all right?"

I sniffled. "I'm fine." I found the straight pin I kept threaded into the inner seam of my pajama top and pricked it into my forearm. The pain spread outward from the spot, crackling along nerve highways and byways. I poked another next to the first, then another, forming the letter C—*C for Colin.*

"You don't seem fine," Simon said. "You've got snot

running over your lips, and you look rabid. Stop hurting yourself."

"I'm fucking fine, okay? Get out of here. You're not real!"

"Oh, not that old song again," he groaned.

I tucked the pin back into its hiding place and grabbed a tissue off Mom's side-table. I folded it, then lay it flat over the welling droplets of blood. The paper soaked them up, and I had a vague, spreading representation of a C.

Someone knocked on the door. "Gisèle, it's Nurse Bea. I'm coming in." Nurse Bea, the blond with the tits that all men coveted. I thought, *Nurse Busy Bea,* and that made me laugh, tripping along a moonbeam.

Bea entered and said, "Oh, Viviane," as if we were friends. "I didn't realize you were here."

Simon said, "She reminds me of a yappy yorkie."

"A spazzy greyhound," I replied.

Nurse Bea said, "I beg your pardon?"

"I was just heading back to my own room." I tucked the blood-stained toilet paper in my robe pocket.

"I know for a fact that you haven't had your medication this evening."

"It's under control, Nurse Busy Bea." In my head, I was murdering her a dozen different ways.

Nurse Bea insisted on walking me back to my room. "It's so important to have a routine. Every night, before bed, I brush my teeth. It feels good to go to bed with clean teeth. Just you wait and see. You'll feel better as soon as you've brushed."

I mumbled, "No halitosis monkey here."

"After brushing, I wash my face. You can scrub off all the terrible things from your day and start fresh. You'll see. It's magical, really."

"Magical."

"We can do it together."

"I can do it myself."

"We wouldn't want you to feel alone and abandoned, would we?"

"No. We wouldn't want that."

As we entered my room, she said, "Oh, look. Someone sent you flowers and a gift."

I didn't look. I didn't care. I crawled in bed and pulled the covers up over my head.

"They arrived this afternoon. They're from your grandfather. Isn't that lovely?"

I said, "Yeah," but the word was bitter. "Lovely like *I'll be over here when you're done being crazy.*"

"Oh, surely not. Your grandfather loves you."

"He loves me when I'm sane."

On my eighteenth birthday, I'd confronted Abram about my mother.

His response had been, "Stop acting crazy." I wasn't crazy. I was pissed. I shouted at him, "Why didn't you tell me? She's my mom!" I was so furious, I was crying.

"Just settle down." He raised his palms toward me. "I didn't tell you because it was easier that way." He looked afraid, and I savored that.

"Easier for who? Me? Or you?"

"For both of us. You can't imagine how it would've been for you, growing up knowing that your mother was in that place. You were too young. I couldn't do that to you. I wanted you to have a normal life."

"You lied to me!"

"I never actually said she was dead. I said she was gone, and she is gone. I love your mother, but she left us a long time ago."

"Do you visit her?" The words tasted sour, spoiled milk.

He just looked at me.

I said, "Don't lie no more," and I meant every ounce of the warning in my voice.

Abram's voice changed then, coming out through clenched teeth, and I could tell I'd almost pushed him too far. "You saw her. You talked to her. Do you honestly think she has any idea you're there or that you're her kid?"

I was fearless in my fury. "She knows! And she loves me! You never really loved me. You just wanted somebody to cook your meals and do your dishes."

His face turned red, and he clenched his fists. For the first time ever in my life, I thought he was going to hit me, or worse, cry. And I was sorry—immediately and completely sorry. I had gone too far.

But he didn't even shout. He just said, low and intense, "Your mother chose to leave of her own…free…will." He sat down hard in his recliner and reached for the remote. He stabbed it at the television and ignored me.

I stood there, sobbing and hating him with all my heart. I knew he was wrong. My mom would never have left me by choice.

From that day forward, I referred to him as Abram, never again as Grandpa.

Nurse Bea went to the door. "All right, love. I'll come back later. Ring the bell if you need anything."

Simon said, "Jesus H. Christ. I thought she'd never leave. I'm guessing she went into nursing for the captive audience."

I ignored him, got out of bed, and went to the flowers. It was a large bouquet, a symphony of pink, yellow, and lavender, punctuated by curling reeds and sparkled with baby's breath. There was a box tied to the flowers, without wrapping.

The card said, "I thought you might need a new cell phone. I got them to keep your old number for you. Call any time. Abram."

I snorted.

He may as well have said, "I'll see you when you get home." He wasn't even pretending. If they never let me out, I'd never see him again.

"Call anytime, my ass." I ripped the flowers from their vase and tore them stem from stem, spewing petals. The petals floated for a few seconds, then dropped to the floor. The flower heads bounced across the linoleum. They released their perfumes as I ravaged them. I ripped and shredded until there was nothing left but shards.

Staring down at the mess I'd made, I panted. None of it made any sense. The colors were all mixed up. Tiny petals lay upon large ones, and torn stems lay tumbled like pick-up sticks. Leaves landed on every surface, places they didn't belong. They lifted on the air, blowing out of the heater vent, and peeked out from under the bed. They were the days and nights of my life.

Simon asked, "Feel better?"

I crossed to the bed and crawled back in. When I rubbed my feet together, I felt petals stuck to them. My fingers smelled green. I closed my eyes.

The sounds of the Center melded into a distant hum, punctuated by the occasional raised voice or squeaky wheel. I drifted in an insubstantial sea of sound, smell, and passing time. *Tick, tock.* The halls grew still. Everyone was in their rooms or in the rec room.

It was because of the quiet that I heard it—a distant siren, door alarm, or heart monitor gone flat. I tried to ignore it, but it didn't stop. I'd heard it before, and I was pretty sure it was all in my mind.

◆◆◆

# CHAPTER 14

Apart of me wanted to stay in bed, to pull the covers over my head and hide, but a bigger part of me didn't trust my bed. The last time I'd heard that noise, the hag had been in there with me.

I got up and put on my slippers and robe.

Most of the doors were closed along the deserted hallway. Televisions competed with one another from different rooms, and—despite my better judgment—I headed toward the screech.

"Where are you going?" Simon asked, sounding upset.

I ignored him.

Perhaps a recording had gotten stuck on a single note. But no. That wasn't it.

The hag had made that noise when she was suffocating me.

Simon said, "Don't stick your nose where it doesn't belong," and he was deathly serious.

So many times, I'd ignored Simon's advice and regretted it. I already had a feeling this was going to be another of those times. But, I couldn't stop. The sound became a ringing in my ears. Someone was in danger.

I met no one in the hall. Among all the closed doors, one stood open. The sound came from that room.

I crept along the wall and touched the doorframe with my fingertips. My hand shook.

"Viviane," Simon said near my shoulder. "I'm serious. Stop. Please."

That time, I did. I stopped just outside, pressed against the wall.

The unearthly keening didn't waver.

I expected someone to say, "This is a test of the Emergency Broadcast System," but no one did. It just kept going. Other noises came from the room: grunts and groans, definitely human, and beneath it all, the resonant ticking of a clock. *Tick tock tick.*

I stepped into the room.

The keening stopped. A gurgle emitted from the bed. An elderly woman lay there, mouth and eyes open wide. Her entire body was tense with the effort to breathe. I almost didn't recognize Mrs. Dufour, the cookie lady.

I shouted, "Help!" and ran to the bed. "You're going to be okay."

Mrs. Dufour lay spread-eagle on top of the sheets, the warm smell of piss and shit rising from her. She looked at me with eyes gone bloodshot with terror, took a deep breath, and screamed.

I knew *exactly* how she felt.

Her scream was different from the keening. It was uneven, broken, and definitely human. It expressed anguish and horror. She flailed her arms and kicked her legs, tossed her blankets off, knocked over the lamp, and sent a small wooden cuckoo clock flying off her nightstand to shatter on the floor.

I caught her wrists, so thin and fragile in my hands. Her skin, translucent with age, showed the blue veins inside.

"Mrs. Dufour. You're safe now."

She stopped screaming and lay still, but she never made another sound or took another breath.

I watched the life leave her eyes. "Help!"

Nurses rushed into the room and shoved me aside.

I almost tripped on the cuckoo clock, and it made one final, misplaced *tick*. Then, it too died.

They hurried around, administered CPR, and tried to resuscitate Mrs. Dufour. Someone guided me out of the room and into the hallway. People came from all directions: nurses, doctors, guards, orderlies, and patients. They moved me this way and that. I was a leaf caught in the rapids.

All I could think was, *She's dead. It killed her.*

I had to get away. I pushed through the gawkers and made my way to the edge, by the wall. Resting my cheek against the apple-blossom wallpaper, I asked Simon, "What the Hell was that?"

"You don't want to know."

At my elbow, Corona said, "It's a *mara*. I heard it." She bounced on her toes, trying to launch herself higher so she could see through the pressing bodies into Mrs. Dufour's room. The sleeves on her pajamas hung down past her hands, and the pants legs pooled at her bare feet.

"You heard it too?" I asked.

She looked at me but didn't say anything.

"Back to your rooms," shouted a nurse, shooing the crowd of onlookers into a wave that quickly engulfed me and Corona. We got separated.

"Corona!" I cried.

The crowd swarmed me, and I had to shove through it. By the time I broke free, Corona had disappeared.

I cut past the stragglers. "Did you see where Corona went?"

No one had.

The doors on the hallway were all open by then. Nurses had arrived in force and actively calmed patients agitated by the emergency.

Nurse Bea latched onto me. "C'mon, Viviane. Let's get you to your room."

"I'm looking for Corona."

Bea put her hand in the middle of my back and directed me down the hall. "All we need to worry about right now is Viviane. Come along."

Short of punching her—and I did consider it—there was no chance to get away. I let her walk me back to my room. When Nurse Bea saw the flower-petal art I'd made, she stared, first at the mess, then at me.

"I see you've been busy," she said. "Unfortunately, there's no time to deal with this right now." Later, she'd tell everyone that I'd destroyed a "perfectly lovely" bouquet of flowers, and I was sorry—for a second—that I'd done it. Not remorseful, just sorry that I'd given her fuel for her gossip.

She helped me off with my robe, tucked me into bed, left, and shut the door behind her.

I threw back the covers and got out of bed again.

The door opened, and Nurse Bea stuck her head back in. She glowered at me. "Don't be naughty, girlie, or I'll have a talk with your doctor. This is not the time to clog up the halls."

She may have been insipid, but she was right. I would have added to the confusion and chaos, and in an institution for the reality challenged, chaos wasn't a good thing. I sat down on the edge of the bed. Nurse Bea left, and I turned to crawl under the covers.

Corona popped up on the far side of the bed.

I screamed and nearly fell.

Corona shushed me with her finger to her lips.

"You scared the shit out of me. Jesus, I thought you were—"

She shushed me again, then tipped her head to listen. I listened too, but Nurse Bea had actually gone away that time.

Corona joined me on the bed, and we sat cross-legged facing one another. She had a handful of petals—pink, yellow, and lavender. She stirred them in her palm as she looked me over from head to toe and back, as if searching for some clue to me.

I said, "Tell me the truth. Did you really hear the noise too?"

Her eyes flicked to mine and locked there. She said, not without compassion, "Are you freaking out? It's okay. I know how it is when you first fall down the rabbit hole. It can be disorienting."

"Yeah."

She nodded, my wise guru. "You took the red pill."

"Corona, you're not making any sense. Did you hear that high-pitched noise?"

"That's what I'm trying to tell you. You're blooming. You're a rose, and your petals are opening. One day, you'll look back on this, and you'll know that everything started right here, on this spot. One day, you'll be queen. But before that, you have to save the world."

"What?"

"I have faith in you."

"Corona," I said, my frustration making my teeth clench. "Why couldn't anyone else hear it?"

"It's simple. Their ears aren't calibrated for it." She put a hand on my knee. "Their minds can't parse encrypted data as well as yours and mine can.”

“I don’t understand. What was making that noise?”

She withdrew her hand and folded it with the other in her lap. “*Maras* are cousins of banshees, but more aggressive. They sit on your chest until you die.”

“Why are we the only ones who hear it?” I wondered if Corona was stalking the moon. It’d be so easy to dismiss what she was saying as delusion, and I came close to it, but I’d spent the majority of my life hearing things no one else could hear. Never before had I heard something that *only one other person* could hear. That was significant. The fact that Corona had heard it too made it real, triangulated, and three-dimensional. It hadn’t been a hallucination. It could’ve killed me.

Corona’s eyes were huge. She slid off the bed. “There are two kinds of people. Those who can see and hear, and those who can’t.” She touched her own nose with the tip of a finger, then reached over and touched mine. “We can.”

Corona went to the door, looked back, and added, “The night hag is on a mission. Watch your back. Your signature is getting stronger. You know?”

“My what?”

“Your signature.” Corona opened the door a crack, and with her eye pressed to it, she looked out into the hall. “The more you know, the greater the friction between your thoughts and reality. When a swimmer splashes, her movement ripples through the water and attracts sharks.”

"What?"

"The *mara* is a shark. It's drawn to the magick in your blood." She looked back at me one last time before slipping out the door. "That is your signature."

My mind focused on the slow way the door swung shut in her wake. Its click, normally quiet, echoed in my head as if it were agreeing with Corona, supporting her strange revelation with its own certainty.

My sense of security soured. I imagined the misty hag brushing my legs. I remembered the clench in my lungs and gut when I couldn't breathe. When it had attacked me in the hospital, I'd told myself it was just a nightmare, that it hadn't really happened at all. I'd been wrong.

The lights flickered. Was it watching me? Waiting for me? A shiver jerked my shoulder blades. What if it was under the bed? I had to get out of there. I jumped, putting as much distance as I could between me and the bed, and reached the door in three strides.

Out in the hall, the coast was clear. All the commotion was down by Mrs. Dufour's room. I ran the opposite direction, to my mom's room.

Mom sat in the armchair, looking out the window, apparently oblivious to the chaos.

I took my usual seat in the vanity chair, and on cue, she joined me, picking up the hairbrush. She smoothed my hair, my nerves, and my mind with her even strokes.

I hugged myself, chewing on the knowledge that the

hag was real—Corona had corroborated her existence. Eventually, it hit me that Corona and I weren't the only ones who knew about the hag. Colin had known as well. I had just dismissed his claims as delusions.

# CHAPTER 15

They wouldn't let me sleep in Mom's room, so I spent a restless night listening for sounds and making sure my feet stayed covered. As soon as I heard people moving about, I got up and wandered down to the rec room.

The staff members clustered together in small groups, talking in whispers about Mrs. Dufour. The patients seemed calm enough, though definitely affected. Calla sat on one of the couches, cross-legged, with her arms draped over her head. She watched the room with hawkish attention. Dahlia sat at the puzzle table, chewing on a cuticle. Polly made the rounds, asking, "What about the cookies? How are we gonna get cookies?" Iraida sang an Islamic chant in her room.

Detective Stace Hayward was talking to Queen Jones in the nurses' office. He looked all-business, and she looked helpful.

I caught Corona's eye from across the room, but when I started to go to her, Nurse Bea intercepted me. The queen's rook put her hands on my shoulders and turned me around.

"Good morning, Viviane. You just crawled out of bed,

didn't you?"

She was right. I had. Forgetting to groom came with the territory of my illness.

Nurse Bea took me back to my room and insisted she would go with me to the showers. I told her a thousand times I could manage on my own, but she ignored me. Finally, I gave up, and she did the rest of the talking.

"What a night, hm? I'm working a double shift because Francis didn't come in this morning. I don't mind, mind you. I can't believe what's happening." She linked her arm through mine as we walked to the showers, and she kept her voice low. "These things come in threes, you know? Mrs. Dufour was the third death in as many months. Can you imagine?"

"Three?"

"Yes. Three. I imagine you know about the others too. For instance, old Mr. Jackson. He was the first to go. Died in his sleep, he did, but no one found that surprising. He was ninety-four. Then, there was Danny McIntyre. Poor kid was only twenty-two. They think he had an allergic reaction or something. No one's really sure why he died, but there you have it. And now, sweet Melanie Dufour. I'll miss her. See, that's why the police are here." Bea's eyes were gleaming. She loved gossip, both the receiving and the giving of it. She'd been reprimanded for it on several occasions, but she was an addict. "Can you imagine?"

I mumbled, "I have a very active imagination."

"Three deaths. Four, if you count that laundry worker, too." She clucked her tongue. "What are the—"

"Laundry worker?"

She paused a moment, then said, "No one told you? That young Hispanic man who had the seizure in the stairwell. He passed on."

"When?"

"Several weeks ago now, love. I'm sorry. I assumed you knew. He was a coworker of yours, am I right?"

I stopped listening to her, my thoughts on Julio and his family, until we arrived at the shower room. By then, Bea was saying, "…asking about you too, since you were the one who found Mrs. Dufour. They wanted to question you, but Dr. Reuter told them no. Detective Hayward is leading the investigation." She squeezed my arm and gave me an excited look as if we were about to get on a roller coaster or drive off a cliff together. "His given name is Stace. Oh, he's a marvel, that one. Damned good-looking. I quite fancy him. And to think, if I hadn't been working an extra shift today, I'd have missed all the excitement."

◆

When I got back from my shower, Lettie was waiting for me in my room.

"Hey!" she said as I entered. Her skirt and blouse displayed crisp wrinkles from spending the night in her locker, and her hair had the mussed look it got when she had worked in the steamy laundry room all night. Her shift had just ended.

"Why didn't you tell me Julio died?" I asked.

"Richard asked me not to. He said you needed more time."

"I figured that was what it was," I said. "It's okay. Did they have a funeral?"

"Yeah. I went. We all did. There were a lot of people there. I think his whole church was there. His mother. His sister." She sighed. "It was kind of awful. You're lucky you missed it. Are you angry I didn't tell you?"

I shook my head. I couldn't find it in me to be angry. I set down my shower basket and went to her. I took her in my arms, and we hugged for a long while. She smelled like the laundry, of sweat and bleach.

I said, "I'm glad you came."

She held me at arm's length and looked me over from head to toe. "You look tired."

"I didn't sleep very well last night. One of the other patients—"

"I heard."

We sat facing one another on the bed.

Lettie said, "Remember that white chick he was dating?"

"Yeah. Was she there?"

"Uh huh. Crying and dropping petals in the coffin with

him and shit. I saw his mom pick them out after she left."

"Mrs. Dufour makes five, you know?"

"Five what?"

"Five deaths in three months."

Lettie sat up. "I don't understand. Five?"

I looked down at my hand as if I had notes marked there. "Julio. They said it was a seizure, but he had no history of seizures. Then, there were the two guys from the men's wing who died, supposedly of natural causes. There's Colin, and last night, Mrs. Dufour. That's five."

"Honey, the Center is a place for unhealthy people. It's normal for people to die here. It's just a coincidence that it all happened at the same time."

"No. Two deaths is a coincidence. Five is a pattern, Lettie."

"A…pattern? That's…a stretch." She cocked her head, expression thoughtful.

"Maybe."

"You think there's something sinister going on?"

"I do." I leaned forward and met her gaze directly.

Lettie chewed her bottom lip, then said, "You almost died in that wreck too, you know."

"But, I didn't. Someone took the trouble to pull me out of the water, but then they just left me there. Isn't that strange?"

Lettie said, "What if it was the guy who jumped in front of your car, and he didn't want to get in trouble for causing the accident?"

We stared at each other in silence for a long minute, then Lettie asked, "When can you get the fuck out of here? This place is making you paranoid."

"I wouldn't mind getting out," I said.

Lettie tapped the hot pink nail of her index finger against her front teeth, thinking hard. After a moment, she asked, "What would it take to get you released?"

"Richard's signature, I suppose. But he won't do that. Not until he's convinced I'm better."

I hadn't told Lettie anything about the hag yet. I normally didn't keep things from her, not even my hallucinations, but this felt real and scary. The words came out of my mouth on their own, "What if there's a monster at the Center?"

"A monster?" Lettie said, laughing. "Honey, hallucinations don't kill people. People kill people. Old age and disease kill people."

"People can be monsters," I replied. "Monsters can be people."

◆

After Lettie left, I returned to my mom's room. She sat at her desk, writing.

From the window, I looked out at the orchard. The trees stood in neat rows, their branches spreading with individualized style. A squirrel ran from tree to tree, a scampering blur with a rippling tail. A blue jay, its raucous call distant, had the crown, the attitude, and the meanness of a thief. It flew back and forth between the highest branches, snatching and grabbing.

The hair on my arms stood up.

Mom was writing, unaware of anything around her.

When I turned my gaze back to the window, it went straight to the source of my discomfort. Nathan stood on the path at the edge of the orchard. A breeze picked up his hair and made it dance around his head. His long, black overcoat covered his white, collarless shirt and black pants. He clasped his hands behind his back, feet slightly apart, and looked straight at me.

A sense of dread washed over me, not dissimilar to the one I'd felt in the stairwell when Colin had frightened me. I yanked the curtains shut.

When I peeked out again a few seconds later, cracking the curtains just enough to put my eye to them, his face was *right there* at the window.

*Right there. At the second-floor window.*

I shrieked and fell back, landing on my ass on the floor. I crab-crawled backward. The curtain fell into place, closed.

Scrambling to my feet, I stumbled to the door. I pulled it open, stuck my head out, and shouted, "Corona!" I didn't know who else to call. I acted on instinct. "Corona!"

After what seemed an eternity, several faces peeked out of several rooms. Luckily, none of them belonged to a nurse. One was Corona's. She came running.

"What's the matter?"

"There's a man at the window!"

"What?" She entered the room. "We're on the second floor."

"Exactly."

She parted the drapes and peeked out. She stuck her head between the curtains and looked this way and that. When she emerged, she said, "I don't see anyone. Are you sure?"

I was as sure as a schizophrenic could be, which wasn't sure at all. I shrugged.

"Well there's no one there now. Do you know who it was?"

"I met him at the hospital, after the accident. He said he was Colin's brother." My hand shook when I ran it through my hair. "I must've imagined it."

She didn't seem convinced.

I kept the curtains closed for the rest of the day.

◆◆◆

# CHAPTER 16

I was seated cross-legged in Mom's armchair, reading a book, when the door opened, and Detective Hayward backed inside, watching the hall. He shut the door.

"Can I come in?" He turned to face me.

"You're already in."

"Your friend Corona told me where you were. I've only got a few minutes, Miss Rose, but I wanted to ask you some—"

"I don't think my doctor wants me to talk to you."

"True. But I thought you might feel differently, considering how I'm trying to figure out what happened to your fiancé and Melanie Dufour." Hayward pulled a digital tape recorder from his pocket and held it up for me to see. He kept it in his hand and thumbed it on. "Do you mind?"

I dog-eared my place, closed the book, and set it aside. "I don't mind, but I don't know how I can help."

"You'd be surprised," said Hayward, "how often I hear that from people who end up giving me exactly what I need to solve the case."

"I hope you're right."

Hayward studied her for a long minute. "Your hair's grown," he observed. "You look different. Less manic."

"Better drugs."

I heard Nurse Bea in the hall. Her accent—as sweet as the richest chocolate, but just as likely, in large quantities, to trigger a migraine—was unmistakable. "Did you see where Stace—I mean Detective Hayward—went?"

Hayward tumbled his question out as if he were trying to beat a buzzer. "Did you see anyone in Melanie Dufour's room last night?"

"No one. She was alone. She couldn't breathe." I had already decided that I couldn't tell the truth and expect to be believed.

Nurse Bea rushed in a second later and said, "Detective. I'm sorry, but I can't let you speak with this patient without approval from her doctor. She's had a rough time lately, and we want to make sure she's stable before—"

Detective Hayward interrupted her. "Look, Bea. Mind if I call you Bea?" He hid the recorder behind his back and stepped closer to the nurse. He made his face go from deadpan to charming with no in-between.

Bea blinked and stopped in her tracks. She was looking up at Hayward like a kid looking at her own birthday cake. "I don't mind."

"Thanks. You and I have been great partners all morning." He winked. "I promise not to upset Miss Rose, but I *need* to get this questioning out of the way. You're welcome to stay. As a matter of fact, I'd be grateful if you did. I'm sure your presence will have a calming effect on her."

Bea blushed but held her ground. "I could lose my job."

Detective Hayward gazed down at her, and his face changed yet again, becoming more serious, though his tone stayed friendly.

"This is a police matter, Bea. I'll take the consequences. I'm not doing due diligence if I don't talk to the person who may have witnessed what happened. I promise I will do nothing to upset her. You may stay or go, as you wish. I won't tell anyone you were here."

Bea considered that, her jaw set. She clasped her hands in front of her and turned to Viviane. "Now, Viviane, you tell the detective everything you know. There's nothing to be afraid of. He's here to help us." Then she shut up.

Detective Hayward had tamed the shrew. He allowed his lips a little smirk before turning his attention back to me.

I vowed never to underestimate him.

He asked, "Viviane, can you tell me what happened?"

I could, but the question should have been, "Will you?" I ran through the truth in my mind and imagined his reaction to it. It wasn't hard to imagine, the look of disbelief, pity, and even disgust. I answered, "I heard a scream, so I went down there."

"Did you see anyone leave her room?" Hayward moved to the opposite side of the bed from Nurse Bea. He was wearing the exact same clothes he had worn when he'd visited me in the hospital: khaki pants, white button-down shirt, and a dark blue suit-coat frayed around the cuffs. He had his badge clasped to his belt.

I shook my head slowly and lied. "I didn't see anyone."

Hayward's eyes narrowed. He didn't believe me, and that surprised me.

Over the years, I'd grown skilled at lying.

He leaned against the bed-side table, casual as a snake in the grass. "I've been wracking my poor, tired, old brain, trying to figure out what's going on here, and I keep coming back around to the same thing, over and over again. There's only one person who had access to all the victims. We in the policing business call that 'means.' Can you guess who that might be, Miss Rose?"

I wasn't sure where he was going, and he obviously hadn't finished, so I just shook my head.

"You, Miss Rose. All signposts point to you."

Nurse Bea gasped. Hayward looked at her. Their eyes locked and a silent communication crossed between them. I could translate it. Nurse Bea warned him not to rock the boat too much.

Hayward ignored her. "You, Miss Rose, had free access to all levels of this building, and according to the nurses, you took advantage of that on a regular basis. You were the one who found Julio, *and* you were a patient in the hospital when he succumbed to his injuries. You've been seen lurking around the Men's Wing at all hours—in contradiction to the institution's rules."

My stomach churned.

Hayward looked down at the floor and kept his voice even. "And then, there's sweet Mrs. Dufour. 'The cookie lady,' they called her, didn't they? Not only were you living here at the time of her murder, but you were first on the scene—yet again."

"I didn't kill anyone," I said. "I swear it."

Hayward nodded knowingly, as if he'd expected me to say that. "The one piece I don't have is motive. I can't for the life of me figure out why you would do it." He raised his eyes directly to me, the hard lines around his irises as defined as inlaid marble. "I can assure you, Miss Rose, that I—"

Someone knocked on the door.

"Come in," I called.

It was Richard. He looked surprised to find the detective and Nurse Bea there. He said, "Hello," but it sounded more interrogatory than greeting. He stood tall in the doorway, dressed in a dark gray suit with a matching heather tie. In one hand, he held a manila folder.

Nurse Bea shrunk visibly, though she said, "Dr. Reuter, you remember Detective Hayward? He's asking everyone on the hall a few questions about Mrs. Dufour."

Richard didn't even look at Nurse Bea. He focused on the detective, offering his hand. "Nice to see you again, detective. I hope your investigation is going well."

"As well as can be expected." Hayward paused a beat, then added, "I wonder. Since you're here, can I take a few minutes of your time to ask you a few questions?"

"I'd be happy to answer your questions, but I'd rather do so in the privacy of my office. I'm here to take Viviane down for her daily session. If you're going to be here in an hour or so, perhaps you could stop by then?"

Hayward asked, "Daily?"

"Yes." Richard didn't bother to explain further. He held the manila folder in front of him with both hands like a shield.

Hayward thought about it. "All right. I'll come by your office in an hour." He checked his watch, then remembered me.

"Thanks for your time, Miss Rose." He held the door for Nurse Bea.

As soon as the door had shut behind them, Richard asked, "What did he want?"

I made an effort to hide how freaked out I was by Hayward's visit. I rolled the tension out of my neck. "He thinks I killed Mrs. Dufour. He wanted to ask me some questions."

"Is that so?" Richard frowned at the door. "I'll have a talk with him. You don't have to answer any of his questions, Vivi. You can tell him to fuck off."

"I can?"

"Yes. If he hassles you again, let me know. I'll get your lawyer involved."

"Won't that make me look guilty?"

Richard shook his head. "No. If he had any evidence against you, he'd pressure me to let him interrogate you. He doesn't. I know this because he'd rather sneak around behind my back."

"Okay."

"You ready for your session?"

"I was born ready for psychotherapy, Dr. Schadenfreude."

Richard chuckled. "I thought we'd go down to my office this morning. I have someone I want you to meet."

"Who?" I narrowed my eyes at him.

"A visiting psychologist who specializes in schizophrenia. I've asked him to consult on your treatment, if you're okay with that."

I stood and rewrapped my robe, double-knotting the belt. "A specialist?" In all the years that Richard had been treating me, he'd never referred me to another doctor.

"Dr. Lamb shares my treatment philosophy. I'm assisting him with his research."

My hackles went up. "What did you tell him about me?"

"Not much, and to him, you're just Patient X. I told him Patient X has had hallucinations since puberty and that they're cohesive and persistent. I told him you've recently suffered a loss, and that you're here only on a temporary basis."

"What else?"

"Nothing more. He's interested in my method of hypnotherapy. He wants, with your permission, to ask you a few questions directly. And I'd like permission to share some of our taped sessions with him."

I trusted Richard more than I trusted anybody else in my life—except Lettie.

"All right," I said. "But don't give him any sex or bathroom stuff, okay? I don't want him hearing any of that."

"Agreed."

"And, if I don't trust him right off, I can say no to it all?"

"Absolutely. You're in charge and doing me a huge favor. I'll need your signature on this Information Release form, and you can refuse, if you choose." He set the manila folder on the desk and opened it.

I smiled at him to ease his mind and because, if I was ever going to get out of the Center, I'd need *his* signature. I signed the form.

We walked together to the main house. Richard held his office door for me, and I stepped inside.

At first, it seemed empty, but then a man made his presence known.

He rose slowly from an armchair in the shadows, unfolding as if moving were an afterthought, his eyes and mind in the lead. By the time he was fully on his feet, he had already assessed me from head to toe. There was nothing sexual in his inventory of me, only professional curiosity.

I gave him the same. To my surprise, he was younger than Richard—mid-to-late 30s. He had thick brown hair left to its own devices. He ran his hand back through it, something I suspected he did often and without thinking, as he came to stand near us.

I was struck with an uncanny feeling of *déjà vu*.

In the other man's shadow, Richard looked frail. He moved away, as if he had made the comparison as well.

"Viviane, this is Dr. Jake Lamb."

We reached our hands out to shake.

His chin dipped, and he smiled crookedly, charmingly.

Our skin nearly touched, and a spark of static electricity jumped between us.

I cried out, "Oh!" and pulled my hand to my chest. Laughter bubbled up in the wake of the surprise.

He was startled too, laughing. He rubbed the spot and said, "I'm so sorry." He had a baritone voice suited for hypnosis and heroics.

"It must be the carpet," Richard said. "Viviane, are you all right?"

I shot him a *don't-be-ridiculous* look and let my hand fall back to my side.

"I'm fine," I said with dignity. "It was just a little static electricity. It's nice to meet you, Dr. Lamb."

His face had more character than classic appeal, nose large and lips quirky. He had incredibly long lashes for a man, and his eyes offered friendship.

He looked familiar.

"Please, call me Jake. I appreciate you letting me sit in on your session today."

I said, "It's no trouble," and sat cross-legged on the couch.

Richard sat across from me in his chair. "I thought maybe we'd talk about what happened with Mrs. Dufour. What do you think?"

Jake took the other chair.

I said, "I don't suppose you'd rather talk about something happier?"

"Afraid not."

No, Richard would rather look at the dark and turbulent elements of my life. They were, of course, the more interesting ones.

I glanced over at Jake to find him staring at me. He didn't bother to look politely away when our eyes met, but he bored into my head with his brown eye lasers.

"All right," I said. "Let's do it."

Richard leaned forward and pressed the button on the tape recorder. He stated the date and the names of those present, then finished with, "Go ahead, Viviane. What happened?"

"Well, I was in my room, I heard a scream, and I went to check it out."

"Go on."

"Mrs. Dufour was in bed, and she couldn't breathe. She was freaking out, waving her arms and kicking. I tried to get her to calm down."

"Could you tell what was causing it?"

My mind pulled back a notch, and I was standing in the doorway to Mrs. Dufour's room again. I saw the hag crouched on top of her, straddling her, one hand at her throat, one over her mouth and nose. Mrs. Dufour's eyes bulged.

I shook my head. I hated lying to him, but the stakes had gone too high.

Richard said, "Tell us about the woman you believe attacked you in the hospital."

I chose my words carefully. "She was out of her mind, I suspect. Old, but strong. And before you ask, she looked nothing like my mother or my old babysitter or my best friend." I hoped a little joke would convey that I was balanced. "I thought she was trying to strangle me."

*Like she did Julio, Mrs. Dufour, Mr. Jackson, and Danny McIntyre.*

I added, "It was probably just a nightmare."

Richard asked, "Have you seen Simon lately?"

"No. Not for a couple weeks."

Jake asked, "Who's Simon?"

"Simon is an auditory hallucination. I've been hearing him for twenty years. When I was a kid, I loved movies about talking animals. I watched *Good Boy* a thousand times, and *Gordy, Marmaduke,* and *Dr. Doolittle.* I was a pretty lonely kid. I lived with my grandfather, who had trouble expressing his emotions."

Jake asked, "What does Simon look like?"

"I imagine he resembles either Sean Connery or a gorilla. Of course, I've never actually seen him. He's a disembodied voice, and I don't believe he's real."

"Why do you call him Simon?"

"That's what he told me his name was."

"Thank you." Jake moved to the edge of his seat. "If you'll excuse me, I think I'll leave you two to your hypnotherapy session. I have some things to take care of. Perhaps some other time, I'll sit in?"

I uncrossed my legs and sat forward too. "Was it something I said?"

Jake chuckled. "Not at all." He came over to shake my hand. No sparks this time, though our eyes met and held when he said, "Thank you, Viviane. It's been a pleasure meeting you."

"It's been a pleasure entertaining you."

He didn't let go of my hand. "Trust me," he said. "The work we're doing here is more important than you know."

I looked down at our hands clasped together and pulled mine away. He wore a ring on his finger—a familiar one.

Large and gold, it had a coat of arms stamped into it. *Secret society,* I thought, and I remembered where I'd seen it before. The dance club.

Dr. Jake Lamb had been the man with the ring at the dance club. As he went out the door of Richard's office, I asked, "Are we done?"

Richard said, "No, not yet. There's something I want to talk to you about."

"Can't it wait?" I wanted to catch up with the stalking doctor and confront him.

"It won't take long. I just wanted to let you know that I'm going away for a few days. Dr. Lamb has invited me to visit his facilities in Oregon. I'll be back on Monday for our regular session."

"Awesome. Have a great trip." I stood.

Richard followed me to the door. "Viviane." He was forty-eight, fit, and had great genes. It was, however, as if he were carrying every day of every year heavily on his face. He seemed sad, tired, and something else—stubborn or determined, resolute. I didn't know what he had to be resolute about, but there was no denying the tight pinch of his lips. "I also wanted to talk about Colin's ashes."

The silence in the room contrasted with the cacophony in my head. Colin was gone, but I had no desire to perform the rituals. The last thing I needed was a reminder.

"What about his family?"

Richard shook his head. "I looked into it. The police

contacted them, but they don't want the ashes."

"Well, that's stupid."

"Viviane, I think Colin would want closure for you. Is there any location you can think of that meant something to him?"

The only place I could think of, other than the Center, was the lake, and that was spoiled for us. I couldn't release his ashes where he'd drowned. "I'll think about it, okay? What's the rush?"

Richard shook his head. "No rush. You let me know when you're ready. I'll keep him safe until you are."

"Are we done?"

Richard took a deep breath. "I suppose. I'll walk you to the tower."

◆

Back in my room, I went straight to the window. Richard had completely derailed my plan to confront Jake. I hoped to catch another glimpse of him—and there he was, as if I'd known he'd be there, down on the patio, leaning casually against the railing, texting on his phone. He stood in profile to me, and I again noted his prominent nose. He had excellent posture, and his body was well-proportioned. Although few women would say he was handsome, he certainly was striking.

Why was he so interested in me, and why had he approached me at the club? How long had he been observing me? Was Richard aware of it?

Richard came out of the building, and they walked together toward Richard's car. Jake moved with confidence. Before he got into the red Mercedes, he looked back at the building, searching the second-floor windows. When he found me, he stopped searching—period—and he winked.

I watched until they'd driven out of sight.

It'd been exactly an hour since Richard told Detective Hayward he'd meet him in his office. I wondered what the detective would think about being stood up.

Later that evening, just before lights-out, I called Lettie on my new cell phone.

She picked up and asked, "How you feelin', sugar?"

I thought about it for a second, then replied, "Tired. I had a strange day."

"Spill it."

"Remember the last time we went to the Midnight Saloon, and there was that guy who was bugging me?"

"Vaguely."

"I met him today. His name is Jake Lamb, and he's some sort of psych specialist."

"No way!"

"Way. He pretended he'd never met me. I didn't figure out why he looked so familiar until he was leaving."

"You think it's a coincidence?"

"I don't believe in coincidence. Everything happens

for a reason. He knew exactly who I was at the club."

Lettie gasped. "You think he's following you? Like maybe he's the killer?"

I gave my paranoia a chance to kick in, but it didn't. I said, "He's following me all right, but not because he's a murderer. I think he wants to study my brain. He left before I got a chance to confront him. And get this, Richard is spending the weekend with this guy, checking out his facilities."

"Ew. That sounds dirty. Is that what they call it these days?"

"I don't think he's Richard's type."

"Phew," Lettie said. "I'm totally creeped out. When are you getting out of there?"

"Soon." I crossed my fingers. "I'm behaving myself."

"You know the rules, girl. When the moonbeams come calling, make it a private conversation. Keep your shit to yourself, and nobody'll know you're stalking the moon."

"Nobody but you."

"Ain't that the truth. I always know when you're about to go Tyler Durden on me."

I replied, "As Tyler once said, 'Only after disaster can we be resurrected.'"

Lettie's voice dripped with sarcasm. "Oh, that's not the least bit creepy."

I said, "Hey, I've been thinking. I don't suppose you'd want to be roomies? You and me?"

She sounded surprised. "I don't know. It never occurred to me. Did Abram rent out your room already?"

"I don't want to live with him anymore. The house smells like twenty-year-old cigars and old-man feet."

Lettie laughed. "Let me think about it. I wouldn't mind living with you, and I am a roommate down now that Nina's gone, but let's see how it goes."

"I gotta get out of here, Lettie. I need a place to go. It'll speed things up."

"You know what you have to do to get out of here—or rather, *not* do."

She was right; I *did* know. "I won't freak out anymore."

"Or, if you do, don't let Richard find out about it. Don't get caught."

"Right."

"I'll come by tomorrow, and we can strategize. It's time for you to stop being a patient and start being a Center employee who just happens to be stay-cationing in one of the bedrooms. Then, we'll work on getting you out."

"Awesome. Thanks."

"It's no trouble. You know I love you."

"I love you, too."

After I hung up, Simon said, "I'll be busy for a while, imagining you and Lettie watching television in your nighties, having pillow fights, and sharing a bathroom."

I ignored him.

◆◆◆

# CHAPTER 17

My sadness weighed me down like a wet wool coat, but I couldn't go on the way I had been. I had to get out of the Center and back to my job and routine.

I started wearing street clothes for my sessions with Richard. I even went to the Center's gym a few times. It felt good to run on the treadmill again. It gave me a chance to think about Colin and what he'd have wanted for me—about what I wanted for myself.

Time has a way of setting you straight no matter how far you go off-track.

During the dinner hour, I went to the women's dining room with my mom. Corona and Polly accompanied us. We sat at a table, waiting to be served, sniffing the wafting food aromas and discussing what surprise was on the menu.

Polly stretched her neck to peer into the kitchen and tugged at her hair. "I'm starving."

"I doubt it." Corona slapped her hand away from her head.

"I am." Polly put her hand in her lap and pouted. "I'm

going to die if I don't get something to eat real soon."

Corona straightened the fork and spoon on either side of her plate. "It would be truer to say that you're going to die someday *whether* you get anything to eat or not."

Polly said, "I wonder what they're bringing us."

Corona looked at me with those kitten eyes of hers and asked, "Have you been training with Jake?"

"No. You know him?"

"Yeah." Corona pinched her mouth into something very serious.

Polly said, "Corona thinks he's hot."

"I do not. Gross."

Polly looked shocked. "You're crushing hard on him."

"No, I'm not." Corona smacked Polly lightly on the arm. "I barely know him. I'm not even sure he's a good guy."

I said, "I think he's one of the good guys," though I didn't fully believe it myself. I asked Corona how she knew him.

She shrugged. "He's interested in my case. He's an expert."

"An expert on what?"

"On the reality challenged." Corona displayed a tiny, but deeply pleased smile. "He says I'm special."

Polly said, "He says I'm special too."

"Don't lie. It's unbecoming. You never even met him."

"So?"

Corona looked at me. "He's from Wyrdwood, Oregon. Ask me how I know."

"How do you know?"

She lifted both her eyebrows and her chin. "He gave me his business card. Did he give you one too?"

"No. Obviously, you're more special than I am."

Corona laughed. "Oh, no. I'm sure that's not it. He probably gave one to Dr. Reuter for you. They're special invitations, you know?"

"I had no idea."

"Your mom says you're leaving soon. Are you going there?"

"Where?"

"To Wyrdwood."

Amused, I shook my head. "No. I've got a job here, and my mom's here." I set my hand on Mom's shoulder. She had her head tipped to one side as if listening to music only she could hear.

The kitchen workers rolled carts between tables. They dropped off a plate of food in front of each patient.

"What is this stuff?" Polly asked.

I replied, "Chicken."

Corona's upper lip curled. "Are you sure?"

"I think so." I poked it with my fork. It resembled chicken.

Corona asked, "Can you be absolutely certain?"

I thought about it and had to admit that I could not be

absolutely certain.

"Of course not." Corona leaned over her plate to eat.

◆

I spent the rest of the evening pondering how to get out of the Center. I figured my best bet was to simply tell Richard that I was ready. I'd been on my best behavior and hadn't had an "episode," that he knew about, for a while. I'd done my time, and Richard would have to agree. I was an adult, after all. He wouldn't keep me against my will—at least, I hoped he wouldn't. I tried not to think about the fact that he *could* keep me there—indefinitely—if he wanted to. Just like my mom. Heaven knew my grandfather wouldn't have fought for me.

I checked on Mom shortly before bedtime and helped her into her nightgown, another white one with eyelet lace and billowy sleeves.

She lay down and settled on her side. "The prince is not what he seems."

I covered her up.

She said, "Beware the prince."

I kissed her cheek, then looked right into her eyes. She was with me. I could tell. I said, "Hi."

Her eyes lit up, crinkling at the corners as pleasure spread across her face.

I said, "I love you."

She was beautiful when present, her face smoothed and happy. I didn't remember her from childhood, and there had been few photos, but I could easily imagine that she'd had that expression while holding me when I was young.

Then, as abruptly as it came, it was over, and she was gone.

I'd arranged my whole life so I could be there whenever her true self shone through. Those moments were falling stars, rare and gone almost before my mind could process them.

Back in my own bed, I didn't sleep so much as wander the territory between Asleep and Awake. My conscious mind struggled in an ocean of unconscious currents. The day's efforts had exhausted me to the bone.

Colin called to me through the water, through the black depths of the lake. "Viviane," he said, "you're mine."

I dove deeper, seeking the dreamlands where Colin waited for me.

I cried, "Colin!" and my own voice woke me up. I curled down into the bed and pursued the dream, but the harder I tried to catch it, the faster it fled.

The ring of a cell phone leaked into my consciousness and pulled me back to the surface. I barely recognized it as my own. Ultimately, it was the physical closeness of the sound that grabbed me. I reached for it.

It rang its last ring before I could tap the button.

Simon asked, "Who'd be calling you in the middle of

the night?"

"No idea." The caller I.D. didn't help. It didn't list a name, and I didn't recognize the number. I set the phone back on the nightstand and flopped onto my pillow.

The phone rang again.

I said, "Son of a bitch," and lurched at it. I thumbed the button. "Hello?"

No one replied.

I repeated, "Hello?" and this time, I was irritated.

Nothing.

"It's the middle of the night, and you've got the wrong number."

A distant voice whispered, "Viviane." It was a man. "Viviane, listen to me."

My heart stopped, full stop. It seized in my chest. I didn't dare believe, and yet, the question that rose to my lips was, "Colin?"

◆◆◆

# CHAPTER 18

Colin whispered it. "I've only got a minute. Talk to me. I need to hear your voice. How are you?"

I couldn't form a complete thought. "Colin?"

"Shit! I have to go," he said. "They're coming."

"No, wait!"

"Viviane, I love you. Check my hiding place. Maybe they didn't get to it. I love—"

The phone went dead, and I sat there gulping air like a fish out of water.

Simon said, "Shite."

A freak-out loomed at the periphery of my vision. It delved for an opening, but I couldn't afford to let it have its way with me. I crawled out of bed, breathing as deeply and slowly as I could. I paced and pinched myself—hard. When that didn't work, I pushed the straight pin into my fingertip. I used every trick I knew to keep from losing it.

Finally, I said aloud, "It was Colin."

"No way," Simon said. "It couldn't have been."

"It was."

"You were confused." Simon was pacing too. His voice

traveled back and forth. "Still half-asleep."

"No. It was him." I watched the phone on the bedside table as if it might leap across the room and attack me.

"Someone's playing a sick joke on you—someone who wants you to lose your mind."

"Who would do that?" I wrapped my arms around myself to control the shaking. "I don't know anyone who would do that."

"You obviously haven't read enough gothic romances. You might be surprised."

My mind raced even faster than Simon's questions and suggestions. My heart could barely keep up, though it did its level best. I flipped open the phone. The caller I.D. gave no name, but it had saved the number.

Simon said, "What are you doing?"

"Calling him back."

"Are you sure that's a good idea?"

The phone rang on the other end.

"No, but it's all I got."

A woman answered. "Hello?"

"Hello. Someone just called me from this number. Colin?"

"Viviane? Is that you?"

"Yes." I recognized her voice.

"It's Bella, dear. Thanks so much for calling me back. I wasn't sure I'd catch you at this hour. I was going to leave you a message, but then I decided to just try again in the morning."

"I don't understand. You called me?"

"Yes, I did. I wanted to see how you were doing. I apologize for not getting in touch sooner, but I've been dreadfully busy. I got roped into teaching, you know?"

"So, *you* just called me?"

"I did. How are you?"

My mind reeled. Possibilities tumbled over one another, confusing me. Had I heard the phone ring and dreamt it was Colin?

Bella said, "I know the past few weeks can't have been easy for you. I heard you were staying at the Center, and I was concerned."

"I'm fine." My body trembled.

"Good, good. Well, I don't want to keep you. I just wanted you to know that I'm here if you ever need to talk. You have my number now, so please call anytime. It's been good talking to you, my dear. I'm sorry I woke you."

"Okay."

"Good-bye now."

I said, "Good-bye," and glanced at the time on the phone. It was 3:52 A.M.

Doubt comes with the territory of mental illness. You ask yourself questions: *Did I hear that right? Did I really see that? Am I being paranoid?* After my conversation with Bella, I had so many questions there was no room left for answers. One question in particular kept bobbing to the surface: *Did I dream it?* Everything in me shouted, "No!"

Then, a quieter voice said, "But…" and I was thrust back into the cloud of questions. I buried my head in my hands and rocked.

I didn't want that infant ray of hope that had birthed in me at the sound of Colin's voice to die. I wanted it to live and grow.

Aloud, I said, "Was I dreaming?"

Simon replied, "It's a distinct possibility."

Tears welled in my eyes. Colin's voice had seemed so real. I flipped open the phone again and pressed a few buttons.

"Now who are you calling?"

"Lettie."

The phone rang a handful of times before Lettie picked up. "Hey, Viv." The laundry machines roared in the background. She was in the middle of her shift.

"I'm totally freaking. Something happened."

"It's okay. It's okay. It's okay." What we say three times must be true. She added, "Breathe."

"I have been. This is me after breathing."

"All right. Hold on. Let me get out of the laundry. Hold on." I heard her shout, "Ajani, I'm going on break. Back in ten." I imagined her crossing the laundry then heard the fire door open and close. The machines became a distant hum.

"There. Now I can hear you. What happened?"

The words stuck in my throat. My anxiety meter was in the red, and my internal alarm bells had begun ringing.

"Viv?"

"Something…weird." I hoped I could ease my way into it.

"Tell me."

"I got a phone call?"

"What? From who?"

The moment of truth had arrived, and I barely believed myself. "From Colin?"

There was a beat of silence, then Lettie said, "I'm sorry. From who?"

"Colin."

"You're kidding?"

"No. Not funny. A cat with a perma-frown is funny. A streaker is funny. A duck walking into a bar is sometimes funny. Getting a phone call in the middle of the night from your dead fiancé is definitely not funny."

"Okay. Look. It's impossible, honey."

"I know. But it was so real."

"Okay. Calm down. It's okay. You're okay. You have to calm down. You're going to ruin everything you've worked for."

I was on the verge of hysteria. "That's why I called you!"

"Okay, okay. Shhhh. It's okay. There's a logical explanation for this. You hear me?"

"Uh huh." I tried desperately to drop anchor.

"Say it. Say, 'There's a logical explanation for this.'"

"There's a logical explanation for this."

Simon interjected, "Maybe it was his ghost haunting you?"

I glared in his general direction. "There's no such thing as ghosts."

"No," Lettie replied, "there's no such thing as ghosts. Look, it's gonna be okay. We'll figure it all out later today. Okay?"

"Okay."

"Go back to bed. Relax. Don't worry. There's nothing we can do about it now. I'll come by after my shift, okay?" How Lettie managed to stay rational and calm when faced with one of my episodes, I'll never know. She talked me back into bed, and we hung up.

I lay there, staring into the darkness, watching visions of Colin and me laughing, loving. An annoying pair of words kept creeping into my consciousness: "What if?" By merely entertaining the possibility, could I influence reality in the direction of my desires? If I wished hard enough, could I make it so?

Simon had gone quiet or maybe just gone.

I was determined to stay awake until Lettie came, but then I woke up.

It was a little after 6:00, and the light coming in the window was a dim combination of natural and unnatural, the sun not yet having brightened enough to shut off the outdoor lights. I lay where I was, staring up at the ceiling. The night before seemed like a dream. I wasn't even a hundred percent sure I had called Lettie.

I went through my morning routine and dressed in jeans, a t-shirt, and running shoes. By the time Lettie showed up, I'd made my bed and was pretending to read. It was about 7:15. The graveyard shift had ended at 7:00.

She stuck her head in and said, "Good morning. Can I come in?"

"Of course, get in here."

The dam broke, and I became a torrent of thoughts spoken aloud. "Do you think he could be alive? I don't dare believe it. I might have dreamed it. Do you think maybe he was kidnapped? Maybe—"

"Whoa there, cowgirl. Slow your roll. You're getting awfully manic. Let's bring this conversation back down to Earth, okay?"

"Okay." I shook my hands as if to dry them.

Lettie pulled a chair over to sit within touching distance, "Let's start at the beginning. Lay it out for me, step by step."

I told her everything exactly as I remembered it all the way through to the part where Doc Bella answered the phone.

At that point, she said, "Hold on."

She tapped her teeth with her fingernail, then asked,

"You mean you called the number back and got Grandma Rosenblum? Isn't she out of town?"

"She left the same day of the accident. She was going on a six-month sabbatical to Boston. Colin didn't tell me much about it, mostly because I didn't care."

"Then what?"

"Then, she thanked me for calling her back and asked how I—"

"Wait. She said *she* called you? Let me see your phone."

She turned it on. "Says here she called at a quarter to 4:00 in the morning? And again a minute later? She called twice?"

"I didn't answer quick enough the first time."

"At quarter to 4:00?"

"Yeah, that's weird, huh?"

Lettie frowned. "10:00 P.M. is weird. 4:00 A.M. is criminal. Besides, you've been in here for weeks. Does she call you every night, or what?"

I shook my head. "This was the first time."

She shook hers, too. "The only people who call you at 4:00 in the morning are the police, hospitals, teenage pranksters, and drunk dialers. Even if you take into consideration that the East Coast is a different time zone, it still would've been 5:00 there. Everybody knows you don't call that early. That's just crazy."

"It's crazy, or I'm crazy?"

"You're crazy sometimes, but not this time. Somebody

called you. It's right here on the phone."

"Colin told me to look in his hiding place. Can we go to his room?"

Lettie chewed on her lip. "Colin had a hiding place?"

"He kept things in the leg of his bed—things he didn't want anyone else to see. It's hollow with a cap on the end. I can't believe I didn't remember it before. Let's go!" I unfolded my legs and jumped up.

Lettie crossed her arms on her chest. "What if there's another patient in there?"

"Lettie, this is important! C'mon. Let's go now, before the place wakes up."

I knew from experience that the best time to sneak around the Men's Wing was between 7:00 and 8:00. The patients who weren't still sleeping were at the breakfast buffet.

I hopped a little. I was excited, and I couldn't help it. "C'mon."

"Okay. But you have to promise me something."

"Anything."

"No matter what happens, you can't freak out on me. Okay?"

I promised.

◆◆◆

# CHAPTER 19

The Center wasn't a high-security institution. The patients were more likely to hurt themselves than each other. Nevertheless, the doors were locked behind an outdated system of numbered keypads. My staff had full access so we could collect the dirty laundry.

Out of habit, I watched Lettie input the code.

We went down first, to the ground floor. The rooms there held exercise and physical therapy equipment, and we passed a pair of bathrooms that led to the therapy pool, sauna, and whirlpools—all abandoned at that early hour. Once we were on the men's side, we climbed to the third floor.

The Men's Wing had an entirely different smell from the Women's. Everything about it was musky and musty. Colin's room was right next to the stairwell, so we shuffled quickly from one to the other and shut the door behind us.

The lights were off inside, and I fumbled for the switch. When they came on, a field of stark white blinded me for a moment. As my vision cleared, I didn't find what I'd expected. The room had been gutted. The bed was a bare mattress on a metal frame built to be sturdy with hollow metal legs two inches in diameter. Nothing remained of Colin's, not even his trunk. The doors on the dresser were ajar and empty. It was as if someone had come along with a bucket of bleach and cleaned away all evidence of Colin—every trace of his presence. The starkness of it cut me to the center of my heart.

Lettie said, "They packed up his stuff."

I got down on my hands and knees by the bed. "Help me. Can you lift this corner?"

Lettie hurried over and raised the bed.

With one hand, I felt around. There was a cap there—a plastic cap that covered the open end of the hollow metal leg. I pulled the cap off, and the end of a ribbon dropped out. I pulled on it, and a roll of papers came with it.

Lettie said, "How about that? A secret stash."

"He was afraid he'd forget everything again, so he used to write the important things down and put them in here. It slipped my mind until he mentioned it."

"Can you get it all?"

I stuck my fingers in as far as they would go, but I didn't feel anything else. "That's everything." I put the cap back on, and we lowered the leg to the floor.

Lettie asked, "What about the other legs?"

"I don't know. It couldn't hurt to look." So we found more.

Lettie and I sat together on the bare bed, and I laid out

the items, one by one, flattening them as much as possible. Among them were his notes, a shipping receipt, and photos of Colin and me—on his birthday, at the lake, and in front of the Center's Christmas tree. I looked at the pictures for awhile, remembering, and then I reached for the shipping receipt.

"What's this?" The shipment had gone to B. Rosenblum at an address in Peoria.

Lettie leaned to look at it. "Is that Doc Bella's home address? He must have stolen it."

I shook my head. "I don't know. Maybe she gave it to him."

"I wonder what they shipped. What's the date on it?"

"The day before the accident."

"It must have been Dr. Rosenblum's stuff? I mean, she's going to be gone for a long time."

We looked at each other for a long minute, then Lettie said, "Let's get out of here before we get caught. The last thing I need is to lose my job."

We went back the way we'd come, doubly careful, and made it to my room without any hassles.

"I need to go," Lettie said. "Are you going to be okay?"

"Don't worry. I'm fine. I'm going to read this and see what I can find out." I nurtured that little spark of hope to the best of my ability, clinging to the memory of Colin's voice on the phone.

Lettie kissed me on the forehead. "Call me if you find

anything interesting. Okay?"

I said, "I will," and the moment she was out the door, I started reading Colin's notes. They overflowed with his everyday thoughts and feelings. As I read, his voice came alive.

> *Some days I think I'll be this way forever. Bella keeps saying I'll get my memory back, that I have to be patient. Patient, my ass. I want it now. This feeling is worse than anything I could ever find out about myself. It's the time between death and birth, waiting for my life to begin. I know I have a future, a destiny so great that it haunts my dreams. I just can't make out the details—not yet. I'm in a chrysalis. I'm a butterfly or maybe a locust. Either way, I'm ready to emerge.*

Colin talked like that, too. It was one of the reasons I fell in love with him. Everything was so…big. His world wasn't limited to a 9-to-5 job and running errands. He dreamed big, talked big, and thought big.

> *Viviane worries I won't love her anymore if I remember, but that's bullshit. The one thing I know beyond a shadow of a*

*doubt is that she is mine.*

Nurse Bea interrupted me when she came trawling for breakfast stragglers. She was in the next room, urging Una out of her corner. I was next.

I stuck Colin's notes in my suitcase, and I locked it. If a nurse found it, she'd tell Richard, and if Richard knew I had them, he'd confiscate them. He'd want to go through them before me and take out anything that might upset me. I wasn't ready to let him invade Colin's privacy.

I hit the breakfast buffet. Doing normal things made me feel and appear sane. It cowed the anxiety and shoved aside the dilemma, for the time being. I took the table in the corner and sat by myself.

Richard had once said, "There are only two possibilities, Vivi. Either what you experienced was real, or it wasn't. There's no in-between. When you learn to recognize the difference, you'll be able to function better in the world." I was nineteen when he said that, and I was usually pretty good at sorting the fantastic from the real.

After that phone call, however, I felt as if I'd gotten off-track again.

To myself, I said, "I want it to be real," and that might've explained everything.

Someone said, "Hi."

Corona stood beside me with a tray of food.

"Hi."

"You're talking to yourself. Don't let them see, or they'll give you more meds."

I glanced around at the nurses, dining staff, and patients. "Thanks."

"No problem." She set the tray on my little table and pulled out a chair. "I'll sit here, then they'll think you're talking to me." She moved her plates off the tray. She had six of them, all small, each holding a different item: scrambled eggs on one, sausage on another, toast on a third, fried potatoes, melon slices, and a single piece of bacon. She placed each plate carefully on the table, and when the tray was empty, she set it aside. She arranged the plates in two rows of three: eggs, sausage, and potatoes closest; toast, melon, and bacon farthest. She lined up her silverware on one side.

On an impulse, I said, "Colin called me."

She raised her brown eyes without lifting her head. "I was wondering."

I lowered my voice to a whisper, and the words tumbled out. "He called me in the middle of the night. He didn't talk long. I don't think he was supposed to be on the phone."

Corona nodded the whole time I was talking.

"And, it was Doc Bella's phone. I know because I called back, and she answered."

Corona said, "I heard Doc Bella say Colin was checking out soon. She said, 'He's overdue for phase two.'"

"What? When?"

"I was in her office for my session. There was a knock on her door."

"Who was she talking to?"

"That old black guy from the laundry—you know him. He and Doc Bella are bosom buddies."

I blinked in surprise. "What black guy from the laundry?"

"You know. The tall, skinny one who works the graveyard shift."

"You mean Ajani? Ajani Jones?"

"Yup."

Memories stirred of Ajani kneeling by Colin, asking me if I was okay. Colin had said, "It's her," and Ajani's response had been, "Are you sure?"

Not "Her who?"

Not "Whatever you say," but "Are you sure?" As if he'd known what Colin had meant.

The hag had been after us in the stairwell. Colin had known it. That's why he'd been so afraid. But Ajani? My head was spinning.

I said, "I think Ajani knows about the hag."

Corona's eyebrows rose. "Ajani is a guardian."

I asked, "I don't understand."

"All I can give is the truth. I'm limited that way." Corona looked me straight in the eyes.

I was beginning to feel more frustrated and angry than

upset and shaken.

"Here's how I see it," I said. "I have two options. I can accept the possibility that Colin is alive, or I can reject it. If I accept it, then I have to dig deeper."

Corona said, "You're at the crossroads between Easy Street and the Olympus Stairway. Choose one and everything stays manageable. Choose the other, and you'll have to overcome your humanity to reach the gods on Mt. Olympus—or die trying."

I wondered what it was about Corona that made people think she was out of touch with reality. She spoke in metaphors, but they made perfect sense to me. I said, "It's not an easy choice."

Corona replied, "It never is when your reality is on the line."

That was how it felt—as if the world, the cosmos, the universe, and my future happiness hung in the balance. If the man I loved were dead, then my version of reality had been corrupted. I wasn't sure I wanted to be part of that anymore.

We sat in silence for a few minutes, then Corona asked, "Do you believe in soul mates?"

"Yeah."

"Do you know what the odds are of meeting a soul mate? If you factor in the size of this planet and the number of inhabitants, then consider time? The chance of them being born in the same generation as you puts the odds against finding your soul mate in your lifetime at a zillion to one."

I stared at her.

She continued without missing a beat. "Maybe, when we all first started incarnating, we had soul mates, and on some level, we remember that. That would explain the irrational yearning. But, it's a wobbly wheel. Over time, our lives get out of sync with each other. In one lifetime, someone dies prematurely. In another, the other does. Before you know it, one is being born just as the other is getting old, and so on and so on."

She paused, staring at me, waiting for a response.

I said, "Wow."

"Then," she continued, "there's the gender remixing. And what if he was born on a different planet or in an alternate dimension? Here's the crux of it, Viviane. If you think you've found your soul mate, and he's not a cranky two-year-old, you have to go for it."

"Wow."

Corona turned her attention back to her food.

I told her about the shipping receipt and how I'd found it.

For the longest time, she had no response, but then she asked, "So, when are we gonna go toss Doc Bella's office?"

"What?"

"That's your next step, isn't it?"

She was right. If there were any clues about what happened, they'd be in Doc Bella's office. "How will we get there? I could call Lettie?"

Corona waved greasy fingers at me. "Didn't you get your friend Lettie's code this morning?"

I stared at her. "Yes. How did you know?"

"You're not as good at sneaking as you think."

"All right. So we can use that to get to the offices, but what about Bella's door?"

"I know that code from my last session. I doubt she took the time to change it before she left."

"What if she did?"

"Then we find another way."

"Someone's bound to see us."

"Nah. We're invisible. I'll show you." Corona wrapped her bacon in one napkin and her toast in another, then put them into the pockets of her pajama bottoms. She piled her empty plates neatly back on her tray.

I gathered my dishes and went with her to the dirty-dish bins.

Corona said, "Act like you belong, and you will. Don't be afraid. Nothing fucks your plans the way fear does." She stood tall and made an ineffective attempt to smooth her hair, then she walked—bold as you please—to the exit doors.

Fearless, she waited for me to tap in the security code, then walked right out into the foyer. I followed her example, grateful that I had put on jeans and a t-shirt that morning. I'd have felt even more conspicuous in my pajamas. Corona, on the other hand, didn't let the fact that she was roaming the Center in slippers slow her down.

We headed toward the main house. As we approached the double doors leading into the foyer, doctors and nurses came and went, escorting patients or reading charts. None of them gave us a second glance. The further we went without getting caught, the more I got into the role.

Bella's office was on the second floor there, just down the hall from Richard's. We went straight to her door.

Doc Marshall came out into the hall, thumbs working furiously on his smart phone. He was short with narrow shoulders, scrawny legs, and a firm, round belly. He looked like a forty-year-old cherub with rosy cheeks, minimal hair on his head, and a love for technological gadgets. He insisted on dressing casually at work, in long shorts and a T-shirt. He said it put his patients at ease. I heard about it often from Richard who found the informality offensive.

I froze and held my breath.

He looked at us. "Good morning, ladies." Then, he walked away.

Corona had correctly guessed that Bella hadn't changed her code, and we were in.

The door locked automatically behind us, and I stood with my back to it. "Oh my god. We did it. We just waltzed in here like we belong."

Corona said, "We *do* belong. I know the P.I.N., after all. It's magic. If you believe it, chances are everyone else will too. Nobody wants to have to think too hard, so they're happy to let you do their thinking for them."

She went to the desk. "Ignore the filing cabinets. Bella's probably got the keys with her." She sat down, turned on the computer, and tugged open desk drawers.

Doc Bella's taste in furniture was different from Richard's. Hers was upholstered with midnight blue fabric, and all the wood was cherry. She had a love for early 20th-century styling. Her office could have been a state room on the Titanic. Bookshelves lined the walls. I tried looking at a couple of the books, but they were all psychology textbooks, psychiatry manuals, and medical encyclopedias.

Corona said, "There's nothing in her desk but office supplies. Let's see what she left on her computer."

"You can get into her computer?"

"Sure. She used to say her password out loud when she was typing it in. You know—old people and computers." Corona went through the log-in process.

I ran my finger around a square left on the desk. Something had been there and wasn't any more. Dust had settled all around it but left the square clear. I noticed other such marks on the shelves.

Corona typed and clicked the mouse.

I went to the couch and lay down on it. Colin must have lain in the same place a thousand times. I settled into the memory of his body the way a ghost settles into a living being. I closed my eyes and waited.

"Here's something," Corona said. "Her calendar. Wasn't she supposed to go to Boston the day of the accident?"

"Yeah."

"Not according to this. She had an appointment at a tailor here in Peoria, two days *after* the accident."

"A tailor?"

"Grandma Bella's a snazzy dresser, but she'd be cross-dressing if she bought her clothes there. One sec." Corona reached over and picked up the phone on the desk. She dialed a number. After a moment, she said, "Hello, yes, I'm calling on behalf of Bella Rosenblum. May I make another appointment?" She listened, and I watched her, fascinated. After a moment, she said, "It's for the same thing as last time." A smile curved her lips, "Yes, that's right. For her son. He needs another suit. I'm sorry. Which boy did she bring in last time? That's the one. Thank you. Next Tuesday would be perfect. We'll see you then."

Once she'd hung up, I asked, "Bella has a son?"

"Yeah." Corona snorted. "A son named Aubrey."

I blinked and sat up straight. Aubrey was the family name Colin had chosen for himself. Could it have been another coincidence? My spark of hope evolved into a small, fragile flame. "My god, Corona. What's going on? If Colin's with her, then why doesn't she tell anyone? Why's she keeping this from me?"

"It's still too early to tell, but the clues are getting weird."

A wave of excitement overcame me. I got to my feet and jumped up and down.

Corona met me in the middle of the room, took my hands, and jumped with me a couple times, then we hugged, laughing.

Someone knocked on the door.

We went still in each others' arms.

In my ear, Corona said, "Shhhh." She kept hugging me, and we both listened.

The person knocked again and said, "Doctor Rosenblum?" It was a man.

I met Corona's eyes. We said nothing.

The man tried the door handle. "Doctor? Are you here?"

I whispered, "What are we going to do?"

"Shhh." Corona rested her cheek against my shoulder. I rested my chin on her head.

The man walked away. We heard him talk to someone down the hall. "Do you know if Doctor Rosenblum is around?"

A woman said, "She's gone for six months. Research sabbatical. If you need to get in touch with her, talk to Doctor Min. He'll know how to contact her."

The man said, "Thanks," and we sighed with relief.

Then, he said, "I thought I heard someone in her office."

We froze again.

"Really? I'll check it out. Thanks for letting me know."

She was coming.

I said, "Fuck."

Corona pushed me downward, none too gently. "Get under the desk."

I hunkered into the cubby hole. Corona sat in the chair and scooted up close. She put a leg on either side of me. She smelled of baby powder.

The lock clicked, and the door opened.

"Corona? What are you doing in here?"

"Doc Bella asked me to defrag her hard drive for her. Her computer's been running slow lately. I told her I'd do it before she got back, and so here I am, doing it."

The woman asked, "How did you get in here?"

"She gave me her code."

"Well, now's not a good time to be wandering around the offices. C'mon. Let's get you back to your room. C'mon."

"Nope. I can't leave this defrag halfway through. It'll fuck up the computer, and you don't want to have to explain why that happened, do you? It's almost done. I'll leave as soon as it is. Promise."

The woman hesitated. "There are police everywhere today. When you're done de-whatevering the whatever, come find me in my office. 215."

Corona saluted, "Yes, ma'am."

The woman said, "I'll walk you back to your ward."

"Sure thing."

The door shut behind her, and the lock engaged—and then I saw it.

A crumpled piece of paper had missed the trash can. It had the partial word "Col…" on it.

Corona scooted her chair back and looked down.

I crawled out.

"What's that?" Corona asked.

I smoothed out the crumpled paper and held it so she could see too. It was a color photocopy of a Center I.D. It had the name Colin Aubrey on it, but someone else's picture, a face I recognized from the laundry.

"Damn," said Corona. "Who's that guy?"

"Jaxon Bellonescu. He works in the laundry." His Turkish coffee eyes looked directly out at me, his mouth serious, jaw tight.

"If that's supposed to be a fake I.D, it'll never work," Corona said. "Everyone knows Colin, and that guy looks nothing like him."

"It's too weird not to be a clue." I folded it and tucked it in my underwear. "Did you find anything on her computer?"

"She's got some weird browser history. She was looking at sites about Wyrdwood and Boston. Her email is sparse. All boring work stuff. Doc Bella's pretty old-school. She doesn't use her computer much."

"Let's get out of here before that woman comes back looking for you."

I waited for Corona by the door. When we left, she went toward 215, and I walked straight back to my room. No one stopped me, and why would they? I wasn't doing anything wrong—or so my demeanor told them. Corona was a good teacher.

◆

Later, Corona came to my room. Simon was already there, pacing back and forth as I told him what we'd found.

Simon asked, "Then what happened?"

"Look at this." I smoothed out the photocopy on the bed.

Corona moved to stand beside me. "It's not paranoia if leprechauns really *are* conspiring against you."

Just behind my right shoulder, Simon said, "Holy shit."

Corona pointed at it. "Look here, how the picture isn't quite in the right place. It was a first draft that failed."

I rubbed my thumb over Jaxon's photo. "What do you think it means?"

Corona's hands fluttered at her neck as she replied, "Well, the literal interpretation, of course, is that Jaxon intended to impersonate Colin, and Doc Bella either figured it out or was helping him make a fake I.D."

"If that's true," I said, "then maybe Jaxon was the one who went to the tailor with Bella." I couldn't keep the disappointment out of my voice.

Corona slapped her hands to either side of her face, mouth gaping. "Oh my god," she said. "Did Colin have any money? Was he rich?"

"Not that I know of."

"Anyone pretending to be him would have access to his holdings."

"Are you suggesting that they killed Colin so they could take his identity and steal from him?"

Corona shrugged. "Stranger things have happened."

"Except," I said, feeling my eyes open wide with the truth of it, "Colin's not dead. He called me."

◆◆◆

# CHAPTER 20

Lettie answered on the third ring. "What's up, Viv?"

"Oh my god, you won't believe what we found. Can you come back?"

"Back to the Center? I just got home."

"I know, but this is really important—*really* important."

"Just tell me."

I sighed. "Okay. Corona and I broke into Doc Bella's office. We found evidence that Jaxon was trying to steal Colin's identity. Here, I'm going to text you a picture."

"You broke into Grandma Rosenblum's office?"

"Yeah. Look."

"Is that Jaxon?"

"Yeah."

Lettie was silent for several long seconds, then she said, "All right. I'll be there soon. Don't do anything stupid."

♦

When Lettie arrived, she found me and Corona sitting on the bed examining our array of evidence.

"So," Lettie said, "let me see that paper." She crossed to the bed, and we offered the photocopy to her as if it were a precious treasure map. She stared at it for a long while, looked up at us, then back down at the paper. Her expression soured.

"It's real." I hovered at her side.

"I see," said Lettie, "a counterfeit ID card. Where did you find this?"

"On the floor in Bella's office."

Corona said, "I know her code."

Lettie's voice was soft and controlled. "Why would Jaxon need a card that identified him as Colin?"

I asked, "Was Jaxon at work last night?"

Lettie's eyes snapped up to mine, and I saw something uncomfortable in them. "Jaxon quit, honey. Ajani said something about him wanting to move back home."

"When?"

Lettie shrugged, thinking back before answering. "I haven't seen him since your accident. I remember thinking that our team was dropping like flies."

"Oh, and that's a coincidence?" Corona said sarcastically. "I'm surprised the police didn't notice." She got up and crossed to the wall, where she inverted into a handstand against it.

Lettie watched Corona. "They might have. They've

been in Ajani's office a lot lately."

"It's adding up to foul play," said upside-down Corona, tone matter-of-fact.

"What else do you have?" asked Lettie. She focused on the clues spread upon the bed.

I described the phone call to the tailor.

As I talked, she went through the items on the bed, ending on Colin's notes. She picked them up. "You mind if I read some of these?"

"No, go ahead."

Lettie searched for the last entry.

I read over her shoulder.

*Viviane and I are taking a mini vacation away from the Center. I find myself packed and ready to go more than 36 hours in advance, sitting here planning how I'll begin making love to her, plotting my romantic moves. It occurs to me that I should ask her to marry me again but do it better than I did the first time. Maybe I could make it a tradition.*

*I suppose I'm excited, and that's an understatement. We're going to have an awesome weekend. It's all about Viviane. I'm going to make it so special she'll never for-*

*get it, and neither will I.*

Lettie had tears in her eyes by the time she finished reading it.

I put my arm around her and squeezed. "It's okay. He's not gone forever. He's coming back."

"I don't know about that."

"I know," I stated. "You didn't hear his voice. I did."

Lettie rested her hand upon my cheek and looked me in the eyes. "That's exactly the problem, honey. Don't you see?"

I *did* see. I could have imagined—or dreamt—the call from Colin. "So, maybe I've lost it completely. Maybe he was reaching out to me from the Great Beyond. Maybe he's been kidnapped." I studied Lettie, considering the idea of telling her about the hag. Corona would corroborate it. My instincts, however, told me it was one step too far. I'd lose her support entirely if she didn't believe us.

I waved my hands over the clues on the bed. "But what about this stuff? You see it too. It's solid, concrete evidence that *something* is going on."

"I just don't know," Lettie said. "It's all so far-fetched."

Corona said, "If you're cuckoo, then I'm cuckoo, too."

I pointed at the photocopy. "What about the faked I.D.?"

Corona sat cross-legged on the floor. "And the tailor."

Lettie chewed on her bottom lip. "That doesn't prove

he's alive."

"I know," I replied, "but it starts the questions. I need to find out for sure."

Lettie's forehead creased. "How do you plan to do that?"

"I'm going to talk to Detective Hayward." I went to the chest of drawers, retrieved my purse, and dumped the contents out on the bedspread. There—amidst the old receipts, chewing gum, loose change, and lint—I found a business card.

Lettie asked, "What do you expect him to tell you?"

"Well," I replied. "If Colin's alive, then who did they find in the lake? The police must have something that proves—one way or the other—who they found."

A slow, flat smile spread across Lettie's face. "I may have gotten the looks, girl, but you got the brains. Good thinking." After a moment, however, her approval faded and was replaced with more worry. "You realize, honey, that if this is really happening, then the people involved aren't the good guys."

"Yeah."

Lettie hid her face in her hands. "I can't believe I'm buying into this. I've seen too many movies."

♦

It took me several tries to get through to Detective

Hayward. When he finally picked up, he didn't say, "Hello," he said, "Hayward."

I said, "Detective Hayward, it's Viviane Rose."

"What can I do for you, Miss Rose?" he asked, wariness in his voice.

"I have a question about Colin."

He paused, leaving a gap of silence between us, then asked, "Does your doctor know you're calling me?"

"I don't need his permission to call you."

Hayward cleared his throat. "All right. Shoot."

"Are you sure the body you found was Colin's?"

"Yes. Why do you ask?"

"How do you know?"

"He had identification on him, and his doctor confirmed it."

"Dr. Rosenblum?"

"Correct. What's this about?"

"I need to know for sure that it was him."

Hayward sighed, sounding exasperated.

"Please," I said. "Call it closure. Call it whatever you want. I need something."

The detective sniffed, then said, "Look. I probably shouldn't tell you this, but we have pictures. I could arrange for you to see them, but I'll need Reuter to make an official request. I'm not gonna be responsible for a set-back in your…recovery." He didn't bother to mask his sarcasm.

Pictures. That was exactly what I'd hoped to hear.

"That would be perfect. Richard will be back on Monday. I'll talk to him first thing, and we'll call you."

Hayward said, "You do that," and he hung up.

Corona bounced excitedly. "What'd he say?"

"He said he has pictures."

"Oh, wow. That's cool."

Lettie was less enthused. "Viv, are you sure you want to look at those?"

"I'm positive," I told her. "I don't think it's Colin, but even if it is, I need to know for sure, one way or the other."

I dialed another number on my phone.

Corona asked, "Now who are you calling?"

Ajani answered on the second ring. "Yo," he said.

"Hi, Ajani. It's Viviane."

Lettie's eyebrows went up, and Corona nodded knowingly.

"Miss Viviane. How's it going?" I listened to his voice, his intonation, and his rhythm. He didn't seem surprised to hear from me.

"As well as can be expected, I suppose. I was just thinking about you and wondering how you were. It's been a while since I talked to you."

"True dat," he said. "Listen, it sucks about Colin."

"Yeah."

After a short, uncomfortable silence, he said, "The laundry's chugging right along. They made me supervisor. Did Lettie tell ya?"

"Yeah, she did. You're the best choice—after me, of course."

"That's right, damn it, though nobody's good as you." He paused, then added, "We miss you here."

"That's sweet of you to say. To be honest, I'm pretty ready to get back to work. If I watch any more Oprah, I'm going to be so well-adjusted I'll have to change my last name to Boring."

Ajani chuckled deep in his throat, and the sound reverberated across the airwaves. It made me smile, and that made me sad. I'd considered Ajani a friend.

He said, "You need to watch more soaps and telenovellas. Better role models."

"Yeah, I think they're all that's saving me right now."

"Look, Viviane, now's not really a good time for me. Can I call you back later?"

"Why don't you stop by? Before your shift? I'd love to see you."

"Will they let me in there with all the women?"

"Only if you promise to behave yourself."

"For you, Miss Viviane, I'll make my best effort. I'll come by tonight. See you then."

"Thanks, 'Jani." We hung up.

♦

Eventually, Lettie left, and Corona returned to her

room. I hadn't showered that morning, so rather than suffer the attentions of Nurse Bea, I stole away to take one before lunch.

The bathroom sat at the intersection where the hall met the recreation room and nurses' station. It had four private shower nooks (with curtains, not doors) and six toilet stalls. Sinks lined one side. On the floor, grout moats separated white tiles. They'd been worn down over the years and channeled the water away to the drain. Once a day, the janitorial staff—I used to be one of them—came in and spread bleach around. It reminded me of the old locker room at the high school, except there weren't any lockers stuffed with smelly gym suits.

I was in no hurry. The shower felt marvelous. I was the only one in there, maybe because it was so late in the morning. The shower curtains didn't close properly, so it was nice to be alone.

When I was done, I turned off the water, dried myself, and wrapped the towel around my body. I yanked the shower curtain aside and—

—came face to face with her. She was upside-down, dangling from the ceiling. Her long hair hung from her head like dusty swamp moss. My eyes were directly level with her mouth. Her lips pulled back to reveal toothless, blackened gums. The hag.

◆◆◆

# CHAPTER 21

I stumbled back, hit the shower wall, slipped, and fell hard on my ass. The hag crawled down the wall to the floor, stalking, and turned right-side up. I opened my mouth to scream, but I had no voice. All I could manage was a choking sound. It—she—came toward me on feet and hands, body naked and angular, back arched upward. Her skin was translucent, colorless. A mist surrounded her. It thickened, obscuring her, then thinned, revealing her in pieces. Her black eyes never left me. The mountain range of her spine was painted by blue rivers of veins and rippled with the upheaval of her muscles. She crawled forward, swinging her hair from side to side and looking up at me from under lashless lids. Her long breasts hung loose, the nipples so gray they looked as if they'd been dipped in ash.

I tried again to scream, but nothing came out, no matter how hard I forced. The effort hurt my throat and made my head spin. I squeezed back against the wall, pulling my feet under me so I could stand up.

The hag reached a crooked hand out and touched my knee. She caressed me, taking her time, as if she knew I couldn't get away or call for help. She stood when I stood and slid her body against mine, pressing me against the wall.

My towel had fallen. The hag's skin felt cold and dry against my exposed front. She moved against me as if she wanted me to want her. Horror held me in place and numbed my mind. I couldn't think. Terror sent the wrong impulses to my brain, and I was far beyond fight or flight.

Her hands moved into the curve of my lower back, down over my bottom, and up along my sides. She cupped one hand over my breast and clasped the other around my throat. She squeezed. The pain broke my paralysis. A wave of anger and disgust washed over me. I shoved hard against her.

She retreated a couple steps, her eyes gone narrow and mean. Then she leaned forward, prepared to strike.

I pointed a finger at her. My voice finally returned, and I said, "Stop," with all my heart. I felt a flash of heat deep in my gut, down where arousal first ignites. It surged up through my body.

She made another move, a jerky lurch as if to attack.

The energy expanded through me and burst out of me with the force of my will behind it. I faced it and screamed, "Leave me alone!"

The hag's eyes opened to full moons, and her lips pulled back in a sneer. Then she was gone.

My body tingled all over, electric with…energy. I had

no idea what it was, nor why it had worked to chase the hag away. I just knew that she'd been ready to kill me, and I'd stopped her.

My legs gave out, and I slid down the wall again. Like the Red Sea crashing back in, fear and horror crushed me in the wake of my short moment of bravery. I burst into tears.

Unfortunately, that was how Bea found me, and they sedated me again.

The next thing I knew, someone pressed lightly on my shoulder, saying, "Miss Viviane?"

A pharmaceutical fog obscured my thoughts. The only person who called me that was Ajani.

He gave me a little shake. "Miss Viviane?"

I forced my eyelids open, just a crack.

"Miss Viviane?"

"Ajani?"

"Rough day?"

"Rough…couple…months," I said, my voice hoarse and soft. "Today…you're pain."

"Tomorrow," Ajani responded, "just a stain."

I fought the effects of the sedative, took a deep breath and blinked wide.

Ajani's expressive face came into focus, his dark brown eyes warm, full lips curved into a smile. He said, "Listen, I can't stay long. I wanted to see you and make sure you were okay. I heard what happened."

"I have…to ask you…a question."

"About what?"

"Colin." I watched him as I said the name, working hard to focus my eyes.

Ajani didn't even flinch. Instead, he brought the chair over by the bed. "If it's gonna be that conversation," he said, "I better sit down. What do you wanna know?"

I waited until he was settled next to me, nestled up against the bed with his long, sculpted arm resting beside me, his hand on my shoulder.

He looked me in the eyes, and I met his gaze head-on.

I asked, "You knew they were going to release him?"

Ajani inhaled sharply, exhaled, inhaled again, and finally said, "Can't get nothing by you, huh?" He patted my shoulder, tone light. "Well, I don't reckon it matters at this point. You deserve an explanation."

"Tell me."

"We were gonna tell you, I'm swearing, but that accident fucked everything up. After that, it was just never the right time."

"Tell me what?"

Ajani said, "Colin started remembering his life before coming here."

"And?"

"Thing is, Viviane, what he was remembering wasn't stuff he could tell just anybody. He…um…had enemies, if you know what I mean."

I shook my head against the pillow. "Enemies? What kind of enemies?"

"The kind that kill."

Viviane heard derision in his voice, scorn for Colin's enemies.

"What? The mafia?"

"You could say that." Ajani swept the back of his long-fingered hand across his forehead. His palm was several shades lighter than the rest of him, a moon flying across the night sky. "We were getting him ready to go underground. If the people looking for him had found him, they'd have killed him."

"What about the accident? Was someone…trying to kill us?"

Ajani shrugged. "All that matters is you're okay."

"But…what about Colin?"

Ajani cleared his throat and watched his own fingers pet my shoulder. He said nothing for long enough that I repeated the question.

"What…about…Colin?"

"Colin has gone to a better place."

My emotions began to boil. My voice took on a manic edge as I said, "What does that mean? No, he's not dead."

"You have to let him go, Viviane." He hung his head, the wide expanse of his brown forehead toward me. I realized he couldn't look at me as, confident and deadly serious, he said, "You'll never see him again."

My face became a font of pain. Tears and snot both welled at the same time. I blubbered. "No! He's not dead. I know he's not."

When Ajani lifted his head, his eyes held the sadness of a thousand dying suns. He rested his hand on my forehead, and his thumb gently stroked the spot between my eyes.

"Shhhh," he said. "It's going to be okay. He's never coming back. If you look for him, those people will notice you, and you'll be in danger. Colin wouldn't want that. You have to let him go."

"What? No. I...can't."

"Yes, girl, you can. You're strong. Do it because you love him and because he loved you."

I threw back the covers, ready to rage around the room.

Ajani's lips formed the words, "Sovran, jélènedra." A vanilla-scented cloud drifted down upon me, and my consciousness slipped away.

# CHAPTER 22

*You have to let him go.*

I awoke in bed with the residue of sedation chemistry in my mouth and nostrils.

Simon said, "I leave you alone for five minutes, and all Hell breaks loose."

I had neither the strength nor desire to ignore him. I was stalking the moon.

I croaked the words, "It's not my fault."

"I know it's not, missy."

"She tried to kill me again."

His voice moved close to my cheek, soft and gentle. "That's why I came back."

"I'm starting to think you know more than you're letting on. I'm starting to think everyone does—except me."

He said, "You've always had a—"

I finished the last part with him, "—very active imagination," and added, "I know."

Kicking off the covers, I rolled to sitting and rubbed my face. I ran my hands through my hair and worked the last lingering bit of fog out of my brain. My brainstem ached.

Simon's voice was right beside me. "We need to get you out of this place."

I couldn't have agreed more. I reached out to Simon, or to where his voice originated, but my hand passed through open air, touching nothing. I immediately felt foolish for almost believing again. "Is the hag a figment of my imagination too?"

He didn't answer.

"Simon? Tell me what's going on."

"I…" he paused. "I… Uh…"

I'd never heard Simon at a loss for words. "What's the matter?"

He sighed, and the sound moved down to the foot of the bed. "Viviane, there are thresholds in this world. Some you cross naturally. Some, not so much. Once you breach them, you can't turn back. These thresholds change you as you pass through them, and when they change *you*, they change your world. Some are man-made, like marriage and divorce. Others are physical. Breaking the hymen and conception, for example. Then there are mental ones, such as the understanding that Santa Claus doesn't really exist. You can never come back once you've passed through an emotional threshold like your first broken heart. There are evolutionary thresholds, consciousness thresholds, and dimensional thresholds."

A chill made my shoulders clench. "What the fuck are you talking about?"

"You ask questions, but I'm not sure you want the answers. Your reality is sacrosanct. It's not cool to fuck with Mother Nature."

"I don't understand."

"Of course, you don't. If you did, this wouldn't be a problem."

My eyes wandered. The biggest challenge of talking to someone I couldn't see had always been where to put my eyes. I wanted to look at him, but there was nothing to see. That produced a conflict in my mind that felt uncomfortable and created discord. So, I looked at my hands or the walls, anything but the location of the voice.

I asked, "What problem?"

"Your reality cherry, lass. Once it's popped, there's no going back. Gone for good. Poof. A distant memory. A friend long lost and sorely missed. And, trust me when I say it's never much fun the first time."

"Just tell me."

Simon huffed. "Your mother's going to kill me for this."

"My mother? What's she—"

Somebody knocked on the door.

"Saved by the knock." Simon retreated.

I told him, "We're not done." And then shouted, "Come in!"

Richard entered and moved to stand beside the bed. He looked down at me with his upset face. I thought I must have been looking back at him with mine as well.

"My flight got in last night. They told me what hap-pened as soon as I got here." He sat down beside me. "I'm back now. Everything's going to be okay."

I blurted my thoughts. "Colin's not dead."

He didn't immediately respond.

"He called me."

"I see." He used that patronizing tone that meant *This is another symptom that I need to document.*

"No you don't." I looked him in the eyes the same way he did me when he was in serious mode. "Colin called me on my cell phone."

Richard paused only a moment before saying, "That's impossible. Think about it. A dead person cannot make a phone call."

"Colin's. Not. Dead."

Richard gripped my upper arm as if he were on the verge of shaking me. "Yes, he is. He's dead. He's been cremated. His body is in an urn at my house."

"I don't think so. That's somebody else. Let me show you." I pushed him away so I could get off the bed, but he pushed back.

"Don't get up. You need to rest."

"I've rested enough," I insisted, starting to get angry. "If you'll just listen to me, I can show you. I found—"

Richard interrupted me. "Viviane, stop talking. Now is not the time to discuss this. I'm going to give you something that'll help."

I knew what that meant. That meant he was going to increase my dosage. I'd made a mistake, and I started backpedaling. "You know, I *am* kind of tired. I think I'm still in shock or something. I—So you heard about what happened in the shower?"

Richard relaxed with the change of subject and didn't seem in such a hurry to write a new prescription. "I heard."

"It was horrible."

"I can imagine. Do you remember what upset you?"

"No," I lied. With the threat of drugs hanging over my head, I was in no hurry to tell him that I'd seen a misty ghost bitch climb down the wall.

I felt sick to my stomach again.

Richard said, "We'll talk about it this afternoon, in our session, okay?"

"Thanks."

He headed for the door. "I have an appointment, but is there anything you need before I go?"

"I need to see Colin's body."

His eyebrows went up, and he thought about it for a second. "All right. I think that's a good idea. I'll bring his ashes with me tomorrow."

"No. I mean, I need to see his body. Detective Hayward has pictures. I want to see them, but he won't show me unless you give him permission."

That surprised Richard so much he turned his back to

me to hide his reaction. He didn't say anything immediately, and when he did, it was noncommittal. "I need to think about that, Viviane."

I knew better than to pressure him. "Okay."

"I'll come back later and check on you."

After he'd left, Simon said, "I'm sorry I wasn't here when you were attacked. I'd have twisted its scrawny neck until its head popped off." He moved around the bed. "Now that we're on its radar, it won't stop until it has destroyed all the special children."

"The special children?"

"The moonstruck. People who can see and hear things no one else can, because they—for one reason or another—have magick in their blood. You, my dear, are one of those."

"Moonstruck? You're crazy."

"That's what most people would think, but most people are deaf and blind to the toe-tickling, ball-constricting wonders of the cosmos."

I rolled my back to him. "You sound like that science fiction geek I went to junior prom with."

Simon chuckled. "Ernie Hapsbaum. I almost forgot about that kid. I got a kick out of him. He had a unique way of looking at life, considering he was a Normal."

Corona slipped into the room and hurried over to the bed. She crawled up on the bed beside me, and we just held each other.

I asked, "How are you feeling?"

"Me? How are *you* feeling? I heard the hag came after you again."

"Yeah. In the shower."

"God, that is so cliché. Although I suppose it could be worse. She could have attacked you while you were on the toilet."

"Don't even say that! I'm freaked out enough as it is."

"Me too," added Simon.

With a quiet snort, Corona asked, "What do *you* have to be freaked about? The hag's not trying to kill *you.*"

"Yes, she is," I said. "She's tried twice now."

"Not you. *Him.*"

I figured she meant Colin. "Technically, in the stairwell, it was after Colin, but in the hospital and the shower, it was definitely after me."

Corona shook her head. "No, no, no. I mean Simon. It's not trying to kill *him.*"

"If it could see me," Simon replied, "it'd be on me like greed on a politician."

I pulled back to look at Corona's face. She was starkly serious.

"What did you just say?" I asked.

She blinked at me. "It wouldn't dare attack Simon. He's more powerful than it'll *ever* be."

Simon said, "Aw, golly, girl. Aren't you all sugar and spice and everything nice. If only that were true."

I couldn't believe my ears. "Who told you about Simon?"

Corona replied, "Nobody. He introduced himself to me when I first came here."

"Huh?" I said.

"Hear that?" said Simon. "That's the sound of cherries poppin'."

Corona petted my shoulder as Simon continued, "Corona, baby, she thought she had me all to herself. The truth is, Viviane, I have a lot of friends. A lot. I'm a popular guy."

I focused my attention on Corona. "My mom told you about him, didn't she, in one of her stories."

Corona snuggled against me. "Nope. She never mentioned him. She wouldn't. He's her secret protector. If she knew he was such a schizo slut, she'd probably punish him."

Simon objected, "I'm not a schizo slut. Well, maybe I am, but Gisèle would never punish me. She loves me. She trusts me."

Corona nodded, her cheek rubbing my arm. "It's true. And that's the only reason *I* trust you."

In that moment, right there, I realized that Corona had answered Simon. She had said something in direct reply to him. Coincidence had not toyed with my perception of reality. No one was pretending.

She *had* to have heard him.

Corona had heard Simon, which meant everything else she had said was probably true as well. She knew him and had known him for years, which meant I had known him for years.

My mouth moved, but no words came out. I thought I might faint.

Corona said, "You've stepped onto the Olympus Stairway whether you meant to or not."

I grabbed Corona's forearm. "Can you see him?"

"No, goddammit. He's never shown himself to me."

"Nobody can see me," Simon said. "I'm under strict orders to remain invisible while I'm here. The last thing we need is some faux schizo seeing me and having a panic attack."

"Oh yeah," I said, sarcasm sharp. "That's the last thing we need, because hearing your disembodied voice isn't creepy at all." I had doubts exploding all over my brain, leaving black char marks. "I'm hallucinating you both." It was the only explanation that made sense.

"Don't be dumb," said Corona. "Here. I'll show you." She pinched my belly. Hard.

"Ow!" I squirmed away from her. "That hurt!"

"See?"

From the end of the bed, Simon said, "You're not hallucinating either of us, darling, and you never have hallucinated me. Welcome to the tea party, Alice."

Corona said, "There is no spoon."

I sat staring at Corona, then at the empty spot that was Simon, then at Corona again. My mind was trying to finish a sentence, but it kept getting stuck on the last word.

Aloud, I said, "If I'm not hallucinating you, then that means you're… That means you're… You're…"

Corona finished it for me. "Real."

Simon offered, "Full of awesome."

Corona said, "Yeah," and rolled onto her back, kicking her legs in the air.

The room spun around me.

"Breathe," commanded Simon.

Corona grabbed the back of my neck and bent me forward. "Put your head between your knees. Are you gonna puke?"

I focused on breathing and *not* puking.

Gradually, the shock faded.

"Oh my god, oh my god," I said. "All this fucking time."

"Duh," said Simon. "You've been working hard to deny it, what with all your schedules and refusing to talk to me for so long. Though, I suppose it's for the best. If you hadn't convinced yourself I was a hallucination, you probably would have tried to convince Dr. Dick I was real, and you'd have ended up in here a long time ago."

"What are you?" I asked.

"You talking to me or her?"

That confused me even more. "Both, I guess."

Simon said, "Ladies first."

Corona tilted her head to one side. "I'm a faux schizo, like you. I can see stuff other people can't. According to Jake, there's a concentration of us in places like the Center, because Normals think we're crazy. Heck, half the time *we* think we're crazy. Sometimes, we really are. Between the meds, the psychotherapy, and the institutions, we usually *do* go crazy." She turned the conversation over to Simon with her hand palm up.

Simon said, "I'm a parachutist. I dropped in from perpendicular."

"From perpendicular?" I asked.

"Yeah, you know—a pocket universe, another realm, a galaxy far far away."

My skepticism was rearing its head, but I went with it. "Okay. Why?"

"Why did I come here? To keep an eye on you."

"On me?"

Simon's tone turned noble. "Your mother asked me to, and I'd do anything for her."

Corona cleared her throat.

Simon said, "Too much too soon?"

Corona nodded.

My mind was icing over. "Jesus. I should have let Richard increase my meds."

Simon said, "There aren't enough meds in the world to stop this train now that you've crossed the threshold, so you'd better get ready for a few revelations."

"I'm not sure I want any more revelations."

"It's the nature of reality," Simon said, "to be fluid. No two people have ever lived the same exact lives. Time, space, and perspective are all subjective. Most of us agree that an hour is sixty minutes, and a day is 24 hours, but remember those long summers when you were a kid, and how the days dragged by? Or how the trip to the theme park was over before you knew it? It all depends on who's doing the counting. You've got your own unique little piece of reality. Why not claim it?"

I stared at my hands. "Why am I learning this now?"

"Because the three of us need to figure out how we're going to take down the hag before it kills anybody else."

"The hag or whatever you call it—is it from…a galaxy far far away?"

Simon said, "Not from mine. I suspect it's an agent of Purgatory."

"Purgatory?"

"The bad guys," said Corona. "Colin's mafia family."

Simon added, "We don't know for sure why it's here or what it wants, but we think it came looking for Colin. It found him, and it also found you. And your mother."

"My mom?"

"Your mother took the red pill too," Corona said. "Her signature is a beacon to the hag."

Simon added, "But you don't have to worry about her.

She's shielded by charms and talismans and voodoo hoo-doo that even I don't understand. It's enough to know that she has the magickal equivalent of Fort Knox around her."

I could do nothing but stare as my mind skidded to a near standstill.

Corona said, "It'd be nice if we could have wards and stuff too, right?"

Simon replied, "I'm afraid they're in short supply these days. But, you're safe in Gisèle's room. Unfortunately, you can't stay there forever, and the hag isn't going to give up. It's already attacked you several times. It won't stop."

"Oh." I was reeling. "Can't we make it go away?"

"Nope," Corona said.

"I did."

"You did what?"

"Made it go away. In the shower."

"You did? How?"

I shrugged. "I just ordered it gone."

Simon chuckled deeply. "I'm proud of you, Viv. Your powers are surfacing."

"Excuse me?"

"Magick, my bonny girl. Magick. You're a natural."

"Magick, my ass." My stomach had begun to churn. I wanted *all* of it to go away. I changed the subject back to the problem at hand. "Can we kill it?"

"Most definitely," Simon replied. "It's dangerous, but not invulnerable."

With a laugh that sounded more than a little hysterical, I asked, "Why don't you just twist its head off then?"

Simon coughed. "I was exaggerating—just a little—when I said that."

# CHAPTER 23

Corona and I waited in the rec room for the call to lunch. Polly and Dahlia sat together watching TV, talking in hushed voices about whatever was happening on the show. Corona joined them. Una was a large presence in the corner of the room, rocking from one foot to the other and watching everyone with suspicion. Iraida Karim, draped in her burka, was hunched over a book at one of the tables.

I went to the piano, and without waiting for an invitation, I sat down beside Eun Hee.

She scooted to give me room. A small tight expression of pleasure came to her face, and she hovered her hands just above the keys before launching into a tune that I didn't recognize. On the second go-round, she started singing.

*Haloperidol makes you itch.*
*Paliperidone makes you twitch.*
*Fat on risperidone,*
*flat on ziprasidone.*
*But without them, you're one crazy bitch.*

*Chlorpromazine blocks dopamine.*
*Ol' clozapine cuts back the mean.*
*Your doc's the controller,*
*And if you're bipolar,*
*He'll make you take olanzapine.*

Several others joined in on the chorus. Their voices produced a discordant harmony, some singing too loudly, some off-key. Iraida's trill gave it an exotic note, and one beautiful voice—Eun Hee's—was the rope that tied them all together.

*So suck it up.*
*Don't chuck it up.*
*You'll spend more time on the stool.*
*But, you won't be down,*
*Not wearing a frown.*
*It's time to stop playing the fool.*

*If Prozacking, try perphen'zine.*
*If yacking, trifluoperazine.*
*Loxapine makes you spit.*
*Quetiapine is the shit.*
*It feels so damn good, it's obscene.*

I couldn't stop laughing. By the second stanza, everyone in the rec room had gathered around the piano to dance, clap, and sing.

Something made the back of my neck spasm. I looked over my shoulder.

Nathan was there, on the far side of the room, dressed all in black. His asymmetrical haircut looked wind-ruffled. He stood with his hands clasped in front of him, watching me with a crooked smile.

"Excuse me," I said, rising to my feet. I crossed to where Corona stood, singing. My ears buzzed. I asked her, "Do you see that man over there?"

"Where?" She looked where I pointed and said, "Oh, yeah."

That was a relief.

He kept his eyes on me.

That wasn't.

"Who is he?" Corona asked.

"He's the one I told you about—Colin's brother, the guy I saw at Mom's window."

"He's invisible."

"What do you mean?"

Corona waved her hand, indicating the other women in the room. "Look. No one else can see him." The other women were all preoccupied. No one, not even Una, not even Nurse Linda, registered his presence. "He's here to see you. I suspect the only reason I can see him is because you pointed him out to me."

"He's not from here?"

"Definitely not. Be careful, okay?"

"Okay." I started toward him. Corona followed.

He looked both young and mature, his baby face beginning to wrinkle at the eyes and around the mouth. He wore eyeliner and maybe even a touch of lip gloss. His skin was so pale, it was worrisome. When we got closer, he bowed to me, actually bowed like an actor at the end of a play, and said with his strange accent, "It's a pleasure to see you, Viviane."

The cat had gotten my tongue, and a rankling sense of danger began to creep up my spine.

Nathan turned his attention to Corona and introduced himself. "I'm Nathan, Colin's brother. I'm trying to find him."

Corona said, "You should talk to the police."

I said, "So you know he's not dead?"

"Shall we sit?" Nathan grinned, and I noticed his teeth. I remembered how white they had been the first time I'd met him—gleaming. They still were. He spread his arms wide and turned to face a grouping of armchairs.

As if on cue, Eun Hee played a strange piano tune, the notes plunky and dancing—a melody from a macabre carnival.

Nathan molded himself to one of the chairs and, with a courtly wave of his hand, indicated we should sit as well. He crossed one knee over the other, his foot dangling. His pant leg rose up, revealing black socks with purple stars. His ankle-boots had pointed toes. He said, "So, you girls don't know where Colin is?"

"No," said Corona. "But—"

I cut her off. "I really want to meet Colin's dad. Is he here, too?"

Nathan's left eyebrow wasn't an eyebrow at all. It was a tattoo, as thick and black as his real eyebrow, but the tattoo ended with a flock of crows breaking apart from it and flying up into his hairline. I hadn't noticed that before. Perhaps it was new. "No, unfortunately not," he said. "Our father is quite ill." His expression shifted into sadness, melting downward as if made of wax. "That's why it's so critical that I find Colin."

My eyes stayed locked with Nathan's for several long seconds. His had the shifting feel of oil on water, black water, water that held no life. I looked away first.

"It really is urgent," he said. "I'm at my wits end, and I find it hard to believe that you girls know nothing about his location."

I asked, "What's Colin's real name?"

"Colin's real name is Aubrey. Interesting how the sub-conscious works in an amnesiac."

I realized I had no way of knowing whether he was telling the truth or not.

"He's in danger," Nathan said. "His family needs him, and there are people who want to use him as leverage against us."

"You think he's been kidnapped?"

"We think they staged the accident in order to take him. Staged his death so we'd stop looking for him."

"Why?"

Nathan pulled a cloth handkerchief from his pocket. Several bits of white confetti, tiny circles, came out with it and fluttered to the ground. He made a big deal of wiping his brow, then asked, "Do you know where he is?"

"No," I replied. "Have you talked to the police about this?"

Nathan's tattoo eyebrow went up. The crows soared. "Those monkeys are too busy flinging feces at moving targets to notice what's right under their noses." His hard eyes softened. "Our father is dying. He begged me to bring Aubrey home, and I'll keep searching until I find him or until my father dies."

The charm left Nathan's demeanor. "Please understand that if you're not on my family's side, then you're on the kidnappers' side, and that makes you my enemy. This is your last chance to do right by Aubrey. Either you tell me what you know or suffer the consequences."

"Are you threatening me?"

"I'm merely pointing out that if I don't find him, he could be lost to us forever. You *want* to be my ally." He held my gaze.

I didn't care for him, I didn't trust him, and I could tell

his threats were sincere.

I told him, "I don't know where he is."

Nathan blinked free of my gaze and uncrossed his legs. "Remember," he said as he stood without using his hands to push himself up, "whatever happens next is because you refused to help me."

"Wow," said Corona. "You've got more bats in your belfry than we do."

Nathan looked cockeyed at Corona. "You don't know the half of it." He handed each of us a business card. "Don't be strangers," he said, then turned—literally—on his heel and strode out.

"Holy shit," said Corona. "He's creepy."

"Yeah."

I looked at the card in my hand. It was black with silver, fancy letters. It said, "Nathanatos," and it had a phone number. That was all.

Corona and I went to the dining room and sat down to lunch at a table in the corner, away from the others. I watched her push her tater tots around her plate and said, "I still can't believe Simon's real. I'm in a David Lynch movie, minus the sex."

Corona frowned. "Plenty of violence though."

"How long have you known him?"

She took a bite of her burger. After a few chews, she said with her mouth full, "Since I got here. He was pretty nice to me when I needed it the most. I don't know what

I'd have done without him."

I realized I'd never heard anything about Corona's history. Until I became a patient, I'd only known her as the sweet schizophrenic who lived down the hall from my mom. More recently, she'd become a good friend. I asked, "How'd you end up at the Center?"

"There was an incident," she answered. She studied me for a moment, as if gauging whether I was worthy of her secrets. Finally, she went back to rearranging her tater tots and said, "I was at M.I.T. when I first started seeing crazy shit. It scared the crap out of me. I didn't understand what was happening. I started thinking my professors or those asshat grad students were experimenting on me. I caught them watching me. I was convinced they were putting psychotropic drugs in my food and water. So I burned down their center of operations."

"Wow."

"Um, yeah. Two steps away from terrorist. I'm lucky nobody was hurt, or I'd be on death row right now." She set down her fork. "My mother paid off the university, and they dropped the charges. Then she sent me here."

"Do you ever talk to her?"

"Who? My mother?" Corona shook her head. "Nah. She remarried right before I went away to school. She's got three other kids now. She figured she botched it so bad the first time, she better just clear the slate and start from scratch."

I could hear the bitterness in Corona's voice, but then she flashed me her dimples.

"It's cool," she said. "I never really liked her much anyway, and now I'm free to be my own woman. Feelings of 'family' are nothing more than genetic drives instilled in us to ensure survival of the species."

I couldn't have agreed less, but suddenly, I understood why she was so drawn to *my* mom. I wondered if she'd let Mom brush *her* hair on those nights when I wasn't there.

Richard came into the dining room, looking collegiate as always in blue corduroy pants and a burgundy jacket, an island of jewel-toned colors in an otherwise faded sea of white coats, bleached robes, and pastel pajamas. I saw him before he saw me, and I watched him.

Several of his patients were there, but his eyes scanned over them, found me, and stuck.

I warned Corona. "Here comes Richard. It's time for my session."

"I know."

"He's got me booked all afternoon. He's scared and in a hurry to get me well."

She spoke through a mouthful of tater tots. "He's afraid of losing you. Just don't tell him the truth about Simon."

"I won't."

♦

"I'm serious about moving out of the Center," I told Richard.

He sat back and tented his fingers on his chest. "I don't think it's a good idea for you to stray too far from your support structure."

I leaned forward on the couch. "Lettie and I are going to share a place."

"Do you really think that's wise? Lettie's a nice woman, but her life isn't exactly stable."

"What do you mean? She's stable. She's got a steady job."

"That's true." Richard looked me right in the eyes. "But, she's also got a steady stream of lovers who pass through her life and disrupt her emotionally and mentally. The last thing you need is to put yourself at Drama Central. You need peace and quiet, Viviane."

It never did any good to defend Lettie to Richard. His opinion of her hadn't changed in twenty years.

"Peace and quiet? With people dying all around me? I can't stay here any longer. I can't. I keep looking over my shoulder. I can't sleep at night, wondering if I'll be next."

"Oh, don't be ridiculous. That's all over now." Richard got up and crossed to sit beside me. "The police have everything under control. You're perfectly safe here."

I shook my head, but I didn't know how to explain that I wasn't safe at all. He wouldn't understand. "You said this was only temporary. You said I'd be able to go home when

I was feeling better. I'm better now. I want to leave." It was getting hard to keep my cool. "I'm not a prisoner."

"Calm down. You're getting worked up over nothing. No, you're not a prisoner, you're a patient, and it's my job to make sure you get well. That will happen on my schedule, not on yours. Your grandfather has entrusted—"

"Fuck Abram." I stood. "I needed to be here after… what happened to Colin. But I'm better now. I don't need this anymore." I waved my hands to indicate the office around me. "We can keep up my sessions, but living here isn't doing me any good." I meant every word of it, though the thought hadn't occurred to me until just that moment. The sudden sense of power over my own destiny was enlightening.

Then, Richard said, "Unfortunately, it's not your call. You were remanded into my care."

"Then fuck you too!" I clenched my hands at my sides, wanting to lash out at him. "This place is no good for me."

With professional nonchalance, Richard looked down at his hands. "I'm not heartless, you know. I understand what you're going through, and I want to help you. There's one possible solution."

My heart beat a little faster. He had my full attention. "What?"

He pushed up out of his chair, slowly, as if afraid to spook me and reached to take one of my hands in both of his. "You could come live with me," he said. "I have an extra bedroom. I'd be right there if you needed me. We could continue our sessions there. You wouldn't have to work. I make enough money to support us both, and I'm willing to do that. It's the perfect solution."

"Have you lost your mind?"

"No. I need more time with you."

"What are you talking about?"

"I love you, Vivi, and I believe—as does Dr. Lamb— that we're well on our way to controlling your illness. If you come live with me, we can do the work in the evenings."

My mind raced a thousand miles a minute. I felt my lip curl in revulsion. My entire being rejected the idea of being under his thumb twenty-four/seven. I tried to pull my hand away from him.

He didn't let go.

"I can't live with you," I said. "You're my therapist."

"I know, but I'm also one of your oldest friends. You've told me so many times. I know you love me too."

Maybe once I had, when I was an impressionable teen, but I'd grown out of that. I said, "We can still do the regressions during our weekly office visits. Not a problem. I want to live with Lettie."

I tugged harder to free my hand, and Richard released me. His face went concrete in a flash, and in a firm voice so quiet I almost couldn't hear it, he said, "That's not going to happen."

The upset built in my chest, rose to my sinuses, and pushed tears into my eyes. "Fine!" I said. I had to get away from him. I headed for the door.

He came around the couch and caught me there, wrapping his arms around me and holding me tightly—too tightly. "I'm sorry. I'm so sorry."

I didn't struggle. I just let him crush me against himself, turning my head to one side and letting my hair spill down over my face.

More gently, at my ear, he said, "Colin is dead. It's time for you to move on."

"Prove it." I hid my face against his shoulder.

"What?"

"I need to see proof that Colin is dead."

Richard's hold on me loosened, but not enough for me to step away. Rubbing my back, he said, "Please, forget I said anything. We'll work on getting you out of here, okay? There's paperwork and tests. I'll have to perform an evaluation, but we'll make it a priority, okay? Okay?"

"Okay."

"Okay." Richard released me and went to the door. "I'll take you back to your wing."

"I need to see those pictures of Colin's body." I wiped my eyes with the backs of my hands.

Richard's expression was one of dark determination. "If that's what you need to move on with your life, then that's what we'll do." He put his hand on the doorknob and turned it. "I'll contact Detective Hayward tomorrow."

We didn't say another word until we arrived at the door to the Women's Wing. Richard held it open for me, but he didn't follow me in. "I'll see you tomorrow for our session."

"Yeah, sure." I felt that, despite his maddening insistence on controlling me, I had won a small victory. I didn't dare show it, however. Richard hated to lose, and I'd need to plow a straight row if I wanted his signature to get me out of the Center.

◆

Corona sat against the headboard in my room, reading a fat paperback. She closed it when I entered and just watched me.

I went to the windows, then back to the door, did an about-face and returned to the window.

"You're thinking so hard I smell ozone," Corona said.

"Richard is fucking with me. He doesn't want me to move in with Lettie. Instead, he suggested I live with him."

"That's uncool."

"Yeah." At the window, I looked out over the circular drive. Bea walked toward the Center from the employee parking lot. She had on blue jeans and a t-shirt. I'd never seen her out of her nurse's scrubs. The clothes and the swing in her step made her look younger. When she got close to the building, she looked up and spotted me. A smile spread across her face, and she lifted her hand in greeting.

I smiled too and waved. She was okay, so long as she wasn't talking.

A movement at the corner of my vision drew my attention. Down where the road cut through the orchard, the wind played in the treetops. A large raven sat at the very tip of an evergreen—or most people would have seen a raven. I saw Nathan. *Nathanatos.* His black coat waved out around him, moving in synchronization with the tree, and his hair ruffled like feathers upon his head. He perched there, avian, weightless upon the tree's slim top, levitating. He was watching the Center.

My hand was still raised from waving at Bea, and I looked back at her. She'd seen that something was wrong, but I couldn't let her think that. I waved again. The last thing I needed was Nurse Bea thinking I still had hallucinations. She'd tell everyone. I moved away from the window.

"Who were you waving at?"

"Nurse Bea. She was coming across from the parking lot."

"Oh." Corona got up and went to the window. "I don't see her."

"She went inside."

"Oh." Corona turned away, then stopped, and did a

double-take. Her eyebrows came together, and she put her nose right up to the glass. "What the fuck is that?"

I went to her side and looked out. Nathan was still there, a black silhouette against the gray sky. "What's what?"

"You don't see that? That bird thing on the thing over there?" She pointed right at Nathan. "It's a man, but he's on top of a tree."

My heart filled my throat with thumping. "You see him?"

"Yeah, though I wish I didn't. He's watching us."

"Yeah."

"That's unnerving."

"Yeah."

As we looked on, Nathan stretched upward. His body elongated, then came back together in the form of a raven. His coat flaps became wings, and he rose into the sky. He soared and made a lap around the treetop before diving toward the ground and disappearing behind a close community of evergreens.

We waited, our mouths hanging open, for him to rise into view again. He never did.

I said, "It's Nathan."

"That creepy man I met? That makes sense. He's a 'chuter." When she saw the look of confusion on my face, she added, "A parachutist."

"You mean like Simon?"

She took my hand and pulled me away from the window. "Just like Simon. Don't you see the patterns? Colin's involved in something really big, so big that he has crazy supernatural beings looking for him. This isn't your everyday, backyard missing person. The risks reveal the stakes. If we aren't talking potential apocalypse here, I'd be seriously surprised."

I sighed. "So what do we do?"

"We find Colin."

♦

Corona and I looked both ways before we headed into the hall and down to my mom's room. Mom was at her desk. I said, "Hi, Mom," but she didn't look up, and she didn't respond. She just kept writing in her journal, methodically scratching letter after letter.

I went to her, pushed a stray lock of her hair back from her face, and studied her. She was still so striking, and I could only imagine how beautiful she must have been when she was younger. Although she was fifty-five, she had the smoothest, clearest skin I'd ever seen on anyone. In some light, it looked almost translucent, although when she got upset, the scarlet rushed up her neck to her cheeks and gave her a splotchy blush. My skin was similar, except years of janitorial and laundry chemicals had left me with a duller, dryer surface that required more care.

My mom was a doll that Abram had put away in the

closet. She'd stayed there, untouched, pristine in her box, for decades.

Corona sat in the big fan-back chair and pulled her legs in sideways with her. "Tell us a story, Lady Gisèle. Please?"

It was weird hearing someone call my mom "Lady Gisèle," but Corona and Polly pretended they were her ladies-in-waiting. Polly especially believed she had a sworn duty to take care of Mom. It was sweet.

Corona's request had an interesting effect.

Mom sat there for a long moment, pen poised over the paper, as if someone had hit the pause button on her movie. When the action started again, she set the pen aside and picked up her journal. She licked a finger and flipped back until she came to the page she wanted.

Her midnight-blue eyes roamed down the lines, searching, then she put her finger to one of them, and started reading.

*The jonquils and daffodils had breached the last of the snow. They were determined to find sunlight and warmth in the wake of winter. Kypris felt the same. She had spent days cleaning her house, washing linens, and scrubbing floors. She wanted to grasp Spring and pull it to her for a long, wet kiss.*

*Her first sight of him left Kypris breathless. He was standing on the street in front of her house, hands on hips, looking up at the sky as if he could command it to hold its rain until he was finished with his errands. He had a regal tilt to his head, and his beauty was beyond compare.*

*Kypris was sweeping her front porch. She didn't know why she looked up, but she was glad she did. Big, fat droplets of rain had begun to fall.*

*Admitting defeat, the man opened his arms and welcomed it. His laughter drew Kypris to the edge of the porch. It was the most uninhibited, happiest sound she'd ever heard. She clung to the post and called, "Hey! You're getting all wet."*

*Dressed only in shirtsleeves and a pair of black trousers, he was soaked to the bone. The downpour showed him no mercy. He called back, "The sky feels I need a bath." He waved and began to walk on.*

*Kypris couldn't bear the thought of him leaving. She called, "Wait!" She would never have done such a thing otherwise, but she felt that if he left, a piece of her fate would leave as well.*

*He stopped and turned to look at her.*

*Kypris didn't know what to say.*

*He waited, and when she didn't speak again, he grinned and said, "I see you're in on the sky's joke. Will I never learn not to fall for a beautiful woman's temptation?" He blew Kypris a kiss and, again, turned to go.*

*She called, "Would you care for some tea?"*

*The man paused...again. The rain ran in ribbons down his face, past his smile, as he looked at her.*

*"You'll catch your death," she said.*

*He replied, "Far be it from me to chase after—much less catch—my death." Then he was on the porch with her, out of the rain. She retrieved a towel for him and watched as he dried his handsome face and close-cropped hair.*

*The silence between them grew tense with her desire. To break it, she said, "I'm Kypris."*

*When he answered, his voice held all the promises Kypris had ever wanted to hear. "Of course, you are," he said. "And I'm Chance, my princess, forever in your debt." He bowed, and Kypris fell in love.*

*They had tea that first rainy afternoon. They talked of wishes, dreams, and the poetry of nature. Kypris dried his clothes for him with a sachet of lavender to scent them and fed him honeyed bread from her larder. Their hands nearly touched more than once.*

*As Chance was leaving, he promised to return the next day, and he did. The second time, they clasped hands spontaneously on the porch. The rain had washed away the lingering snow and its dirt. The world seemed a bright, new place. The afternoon fled, and when it came time for Chance to leave, he stole Kypris's soul with a kiss.*

*The third time he visited, they made love in her bed. For days, they languished in each others' arms, loving and laughing. His every touch and every kiss was a promise of forever happiness. Kypris basked in him.*

*Then, one morning, Kypris awoke to find he had gone.*

*For weeks, she mewled with a cat's heat and wept with a widow's grief. Months passed, and Kypris came to realize that she had retained a part of him inside herself. His child grew in her womb. She did the only thing she could—she called her mother.*

*Her mother knew from the details of the tale that Kypris had been with an unearthly being. The two women set about hiding the child from its father. Even before it was born, plans were put into motion to keep the child safe. Kypris changed her name, for names had the power of finding. If Chance were ever to discover them, he would take the child away, and Kypris would never see it again.*

# CHAPTER 24

The last person I expected to see at dinner was Dr. Jake Lamb, but there he was, looking lumberjack-chic in a plaid flannel shirt, jeans, and heavy boots. Corona and I were sitting at our table when he appeared beside us.

"Hello, ladies," he greeted, brown eyes lit with flecks of gold.

Corona turned a grin on him. "Jake! You're back. I'm so glad."

"Hey, kiddo," said Jake. He offered his hand for a shake, which Corona took enthusiastically. "I hope you're doing well."

"Pretty good," she replied. "Better than Viviane. She got attacked again."

A dark shadow crossed Jake's face, and he shifted his gaze to me. "That so?"

I shrugged. My mind was on the questions I wanted to ask him. He still wore the ring, and it still screamed secret society or fraternal brotherhood. It taunted me, large and uninhibited on his finger.

"Why don't you join us?" I offered. "It'd be nice to get

to know you better. Corona says great things about you."

"I'd be delighted. Tell me about this attack. What happened?" Jake claimed one of the empty chairs.

Corona was eager to share. "It happened in the shower. The hag went for her. Isn't that right, Viviane?"

"It was over pretty quick."

Jake showed concern, but that was it. No disbelief. No condescension. "You're all right?"

"Yeah."

We all looked at each other for a moment, then Jake cleared his throat. "I have a proposal for you, Viviane. I've already talked to Dr. Reuter about it, but I wanted to talk to you in person as well."

"A proposal?" I was suspicious.

He leaned forward in the chair, put his elbows on the table, and folded his hands. "I specialize in a certain type of schizophrenia. I work with patients who present specific symptoms."

"What kind of symptoms?"

"For example, long-term friendships with people no one else can see. Or, the recurring paranoid delusion of being followed or even attacked by monsters."

"Uh huh. Because if someone thinks they're being stalked, say…while they're at a nightclub, they must be delusional, right?"

He got my reference. "I was beginning to think you hadn't recognized me."

"I didn't right away, but eventually… Why were you following me?"

Jake leaned forward and lowered his voice. "I had to confirm that you fit our profile. But. If you tell anyone, I'll deny that it was anything other than a coincidence."

"How long have you been watching me?"

Conversation paused for a moment as one of the kitchen staff rolled her cart to our table and set out three plates of spaghetti and meatballs, along with silverware and a plastic cup of water for each of us.

"Not that long," continued Jake after the woman had moved on. "I arrived in Peoria a week before I met you at the dance bar. I was actually here looking for Corona when you appeared on my radar."

I glanced at Corona, and she gave me a bright smile. She wasn't even remotely surprised by any of that. I said, "What you did at the club was rude."

"Sorry. I'd planned a better introduction, but you escaped before I could do it properly. Unfortunately, I have a tiny penchant for drama. I come by it honestly, but yes, I got carried away."

Some of my anger dissipated. "What do you want from me, Dr. Lamb?"

He pointed at me and wagged his finger. "Now, *that* is a very good question. I don't want anything *from* you. I want to do something *for* you. And, please, call me Jake."

"What can you do for me, Jake?"

"I can teach you how to control and understand your schizophrenia."

I laughed. "I don't need your help with that."

"Really? Then why are you in here?"

My temper flared again. "Because I had a car accident and thought my fiancé had been killed. I was upset. These are not normal circumstances."

"I see,' he said. "And under normal circumstances, you hold down a job and take care of a home, a catatonic mother, and an amnesiac boyfriend. I'd say you were quite the Wonder Woman, under normal circumstances."

"That's right."

Jake looked at me intently to underscore the importance of his next question. "And where, in all that caretaking, does Viviane fit in?"

He'd made an abrupt turn that I hadn't expected.

When I hesitated to reply, he said, "Hiding behind everyone else's problems isn't the same as controlling and understanding your own situation. If you keep making choices based on other people's lives, your life will stay as it is—one long series of sacrifices for someone else."

When I started to speak, he raised his hand to forestall my comment. "This isn't a criticism. I respect what you've done. You've given up so much to be near your mother. I admire that. However, I would also ask you to consider whether it's time to remember your own dreams and to pursue them again, maybe in small measure at first. I'm here to offer you the chance to do that."

Corona leaned toward me. "Hear him out. You won't be sorry." She had spaghetti sauce on her chin.

To Jake, I said, "Go on."

He leaned back in his chair. "I run the Lost Lamb Halfway House in Wyrdwood, Oregon. The only people living there are special like you. We offer classes and support one another. You could join us."

A thousand reasons came immediately to mind for why I didn't want to go with him. My mom was at the top of the list. There was no way I'd leave her. And then there was Colin, who I believed was alive and being held against his will somewhere. I had a job I intended to go back to, and what about my sessions with Richard? I'd been doing them for so long, I was half afraid I'd fall apart without them. I could go on and on—I had so many reasons *not* to take his offer.

Jake said, "We can get you integrated back into society. You could take university classes. The halfway house is funded by grants, and your stay would be free to you. You wouldn't pay a cent for room or board. The house isn't an institution, it's a home, and we treat it that way. We don't force you into bed at a certain hour or lock you inside. We work on a system of mutual respect."

I interjected, "What did Richard say about it?"

Jake inhaled. "Well, he didn't like the idea. As a matter of fact, he told me in no uncertain terms he wouldn't allow you to go."

I snorted, not the least bit surprised, and said, "So you figured you'd come straight to me and work around him, is that it?" At that moment, I wasn't sure who was the lesser of two evils.

Jake leaned forward again, intently lowering his voice. "He's wrong, Viviane. He's trying to control you at the expense of your well-being. Surely, you see that?"

"And you're not?"

"No," said Jake.

I rested my palm flat on the table and looked him in the eyes. "I don't even know you. Richard has been my doctor for twenty years. He knows me better than anyone."

Jake shook his head. "He really doesn't. He can't even begin to understand what's happening to you."

"Oh, right! And the stalker guy I just met does?" Amused, I put a snarky smile on my face. "Please. I don't know what you want from me, or what you think makes me special, but I'm not going anywhere with you. My life is here."

Corona poked apart a meatball in her spaghetti.

Jake nodded. "It's your call. But, if you need anything, I'm staying here in Peoria for a while." He pulled a card out of his breast pocket and handed it to me. On it was his name, an address, and a phone number. "Call me any time. I can help more than you think." He checked his watch, pushed back his chair, and stood. "Bon appetit, ladies."

"Bye, Jake," said Corona with a small wave.

"Bye, Corona."

Once he was out of sight, I tore the card in half and left the pieces on the table.

# CHAPTER 25

The next morning, shortly after breakfast, Detective Hayward stuck his head into my room. "I heard you had another break-down, Miss Rose."

I looked up from where I was sorting through my notes on Colin's disappearance. "You could call it that."

I waved him in, and he entered, gaze drifting around as if he were in a museum. He didn't look at me as he said, "You know, it's funny, Miss Rose. Most people ask me, first thing, whether I've found the killer or not. You've never asked me that. Why is that?"

"Because if you'd figured out what happened, you'd have a less stressed and more smug look on your face."

"Good answer."

"You've decided they were murders?" I asked.

"It would seem so. The bruising kind of gives it away." He strolled over to the bedside table. "So, you've got everybody convinced you're nuts, huh?"

"God, I hope not."

"Well, I'm not convinced." Hayward ran his hand along the metal footboard as he rounded the bed. "Your unhinged act is impressive. One might even say, 'finely tuned.' Have you had a chance to make a fuss yet over the pictures of Mr. Aubrey's body?"

"Excuse me?"

"I figured that's why you wanted them—so you had another opportunity to lose your mind."

"I haven't seen them."

"I had them delivered yesterday morning to Dr. Reuter. He hasn't shown them to you? Mm. Probably trying to protect you. If he isn't your accomplice, then he's completely bamboozled by you. Personally, I think he's in love with you, but that's me."

I said nothing.

Hayward put one hand on the back of my chair and leaned over me. He lowered his voice to a friendly whisper and said, "I know what you've been up to, Miss Rose. You may be able to fool everyone else, but you don't fool me. I see the sanity in your eyes, the cunning. If you're the one who committed those murders, I'll prove it. Don't think for one second that you can hide behind an insanity plea. You're more transparent than you think."

"I didn't kill anyone."

"Save it for your doctor." He saw the papers on the desk. They were my notes, documenting the hag and its victims, the accident, Nathan, Colin, Doc Bella, and Ajani.

"Keeping notes for when you write your memoirs from prison?" Hayward smirked and headed for the door. "I'm guessing it'll end up in the Fantasy section at the bookstore."

♦

I had to see those photos. If Richard had them, they'd be in his office somewhere. He hadn't mentioned them during our session the previous day, so I had no faith that he'd show them to me later that afternoon. I decided to hedge my bet.

I had an idea for how to get him out of the office so I could search, but it was risky, and I needed a helper.

Richard and I had just entered his office for that afternoon's session. "I've got something I want to show you today," he said. "Why don't you make yourself comfortable."

I got a little zing, a combination of dread and excitement. Was he going to show me the photos after all? "What is it?" I asked, trying to keep my voice even. I sat in my usual spot on the couch, but it didn't feel as welcoming as usual. I perched at the edge and clasped my hands to hide their trembling.

He waited until I was seated, then he picked up a cardboard box just big enough to hold a human head. He carried it over and sat down beside me.

*How many pictures were there?* I wondered, eying the box.

He watched me closely for a moment.

"Well?" I prompted.

He opened the box top. Reaching inside with both hands, he said, "I want you to know that you're safe here. No matter what, you're safe here."

He pulled an urn from inside the box. The cardboard fell to the floor with a hollow bump, landing on its side. I saw the stamp of Dolce Riposa Mortuary on the side.

To his credit, Richard said nothing else immediately. He just handed me the urn.

I took it automatically.

The urn's brass was cold and smooth. It curved upward and had a sealed lid on top. I held it in front of me and looked at it. There was an engraving. It read:


Colin Aubrey

10006593-3667IL

My face was reflected back at me, distorted by the curve and color of the brass.

Richard said softly, "This is what I've been trying to tell you."

I held the urn to my chest, hugging it. I didn't care who or what was in it. It represented my Colin and all the terrible things that had been happening. Besides, I had to make Richard believe my reaction.

Richard put his arm around me. "It's going to be okay. I've got you. We're going to—"

A knock on the door interrupted him. He looked up.

The second knock was more insistent.

Richard shouted, sounding irritated, "I'm in session."

"Dr. Reuter?" It was Corona, right on time.

"Go ahead," I said. "I'm fine. I'm just going to sit here for a minute."

After a brief hesitation, Richard stood, smoothed his jacket sleeves, and walked to the door. He opened it to reveal Corona.

She looked freaked enough, but not too much. "Dr. Reuter! I just saw Henry Tomkins running down the hall with a black permanent marker." Henry was one of Richard's patients, and he had a compulsion for drawing giant penis graffiti.

"How did he get… Never mind." Richard shook his head. To me, he said, "Stay here. I'll be right back."

"Okay," I replied, casual as pajamas.

Corona gave me a wink as Richard headed out, leaving the door ajar. She followed him, saying, "He went that way."

I set the urn aside. I had a mission, and I couldn't let anything get in the way of it. I quietly shut the door, and it locked automatically.

Corona's distant chatter moved down the hall.

Richard had no intention of showing me the photos. I knew he had them, and I knew they were the key to solving the mystery. But he didn't know I knew.

Fingers nervous and clumsy, I went through the papers on the desktop first, looking for an envelope or folder. When that proved fruitless, I started going through drawers. I found a file with my name on it and pulled it out. Inside it, on top, was a document—a Petition for Involuntary Admission—signed by my grandfather. It confirmed what I already knew—that he believed I'd lost my mind and wanted nothing to do with me.

I was in the process of flipping the page when something caught my eye. I stopped and looked at it more closely.

The signature at the bottom read "Abram Rose." It was my grandfather's usual, prim handwriting, except he never signed his name "Abram." On legal documents, he always used his full name, "Abraham."

I wasn't sure what it meant, and I didn't have time to think it through just then, but something turned screwy in my stomach. I folded the paper and stuffed it down the back of my pants.

The next set of pages was a progress report to Dr. Min, written and signed by Richard.

*Viviane is showing no sign of improvement. Her symptoms have increased in frequency and severity. It's my conclusion that her psychosis makes her a danger to herself and others, and I recommend that she continue her residence and treatment regi-*

*men for another twelve months, after which time, I
will perform a reevaluation.*

The report was dated and time-stamped that very
morning, after he'd promised, the day before, to work on
releasing me.

He had no intention of letting me go—not then, not
ever.

Pages stapled to the report included a transcript of one
of our hypnosis sessions. I recognized it immediately as
one from a week or so earlier. I didn't, however, remember
saying that I wanted to kill myself. I also didn't remember
saying that I'd hallucinated a visit from my dead grandmother who wanted me to go back to Hell with her and
bring my mother along too.

It was like reading someone else's therapy—someone
much sicker than me, a suicidal, homicidal maniac.

I took those papers too.

Shuffling through the rest, I saw no photos, so I put
the folder back and kept looking. I pulled out the middle
drawer, and there in the center of it was a white envelope
addressed to Richard. It had the police logo on it, and it
had been opened.

My hands shook as I pulled the photos out and looked
down at them. There were only three. One showed a man
lying in a half-zipped body bag at the lakeshore; the other
two showed the same man on a coroner's table.

The man in the photos had coffee-colored hair and shadowed skin, so different from Colin's ginger curls and Gaelic pallor as to be immediately discernible.

It wasn't Colin.

Joy and relief swelled inside me, threatening to over-flow without restraint. I held the photos to my chest, torn between the urge to shout "Thank you!" to the Heavens and the urge to cry with relief. I landed on a combination of both, tears brimming, my gratitude flowing out in a gush of mumbled thank-yous.

If Richard had looked at these, then he knew it wasn't Colin.

I recognized the man in them. His face was swollen and the wrong color, but there was no denying it. The man in the photos was Jaxon Bellonescu. He was dead. Some-one had faked my fiancé's death by putting another man in his place. Suddenly, the false I.D. made sense.

Out in the hall, Corona said, "I think he might've—"

"I'll find him later, Corona. Right now, I need to get back to my session with Viviane."

I quickly stuffed one of the morgue pictures into my jeans.

"But wait, Dr. Richard," Corona said quickly.

"What is it?" Richard asked, right outside the office door.

I put the other two photos back in the envelope.

The door's lock clicked.

Corona said, "I remember now. He definitely went this way."

I shut the drawer too fast, catching my finger just at the edge and pinching it. An explosion of pain reverberated into my mind, and I couldn't keep from exclaiming aloud.

"Don't worry," said Richard. "I'll find him after my session. He can't do too much damage."

I shook my hand in a failed effort to make it stop hurting and hustled around the desk toward the couch.

The doorknob started to turn.

Richard said, "Go on back to your room, Corona," as he pushed the door open.

By the time he stepped in, I had landed back on the couch. I wiped my eyes of the tears that had come with the pain and held the urn held to my chest.

Richard made a sympathetic sound as he closed the door behind him.

Getting through the rest of that session was one of the hardest things I'd ever done. I wasn't fully successful, but I couldn't let Richard see that anything was wrong. I had to get out of there with my treasures intact.

Richard noticed that I was distracted. He had a hard time putting me under hypnosis. I paid close attention to what happened during the session, and it made me less susceptible to suggestion. I had lost all trust in him.

When the time came for me to go back to my wing, I tried to take the urn with me.

Richard wouldn't let me. He pulled it from my arms and set it on the bookshelf by the door, like a trophy. "I'll keep it here for you. That way, it'll be safe. You can come see it whenever I'm here."

"Him," I corrected. "See him."

"Right. Him." Richard guided me out into the hall. He checked that the door had locked behind him, something I'd never seen him do before.

We walked in silence, side-by-side yet separated by a vast new distance. Something had broken. I saw Richard's manipulation for what it was, and for the first time in my life I didn't just doubt, I *knew* he didn't have my best interests at heart. He didn't respect my wishes. I wished I knew why, but ultimately, it didn't matter. I had enough evidence safeguarded in my pants to prove my sanity.

We arrived at the doors to the Women's Wing. Beyond them, Corona sat at a table and pretended not to be waiting for me.

Richard pushed the buttons on the keypad to unlock the door.

I said, "Everything's going to be okay."

Reaching for the door handle, Richard replied, "Famous last words."

♦

Back in my room, Corona and I held hands and jumped

for joy.

She said, over and over, "I knew it!"

It was easy to say "I told you so" *after* you found out you were right. The truth was that you'd just been hoping really hard. Pandora opened a box and the last thing to emerge was hope, but a whole shit-ton of nastiness came out first. Despite my joy at learning that Colin was alive, I suspected that some of Pandora's fallout was waiting for me.

Simon said, "He's not out of the woods yet, my little chickadees."

We stopped jumping.

Corona stopped singing her *I Knew It* song and looked at me.

I smiled—big.

Corona grinned back at me.

"Now, I just have to find him," I said.

Simon warned, "You're going to have to play this carefully."

I knew he was right. Richard had no intention of showing me those photos. He knew it wasn't Colin in them, and yet, he'd said nothing to Detective Hayward. He wanted Colin to stay dead.

Maybe it *was* better if he were. Someone bad was looking for him. Nathan was looking for him, but I didn't know whose side he was on.

"I need to think," I said, shooing Corona, and presumably Simon, out the door.

◆◆◆

# CHAPTER 26

Late in the afternoon, there was always a lull in activity at the Center. Naps claimed some people. Oprah claimed the rest. I heard the siren call of Oprah's theme song, and I got up to shut my open door.

I needed time to figure things out, to think, but then I heard another sound, a ringing in my ears. It was quiet at first, and I stuck my finger in my ear and wiggled it around. The sound didn't go away. It got louder.

I put my head out the door and looked up the hallway. No one was there, so I headed toward the keening. The closer I got, the more obvious it was that the sound was coming from Corona's room.

I walked faster and then faster until I was running.

I skidded to a stop at Corona's door and looked inside.

The hag stood in a cloud that swirled at her feet. Her skin glistened with rainbows, like rotting meat, and was pulled taut to the bone. Seeing her, I was struck with the urge to vomit—the same urge you get when you find half a worm in your apple. It was the sick realization that your worst fear has already come true.

The hag had Corona by the throat and was lifting her off the ground.

Corona's legs and arms dangled. Her pajamas hung long and covered her hands and feet. A wet stain had spread between her legs, and urine dripped out of her pant-leg onto the floor.

The hag's sharp thumbnail cut into Corona's cheek, drawing blood.

Corona was a rag doll that had been dragged around one too many times. Her face was lifted toward the ceiling, mouth open, tongue sticking out. Her enormous eyes bulged.

If only I could have looked away, even blinked, then maybe when I looked back, it would've been gone.

But I couldn't.

The hag turned her head toward me.

I shouted, "No!" and rushed at the monster. I threw myself at her, clawing and hitting as hard as I could. "Let her go!"

I didn't stop until I heard my name.

Someone shouted, "Viviane!"

I was breathing hard.

The hag had released Corona. She crawled up the wall on all fours, until she reached the far corner of the ceiling, watching me with those terrible eyes.

Someone said, "Viviane! C'mon! Let's go!"

I dared a glance behind me.

It was Polly. "I've got her!" She had Corona around the waist.

Corona coughed and gagged. She had thrown up on herself.

I said, "Get out of here," and I locked eyes again with the hag. I backed toward the door.

The hag watched me, a predator gauging its prey, waiting for her chance.

"Go toward the rec room," I said. "That's where everyone is."

Corona and Polly moved out into the hallway.

I kept backing, slowly.

The hag edged forward. Her stringy muscles stretched and bunched with each inch she reclaimed.

I bumped into the doorframe and only broke eye-contact for a fraction of a second. That was all it took. The hag launched herself at me.

I screamed and turned to run. I grabbed the door as I went, pulling it shut behind me. Red-hot pain streaked down the back of my shoulder, and I stumbled.

Corona and Polly were ahead of me. They stopped to look back.

"Go!" I hung onto the door, and the hag's nails gouged the back of my hand. I screamed again and let go, but only for a moment. I took hold of the door handle and tugged on it as hard as I could.

The door slammed on the hag's arm.

It shrieked, and the arm withdrew inside.

The door shut completely.

I ran down the hall, cradling my bleeding, throbbing hand against my chest.

Corona and Polly hobbled along ahead of me as if in a three-legged race.

I heard a door open behind us.

The rec room was in sight. On the television, Oprah was talking about how important "right thought" was to living a healthy life.

I caught up with Polly and Corona. Corona could barely walk by herself. She was sobbing. Polly was almost carrying her.

I looked behind us—I couldn't help it—and saw the hag hulk out of Corona's room, in no hurry. She knew we had nowhere safe to go.

Just then, Nurse Bea emerged from one of the bedrooms, carrying sheets. She was a surreal vision, out of place, a ghost. She walked right by the hag without seeing it and headed toward us.

"What are you three doing? Oh dear Heaven, Corona! Are you ill?"

The hag followed her.

I cried, "Watch out!" but it was too late. Bea couldn't see the hag, but that didn't mean it couldn't hurt her.

The creature grabbed the nurse and slammed her face-first into the wall. The thud of skull hitting plaster and the crunch of breaking cartilage were the only sounds she made.

Nurse Bea went limp and fell to the floor, leaving a smear of blood where her face slid against the apple-blossom and peach wallpaper.

The hag looked at me with intent.

Corona and Polly loped toward the rec room. I backed that way more slowly, ready to stall it until the others got to safety.

The hag's gaze moved from me to them, and then she jumped past me. It happened so fast. She clung to the wall and crawled near the ceiling toward Corona and Polly.

I tried to warn them. I opened my mouth and cried, "Polly!"

Polly turned just as the hag got there.

The creature reached for Corona, but Polly put herself between them and shouted, "Keep away, you bitch!"

I ran and shouted, "Get away!" My whole body buzzed, my belly full of wasps. I stopped in place and pointed at the creature. "Go away!"

A shiver ran through the hag's body. She cringed and turned to look at me.

I met her eyes, and with clenched teeth, said, "Go away."

Her face reddened. Her neck muscles clenched, and for a second, I thought she would attack me instead, but she didn't. She raised her arms and spun in place, a single rotation.

Her claws cut across Polly's neck.

A spray of blood hit the wall.

And then, the hag was gone.

Polly folded to the floor.

Corona began to scream in great, gulping bursts.

I fell to my knees and crawled to Polly.

Her eyes were already vacant, her mouth open with surprise. I put my hand over the wound in her neck and felt the blood, hot and wet, pulse against it. The hag had sliced right through her burn scars.

Corona kept screaming. I looked over and saw the horrified expression on her face, the terror in her eyes. She had her hands to her mouth, balled into fists. She was seated on the floor, pushing herself backwards, away from Polly. Where she scooted, she left a streak through the blood spatter.

Polly's blood stopped pulsing and just flowed smooth, thick, and red. Dead Polly—willowy and limp—was the most awful thing I'd ever seen.

I tried to suck in breaths through my open mouth, but I couldn't get much air in. I panted with an irregular rhythm, unblinking, disbelieving.

A hoard of nurses surrounded me. They were a murder of albino crows, raucous and ravenous. I wasn't big enough nor strong enough to shoo them away. They tugged at me, pulled at my clothes, and carried me away. They scratched at the cuts on my back and hand. They stuck me with pins and needles.

♦♦♦

# CHAPTER 27

Awake, but not quite sure I was alive, I took inventory. I was in a bed. My head felt fuzzy. My mouth was dry. They had sedated me. I was nauseated, and I remembered.

*Polly.*

I got out of bed, unsteady on my feet. I hurt. There were bandages wrapped around my hand and more on my back. It hurt more when I touched them.

Everything moved in slow motion. I dragged myself to the door and pulled it open. The far end of the hall was cordoned off with screaming-yellow police tape, and they'd rolled in curtained screens to hide the stain where Polly had died.

My vision swam, and I leaned heavily against the wall.

"They moved her." Eun Hee said quietly from her own doorway. "Corona's in 210 now."

"Thanks."

Eun Hee added, "We're not allowed to leave our rooms. We have to go with a nurse, up the back stairs to the third floor, to use the toilet."

Dahlia's door cracked open and her nose peeked out. She stage-whispered, "What the fuck happened to you guys?"

"I smell blood," said Iraida, voice throaty, from her doorway.

"They're going to serve us breakfast in our rooms tomorrow," said Calla from behind her door. "It's grapefruit day."

Eun Hee said, "If you want to see Corona, go now before the guard gets back."

I hustled down to room 210.

Corona was in bed, unconscious. She was alive, but her neck was dark with bruises. She had dried drool on her chin and dried tears on her cheeks. She was wearing baby blue pajamas with pandas on them. They fit her body, but not her soul.

Crying, I curled against her and rested my head on her shoulder. I draped an arm over her.

She made a small noise and whispered, "Please don't leave me."

"I won't. I promise."

We slept—

—until something woke me. Someone pulled on me and moved my arm. I was afraid. I fought, and my elbow smashed into someone.

I heard, "Fuck! Viviane, calm down. You can't stay here."

And, "Give me the syringe."

A woman whispered, "Shhhh. It's okay. You're going to be fine."

"Take her back to her own room."

And I said, "No, please. I can't leave her. Don't make me leave her."

They carried me, and the world tilted sideways.

◆

"Viv."

"Viviane."

"Viviane Rose."

I fought my way back to consciousness and blinked my eyes open. The bed spun beneath me, and I hung onto the cold, metal headboard.

"Viviane, wake up." It was Simon.

"Where's Corona?" I asked.

"She's safe. She woke up a couple hours ago. I guess they didn't use as much sedative on her. She and I had a long talk. She's going to be okay, but she's shifting from freaked out to pissed off pretty quickly. I need you to wake up before she does something stupid."

"Can she come in here?"

"They've shut everyone in their rooms and posted a nurse in the hallway," said Simon, "but I can be her look-out. We just have to wait until the monitor goes to the toilet. The police aren't back yet, but they will be. You're both lucky you aren't in straight jackets. Fortunately, that nurse vouched for you. Said someone came up behind her."

"Go get Corona," I said.

The room went quiet, and I drifted back to sleep. The next thing I knew, Corona snuck in and said, "We've got to kill it. Now." Her voice had a scratchy quality, as if she'd been screaming for hours or smoking for decades. "I'll go after it myself. I'll get a chainsaw and chop it up. I'll pour acid on it. I'll—"

"—call it bad names until it cries?" Simon interrupted. "Or strangles you again?"

"Shut up, shut up, shut up!" Corona shouted. "Asshole. You didn't see what it did to Polly."

I sat up and opened my eyes as wide as they would go. "Shhh… What time is it?"

"A little after six in the morning," Simon replied, voice quiet.

Corona paced at the end of the bed, gesturing on each beat. "I know two things that will probably hurt it pretty bad. Silver and salt."

Simon added, "Two of the most magickal substances on Earth."

"What about Nurse Bea?" I asked. "Is she okay?"

"They took her to the hospital," Corona replied.

"But, she's alive, right?" I remembered the sight of Bea's face hitting the wall.

"Yeah," answered Corona. "She's alive."

"This is crazy." I rubbed my hands over my face.

"No," said Corona with the intensity of a doomsayer. "This is as sane as it gets."

"Okay," I said. "So, we're going after it?"

Simon said, "In order to kill a hag, you have to be a stronger predator than it is. You become the aggressor. The hunted hunting the hunter. It's the only way."

I didn't appreciate the sound of that. *"You* can kill it, right?"

Simon huffed a small sigh. "Best I can do is make it back off temporarily. I can't actually hurt it."

"Can *I* kill it?" I asked.

"Probably. With the right weapon."

I nodded. "In for a penny, in for a pound."

"A pound of flesh, I'd say," said Simon, sounding irritated.

We shared a few minutes of congenial silence, each in our own thoughts, until Corona said, "That police detective asked me if you attacked me."

"What did you tell him?"

"I told him the truth—that you saved me."

◆

Richard came by my room just before lunch to check on me. He said he was keeping Detective Hayward on a short leash, but Richard's own questions were just as invasive. *What happened? Who did it? Was the attacker male or female? Did I remember anything at all about the attacker? Where had everybody else been at the time of the attack? Why hadn't anyone seen who did it? Had the attacker said anything?*

I did not follow Corona's lead. I lied through my teeth and said I didn't see the attacker. Richard, of course, was fascinated. He leaned toward me with a hungry expression on his face.

"Let's go to my office, and I'll regress you back to yesterday afternoon," he said. "Maybe we can pull details out that you've consciously forgotten."

"No. I'm not going to relive that."

"Don't you want to catch Polly's killer?"

"Of course, but not like that."

"Okay. Maybe tomorrow."

Not tomorrow, not ever.

# CHAPTER 28

By dinner time, we were freed from the lockdown. The police had gathered all their evidence, and the cleaning crew had tackled the hallway and removed the sheeting. The smell of bleach remained, but the blood was gone.

*Today we're pain.*

I stayed in my room, not wanting to be bombarded with questions.

At three a.m., on the nose, Corona came into my room. "Viviane, wake up. It's time." She tugged on me. "We have to go."

Simon was waiting for us in Corona's new room. The bed held an array of devices: pieces of tarnished silverware (forks and butter knives), syringes, squirt bottles used by the janitors, a carton of table salt, a handful of silver necklaces, and a silver vase of the tall and narrow variety meant for a single rose.

I stared in wonder. "Wow."

"If we ever have an apocalypse," Corona said, "I'm your girl."

"Where'd you get it all?"

Simon said. "Corona's been busy while you were sleeping."

"I borrowed it from all over," Corona explained. "I stole the silverware from that display cabinet outside the staff lounge. I think it belonged to the Malums. They probably won't even notice until the cleaners go to dust it. And I got squirt bottles from the janitor's closet, salt from the pantry, necklaces came from Dahlia, and the vase is Calla's."

"Where'd you get syringes?"

"That was the hardest. I had to knock over Nurse Medhead's cart. She was pissed 'cause then she had to go refill the med cups from scratch, but I snuck a few syringes into my pockets. I'm hoping she's so pissed she won't notice they're missing."

Simon said, "She didn't notice. She'd have been in here by now."

"It helped that Simon was my look-out and that two of the day nurses didn't show up for work this morning. I doubt we'll ever see them again."

"Nice job," I said.

Corona came over to stand close beside me. She held my hand. "Simon and I have been talking about our plan. Want to hear it?"

"Sure."

"We figure we'll need to bring the hag to us." She

looked up at me with her eyes wide and excited. "Then, when it comes, we'll jump it and kill it. It won't be expecting an ambush."

"That's a pretty simple plan."

Corona nodded. "Elegant."

"The back stairwell," Simon said, "will be our best chance. It's been spotted in there before. Besides, no one ever goes down that way, so we won't have innocent bystanders."

"Or witnesses," added Corona.

"So," I said as if it were a foregone conclusion, "I'll go in first, and when the hag comes after me, you guys help me kill it."

Simon objected. "What? I don't think so. I'll be the bait."

"That's dumb," Corona argued. "It's not after you. It can't even see you. *I'll* go in first."

I raised both hands. "No way."

"It's after me." Corona locked her hands firmly on her hips.

I shook my head. "It's after me, too. I'll be the bait. No arguing."

Simon said, "Right-o." He insisted we each put silver necklaces around our necks and on our wrists to keep the monster from touching us there. Feeling ridiculous, I took my share of syringes primed with salty water, and stuck a fork and butter knife into my pocket. I knew nothing about magickal beings and their vulnerabilities, but I trusted Simon and Corona.

He said, "Just get the salt water on her however you can."

I said, "I'm Harry going after Voldemort."

Corona replied, "More like Harry going after Bellatrix Lestrange. This hag is just a nasty servant to your nemesis."

"I have a nemesis?"

"Don't all heroes?"

"I'm no hero."

"Sure you are. You saved my life." Corona said it as if it were a cosmic truth.

We eased out into the hallway, trying not to clink or clank, and crept along.

The other patients were all asleep at that hour, and the only staff on duty were the security guards monitoring the camera feeds, the night nurse, and an orderly named Marsha. Usually, Marsha watched TV all night in the rec room, and Nurse Andrea read a book or surfed the web in the office. That was, at least, what we had been expecting.

As we advanced down the hall, however, we heard voices ahead, coming from one of the rooms. It was Dahlia's room. She and Marsha were arguing about her getting back into bed.

Corona and I froze in place.

"Let me look," whispered Simon.

I crept forward in his wake. Dahlia's door was mostly

closed, but through the crack, I saw a sliver of her space. She passed across it, then Marsha did the same.

"I'm an adult," said Dahlia.

"Just shut the fuck up and get into bed, Dahlia. I'm missing my show."

"You think I fucking care about that?" Dahlia crawled across her bed, fleeing from Marsha.

"This is not the time to be wandering around. Remember what happened to Polly."

"Like you care."

"You know the rules."

"I know you can shove the rules up your ass, bitch." Dahlia crouched on all fours in the middle of her bed.

"Don't call me that."

"Bitch." Dahlia spat the word, her New Jersey accent adding venom to it.

Marsha back-handed Dahlia.

The blow knocked Dahlia to one side. She lay there on the bed, holding her jaw and staring at Marsha with accusatory hatred.

"Sorry," said Marsha, her voice smug. "I didn't see you there."

I was going in, all guns firing—and would have, if Corona hadn't stopped me with a quiet, "We can't. We have a more important mission."

"Stay there, Dahlia," Marsha commanded. "Don't make me come back in here."

When I peered in at Dahlia, she was looking right back at me.

I put my finger to my lips.

Marsha was coming.

Corona and I looked around desperately for a place to hide. We were doomed little mice, trapped in the path of the lean, mean cat.

Panic rippled up my spine, and I nearly ran back up the hall.

Then Dahlia said it again. "Bitch."

Marsha made an about-face and stormed across the room to grab Dahlia by the hair. She growled when she said, "Get under the fucking covers."

"C'mon," said Simon. "This is our chance."

I caught Dahlia's eye as Marsha wrenched her onto her back. I mouthed, "Thank you."

Dahlia smiled. She actually smiled, then said, "Okay, okay. Knock it off. I'll behave."

We hurried to the exit, and I input the code to let us out of the Women's Wing. The rest of the halls were deserted at that hour.

"I can't believe that," I said.

Corona said, "The vampires come out at night."

"Marsha's always that way," said Simon. "Especially with Dahlia. Dahlia isn't so good at following orders."

"Still, she can't get away with that. I have to tell somebody."

"You can't," said Simon and Corona simultaneously. Simon continued, "How are you going to explain why you weren't snug in your bed?"

He had a point.

We kept to the walls and shadows until we reached the door to the back stairs.

Simon said, "Okay, we'll wait here. Hang onto the vase. If the hag silences you, just drop it. We'll hear it and come running. If you can, lead the hag here, and we'll cut off its exit."

Corona used the belt from her robe to tie one of the squirt bottles around my waist. It hung down on my hip, a gunslinger's Colt.

Before I could change my mind, I entered the stairwell. I descended halfway down to the landing between the second and first floors. Nothing happened. I scanned the walls for moving shadows and listened so hard I could hear my own blood.

Nothing.

I waited and waited. *Tick tock.* Time passed without incident. I imagined I was sending my signature out in waves, but I had no idea what I was doing.

Simon called out from above, "Viviane?"

"Still nothing." I was wondering if we were wasting our time, and then I remembered something Colin had said to me. "She nests on the roof."

I reversed my steps and climbed. I passed Corona peering at me through the crack in the door, gave her a nod, then continued upward, pausing to listen between each step. One hand clutched a butter knife and the other trailed along the handrail. I climbed back to the second floor, and nothing happened. I got to the third floor. *Nada.*

The building had four stories. I looked up to where the ceiling capped the stairwell. I couldn't see the door leading to the roof, but I could hear the wind beyond it, howling and beating against the door.

I went up one more flight to the fourth floor, and I waited.

Nothing.

One more set of steps to the roof door, where I entered the security code and pushed it open. As soon as the latch released, the wind caught the door and jerked it from my grasp.

It slammed against the wall with a loud crash.

"Viv?" Simon called, his voice echoing and distant.

"I'm okay! Stay there!"

Out on the roof, the wind whipped around me, lifting my hair and flapping my pants legs. The roof was a grim platform. Beyond it was a sea of moving trees lit at their edges by the glow of dawn's burgeoning light.

I shouted, "Are you here?"

The door slammed shut behind me, and there she was, a tornado of mist and hair, directly in front of me, baring her teeth at me, death in her eyes. Those eyes were too round. A slimy film swam across them whenever she blinked, and her irises were faded and hard, white, dead eyes that rejected all light. Despite my fear, or perhaps because of it, I was ready when she leapt. I swung the vase and hit her on the side of the head.

Her claws raked my arm, but she fell to one side.

I cradled my arm against my body, turned, and ran to the door. It wasn't locked from this side, and I grabbed the handle, smearing it with blood.

Gravel crunched right behind me.

I turned to face her, and she was on me. Her hands closed around my throat.

I swung the vase at her head, but her arm was in the way. She pinned me back against the door. The vase fell from my hand.

The keening had begun in my head, the sound that always accompanied the hag's attacks.

Desperate, I fumbled for the squirt bottle and wrapped my fingers around the trigger. I got it turned to point toward her and squeezed. Water exploded between us and dampened my clothes. I squeezed again. Water ran down the front of my leg.

She howled and cringed away from me. I pulled the bottle free and held it out like a gun. I squirted her again, forcing her back.

She glared furiously at me.

I fumbled for the doorknob, turned it, and pulled the

door open. I hurried through and turned to pull the door shut behind me. I got one last glimpse of her.

She was staring at me, lips black and angry, pulled back. Red welts had formed where the salt water had touched her belly, and her eyes had gone from dead white to blood red. I had pissed her off.

I fled inside and was halfway down the first set of stairs when the roof door opened and then closed again. She was inside.

"Simon!" I shouted. I tore down the stairs and made it to the third floor before she caught me.

She grabbed a handful of my hair and yanked me back. My scalp was on fire.

I shrieked in pain and latched onto the handrail to keep from falling. At the last moment, I swung around and aimed the spray bottle. I squirted, but she had learned.

She released me and dodged aside, avoiding most of the water. She had some of my hair between her fingers.

I shouted, "Fuck!" and sprayed at her again.

She dodged, leapt past me, and dropped low to the stairs below, cutting off my descent. She slashed at my legs.

I jumped back, half-stumbling up a step. I wasn't fast enough.

Her claws cut across my shin, tearing my pants and lacerating me. I screamed and fumbled, landing on my ass on the stairs. I kept squirting at her, but the bottle was running out of water.

The hag launched herself at me and knocked the bottle to one side. It went flying, bounced off the wall, and fell down the stairs with a dull clatter.

She grabbed me by the shoulders.

I crab-crawled backwards, trying to get away from her, but she pushed me down, hard, onto my back, on the stairs, and I hit my head against the edge of a step.

She knelt on top of me, her knees in my gut, clawed hands pinning my shoulders.

*This is it,* I thought. *This is how I die. I don't want to die.* Tears blurred my vision.

The monster reared back, clawed hand raised high and tense.

I cringed and squeezed my eyes shut, focusing on pulling out the syringes in my pockets. One in each hand, I stuck the syringes between the hag's ribs, and I pushed in the plungers.

I opened my eyes. "Die!" I said, watching surprise spread across the hag's face. "Just die!"

The monster's mouth and eyes opened wide. She leapt away from me. She dug at her sides, at the syringes still hanging there, at the pain.

I ran past her, stumbling down the stairs in a panic. I felt her latch onto the back of my shirt, pulling me back just when I'd stepped off the next stair. Off-balance, I fell back toward her and banged my elbow hard on the railing.

I twisted free, flailed and rolled, managed to get up onto one knee, facing her. I slid the silver butter knife out of my pocket. My mouth was dead dry. My nose was running.

The hag and I were eye to eye.

She tensed a clawed hand, ready to strike, and I reacted. I raised the butter knife up next to my ear.

The hag saw it coming.

I shoved the knife into her eye, then hit it with the palm of my other hand, driving it even deeper. I hit the hilt again and again, each time sending it further in.

Simon said, "Viviane, you can stop now."

The hag's movements had stopped. She was dead. I'd killed her.

I turned toward the sound of Simon's voice and shouted, "Where the fuck were you?"

"I got here as soon as I could. You didn't tell me you were heading upstairs. I thought you were still down below."

Corona came running up the stairs, panting.

I leaned heavily against the wall and descended a couple stairs. My legs were shaking. My hands too. I sat down, bottom-heavy.

A hiss sounded from the hag's body, startling me. I tensed, ready to move, but there was no need. The body was melting into mist, slowly at first, then more rapidly. She became a fog that rose upward, broke apart, and drifted into nothingness.

Corona said, "I knew you'd do it." She sat down beside me, wrapped her hands around my good arm, and bounced up and down.

"Keep that up," I told her, "and I'll puke on you." It wasn't an idle threat.

◆◆◆

# CHAPTER 29

After the fight, Corona and I cleaned my blood out of the stairwell and off the roof, then the three of us snuck back to the Women's Wing. No one noticed us. After gathering my pajamas, a robe, and my basket of soaps, I showered, the water stinging my wounds. Corona helped me cover the deepest one with a washcloth and affixed it to me with scotch tape. She retrieved my pajamas and a robe, then we returned to my room.

We ate cookies in honor of Mrs. Dufour and dedicated the hag's death to Polly. We were giddy with triumph.

◆

The next morning, awareness came gently. My mind led the way toward getting up, exploring memories of the night before. It seemed surreal in retrospect.

Monsters. Magick. Salt and silver.

I hadn't done anything right during the car accident. I hadn't saved myself, and I hadn't saved Colin. This was different. I felt powerful.

I sat up on the edge of the bed with the growing belief that my work wasn't done. I had momentum, and I had to follow through. The hag was gone, but there were so many other things wrong with my world, the most important of which was that Colin was out there somewhere, possibly being held against his will.

I had to do something.

My wounds hadn't been as bad as they'd felt. I looked them over more closely. I had scratches on my shin and puncture wounds in my shoulder where five clawed fingers had held me down, but the worst were the three parallel cuts on my upper arm. I'd be wearing long sleeves for awhile until they healed. I probably could have used a couple stitches, but I didn't need anyone finding out there'd been another attack. Scotch tape would have to do.

I dressed in jeans and an evergreen Henley t-shirt. It was a turning point. I wasn't the same woman I'd been twenty-four hours earlier, though I wasn't sure what I'd become.

Simon had said I was a warrior. All I knew was that I wanted to be ready to defend myself, if necessary. I still didn't feel safe.

I laid out the papers I'd stolen from Richard and picked up the photo of Jaxon's body. I looked at it more closely. Jaxon had been such a large and strong man, but in death, he seemed smaller.

He could've been one who'd saved me from the lake. I

remembered the hands on my body, turning me, swimming me up to the surface, the legs kicking hard at the back of my knees, the chest pressed to my shoulder. I remembered my savior's strength. *Had it been him?*

On the morgue slab, he was anything but heroic. Had he gone back after Colin? Had he swum him to shore too? Did he have a moment of pride that he'd saved two lives, then a moment of horror when he realized they were going to kill him?

"Here he comes," I'd heard the woman say. "Do it."

Doc Bella. She'd given the order to kill Jaxon. The photocopied I.D. told me she'd known she was going to do it—premeditated murder. She needed a body for the police to find. Doc Bella had then misidentified the body.

A quiet knock preceded Corona. She slid into the room and shuffled over to me, vibrating with barely contained excitement. "We did it, right? I didn't dream it?"

"No, you didn't dream it. I've got the wounds to prove it."

Her expression changed briefly to worry, then back to pleasure. "You're a hero."

"I got lucky."

The sound of patients moving around crescendoed. The breakfast hour was in full swing.

I put my hands on top of my head and took a deep breath. "I need a plan. I have to do something. I have to get out of the Center and find Colin."

"Yeah!" answered Corona. "But the way I see it, you've got one major bandwidth blocker in Dr. Reuter. You know he's writing a book about you, right?"

"What?"

"I heard him talking to one of the other doctors."

"Why would he write a book about me?"

"Because you're a faux schizo, and that makes you special. He doesn't understand what it means, but he recognizes that there's something different about you. He thinks he's discovered a new type of schizophrenia—our type."

"He never mentioned that to me."

"Your mom's in the book too. He's calling it 'The Rose Legacy.'"

I stared at her with my mouth hanging open. "I can't believe he'd do that!"

"Believe it. The good Dr. Reuter isn't nearly as good as he pretends. He's been writing articles about you since forever."

"Why didn't you tell me this before?"

Corona shrugged. "It never seemed important, besides I figured you knew. That was before you found out he was forging signatures."

A book. I remembered signing release forms back when Richard was still in grad school. He'd said he needed them for his dissertation and academic publications. Richard had my life—my entire being—recorded on tapes in his office. I suddenly wondered how much he'd been sharing.

Corona said, "He's afraid his entire career will be ruined if it turns out you're not as delusional as he's claimed."

"Oh my god."

Corona suggested, "You could take everything you know to the police. The cops will be pissed that Dr. Reuter didn't say anything." Corona bounced happily on the bed where she was seated. "Maybe they'll even start suspecting him."

"I need to think about it. Richard can be cunning. If I'm not careful, he'll convince everyone I'm a lost cause. I need to get out of here."

"We've got this!" cried Corona, raising her arms overhead. "Tell me how I can help."

"All right. We need to gather the troops. I'll call Lettie. Simon, are you here?"

"I'm here."

I shook my head. "Eavesdropping bastard."

"Hey," said Simon. "It's my job."

◆

Once Lettie, Corona, Simon, and I were in the same room, we came up with a plan. I'd already figured out most of it, and they helped me see and fix the weak spots. I spent the rest of the morning prepping, checking off each item on my To-Do list as I completed it. The first was "Send evidence to Hayward." I captured pictures on my phone of the Jaxon morgue photo and another of Colin and me standing in front of the Center's Christmas tree. I wrote a text message that said: "Man in picture with me is Colin. Get 2nd opinion on identity of dead man. Pls trust me."

I wished I could have been there to see the look on Detective Hayward's face when he realized the truth.

The second item on the list was: "Write Mom's lawyers." I took my time, rewriting an email several times—with much advice from Lettie, Corona, and Simon—so that I clearly expressed my wishes and the seriousness of the situation. Mom had hired the law firm of Bagley, Smart, and Cobb to handle her affairs just before she was committed to the Center. They were the ones who'd informed me she was still alive. I didn't know if they still considered her a client or not, but I was hoping they would look in on her and care for her if it turned out that I couldn't.

I asked them to look into my involuntary commitment, and for good measure, I enclosed a picture of the form with Abram's forged signature.

I hit "Send" on both.

Next, I packed a gym bag with things I'd need if I ran away. I took it with me when I went to the rec room to meet Richard for my afternoon session. I was there, bag in tow, when he came looking for me.

He walked through shadow, light, and shadow again on the checkerboard of dim sunshine coming through the windows, and he was a stranger to me. The man I had trusted for twenty years had been using me. How many journal articles had he written about me?

"Hey," I said. "I'm ready when you are."

He glanced at the gym bag as he led me toward his office. "How are you feeling?" I smelled his cologne, a spicy blend that reminded me of fireplaces and snow.

"Better," I replied. "Clearer than I've been in a long time."

He shot me a sideways glance. "Good. I'm glad to hear that." He didn't sound glad. He sounded thoughtful. Along the way, he made a point of saying hello to several people we passed to avoid talking to me, and eventually, we arrived at his office.

I had no idea how the confrontation would go down, and I didn't know whether he had discovered the missing papers and photos or not.

"I plan to do an extended regression today," Richard said, "since you're feeling better."

I scanned the room as I sat down on the couch, setting the bag beside me, and I found what I was looking for—the urn of ashes. The box containing it stood on a bureau of drawers near the door.

Richard went to his chair.

"Actually," I replied, "I wanted to talk to you about something."

Richard considered me for a moment, then sat back

into shadow, letting it shield his dark eyes from me. He wove his fingers together, elbows on the arms of the chair.

"Okay. What?"

Phase Two of The Plan had three parts. In the first, I tried giving Richard a chance to do the right thing for the right reasons.

"Richard, you and I have known each other a long time. You know me better than anyone. We've had a lot of history flow under our bridge."

He tipped his head. "That's true. And I care about you."

"I know how hard you've worked to keep me sane. I want to thank you for that. But—"

"But?"

"But I need you to release me from the Center. I want to go home. It's time. I've been here long enough, and instead of making me better, this place is dragging me down. I'm not exaggerating. Please. Release me today."

Richard inhaled deeply. "I'm working on it. There are protocols and so much red tape it would make you cry. I can't just decide overnight that you're well enough to return home. My professional reputation is on the line. I have to follow procedure. I'd be remiss in my duties if I didn't. I took an oath."

I was disappointed, but only because the conversation was going exactly as I'd expected it would. I leaned forward, resting my elbows on my knees.

"You said I wasn't a prisoner, and I'm calling you on

that. I want out of here, today. Now. I want you to sign the release papers. Please."

Richard sat forward too, pleading with his hands and eyes. "I can't. You're ill. You need help, and this is the best place for you to get it. I'm the best person to give it to you. You can't see how all this trauma has affected you. You think you feel clear right now, but you're still in shock over Polly. Your blue sky is an illusion. You're seeing it through the window of your illness. Before you know it, the storm clouds will close in again."

I shook my head. In the second part of Phase Two, I tried to corner him.

"Can I see the pictures of Colin's body?"

Richard couldn't have been more shocked. He blinked wide, then turned away from me to hide his surprise. He must not have noticed that I'd taken one of them.

He stood and went toward his desk. "I told you I'd think about it," he said. "I haven't made my decision yet."

"Detective Hayward told me he sent them to you. I demand to see them. It's my right."

"Perhaps it is. But I have a responsibility, and I think the photos will upset you too much. They're…gruesome." He didn't look at me.

"Is it really Colin? In the photos?"

To his credit, Richard didn't answer immediately. After a moment, he crossed to sit beside me on the couch. "Colin is gone, Vivi, and he's not coming back." He tried to take my hand, but I pulled away.

I repeated, "Was it Colin's body in the pictures?"

"Oh, for crying out loud," Richard exclaimed. "Listen to yourself. You're obsessed. If this doesn't prove to you that you're not ready to leave the Center, then I don't know what else I can say. I'll simply have to take matters into my own hands. I'm sorry, Viviane, but you can't be trusted to make decisions for yourself."

He stood, straightened his tie, and returned to his chair across from me.

I said again, my voice steady and clear, "Was it Colin in the pictures?"

Angry, he glared at me. He resembled a wild panther, cornered, and ready to strike. "Yes," he said. "Is that what you want me to say? Yes, it was Colin. Beyond a doubt. He's gone, and it's time for you to get on with your life."

That sealed it. That was what I needed to move on to Phase Three. Richard had gone too far. That morning, when I'd shown the photo I stole to Lettie and Corona, they'd reacted just as I'd expected. Lettie had confirmed that it was Jaxon in the photo.

I wondered how many other things Richard had lied about over the years to keep me near him, how many other manipulations he'd performed on my mind to keep me under his control. A volatile mix of sadness and anger at his undeniable betrayal festered. Later, I'd examine it more closely, but at that moment, I didn't have time.

I stood. "You're right. It's time for me to get on with my life." I slung my bag over my shoulder and headed for the door. The bag was part of my plan to get Richard off my back.

With three strides, he was beside me, one hand on the bag, one on my arm.

"Where are you going?" he demanded.

"Away from here," I told him, matter-of-factly, "to get on with my life."

"What's in the bag?" He started trying to pry it from my shoulder.

I fought to hold onto it, but not too hard. Just enough so it seemed convincing.

He took it away from me and carried it to his desk.

I protested, as he'd expect me to do. "That's my stuff. You have no right."

"I have every right," he said. "I'm your doctor. I can look into any nook or cranny I want, if I feel it serves your health." He opened the bag and began to pull things from it—clothes, toiletries, food bars, a twenty-dollar bill, and a photo of Colin—things I'd need to run away.

I watched him empty the contents onto his desk.

He picked up the money and waved it at me. "How far do you think you'd get with twenty dollars? Have you lost your mind?"

Richard didn't see the irony in his question, though I did.

I replied, "Apparently so." I waited a beat, then commanded, "Give me back my stuff."

He put the clothes, toiletries, and food bars back in the bag. The money and photo of Colin, he left on his desk.

"If I can't trust you, then I'm going to have to keep these things. It's for your own good." Richard offered me the bag. At that moment, I knew I'd won. He thought he was still in charge.

I ignored the bag and made a grab for the items on the desktop.

Richard put his body between me and them. "No. You can't have them." He shoved the bag at my chest so that I had to take it. "I won't let you run away from me, Viviane."

I glared. "I hate you." That, I meant.

He flinched, and for a moment, I thought I saw a shimmer of remorse in his eyes. He turned his back to me. "No, you don't. You're just angry."

I backed toward the door. "I want my stuff," I insisted.

"We can talk about it later," Richard said. "Once we've both calmed down." He opened a cabinet on the back wall and began putting my things in it.

By then, I'd reached the bureau by the door, and with one eye on him, I snatched the box holding Jaxon Bellonescu's urn and quickly slipped it into my bag.

Richard closed the cabinet, locked it, removed the key, and turned toward me. "I'll give your things back as soon as you've proven you can be trusted."

I held the gym bag with both hands behind my back.

Richard came toward me and entered my personal space. He backed me against the door, took my chin in his hand, and looked me right in the eyes.

"I want you to remember one thing, Vivi." His voice was deadly serious. "If you try to run away, I'll find you, but you'll have damaged my trust permanently. I don't see how, after that, I could allow you to see your mother. You'd be too much of a risk. I have to protect her."

I shoved aside the acidic response I wanted to give him, and instead said, "No, don't do that. Please. I'll be good."

"I know you will. You're a good girl." He reached behind me, and for a moment, I was afraid he was going for the bag, but he just grabbed the doorknob and turned it. "I'm *trusting* you to get back to the Women's Wing on your own," he said. "We'll talk at your next session."

"I'll go straight back," I promised.

"Good," he said.

As I walked away, I held the bag to my belly, but I didn't hear the door shut, and before long, Richard called after me.

"Oh, and Viviane," he said. "Detective Hayward is coming with a warrant tomorrow. He's going to ask you some questions."

I didn't look back, and when I reached the top of the stairs, his door closed with a firm click.

◆◆◆

# CHAPTER 30

I spent the rest of the day behaving normally. It was a good call. Richard came by several times to check on me, whenever he dropped into the Women's Wing to pick up one of his patients. He ghosted around my room, looking at things, as if searching for something.

He found nothing incriminating. I'd hidden my purse in Mom's room and the urn box in Corona's.

Around five p.m., I started watching out my mom's window for Richard to leave the building. I saw him go and hid behind the curtain. He drove from the lot as usual.

After that, it was Nurse Linda on Viviane Watch. She seemed unusually concerned with my mood, and I suspected that Richard had told her I was feeling suicidal.

We had dinner in the dining room. Women from the other two floors were there as well, creating a chaotic clatter. The usual group sat together at the same long table.

Polly and Mrs. Dufour were conspicuously missing. Their absence broke the rhythm. The friendly banter was gone. Any attempts to resurrect it ended with a gap that couldn't be breached, a spot where either Polly or Mrs.

Dufour would have chimed in to keep the conversation going.

It didn't matter. That night, I had a particular topic I wanted to broach. Once we had all been served, and the staff had moved away to a safe distance, I announced, "I'm going to break out of here."

Five pairs of eyes turned to me. Only Una and my mom kept their gazes elsewhere, though I knew Una was listening. She had stopped chasing her food with her spoon.

"Why?" asked Eun Hee. "In here, you can roll around in the lusty, luscious joy of insanity. Out there, it's dark and dreary, and they punish you for being different."

"I have things I need to do," I said. "I have to find my fiancé."

Dahlia said, "Yeah, I give you a week, assuming you can even get out. You'll be back."

"How are you going to do it?" Calla asked.

"I've got a plan. I'm leaving tonight, but I need your help."

Calla's eyes got big. *"My* help?"

I nodded. "Everyone's. I need help from all of you." I laid out my plan for them and explained their roles. They all agreed. Even big Una, who spent her days standing in corners mumbling to herself, gave me a nod of acknowledgement. It was the first time I'd ever seen her directly communicate with anyone.

◆

I spent the rest of the evening with my mom. While she worked on her journal, I went over my plan again and again, looking for holes in it.

It was always so peaceful around Mom. Unless she was reading to me, she rarely spoke. In the early days, I had done everything I could to engage her in conversation or even just to get her to respond. I failed miserably, month after month, year after year. In the end, I gave that up. I eventually learned to abide in the silence, and I found it healing. It comforted me to be in her presence, as a child should be comforted by the sight and smells of their mother. If she had taught me anything over the years, it was that you didn't need to talk all the time.

I sat in front of the mirrored dresser, and she brushed my hair. I had changed since coming to the Center. My face had sunken in on itself, cheeks and eyes shadowed. My hair had grown. It hung a couple inches past my shoulders, thickening and straightening the longer it got.

I teetered at the edge of a precipice. My life, up to that point, had been so predictable. Jake Lamb was right. I'd been tethered to the Center long before I'd moved in, and I hadn't experienced much outside that orbit.

I had resigned myself to a future that involved caring for my mom to the end and marrying a man I'd met on the Center's lawn. I hadn't dared dream any bigger for myself or for them.

More recently, however, I'd begun to dream. Although my escape plan wasn't going exactly as I'd hoped, it wasn't failing either. So many things could have gone wrong. I could've ended up incarcerated at the Center for the rest of my life—or worse, Richard could've followed through on his threat, and I might never have seen my mom again. That was a possibility I couldn't ignore.

How could I have known that the stakes would get so high? And I had no idea how it would all turn out. What mattered was that I had to try. If I hadn't, then I'd have been living in as dark a catatonic state as Mom was.

I'd have been lying if I'd said I wasn't terrified and excited in equal measure.

◆

My hair shone after an hour of brushing, its golden highlights emerging and making it almost pretty in the light from the lamp.

Mom was the first to move away. She put the hairbrush down and returned to her seat at the desk, where she picked up her journal and thumbed through it.

I took a magazine to the couch. I didn't intend to read, but I felt it would look better if Nurse Linda poked her head in again.

Not five minutes had passed before my mom started

reading aloud. "Kypris could feel the life growing inside her."

I set aside the magazine and stretched out. I hadn't heard this before—it was new, maybe even something she'd written that day.

She read:

*Chance had disappeared as abruptly as he had arrived, never to be seen by Kypris again. In his wake, he left uncertainty and a child. When Kypris told her mother about her lover, it took no time to figure out the child's fate. Kypris's mother, Moira, knew of the Gehenna realm. She knew more about it than Kypris did, and she knew that if the lord of Gehenna ever discovered there was a child born half of darkness and half of light, he would take it away to where Kypris wouldn't be allowed to follow.*

*All the better to hide, Moira became Mirabella, and Kypris took the name Gisèle. Secrets piled upon secrets, cloaking the family from view, until one day, the child made its will known. It was ready to come into the world.*

*The baby was born in Mirabella's sanctuary, upon silk sheets, with pixies in attendance. The child cried her first cry to a wave of applause from tiny fairy hands.*

*Those were the best days. Gisèle had given*

*birth to a daughter and watched with eager eyes as the baby awoke to wonder. She named her child Viviane, invoking life itself to protect and guide her, to give her the strength she would need to change the world.*

*But they couldn't stay there forever. Word came that the evil queen of Gehenna was looking for the child. She could track Mirabella and would do so.*

*Mirabella and Gisèle had sobbed together that night, for they knew many years would pass before they saw each other again. The pixies sang lullabies and braided their hair, but it could not ease their pain. The next morning, Gisèle packed up the baby and went to live with her father.*

*The evil queen would never find Abraham Rose. Abraham had already been hidden for a quarter century. Such was the power of the magick that cocooned him, and so long as Gisèle and Viviane were under his care, the queen could not find them either.*

*For seven years, seven months, and seven days, the Rose women lived under Abraham's roof, and Gisèle watched her daughter grow. They talked for hours and made up stories that they then acted out, stories about kittens, fairies, and flying horses—stories about trolls, demons, and the bones of little children, stories about a prince who rode a giant turtle and kept cupcakes in his pockets, just in case, and stories about an evil queen and the princess who had to stay hidden from her—forever.*

*Then, one day, the evil queen's scouts came calling. Gisèle had let her guard down. She had allowed herself to believe that enough time had passed, but she had forgotten that time did not soften evil.*

*When the scouts caught her scent, Gisèle did the only thing she could do. She left her daughter with Abraham and led the dogs away. They followed her trail, baying their hunger, and when they caught up with her, they cornered her in the darkest of woods. There, they kept her prisoner until the queen's son could tumble her off the edge of the world and force her into Gehenna.*

*The raven man made one mistake, however. He did not see that Gisèle had anchored herself. She kept one foot on the floor, one hand on the wall, one thought ever touching the ones she loved, and thus, her soul was divided.*

*Stretched thin across the barrier, she could shift between realms, though at great cost to herself. The evil queen imprisoned her, but like Rapunzel, Gisèle had a link with the outside. The tether grew from her heart, not from her head. Hers was the love she had for Viviane. It alone, kept her from being lost, completely, forever.*

I didn't dare make a noise or movement, for fear of startling Mom into stopping. I wanted her to keep going, to tell me more, so much more.

When it became obvious that Mom was finished reading, I got up off the couch and crossed to sit at her feet. She'd retreated back into herself.

The journal lay open on the desk. I re-read the words but understood them no better. Eventually, I rested my arms and head upon Mom's knees. I lifted one of her hands and placed it on the back of my neck. It lay there, still, cool, and heavy.

I must have fallen asleep, because I awoke to a quiet voice. It was my mom. She whispered, "Viviane. Viviane, wake up, sweetheart. Wake up."

I blinked my eyes open and wondered if I were dreaming.

She said, her voice so quiet that I almost couldn't hear it, "Wake up. I have to talk to you." Her fingers wove into my hair.

I was awake in an instant, wide awake. "Mom?"

She smiled. "I'm sorry about Polly."

I envisioned the whippoorwill girl who would never grow up. "Me too."

Mom tilted her head to one side, expression soft and loving. She touched her fingertips to my cheek. "There's so much I wish I could tell you and so little time. One day, you and I will have all the time in the world."

"That would be nice." My heart hammered. I'd never seen her so lucid.

She nodded in agreement. "But not tonight. There are gears in motion that you know nothing about, age-old debts and grudges that I've tried to keep you safe from."

"What are you talking about?"

"Shhh," she whispered. "I don't have time to explain. You have to trust me. Leave this place. Go to Wyrdwood. You'll be safer there. And no matter what, stop looking for Colin. His danger will become your danger, compounded."

"I don't understand, Mom."

"You will," she said, then looked over her shoulder at the wall. "I have to go." She brought her gaze back to mine and whispered quickly, "I love you."

"Mom!" I pushed up onto my knees and put my hands on her shoulders, but she was already gone. Her eyes shifted and a light went out inside her.

I sat petting her hand for nearly an hour, waiting, hoping she would come back. I didn't beg or even coax—I just waited, but she didn't return.

When the time came, I helped her into her nightgown. Doubts nagged me. I wasn't sure that Richard wouldn't take his anger out on her when he discovered I'd run away. I just hoped that my email to the lawyers would keep him in line.

Eventually, Corona stuck her head in and asked, "Are you ready? They'll be checking beds soon."

I nodded, but I couldn't move. I sat there, paralyzed with fear, afraid to leave my mom, afraid that I'd never see her again.

Moving to my side, Corona said, "It's going to be okay." She took my hand.

"Famous last words," I replied without thinking. I bent and kissed Mom good-bye, rubbing my cheek against hers.

I whispered, "I love you," then accompanied Corona into the hall.

The door to Mom's room closed with a click of finality that sent a shiver rocketing down my spine.

◆◆◆

# CHAPTER 31

Corona went to her room, and I to mine. I got into bed, turned out the lights, and pretended to sleep. When someone looked in on me, I didn't move, and they were appeased.

Third shift came on duty at 11 p.m., and the staff roster was reduced to a nurse, an orderly, and a couple security personnel who roamed the halls. Every night, like clockwork, *tick tock*, Nurse Andrea made her rounds and then joined Marsha, the orderly, in the rec room with the TV.

Nurse Andrea also peeked in at me before moving on to the next room.

That was my cue. I got quietly out of bed.

I changed from my pajamas into jeans and several layered shirts for warmth, put my hair in a bun, and strapped my purse to my torso. It held my cell phone, all my photos of Colin, the evidence, and the money Lettie had given me, minus the twenty I'd used to bait Richard.

I stuffed clothes and a pillow under the blankets to make it seem I was still in bed, in case anyone checked. The homunculus wouldn't stand up under direct scrutiny, but it was improbable that anyone would look that close.

"Simon?" I whispered. "Are you here?"

Simon said, "I'm here, my love. Are you ready to go?"

"I'm ready. Can you see if the coast is clear?" I picked up the gym bag and double checked the contents, which now also included Jaxon's ashes, then zipped it shut. I tucked my cell phone into my jeans pocket.

A moment later, I cracked the door open and peered out into the hall.

"There's no one," Simon whispered. "I'll head down to the exit and warn you if you're in danger of being seen. Just keep going until you hear otherwise."

"Okay." I started down the corridor.

Several doors down, Simon hissed a warning. "Wait here."

After a few long seconds, he whispered, "Clear."

I tapped twice on Dahlia's door and it opened. I did the same on six of the other doors. By the time I was done, all my ladies had shambled out into the hall and were gathered in a motley mob, silent and serious.

Eun Hee approached me and gave me a hug. It started a series of hugs, one from each woman. Only Una didn't participate.

Then Dahlia led them silently into the rec room where Marsha was lounging to watch a late-night talk show.

I held back, peeking around the corner at them.

Una took up her position in the corner, keeping an eye

on everything and everyone, a stalwart and stoic guardian.

Dahlia snuck up behind Marsha and tapped the orderly on the shoulder.

The orderly hadn't heard Dahlia approach. She turned in surprise.

Dahlia punched her, right in the nose.

Marsha fell back onto the couch, arms flailing.

Dahlia said, "Sorry. I didn't see you there."

Iraida and Eun Hee took Marsha by the arms.

"Don't worry, Marsha," said Eun Hee. "We just want a midnight snack. Then, we'll go right back to bed. We promise." They turned Marsha so her back was to me and the exit.

Marsha let loose a string of curses and threats that echoed in the large room.

Nurse Andrea hurried out of the nurse's station. Hands raised, she tried to talk the patients down. Calla took one of the nurse's arms and twisted it behind her back. She turned her to face away as well.

Dahlia went to the dining room doors and input the security code to open them.

Nurse Andrea asked, "How did you get that code?"

"Oh, please, bitch," replied Dahlia. "You think we don't pay attention?"

Led by Eun Hee, they started singing the "Haloperidol Hoochie Koo."

*Haloperidol makes you itch.*
*Paliperidone makes you twitch.*
*Fat on risperidone,*
*flat on ziprasidone.*
*But without them, you're one crazy bitch.*

"Bitch!" repeated Dahlia at the top of her lungs.

Simon whispered, "Go now. Now."

I scuttled across the rec room to the exit and tapped in the security code. The door unlocked. When I opened it, the bell dinged, but it was drowned out by the cacophonous song.

I hurried through, and when I would have pulled the door shut behind me, I was halted as a small hand took hold of it. The door opened wider, and Corona slipped out.

"You can't come with me," I whispered.

"Why not?"

"It's too dangerous."

Corona pulled the door shut behind her. "You shouldn't be going alone."

"What about Jake? And going to his place?"

"That can wait. I'm coming with you. Now get moving before somebody notices us." She was carrying a pillowcase half-filled with her belongings.

I hesitated, but the truth was that I was glad to see her. "All right, but stick close." I opened my gym bag and indicated that she should put her things in there.

Corona scooted close, stuffed her pillowcase in the bag, and then took hold of my shirt tail.

Though muted, the song trailed after us to the stairwell door.

*No more voices.*
*Your doc rejoices.*
*It's the cocktail of the week.*
*They're gonna fix you.*
*Gonna remix you.*
*Your meds gonna make you oblique.*

We made our way out of the Center. Once outside, we ran to the orchard and hid ourselves among the trees. No one stopped us. Phase Three of Operation Freedom was going without a hitch—so far.

We followed the long driveway out to the main gate, sticking to the shadows at the edges. I swiped the employee badge Lettie had loaned me, then hid it where I'd agreed I would.

The gate opened with a clatter. We skirted the road, rather than walk down the middle of it, and watched in all directions for cars. The buses didn't run that late at night, not that far out of the city, so we had a long walk ahead of us. I figured once we hit a landmark, we'd find a phone and call for a cab.

Beyond the Center's drive, the countryside was dark. Night bugs hummed in the background. The mist—not quite rain—felt good on my skin, like it could get into me through my pores and plump me up.

As we walked in damp darkness, the full moon squeezed through clouds intent on forming a barrier to silver light and illuminated the fields surrounding us.

The scene had a surreal quality. Corona and I were the only two people in sight, looking down the long expanse of road in both directions, corn fields on either side. The only man-made lights came from the distant Center.

Corona said, "Have you ever felt," and her voice had an ageless quality, "like you're standing at the edge of the world, looking out into endless possibility?"

The question made me uncomfortable, and I didn't answer.

A car came from behind us. It could have been anyone. The mist made auras around the car's headlights. It was a scene from a Hitchcock movie.

I grabbed Corona's arm.

She said, "I see it."

"C'mon. Let's get off the road." I led her into the ditch, then up the other side where tall weeds stuck burrs to our clothes.

I willed the car to keep going, but it slowed, then pulled up—and I recognized the black sedan with tinted windows.

"It's Nathan," I told Corona.

"What does he want?"

"I don't know."

We started walking again, our pants getting wet all the way to the knees in the tall grass, unable to cross into the field without tackling a barbed wire fence.

The car followed us, creeping along the shoulder that ran parallel to the ditch, a pair of smearing headlights upon a black hole of mystery and danger.

After awhile, it zoomed ahead a short way and stopped. We had no choice but to go back the way we'd come or pass it.

I said, "This is starting to freak me out."

"Starting to?"

The back door of the car opened, and Nathan got out. The night enclosed him in camouflage, embracing him as if he were an old friend. Only his face stood out in contrast, a cratered moon reflected on a deep, black lake.

He called, "Hello, my dears. What a pleasure to see you both. You look well…for fugitives."

I told Corona, "Just keep walking," but that strategy didn't work.

The driver's door opened, and an enormous man got out, dressed in black pants, tailored white shirt, and suspenders. He moved like a warning without even trying. I found myself wishing for Nathan's other, less scary driver—the one who'd worn leather chaps.

We stopped a short distance away.

I asked, "Did you find Colin?"

Nathan replied, "His name is Aubrey, and I did indeed. His father is so pleased. We expect Lord Rebus to make a full recovery now that he knows his son is safe."

Hope filled me. "I want to see him!"

"No, Viviane," whispered Corona.

Nathan smiled a white, toothy invitation and put his hands together as if in prayer. "That's why I'm here, lovely girl. I've come to deliver you to your sweetheart." He indicated the open backseat door.

I hesitated. I didn't trust him, though I didn't know for sure that he didn't have Colin's best interests at heart. No matter what, he could be a means to an end. Anything that moved me closer to Colin worked in my favor.

I said, "C'mon, Corona. Let's go." She and I walked slowly toward the car.

Simon protested, "Viviane, don't."

"Shut up, guardian," said Nathan. "Would you stand between the girl and her true love?" He chuckled.

Corona asked, "Are you sure?"

I walked right up to Nathan. "Is he okay? Where is he?"

Nathan latched onto my wrist with surprising firmness.

I stared at him. "You don't know."

A slow smile spread across his lips.

I took a step back, but I was too late. Corona squeaked behind me, and I turned to see the driver holding her by the arm.

"As soon as I saw you two walking along the road, I had to wonder. I don't imagine they permit you to roam the countryside at your whim. So, what would make you leave the sanctuary? It must be a very important mission indeed. I'm guessing you think you know where Aubrey is, and you're off to find him."

I said nothing.

"Tell you what. How about we find him together," said Nathan. He waved his hand toward the car. "My chariot awaits."

I shook my head.

"This, sugarkin, is the part where you acquire a full understanding of just how dedicated I am to finding my brother." He kept his tone light, but the underlying menace was clear as a bell. "Tell me. What do you know?"

"Nothing," I answered, horror building in my chest. I'd made a huge mistake.

"I don't believe you."

I looked into Nathan's eyes, black as a starless sky. He waved his hand toward Corona and the driver.

The unmistakable crack of breaking bone fractured the night, followed instantly by Corona's howl of pain. I swung around.

Corona sank to her knees, cradling her forearm against her chest.

"Stop it!" I shouted at the driver and would've rushed to put myself between him and her, if Nathan hadn't latched onto the back of my shirt.

He held me easily in place, the neck of the shirt biting into my throat until I stopped pulling. Almost lazily, he said, "Have you ever heard the sound of a neck snapping? It's not dissimilar."

"You wouldn't," I said through gritted teeth.

Nathan moved in close to me and growled. "I wouldn't. He would." His breath smelled of dry, dead leaves. "Gimme." He pulled on my purse, and I let him take it.

"Let us go," I commanded.

He ignored me, his attention on the contents of my purse. He tossed my money out, my cell phone, and my pictures of Colin. Then, he came across the shipping label with Bella's address on it. "What have we here?" he purred.

An aura of efficiency came over him. He threw my purse down, grabbed me by the arm and tried to shove me into the car. His touch was cold and clutching.

I resisted, dropping my weight.

He hissed in my ear. "Get in the car, or Missy-miss has her necky-neck go snappy-snap."

"I'll go with you," I said. "But leave Corona. She needs a doctor." Corona was sobbing, rocking herself, and she'd gone pale. "Please."

Nathan studied Corona with disgust on his face. "Get in, and we'll leave her here. If she blubbers that obnoxiously in the car, she'll be dead before we reach our destination anyway. Get in.”

I slid into the backseat and turned to watch through the back window.

The enormous man left Corona behind and walked to the driver’s side. I breathed a sigh of relief. “Simon, stay with Corona!” I commanded and hoped that Simon would do as he was told.

“He sure as hell isn’t coming with us,” said Nathan with a smirk in his tone. “Not if he values his disembodied self.

The driver got behind the wheel and started the car.

Getting into the backseat beside me, Nathan said, “Take us to this address.” He handed the packing slip across the front seat.

I watched Corona through the rear window until I couldn’t see her anymore. She shakily got to her feet and watched us drive away.

# CHAPTER 32

We drove through the countryside and penetrated the city limits, streaking along I-74, headed for the living heart of the city. The drive took approximately half an hour, making it almost midnight by the time we arrived.

"We're here," said Nathan. The car pulled into a parking spot on the street. The driver opened his door and got out, looking around.

Nathan straightened his sleeves. "Ah, the Monsieur Hotel, one of the oldest, most magickal buildings in Peoria. You'd better hope this isn't a dead end."

The driver leaned down and looked into the car. His face was harsh. When he spoke, his mouth barely opened. "The path is clear."

Nathan drew a knife from inside his coat. He pressed the tip to my throat, just below my ear. It stung, and I leaned away.

"We're getting out and going inside," he told me. "If you try anything, I'll slit your throat from ear to ear, and you'll never see your beloved again."

I nodded acquiescence, and he put his knife in his pocket, then got out of the car, pulling me along after him.

Standing on the sidewalk, I touched the spot where he'd jabbed me, and my finger came away with a stain of scarlet.

Nathan lifted his nose and took a deep breath. "He's here." There was something animal in the way he smelled the air, and his eyes took on a steely intensity, unblinking.

Normal people walked by, traipsing between bars or heading home after an extended happy hour, unaware of the drama happening in their midst.

People got out of our way without even looking at us. I wondered if the driver was invisible, too. Did I seem like I was alone to them? Just another woman getting out of a car.

"No one's going to help you," Nathan hissed. "Normals are oblivious."

"Normals?"

Nathan tugged on my elbow, and we headed straight for the front doors of the hotel. "The non-magickal." He gave me a judgmental look. "Have you been living in a cave all your life?"

"Kinda," I replied.

The lobby was luxurious and spacious, with marble flooring and a second-story gallery that looked down upon arriving visitors. A uniformed clerk stood behind the counter, talking to an elderly couple. It occurred to me that maybe I could say something to…

"Don't even think about it," said Nathan, jabbing me in the ribs with the handle of his knife. "It would take one second for me to kill you, and while they were trying to figure out what had happened, I'd continue on as planned."

"I get it," I said, stumbling a little. I probably seemed impaired to anyone who did look at me.

"This way." Nathan's grip tightened around my waist. We crossed the lobby to the elevators, and he pressed the call button.

It felt unreal, standing there in the serene lobby, listening to ambient jazz.

While we waited, Nathan pointed up to the giant mural over the elevator doors. It showed a missionary standing in a canoe, preaching to half-naked primitives on the shores of the Illinois River. He hissed, "This is why Apfallon left your world. Look at the arrogance. You still honor someone who invaded and imposed his culture upon the native people."

"Apfallon?" I knew that word.

Nathan smirked at me. "The land of apples and honey. The holy grail of neighborhoods. Your ancestral homeland."

"Mine?"

"Half of you. The other half is from my homeland, Gehenna."

The elevator arrived with a chime, and Nathan pulled

me into it. The driver stepped in last and pushed the button.

"What are you talking about?"

"You are so cloaked in Normalcy, it makes my teeth hurt." Nathan came close to my face, his eyes intense. I turned my head away, and he spoke at my cheek. "They imposed ignorance upon you, sweetling. I can't wait to see how you feel about that once you realize how much they wronged you."

"I don't understand."

"You don't have to. Not yet. You'll see it all when we get to Gehenna."

"You're insane."

"Oh no, precious. I'm as sane as you are." He gave a screechy sort of laugh. "Though I guess that's not saying much, is it?"

As we exited the elevator, Nathan paused and looked at the shipping receipt in his hand. "1402," he said. "Stay alert. And you, don't try anything."

"All right," I said. "Stop poking me."

We followed the signs to suite 1402.

Nathan bent and put his eye to the keycard mechanism, then stood aside and nodded to the driver.

The large man in suspenders kicked the door in.

Nathan pushed me in ahead of him.

I stumbled slightly when Nathan released his grip on me.

The suite looked more like an apartment than a hotel

room. It had a kitchen visible to one side and matching leather couch and chairs. A dining table occupied the far end of the main room, just past which was another door that I assumed led to a bedroom. Tall windows lined one wall, the lights of Peoria visible through sheer drapes.

A loud thud and grunt resounded in the hall behind us. We both turned to face the open doorway.

Colin charged into the suite, shoulder in the lead. He plowed into Nathan, and the two of them went down to the floor. Colin quickly moved to straddle Nathan and punched his brother.

I gave a whoop of pure joy.

Then, the knife gleamed.

"Colin!" I rushed forward.

Colin caught Nathan's arm in mid-swing and managed to hold it away from himself.

Adrenaline coursed through my veins, pushed on a hyper heartbeat. I grabbed for the knife.

Nathan twisted his hand around and brought the blade across my forearm. I saw a red bloom, and white-hot pain followed. I pulled back just in time to avoid a second cut.

"Viviane, stay back," Colin shouted.

They rolled, and then Nathan was on top.

"Don't do this, Aubrey," Nathan warned harshly. "The repercussions aren't worth it."

"You're wrong." Colin pushed with one foot and rolled.

Nathan used the momentum of the roll to bring his elbow around into the side of Colin's head. The blow knocked him off-balance, and Nathan came up on top again. Colin held Nathan's arms away from himself, hands on the other man's forearms.

For a moment, the fight paused, both men breathing hard.

Nathan said, "This world's magick tastes like puke, but you'd rather have that than—"

"—than war? Yes, brother. I would."

"That's why I have to take you back, alive or dead. It's up to you."

Nathan twisted his blade-wielding arm free and carried through with a deadly arc aimed at Colin's neck.

Colin somehow blocked it, and rolling yet again, he straddled Nathan, reared back, and hit the other man in the jaw with weight behind the punch.

Nathan went limp, unconscious.

Colin climbed quickly to his feet, shaking the pain out of his punching hand. He reached for me. "C'mon!"

We ran into the hallway. The driver lay unconscious on the floor.

"Colin! Are you okay?"

"Not now. Keep moving!"

I tried to concentrate on running, keeping up with Colin, and staying on my feet. He led us to the exit stairwell, but instead of turning downward, he climbed up.

"Where are you going?" I cried, tugging back on him, wanting to run down toward the exit instead.

He halted and touched a brief kiss to my lips. "Trust me. C'mon. There's no time to argue."

We had only one flight of stairs between us and the top floor. Colin extended his hand in front of him, mumbled something I couldn't hear, and the door swung open before we got to it. We rushed through into the roof-top bar, threading our way between people dressed in suits and sequins.

I gasped, but Colin didn't notice and didn't stop.

We passed a man in a tuxedo playing a baby grand piano. Beyond him, a bank of windows separated the bar from the cityscape beyond.

Colin halted in place, facing the windows. He raised his hand again, palm facing away, and said something in a language I didn't recognize. I barely had time to register that he was even speaking when the window exploded outward. An enormous crash inspired screams and shouts from the crowd. People lurched away from the point of commotion.

Wind whipped into the room—a demon freed from ages of captivity. It careened around people's bodies, disturbing their hair and hems. What glass remained clinging to the upper edge of the frame fell straight down and into the bar, scattering over the floor.

The bartender picked up the phone. People piled up at the elevators or cowered on the far side of the room. Two or three brave souls took out their cell phones pointed them at us.

Colin climbed into the window frame.

I rushed forward, grabbed at him, clawed at him, and tried desperately to anchor him inside. "What are you do-ing?"

"Trust me!" he said, taking hold of my shoulders and looking me square in the eyes. "We have to get off this building. Nathan will be coming after us any second!"

Someone shouted, "Stop!"

Someone else cried, "That's suicide!"

Broken glass crunched and slipped under my feet.

Colin stood at the window frame, one leg out, one leg in. At the edge there, the wind was stronger. It whipped my hair back from my face.

He said, "I can't go back with them. I can't. They'll kill me."

"Why? Why would they kill you?"

"I'll explain everything." He pressed a kiss to my lips, then looked me in the eyes and said, "Don't worry. I can fly."

He wrapped an arm tightly around my waist, and I felt his knees bend.

"No!" I cried, pushing myself away from him. I al-most managed to pull him inside, but then he released me. I stumbled backward into the arms of a stunned waiter.

Colin turned toward the open air, spread his arms, and jumped.

I heard screams from all around and cries of, "Oh my God!" and "He jumped!"

The waiter moved me out of his way, stepped to the opening, and looked down toward the street, fifteen stories below.

My life with Colin flashed before my eyes—our past together, and all my dreams for the future. I stumbled to the gaping hole and clung to the frame, swaying there with my hair whipping around my head.

A morbid need to see made me look down at the concrete so far below.

I saw him.

# CHAPTER 33

Colin rose from below on glossy raven wings. They flapped and lifted him, then he rode the air currents like river birds did, letting them hold him aloft. He said something, but I couldn't hear him over the wind and the crowd. He held his arms out to me, and that I understood. He wanted me to jump to him. He wanted me to fly away with him.

I wanted it too. I wanted to be with him. I stood, using the frame for support.

Colin was beautiful—an angel. The sky opened wide behind him, the heavens full of stars and moon-kissed clouds.

"Take my hand," the waiter said. "He's gone. There's nothing you can do." He didn't… He *couldn't* see Colin.

Colin swooped close, then rose again, hovering just out of reach. I held first one hand, then both, out to him.

"No!" shouted the waiter.

Colin's lips moved around the word, "Jump." I heard it in my head.

For the briefest moment, I wondered if I'd completely

lost my mind. The thought that I might be hallucinating him hit me like lightning, a blinding flash, and then gone again, leaving only the negative image of it on the backs of my eyelids. I knew then and there that I had a choice. I could remain locked in a colorless world of gray and black, *tick tock,* where everything was a burden or an injury. I could return to my familiar routine and to the daily grind of hiding who I am from the real world.

Or, I could choose to believe in beauty, wonder, and magick.

The stars above twinkled, and Colin hovered there, his eyes worried and afraid. He held his hands out to me, beckoning, promising to catch me.

I bent my knees, and—

I took a leap of faith.

As soon as my feet lifted off the floor, I sensed the building had abandoned me. The wind took me, but it wasn't enough to hold me up.

A second later, I was plummeting toward the street, fifteen stories below.

I thought, *This is it.*

Ahead, tiny cars moved from stop light to stop light and people streamed along, ants carrying the crumbs of their lives. They got bigger as I got closer. The cracks in the sidewalk rose to greet me.

I thought, *Today you're pain...*

And then, Colin was there.

He wrapped his arms around me from behind and re-directed my downward momentum with a harsh jerk that knocked the air out of me. One of my shoes fell off and was swallowed by the Peoria streets. I was rising, up over the city, gasping in lungful after lungful of life.

I slid in his grasp until he had me by the armpits, his embrace tight around my chest. With each downward stroke of his wings, we lifted higher, the air rushing past us, cold and crisp.

The Monsieur Hotel grew small and distant. People at the broken window all looked down, hands over their mouths. One single face, however, was lifted to search the sky, his black, asymmetrical hair ruffled, blowing in the wind.

As I watched, Nathan spread raven wings and took off through the same broken window.

I shouted over the roar in my ears, "He's coming!"

Colin said nothing, but his body tensed. I clung to his arms, doing my best to ignore the pain of muscles stretched to their limit. His wings stroked harder, pushing us forward harshly with each flap.

I searched the sky for Nathan, and when I didn't see him, I knew he was at our backs.

The city was a sea of lights below us. Tiny cars on the highway created a streaming river of blood red and white gold. It blurred together as my eyes glazed with tears brought on by the wind and my fear.

Jarred, Colin jerked us to one side. My legs swung wildly, and I craned my neck trying to see.

Nathan had caught up to us. He was faster, more agile.

Colin was burdened by my body's weight. He veered again, and my body swung to the opposite side. Colin's grip loosened. I was slipping.

A great black form cut directly in front of me. Feathers raked my face, too close to my eyes for comfort, and a searing pain lit up my left thigh. The roar of wind and wings swallowed my cry.

Colin changed directions again, tearing me away from the onslaught.

My head spun, and before I could recover my equilibrium, another assault sent us diving downward. For a moment, we were outpacing gravity itself. Bile surged into my throat, and I swallowed it back. Coughing, I blinked at the ground far below, rising to meet us.

Colin changed course abruptly, pulling out of the dive and flying upward.

A great raven's caw split the night.

We flew up, ever higher, into darkness, into clouds, into the heavens.

A shadow appeared to my right, bearing down on us with ferocious intensity. Nathan's face, twisted with cruelty, came out of the darkness. His black wings obscured the moon, but I saw that he still had the shimmering blade in his hand.

"I'm sorry," Colin shouted. "I need my hands."

And he released me. It happened so fast I didn't have time to clutch at him. One second, my back was pressed to his chest, and the next, I was dropping in open air, falling straight down through misty tendrils of cloud that clung to my skin and clothes, wet and chilled.

It took my mind a moment to catch up and realize that I was falling and screaming at the top of my lungs. The wind howled in my ears, assaulted my face and flapped my clothes sharply against me. With each passing second, the ground below grew closer, bigger, and more detailed. I fell straight toward suburbia, spinning head over heels.

Time stretched oddly. I had only a few seconds, or was it minutes? My thoughts focused on what was below me. The people down there went about their lives as I plummeted toward them. *If I hit one of their houses,* I wondered, *would I break through into a bedroom?* There was a swing set in a back yard. *Would my sudden appearance scar a child for life?*

That, very probably, would have been my last thought, but a flash of lightning lit the roof of the house below, and thunder cracked at my heels.

A moment later, someone slid up my body and wrapped arms around me from behind. We swooped upward, my legs dangling wildly as I was forced to change direction. My stomach lurched again.

"It's okay. We're okay," said Colin next to my ear.

"He's gone—for now."

Colin's body was a warm comfort against my back, but the rest of me was freezing, quaking with the rush of adrenaline.

"Put me down!" I shouted.

"Let me find a good spot," he replied.

He flew along the Illinois River. I tried to relax, but my fear wouldn't let me. Every muscle in my body was tense, some on the verge of cramping. I couldn't stop shaking.

# CHAPTER 34

We spiraled downward, passing between Peoria's skyscrapers. Gradually, we descended, until finally, Colin landed us on a rooftop. Gravel crunched underfoot, painful to my shoeless one.

As soon as I was standing on my own two feet, I turned around and screamed at him, "You dropped me!"

My body was shaking so violently that my legs gave out and I sat down hard. "You dropped me!" And then, I was sobbing. My fury at him for leaving me had been building for months. "I can't believe you fucking dropped me!"

"I'm sorry," he said. "I'm sorry. I had no choice." He put a hand on my shoulder and crouched beside me.

I ran out of steam and collapsed into Colin's arms. Bombarded with emotions I couldn't control, my body racked with wet sobs like sucking wounds, I couldn't do or say anything else. I leaned on him, and he held me. I realized then that, even though I'd pretended Colin was alive, I hadn't fully believed it until I'd seen him. Relief sifted in amidst the fear, anger, and shock as I clung to him. He was solid, warm, and breathing, not a hallucination. I inhaled his scent deep into my body. My hands curled of their own accord in his shirt, as if they might refuse to let go when the time came.

We stayed there for the longest time. I had no words.

Then, as my tears subsided, and my brain picked up—more or less—where it had left off, I felt another great wave of anger rising in me.

I shoved him away. "You let me believe you were dead!" I said, voice pinched with accusation. I stumbled to my feet.

"I'm sorry." He stood too and stepped toward me, reaching to brush at an errant strand of my hair. "Bella faked my death to protect me from Nathan. I hated lying to you, but it was for your own safety."

I shook uncontrollably, arms wrapped around myself. "Why? Why is he after you? This has gone way beyond a sick dad trying to find his amnesiac son."

"I can explain," he said. "I *will* explain, but you're bleeding, freezing, and possibly in shock. We need to get you somewhere warm."

Darkness oozed in at the corners of my eyes, and as my knees began to buckle, I said, "You can fly."

"Told you so," he replied.

The ground dropped out from under me yet again.

♦

When I came to, I was in a bed, covered with a heavy down comforter. It smelled good, felt warm, and I had to fight the urge to snuggle deeper and go back to sleep. Memories of Colin and our flight pulled me all the way to consciousness.

I was wearing a man-sized t-shirt and thick baggy socks, and someone had bandaged my wounds. When I moved, I was sore all over, especially my back and shoulders. I threw aside the covers and a chilly draft put goosebumps on my skin. I wrapped the comforter around myself.

Beyond the room's window, a pall of darkness obscured the surrounding landscape. The moon had fallen out of sight beyond the horizon. I wondered if Corona was okay. I hoped she had called Lettie for help. The sound of her arm breaking and the sight of her shrinking into the distance, face distorted with anguish, haunted me, and my stomach went uneasy again.

I found the door ajar and voices murmuring beyond it, so I crept over and pushed the door a bit wider. Beyond, a long corridor extended, lined with other doors.

Colin said quite clearly, "…supposed to do, Bella? I had no choice. Nathanatos showed up at the Monsieur with her."

I recognized Doc Bella's voice. "How did he find you?"

"I don't know. It doesn't matter. We're all here now, safe and sound."

I slipped into the hallway and padded toward their voices.

Bella's laugh held tension. "Safe and sound? You think so? It's only a matter of time before he tracks you here."

"So, we leave a little early. What can it hurt?"

Colin stood by the living-room fireplace, his hand on the mantle. He had exchanged his wet clothes for a pair of jeans and an emerald cable-knit sweater. His hair had grown. A mass of auburn curls haloed his face, chaotic and untamed. Otherwise, he looked exactly the same.

Bella wore an old-fashioned housecoat, and her white bony legs showed between its hem and the fur-lined slippers on her feet.

The final face in the room surprised me the most. Ajani leaned against the wall by the window, holding open a crack between the drapes so he could see out, as if on guard duty. He glanced over his shoulder, dark eyes landing on me, and his lips curved into that old familiar smile. He resembled my friend, the man I'd sweated with five days a week, for more than thirteen years. But he wasn't and had never been that man. I didn't know how I could ever trust him again. I didn't see how I could trust any of them.

"I guess," said Bella to Colin, "we have no choice. I'll start—"

Ajani cleared his throat, then said, "Miss Viviane. You're awake."

All eyes turned to me, and Colin crossed the room in a

handful of strides to put an arm around me. "Viv, how are you feeling? I was so worried."

"I'm feeling very ready for that explanation you promised me."

"Sit down, dear," said Bella. "I'll make us some hot chocolate." She stood. "Ajani, if you would help me, please?"

Feeling like Alice through the looking glass, I let Colin lead me to the couch.

Ajani followed Bella from the room, and Colin sat with me.

Colin asked, "Are you warm enough?"

"Yeah." I touched his face, his neck. "I can't believe you're here." Moonbeams glowed inside me, taunting me, daring me to follow them. I was tempted, and it would have been so easy to catch them, far too easy.

Colin laughed. "I know. I'm sorry. If there'd been any other way..." He pulled the blanket more tightly around me.

I studied his face. "You need to tell me what's happening."

"I know. I want to tell you everything, and I will."

"How about we start with the wings?" I reached for his shoulder and pushed it away from me, twisting him so I could see his back where the wings had been.

He chuckled. "I put them away."

"You mean they come off?"

"No. I fold them into a…magickal pocket."

"Bring them out."

"Now?"

I nodded, though my heart had started a pitter-patter of protest.

Standing slowly, eyes locked on me, he moved to the center of the room. He didn't even need to concentrate. Suddenly, the wings were just there, unfolding. They spread large behind him with a whoosh and a crack—the sound of clean linens flapping on a clothesline.

My mouth opened on a huff of breath.

Colin tipped his head back and laughed. "You should see the look on your face."

"You should see the wings on your back!" Breathless, I asked the only thing that came to mind, "Is it unlucky to bring them out in the house? Like an umbrella?"

Colin laughed. "No. I just have to be careful not to break anything."

A moment later, they were gone again, tucked back into their pocket.

"Why do you have wings?" I asked.

He sat back down beside me, closer this time, and took my hand in both of his. Slowly and carefully, he said, "Think of it this way. If you imagine our reality is a house, then most people only ever know one room in that house. Some rooms are locked, and you'll never get inside them without the right key. Others are open wells you can fall into, maybe even drown in. Trap doors, secret passages, and cubby holes."

Bella returned with a tray of mugs. "That's a very basic analogy of what Reality is, my dear, but not a bad one for a beginner's introduction."

"Thank you." Colin bowed.

Ajani appeared in the kitchen doorway also, leaning loosely and crossing both his arms and ankles.

I asked Colin, "So you're from a different room in the house?"

Both Colin and Bella said, "Yes."

"Gehenna?" I asked.

Bella set the tray on the coffee table. "Where did you hear about Gehenna?"

"Nathan mentioned it."

Ajani grunted. "Figures."

I said, "The things I see…"

"Are real," Colin finished for me when I stumbled onto the truth.

"Faux schizophrenics," I said, thinking aloud.

"Yes." Bella put a spoon in each of the mugs and gave them a stir. "Your symptoms are not signs of illness, but signs of a gift—a gift that runs in families."

"You mean my mom?"

Bella nodded. "And your grandmother."

"I never knew. Is that why Mom is so lost?"

"No," replied Bella. "Your mother is in a unique situation. Her mind is trapped. There's nothing anyone can do about it, for now, but I have every confidence that she'll be well again one day."

I smiled at her, despite myself. That was news I wanted to hear. This was all news I wanted to hear. It explained everything and made it all seem romantic and wonderful. I was Dorothy in the Emerald City, dancing through the streets in my ruby slippers and running from flying monkeys. The happy ending was surely just around the corner.

I took the mug when Bella held it out to me and asked, "Why are you hiding from your family?" The comforting aroma of chocolate drifted up to my nose.

"That's a long story," Colin replied, "but the short of it is that I don't agree with my father's methods. The amnesia was supposed to hide me from them."

"You don't really believe they'd kill you if they caught you. Do you?"

Colin sighed. "They would if I refused to help my father. "

I looked down at the mug in my hand. I remembered the lake. "We nearly died in that accident," I said. "Someone *did* die." I put the mug down without taking a sip. "How could you?"

Bella raised a hand to forestall Colin from responding. "Let *me* explain."

She sat down in an armchair. Her eyes were dark, their usual gleam lost to gravity. "I never meant for you to be in any danger. I had people all over the area, ready to pull you out. It just didn't work out that way. I would never hurt either of you on purpose." She addressed Colin. "You know that, right?"

Colin said, "I know."

Back to me, Bella said, "It turned out to be more harrowing than I'd intended, and for that, I apologize."

"What about Jaxon?"

Colin and Bella exchanged glances again. Colin said, "He gave his life for something he believed in."

"You knew about it?" I was horrified.

"Jaxon was a warrior," Bella said. "He volunteered to sacrifice himself. He felt the cause merited it. When a soldier dies in war, it isn't murder."

I said, "That doesn't seem right."

"If it's any consolation," Bella continued, "he didn't suffer for even a second."

Colin said, "What you have to understand, Viv, is that I was starting to remember, and that changed my signature—made me findable. If Nathan had gotten to me before I fully remembered who I was, I'd have been vulnerable. He'd have taken me back to Gehenna, where I'd have been executed for treason."

"Treason? For not agreeing with your father?"

Colin and Bella looked at one another. Bella nodded as if giving him permission, and Colin said, "My people were exiled to Gehenna long ago, and they want to take back their homeland. My father will stoop to anything to make that happen, including going to war. I refuse to be a party to that. If Bella hadn't *faked* my death, I'd be dead for real."

"War with who?" I asked.

Colin and Bella exchanged looks, but it was Colin who replied. "The inhabitants of another pocket realm known as Apfallon."

The world where Mom's stories took place.

Bella continued, "Apfallon is hidden. Colin's father is trying to find it."

*Tick. Tock.* The clock on the wall filled the empty space left in the wake of our conversation. *Tick. Tock.*

Colin was the first to speak again. "There's something I want to ask you, Viv." He reached out and touched the wound on my back, the hot pink claw marks of the hag, and said, "I saw your wound when I undressed you. Did Nathan do that?"

I shook my head. My stomach was upset, as was I.

Colin turned my face toward him. "Viv? What happened?"

"It wasn't Nathan," I said. "It was the hag. I fought it and killed it."

Three pairs of eyes blinked at me, then Colin and Bella both turned to Ajani.

Ajani raised his hands in surrender. "Simon told me *he'd* killed it."

Bella said, "So he lied about that too, did he? I'm not surprised. He probably guessed Colin and I would be unhappy if we knew you were fighting a hag."

"It was a group thing. I had help." I yawned, unable to suppress it.

Bella slapped her hands down on her thighs and stood. "Let's talk about this more tomorrow. I, for one, am pooped. I think we could all use some rest."

Colin put his hand on my arm. "Why don't we go to bed? You're exhausted."

I didn't want to lie down, but my body did. "I should call Lettie and let her know I'm okay, and check on Corona. They hurt her when they grabbed me."

"Leave it to me," Bella said. "We have to be careful."

Colin followed me down the hall to the guest bedroom. Once we were inside, he closed the door, and its click shut us off from the rest of the world. At last, we were together again, and alone.

In those first few seconds, I became vitally, physically aware of his presence. My breath quickened, and—with my back to him—I listened for his movement. It took him three, slow steps to reach me, and a full other second before his hands moved cautiously around my waist to rest on my belly. I knew then that he wasn't sure how I would react.

And before I could wonder myself, I turned toward him, into his arms. Our mouths came together with all the warmth and blinding sparkle of summer sunshine. I was home after an excruciating day at work. I settled into his body as I would my favorite pajamas, fingers exploring my favorite paths. It was all so familiar.

What little barrier they raised, our clothing was no match for us. We half-stumbled in increasing nakedness to the bed. I hit it first and fell backwards onto the down-padded nest.

Colin rushed forward to drape himself upon me, his mouth and hands hot wherever they touched.

I spread my legs and welcomed him to me.

Our passion was a flash fire that burned white hot, flared with explosive power, and left us trembling in each others' arms. We gave no thought to tomorrow. There was no passage of time. There was only *now*.

When our hearts had slowed to a more normal pace, Colin slid to one side of me and propped himself up on his elbow. He rubbed his other hand in circles over my sweaty stomach.

I watched him, thinking I could anchor him in place with my eyes. His curly red hair had the craziness that only my hands could inflict upon it. It made him a wild man, a Scot from the deepest moors.

My fingers played in the matching mini-curls on his chest, making swirls of auburn against his pale skin.

He said, "I want to bathe you."

Those words and the heather softness of his eyes re-awoke my desire.

I didn't know how to reply.

He got up, and I watched him walk naked into the bathroom. I had already forgiven him.

◆

Colin and I spent the rest of the evening alone together. We made love again until we both passed out from exhaustion.

When I awoke the next morning, Colin was gone from the bed. My first thought, my first fear, was that I had imagined everything or dreamt it.

Colin's clothing lay on the floor where he'd left it.

I was in the bedroom at Bella's place, nestled under the down comforter and shielded by half-drawn bed curtains. I could still feel the physical signs that Colin and I had made love.

I heard the shower running in the attached bathroom, and then, Colin's hum.

Tears brimmed of their own accord, and I cried with relief.

Colin was alive. It hadn't been a dream.

The shower shut off, and he came out with a towel wrapped around his hips. He took one look and came straight to me. "Are you all right?"

His skin was warm and moist from the shower.

"I am now."

He kissed me with all the care of a surgeon stitching up a gaping wound. But, when I tried to pull him back into bed with me, he retreated.

"Bella's fixing breakfast," he said. "The shower's free."

Under the guise of thinking about it, I stretched luxuriantly. It felt good, even though I was still stiff and sore. The light coming in the windows had a magical quality—it was a lovely shade of brand-new-day.

I realized I was starving and said so.

"Well, hurry up then. I'm pretty sure Bella's frying bacon for you."

That got me moving. I swung out of bed and turned on the shower, then stood naked in the doorway watching Colin dress. "So what now?"

Colin pulled his jeans up and buttoned them. "Now, we go into hiding. Nathan won't stop."

"Why don't you just call your dad? Explain to him what's been going on, and tell him to call off his spooky henchman."

Colin shook his head. "It's not that simple, honey. Besides, neither phone lines nor cell coverage extends between realms."

With my arms crossed on my chest, I frowned at him. It didn't have quite the effect I'd hoped.

He laughed, came to me, put his hands on my arms,

and said, "I've missed you."

I melted and lifted my face for a kiss.

He gave me a peck on the lips, then said, "Go on," and turned me toward the bathroom. With a pat on my behind, he shooed me in and shut the door between us.

♦

I kept my shower short. I still wasn't entirely comfortable alone in a bathroom. My thoughts inevitably drifted to the hag, and every sound gave me the creeps.

Feeling much more awake and less sore, I dressed in the same jeans I'd arrived in and the man's t-shirt from the night before. As I emerged from the bedroom, I meandered, checking out the artwork and furniture. It was all from a different time, turn of the last century, just like Bella's office. The décor had an old-world charm that made me a little afraid to touch anything.

I heard their voices before I got to the kitchen.

Bella scolded someone. "Don't forage. I'm making a nice breakfast."

"Yes, ma'am," Colin replied, sounding chipper.

I stopped in place, riveted by the sound of his voice, so sane and clear.

"Where's Viviane?" Bella asked.

"In the shower."

"Good. I need to talk to you. I'm furious with you."

"Why?" asked Colin.

I didn't mean to eavesdrop, but the conversation took such a sudden turn for the serious that I didn't know what to do, so I did nothing.

"Do you realize," asked Bella, her tone too even, "how close you came to getting her killed?"

"Nathanatos wouldn't have done that."

"Don't be a fool, Aubrey. Your brother is a killer. He kills people for fun. What made you think he wouldn't kill her in front of you, just to remove any desire you have to stay away?"

Colin didn't answer immediately.

I almost took a step, almost made a noise, but then Colin said, "He knew if he did anything to her, he'd have to kill me too."

"And you, you arrogant idiot, assume that he wants you alive?"

"I didn't know he'd snatch her."

"Pfah! You left her clues so she wouldn't give up trying to find you, and Nathan figured it out."

"It all turned out okay," Colin responded. "She's here with us, safe and sound. Nathan lost this battle. We can disappear and live happily ever after. Viviane is my betrothed. I had to have her with me."

Bella let out a puff of air through her nose. There was a long pause, then, "You realize…you know she *can't* go with us. Right?"

"Of course, she can," said Colin. "She has to go with us. She belongs to me."

"That's exactly why she can't go with us." Bella's voice had taken on an edge of emotion that I couldn't identify. "With her parentage, we can't risk your father ever getting his hands on her."

"She'll be safer with me, and that's that."

I'd had enough of them talking about me behind my back. Without masking my steps, I headed straight for the kitchen.

"Your bacon's burning, Bella." Colin said.

"Good morning," I said from the doorway. "Something smells delicious."

Bella uncrossed her arms—she had been squeezing them tightly across her chest—and put a smile on her face. "Good morning, dear. Come in. I'm making breakfast. Coffee?"

I moved to stand beside Colin. We exchanged a kiss, and he pulled me into the circle of his arm.

"Yes, that would be awesome," I said. "I can get it."

Bella waved dismissively. "No, you sit down. Do you take cream or sugar?"

"Neither," I answered. "Black. Can I do anything to help?"

Bella crossed to the coffee maker and upturned a clean mug. "I've got it under control, but thanks."

Ajani appeared in the doorway. "Mornin', sunshine."

"Good morning," I replied.

Colin squeezed me around the middle and I huffed out an unexpected breath. I covered it with a cough, poking a gentle elbow in his ribs. He hammed an injury.

"Ajani," I asked, "are you from this room or a different room?"

"The better question is," Colin corrected me, "are you a magick wielder."

Ajani smiled, "I'm like you. A wielder. I can see and do things others can't."

"Corona calls us *faux schizos.* False schizophrenics."

Bella said, "What you—charmingly—call a *faux schizo* is just someone attuned to magick, usually because they have a magickal ancestor. When you have magick in your blood, your mind ceases to obey Normalcy barriers."

Ajani went to a drawer in the hutch and opened it. He began to withdraw silverware, but then abruptly stopped and turned his head to one side, listening.

His voice strained with urgency, he said, "They're here."

♦♦♦

# CHAPTER 35

Everyone went skittish—everyone else first, then me. "Who's here? Nathan?"

I got no answer, only a hand under my armpit urging me up out of my chair.

They had a plan, it was obvious. Each of them had a job to do, and they did it with precision, zipping from room to room, gathering books and papers quickly into large gym bags.

I stood in the middle of the living room, watching them skirt around one another like square-dancers.

The first bang on the door didn't break it in. Ajani, closest to the door, wheeled on it and took a deep breath. An insanely long knife appeared in his hand.

The second bang sent the door crashing inward. It swung and hit the wall, fell off the bottom hinge and dangled crookedly.

Nathan's large driver filled the doorway, dressed in black pants and suspenders as when he'd driven us to the Monsieur. He had his arm extended at chest level, palm forward.

Colin shouted, "Viviane!"

Bella mumbled something in a language I didn't understand.

It happened so fast.

Ajani struck, jumping forward, his blade slicing twice in an X across the driver's palm. The stricken flesh parted and blood flowed from the cut.

The driver stumbled back on his heels and faltered, but only briefly. His face twisted into an expression of focus, and he raised his other hand beside the first.

As Ajani moved in for his second attack, static electricity made my scalp tingle. A blast of energy coursed from the chauffeur's hands and hit Ajani square in the chest. His chest caved in and his head was thrown back impossibly far. I knew beyond a shadow of a doubt that Ajani was dead before he hit the floor.

Blood welled in his mouth and overflowed.

My voice came free, and I cried, "Ajani!" I started to go to him, but someone had hold of my wrist and was dragging me in the opposite direction. Another wave of static lifted my hair, and I saw, out of the corner of my eye, a flash of silver shoot from Bella's general direction, at the driver.

The big man roared.

I turned to run with Colin toward the back of the house. "What about Bella?"

"She'll be all right. She's going to buy us some time. If

she gets in trouble, she'll chute out. C'mon! We have to go!"

We rushed through the kitchen and out the back door onto the lawn.

Clouds loomed overhead, heavy and ominous. They released a few fat droplets of rain with the promise of more to come.

Colin opened his wings. They unfolded from his back as if they'd been there all along. The feathers gleamed, all the rainbow's colors contained in the black.

"C'mere," he said and held his arms out to me.

I couldn't have been more than a step or two away from him, but before I could reach him, a force slammed into my body and threw me to one side. It knocked the wind out of me and left me sprawled in the dirt, gasping for a breath, a sharp pain in my side.

"Aubrey," said Nathan. There was no mistaking his voice. "Don't you think you've been naughty enough for one century?"

"Fuck off, Nathan. Why don't you go back to Gehenna and tell Father he can—"

"Do stop. I don't share your appreciation of Earth colloquialisms. I find them crude and distasteful. Turn around so I can bind your hands."

"Never."

"We've danced this dance before. You know you can't win."

Colin's voice took on an added edge. "No way I'm going with you, Nathan."

I finally managed to take a breath, and immediately regretted it as a spark of pain lit up my side. I gasped in shallow bursts.

"Hm," Nathan replied. "That may be so, but what I do have is your lady love. If you don't go with me, I'll kill her dead, dead, dead. Go on, I dare you. Give me a reason to melt her insides."

Colin growled on an inhalation. It was the scariest sound I'd ever heard him make.

I tried to sit up, but the best I could manage was to roll onto my side and lift up onto an elbow.

Nathan and Colin stood facing one another, staring into each others' eyes, but the palm of Nathan's hand was aimed toward me.

Colin shouted, his face red and twisted with anger, "Can't you see? Father is going to war with Apfallon. Is that what you want?"

"Whatever it takes," replied Nathan. "All I want is to get out from under this curse. We've suffered enough. Apfallon is our birthright."

"I'm living proof that we don't have to stay in Gehenna. We can live here, among the Normals."

Nathan laughed. "Here? Normals are a scourge. They systematically destroy wielders. If our people came here, we'd be sentencing them to a life without magick. It would be the end of our race. We need Apfallon."

Colin shook his head slowly. "Some Normals have more heart than you'll ever have. With a little encouragement, we can bring magick back. They'll believe again."

"You're wrong, brother. You do remember the Inquisition, don't you? How about the Vatican? The KKK?"

Colin glanced over at me. "Times are different now. Let us go, and I'll prove it to you."

"I can't do that. You know I can't do that." Nathan straightened his arm, tensing it, and his fingers crackled. "Don't make me. I was just starting to tolerate her."

Doc Bella had predicted this moment so long ago in her office. Colin's battle, his war, was my own by extension, because I loved him, and because I'd promised to be his partner. If he was willing to die for his cause, then so was I.

"Go, Colin! Leave me! He won't hurt me after you're gone."

Nathan hissed, "Oh yes, I will."

Troubled, Colin hovered between leaving and staying. "Viviane, I…" His hair shone with brilliant copper highlights in the sunlight, the curls thick. The color had drained from his face, leaving him pale, his freckles standing out in sharp contrast.

I hesitated only a moment longer, then said the words Bella had armed me with in the midst of her warning: "I'm not worth the sacrifice."

Colin twitched as if waking from a trance. "I'll never

forget this, Nathanatos. Never. And one day, you *will* pay for it!"

Colin flapped his wings hard and lifted up off the ground. "Chase me if you dare, Nathan." He waved sparking fingers in an arc that sent a bolt of lightning toward Nathan, thunder as immediate as life.

Nathan dodged, rolling to one side. It took him a moment to reorient himself and get to his feet.

"I'm not the one who will pay!" Nathan shouted. He watched his brother rise, but made no move to go after him. "I'll catch up with you later."

Colin's voice grew distant as he cried, "Viviane! I'll come for you!"

Nathan glared at me with all the terrifying threat of a predator, and I was the prey.

My voice croaked as I said, "You. Need. Me."

His jaw tensed on one side. It pinched his face into an expression of rage.

"No," he said. "I don't." He strode over to me, bent, and grabbed me by the throat, lifting me up onto my feet with one hand, his strength supernatural.

I couldn't speak. He'd cut off my air and the blood supply to my brain. I stood on tiptoes to lessen the pressure under my jaw. If I'd doubted it before, I no longer did. I was going to die.

He eyed me up and down as if I were a dirty rag and said, "You have no idea what you just unleashed upon your realm. Sadly, you won't live to—"

Before he could finish, Bella shouted from the back door. She stretched both hands toward Nathan as if she could push him from afar. Her words came out garbled.

A shimmer moved through the air, a heat wave, heading straight for Nathan and me.

Before it arrived, he raised his free hand and said a single word I didn't recognize. The shimmer reversed course and sped back at Bella.

She saw it coming but had only a second to respond. She took a step back, and her foot kept going down as if there was nothing under it. She fell out of sight as if into a well.

The shimmer passed through where she had been and dissipated.

Nathan harrumphed.

When he turned back to me, I was ready. I pushed the straight pin into his eyelid. It slid all the way into the head.

Nathan howled and released me immediately.

I fell to the ground, gasping for breath. My only thought was escape, and I crawled toward the house. Every breath, every movement, was accompanied by pain in my ribs.

Abruptly, Nathan's howling ended, and he was gone—just gone.

The taste of blood was bitter in my mouth. I had no strength left.

Then Bella was there. She bent over me. "Viviane? Are

you all right?"

My voice came out as a hoarse gasp. "I'm alive. Where's Colin?"

Bella's gaze scanned the skies. "Far away, my dear."

"Nathan was going to kill me."

Bella nodded gravely. "Yes."

"Where did he go?"

"He chuted back to Gehenna. We're safe for now."

I thought of Ajani. He wasn't safe.

Bella got an arm under me and helped me to sit up. It made it a little easier to breathe.

She said, "It's time for you to go home."

"I don't have a home."

"You can still have a normal life."

"I don't *want* a normal life." I never thought I'd say that, but there it was, and I felt its sincerity all the way to my core. "I want to fly away with Colin."

A gust of wind lifted Bella's curls, more silver than auburn. They danced briefly before lying still again. "I know. But your mother and grandfather need you. Colin doesn't need you. He may want you, for now, but that's different. His selfishness nearly cost you your life." Bella ran her fingers down my cheek. "I'm so proud of you, Viviane. You handled this whole mess with courage, strength, and good heart. Your mother will be proud, too. I'm sure of it."

A shout sounded inside the house, and Bella glanced back over her shoulder. "I have to go," she said. "Take care, my dear. Your future is in *your* hands now." She lay me down, then stood and backed away a few steps.

"Wait," I said, but to no avail.

Bella stepped back one last time and fell out of sight.

I laid my head down on my arm and focused on breathing.

◆

Some unknown time later, Detective Hayward crouched down beside me. "Help's on the way."

"Why…are you here?" I asked on a wheezy breath.

His voice had none of the sarcasm I normally heard in it. "I got the pictures you sent." His hand came to rest on my shoulder, a light, comforting presence. "I came to take Dr. Rosenblum in for questioning."

"You believe...me?"

"I believe the evidence."

When the paramedics arrived, he backed away.

They rolled me out on a gurney, around the house, saving me from having to see Ajani's body. In front, the ambulance and police lights flashed red, white, and blue in my eyes, turning the whole world into an emergency.

◆◆◆

# CHAPTER 36

Everything felt wrong. My side hurt, my chest ached, and my head pounded. I moved a little, but it hurt more. I couldn't think. I drifted in and out of consciousness, drugged and exhausted, but I remembered seeing Richard talking to doctors, giving orders, and overseeing my treatment. He was, after all, my physician on record.

They rolled me into an ambulance and took me back to the Center. Jared, the receiving clerk, came into view, concerned.

"You're going to be all right," he said—or something like that.

♦

I awoke in my bed at the Center, restrained. The last place I wanted to be was back there. If I could've turned back the clock, I'd have begged Colin to take me with him. But that wasn't what I did.

Richard came in, his smile insipid and condescending. "You're awake. How are you feeling?"

"I had a collapsed lung and three broken ribs, and now I'm back here. How do you *think* I'm feeling?" I was all acid and attitude.

Richard took the desk chair and swung it around to face me, then he sat. "I heard you had quite an adventure."

*Quite an adventure.* That was psych talk for *I heard you went bat-shit crazy.*

I replied, "Today I'm pain. Tomorrow, a stain."

"Okay," he said, his tone controlled. "How about we build up to it gradually?"

Richard was mad at me. I could see it in the tightness of his face and posture.

I took the bull by the horns. "Why are you mad at me?" I asked.

"Maybe because you ran off and tried to kill yourself? Christ, Viviane."

"I didn't try to kill myself."

"You let yourself get so deep into your delusion that you almost died."

I resented that. "It wasn't a delusion. I found Colin."

Richard looked down at the floor and sucked on his teeth. That meant he was trying to regain control of himself. "This is my fault. I saw it coming. I knew I should have increased your medication. No matter. You're back on it now. We'll build the dosage gradually and stop when it's right."

I narrowed my eyes at him. "Don't I get a say in this?"

Richard said, voice tense, "You were found out in the middle of nowhere, at some farmhouse, having been assaulted and raped. That is not my definition of fine."

"I wasn't raped."

"We found evidence that you were."

The horror built in my stomach. "How do you know that?"

"I know because I had them do a rape kit at the hospital. I didn't know what you'd been through."

Silence hung in the room, heavy and thick, as I processed what he'd just said.

Eventually, I told him, "I was with Colin."

He sighed heavily. "Colin is dead." The words held no real power, and they came out flat. We both knew Colin wasn't dead.

Richard took a deep breath. It was the patience-inducing breath he had taught me, in through the nose and out through the mouth. "Vivi, listen to me. You have a mental illness that causes you to hallucinate and have delusional thoughts. You know this. You know that not everything you see and hear is real. It's chemicals and neurons misfiring in your brain."

"Not this time."

"You were babbling at the hospital about flying with Colin. You said he had wings. What part of that wasn't a hallucination?"

I knew how it looked, and it terrified me.

Richard said, "How many men have you known who could sprout wings and fly?"

"Two."

Richard smiled a little like he thought I was being cute. "Don't you think it's more likely that your subconscious twisted him into an angelic hero who was there to rescue you from the man in the car?"

I knew it sounded made-up. In my old reality, people didn't get kidnapped by their doctors. They weren't hunted by their brothers. They weren't princes from other realms, and they didn't have wings.

Richard pushed onward. "If you believe the voices and the visions, then you feed them, and they get worse."

In my old reality, ghostly hags didn't kill people.

Richard said, "Your grief has made you vulnerable. You're in the midst of an episode. But, you're going to pull out of it."

In my *new* reality, however, help was just a knock away. A double rap sounded on the door.

Richard shouted, "In session!"

The door opened anyway, and Detective Hayward stuck his head in.

Richard stood abruptly. "You can't talk to her right now, detective. She's still in a fragile state. You'll have to come back later."

"I don't think she's nearly as fragile as you want her to be, Dr. Reuter." Something in Detective Hayward's tone made me look more closely at him. For a change, he wasn't studying me. He had Richard in his sights.

Richard walked toward the detective "She's been through a lot. I think you should go."

Hayward stuck his tongue in his bottom lip, gaze dropping to the floor. After a moment, he said, "I can't deny that Miss Rose has been through a lot, and to be honest, I can't think of a good reason to bother her right now. However, I do have some questions for you, Dr. Reuter."

"For me?" Richard's surprise was evident. "I don't have time for that."

"I'm afraid you'll have to make time. Would you come with me, please?"

Richard's cheeks went splotchy, as if he had a rash. He didn't move. "It will have to wait. I'm in the middle of—"

"I'm not asking, Dr. Reuter. I'm telling. You're wanted for questioning. I'm here to accompany you down to the station."

"Whatever for? If you insist on talking to me, then we can do it in my office, I suppose."

"No, sir. We can't."

Richard crossed his arms on his chest. "What the hell is so damned important?"

Hayward sighed. "Why don't we start with the fact that the body in the photos I sent you wasn't Colin Aubrey. I have to admit, I'm very curious about why you didn't say anything."

Richard's mouth opened on a half-formed word. He changed his mind and closed it, then started again. "I never looked at those photos. Are you saying it wasn't Colin they pulled from the lake?"

Hayward gave an amused chuckle. "You need to come with me, doctor." He opened the door and waited for Richard to accompany him. "Let's not impose any more unpleasantness on Miss Rose."

"I didn't identify the body. Rosenblum did. Why don't you talk to her?"

"Trust me. When we find her, we'll have a ton of questions for her. Now, please, if you would come with me."

Richard turned to me and said, "I'll be back later."

Just before Hayward closed the door, one side of his mouth quirked up, and the detective winked at me.

As if she'd been waiting for them to leave, Corona rushed in a moment later. She came straight to the bed and started undoing my restraints, no easy feat with one arm in a cast and sling.

"Wish I could help," said Simon from the end of the bed.

I was happy to see them. "I'd hug you, but I'm on a no-hug diet for awhile."

"Then kisses it is." Corona planted one right on my lips. There was nothing sexual about it. It was warm and soft, sweet and full of love. It brought tears to my eyes.

Corona asked, "Did you hear they fired Marsha? A lot of things came out about her."

"That's great. But, how did you end up back here? How's your arm?"

She waved her good hand all around. "Don't worry. It's no big deal. I called Jake. He worked things out for me."

"Worked what things out?"

"I'm going to live at his haven in Wyrdwood, Oregon. He'll be my doctor from now on." Her eyes shone with excitement.

In my old reality, psychologists didn't rescue you from cruel institutions.

She put her hand on my cheek and her nose to mine. Her eyes crossed. "You should come too."

"It sounds nice." I was a bit in awe of Corona. She had so much hope.

"Talk to him. Besides, he's got the ashes. I left them with him, for safekeeping." Corona dug in her pocket and pulled out the business card I'd thrown away. She held it out to me. She had taped it back together. Printed on antiqued card stock, with old-fashioned lettering, it said "Jake Lamb, M.D., Wyrdwood, Oregon." It had his phone number on it.

She produced my cell phone from her other pocket. "I snuck this back in with me. Call him. What have you got to lose?"

"Just so I can get Jaxon's ashes back," I said.

I took the phone and carefully dialed the number.

Corona bounced.

When Jake answered, he said, "Lamb, here."

"It's Viviane. Viviane Rose. I'm calling about the gym bag Corona left with you."

"Hi. I'm glad to hear from you. How are you?"

"Recovering." My whole being was vibrating. "Corona tells me you're taking her to Oregon."

"True. There's a spot for you too, if you'd like."

"Answer me this. Have you ever been to a place called Apfallon?"

Jake was silent. When he answered, his voice was soft, as if he were afraid to spook a nervous horse. He said, "Yes. Many times."

My heart skipped a beat. "Can I bring my mom with me?"

"Absolutely. I wouldn't have it any other way."

His answer lifted a weight off me, and I inhaled as if I'd been holding my breath. Peoria had lost me.

I could never go back to the laundry, to the daily—*tick tock*—grind that I'd used to shelter myself. I wasn't that woman anymore. I had uncovered aspects of myself that I couldn't put away again. I'd had a glimpse into the world beyond, and I wanted more.

◆◆◆

# CHAPTER 37

Later that morning, alone in my room, I received a call from Mom's lawyer Divana Smart. She had a cool, casual voice with just a hint of old-fashioned manners. It had been fifteen years since I'd received the letter from her about my mother being alive.

"Miss Rose," she said, "what a delight to speak with you after so many years. I trust you're well?"

"Yeah, I'm good, thank you. Uh, and you?"

"I'm wonderful." She paused just long enough that a redirection to the business at hand wasn't rude, then said, "I'm calling with regard to the letter you sent the firm. I've made some progress on your request, and I wanted to warn you that I'll be coming by the Vince Malum Residential Living Center shortly after midday to serve papers to your psychologist, Dr. Richard Reuter, and to get you and your mother out of there."

I couldn't have been more flabbergasted.

She must have sensed it or deduced it from my utter silence, because she said, "I realize this may be something of a shock, and I apologize for ambushing you, but it was imperative that we move quickly. If you do not wish to leave the Center, please tell me now."

"No. Yes, I want to leave."

Divana Smart chuckled—an alto, feminine sound that made me smile. "It's long overdue, Miss Rose. I was dismayed to learn that you were being held against your will. Dr. Reuter's misconduct came as quite a surprise. He may be facing jail time for the forged papers, and he'll undoubtedly lose his license to practice. Richard Reuter is an intelligent sociopath who thinks of you as nothing more than a possession."

"Well," I said, "when you put it like that…"

"I'm not the only one who thinks so. The courts agree. I have a court order remanding you to your own guardianship and putting your mother under your care. Thanks to the evidence you sent us, it wasn't difficult to convince a judge that you were being railroaded."

"Good."

"I spoke with your grandfather, and he's eager to have you and Gisèle both back in his home. I'll take you there for starters, and if you want to go elsewhere after that, it'll be entirely up to you."

"Thank you." A mix of excitement, gratitude, and fear overwhelmed me. My whole world was changing.

"Wow," said Simon as I hung up. "So, you're getting out, are you?"

A smile spread across my face.

"This is a big moment." Simon was moving across the room in front of me.

"It's going to be a new start, for all of us."

Simon said, "Too bad I won't be going with you."

I hadn't expected that. I'd assumed that Simon went where I went. "What do you mean?" My voice had gone airy.

"I have things I need to do."

"What kinds of things?"

"That's not really your business, now is it?" He stopped near the door. "I don't know how long it will take me, but I'll visit you as soon as I can. For now, I just want you to know how proud I am of you. You've handled yourself like a champion these past few months."

"Wait, you're leaving right now?" I had a lump forming in my throat.

"You won't be alone. Corona will be with you. You can rely on her, you know? She's a saucy little wench, and she's got a good head on that scrawny neck of hers. You'll be fine."

I was silent for a long moment, trying to think of something to say to keep him with me, but nothing came to mind. He had always dropped in and out of my world, though this was the first time he'd warned me and bothered to say good-bye. That made it somehow more serious.

Simon said, "I'll see you in Wyrdwood."

I blinked back tears and confessed, "I'll miss you."

"I'll miss you too, sweet Viv."

I waited, listening, and after a moment, the words came of their own accord. I said, "I love you, Simon," though I had no idea whether he was still there to hear them, or not.

◆

I stood at my window and watched a white Mercedes cruise up the driveway to the circular turn-around in front of Vince Malum Residential Living Center. It parked close to the entrance, ignoring the "No Parking" signs.

As the woman emerged from the car, she tossed her long blond braid to her back. The starkness of its style suited her, as did the crisp, linen pantsuit—cream with a white blouse. Although she was younger than I'd expected, I had no doubt that she was Divana Smart.

She took her time, tucked an envelope under her arm, and browsed the main house's façade as she approached and entered it.

I'd spent the previous few hours packing and getting Mom ready to go. None of the nurses had bothered with us. Lunch came and went, and Corona joined me in the waiting. She was more antsy than I was.

"Let's go down to the rec room and wait," Corona suggested, so we did.

The ladies were all there, languid in the after-lunch haze. Eun Hee played a quiet and haunting tune on the piano. Calla and Iraida bent over that week's puzzle, an antique map of the world. They were a salt and pepper set, Calla pink and fair, Iraida dark and draped in black.

Dahlia was curled up on a couch, reading a book and chewing on the nub of a fingernail. Una stood guard in the corner, rocking from foot to foot, keeping an eye on things. She was closest, so I approached her first. She kept her gaze everywhere except on me.

"I'm leaving today, Una," I said. "For real. I'll think of you often."

She didn't respond, but as I turned away I caught a flicker of movement at her eyes. She looked at me. That she had looked said it all.

"Hey, Dahlia," I said, moving to stand beside her. "I'm out of here today."

"I've heard that before," she replied.

"No, I mean it this time. There's a lawyer coming with papers to get me out."

"Uh huh." She looked up without moving the rest of her face and lowered her book into her lap.

"Look, I just wanted to say thank you." I smiled. "You've been a good friend."

Dahlia shrugged, stoic. "No sweat," she said. "You're the most interesting thing to happen around here in years. I should be thankin' you."

That made me laugh. "Maybe I'll see you again some day."

"I hope not. That'll mean they brought you back here." She picked up her book and turned her attention to it. I'd been dismissed.

I skirted around the couch and joined Calla and Iraida at the puzzle table.

"Hey," I said.

They looked at me without saying a word.

"I'm leaving today, for real, for good, and I wanted you to know how grateful I am for your help with the break-out and everything."

"It was no trouble," said Calla. "Don't come back this time."

"I won't."

"As-salaamu 'alaykum." Iraida's face was half-hidden by a veil, but her eyes were soft and gentle. *Peace be upon you.*

I mush-mouthed my way through the response, unsure if I was getting it even close to right. "Wa 'alaykum as-salaam." *And upon you, peace.* The inverted wording of the call and response always felt magical to me, somehow representative of my world, of the looking glass through which I saw everything, not as it was, but somehow flipped.

The crinkles and sparkles in her otherwise pitch-black eyes told me she was pleased.

I crossed to the piano where Eun Hee still played softly. She indicated I should sit down beside her. I did, and she adjusted her playing. The mysterious, gentle tune settled down into a familiar plinking, into a memory from childhood, and now from the Center. I'd never hear "Chopsticks" again without thinking of Eun Hee.

I joined her, taking the melody away from her and letting her soar on the harmony.

After a minute of playing together, she leaned toward me and, without looking at me, said, her voice gone husky, "I'm a little bit in love with you. You better take care of yourself." She leaned back and took the dance of notes to a whole new level.

I smiled, but I didn't think she saw.

The entrance buzzer rang, cutting short our song. I released the melody, and Eun Hee brought the harmony to a satisfying conclusion. With a hand on her shoulder, I stood, my gaze locked on the door, as was everyone else's, even Una's.

Nurse Jones—the white queen—came out of her office and stalked toward the double doors. No one ever rang the buzzer, so she cocked her head to see who it was, long before she got close enough. One of her medical tennis shoes squeaked on the linoleum, loud in the silence that had descended upon the room.

All eyes watched.

The glare on the glass obscured the person on the other side, but—when Nurse Jones pulled open the door and asked, "May I help you?"—everyone got a good look at the blond, beautifully statured woman who stood there.

Several caught their breath just at the sight of her, and several others gasped when she said, "I'm here to free Viviane and Gisèle Rose," and handed Nurse Jones a copy of the court order.

# CHAPTER 38

Abram came out of the house as soon as Mom and I pulled up in Ms. Smart's fancy car, as if he'd been watching for us. By the time he got to the curb, Mom and I were both out on the sidewalk, equally eager.

I couldn't have been more shocked when he hugged Mom to him and cried in her hair. I'd never seen my grandfather so emotional. It was as if a dam were breaking, a dam he'd shored up time and again over the years.

I heard him whisper to her, "I kept my promises. I kept them all."

She neither said nor did anything to indicate that she knew he was even there, but it didn't matter.

After awhile, he hugged me too, and although I was tempted to give him the same cold response that my mother had, I discovered that, after everything that had happened, in his arms I was a kid again, full of love for my grandfather.

By the time we got into the house, he had aged another ten years. He was shaking. Ms. Smart and I helped him into his recliner. The lawyer crouched beside him and asked, "Mr. Rose, is there anything I can get you?"

He shook his head, unable to take his eyes off my mom. "You already answered my prayers," he told her. "Thank you."

"It's my pleasure," said Ms. Smart, "but all I did was file paperwork. It was your granddaughter who saw through Dr. Reuter's lies. She's the one who pulled the plug."

Abram said, "He lied to me too," and his eyes filled with tears again. He hid them behind a hand.

Ms. Smart said, "I need to go." She came to me. "Viviane—may I call you Viviane?"

"Of course."

"Please call me Divana. And please, don't hesitate to ring if you need anything at all from Bagley, Smart, and Cobb. We're here for you." Up close, she had the most amazing green eyes and ageless skin I'd ever seen.

I accompanied her to the door. "Thank you, for everything."

"You're quite welcome," she replied, resting a hand lightly on my shoulder. She smiled at me, and I found myself automatically smiling back.

She turned away and headed down the walkway, calling over her shoulder, "Look me up when you get to Wyrdwood. I may have a job for you."

I stood there blinking, watching until she'd driven out of sight. When I returned to the living room, I found Abram on the couch with my mom. She was *there*, with him. I could see it in the tilt of her head and the awareness in her eyes.

"Don't cry, Dad," Mom said. "Someday, she'll understand."

"I promised," he said.

"Yes, you did." Mom reached out and laid her hand on his, then she looked over her shoulder at the wall. "I don't have much time." Leaning forward, she kissed Abram on the cheek.

"Don't go."

"I have to. I'm sorry. I know how hard this has been on you."

Abram straightened his back and shoulders.

Mom said, "You have to let us go for now, both of us. But we'll come back to you, and when we do, we'll be able to stay, all of us, together."

"Promise?" asked Abram. He studied her face as if he were starving for the sight of it.

"I promise," said Mom. She rested a hand on his cheek. "I love you, Dad."

She was there a moment longer, a breath in and out, and then I saw the spark leave her eyes, her facial features relaxed, and it was as if something had cast the tunnel to her consciousness into darkness.

"But, baby girl, I'm all alone here." Abram pulled his daughter to him and rocked her like the child she had once been. I'd never seen my grandfather with her, had never seen that sorrow and love on his face. I was immediately ashamed of all the terrible, mean things I'd said. It stuck in my throat and made my jaw ache.

I knelt at his knee. "What did you promise?"

Abram looked at me with watery, old man eyes, and several seconds passed before he answered. Finally, he sniffed and said, "I promised your mother that I'd stay away from the Center."

"Why?"

"So they wouldn't find *you*. They've been searching for years, waiting for you to appear. Your mother left us because she thought it would keep you safer."

"They?"

"Your father's enemies." Abram set Mom gently back against the cushions and turned to face me. "They're dangerous, Viviane. If they ever found you, they'd take you away, and you'd never see home again."

I sat back on my heels. "I don't understand. I've been going to the Center for twenty years. I'd think they'd have found me by now if they were looking that hard."

Abram shook his head dourly. "They're not familiar with the sound of your heart strings. They know Gisèle's, and my own are also familiar to them, especially the tones I put out when I'm with her. We're taking a huge risk—she and I—being here in the same house together. I hope the charms hold until you and Gisèle can get underway."

"My father's enemies?" I asked. "Are they…do they…

do you know about the other realms?"

Abram's gaze lifted sharply to my own and locked there. "Yes. You?"

I grinned. "Oh, yes."

My grandfather took a deep breath and shook his head in wonder. "That's a relief. Are you aware that your father was from a place called Apfallon?"

I felt heat rising to my cheeks and heart, anger and other emotions fighting for dominance. *Why had no one told me?* The pieces were finally coming together.

"That's," I said, "why I can see things other people can't." My mind went to my mom's journal entries.

"Yes," Abram said. "You see things because you're half Apfallonian."

"All this time—"

"Now, hold on," he interrupted me. "Before you get mad, let me explain why I couldn't tell you."

"Go on," I prompted.

"Right now," he said, "you're thinking it would have been easier if you'd known what you were seeing was real, but you're wrong. You think you felt different from other kids because you had hallucinations? Just imagine for a minute how you'd have felt and acted if you knew they were real. Now, imagine what would have happened if you'd told somebody you believed they were real. They'd have locked you away much younger." He rubbed his hands over his face. "What I did, keeping this from you all those years, might've been evil, but it was the lesser of two evils. Sometimes, when you love somebody, you have to do wrong in order to do right by them."

Suddenly, I understood. I thought of Lettie. I knew I couldn't tell her I'd flown with Colin. My own best friend would think I'd gone off the deep end.

"I need to lie down," I said quietly.

Abram agreed.

# CHAPTER 39

We stayed with Abram for a week longer, protected by charms placed on the house. Lettie came over nearly every day, and we hung out like we had before my world cracked. On our last morning together, I made her breakfast after her graveyard shift in the laundry. She sat at the counter and said, "I can't believe you're leaving."

"It's surreal, I know." I sat beside her and set our omelets in front of us. "It's all happening so fast."

She put her hand on my arm. "Are you sure about this?"

"Positive. Jake has this amazing new therapy. It's exactly what I need."

"Well," Lettie said, "I'd rather you be healthy and there than sick and here. But, do you really have to go that far?"

"I need to get out of here."

"Okay." A tear dropped off the end of her nose, into her omelet.

"Oh, honey." I put my arms around her. "It'll be okay. You can come visit. I've heard it's beautiful out there. They have mountains and ocean."

"I will," she said, her voice tremulous with emotion.

"I'll visit. A lot."

We hugged for a long while, both crying our good-byes.

◆

Abram drove us to the airport. Mom sat in the front seat. Corona and I sat in the back with luggage on our laps.

I watched Peoria slide past, outside the car, the stream of time flowing onward, my history falling away behind me.

I thought of Lettie. I was going to miss her so much, but when I couldn't tell her the truth, I realized she couldn't be as big a part of my life. It was one thing to ask my best friend to believe my fiancé had been kidnapped. It was another entirely to ask her to believe he was a prince from another realm who could sprout wings and fly. According to Corona, the minds of pureblooded Earth natives had their limits, and what Lettie didn't know couldn't hurt her.

Abram came into the main terminal with us, pulling Mom's suitcase behind him. He couldn't go beyond security, so he said his good-byes there. He hugged Mom, and I could see he was using every ounce of his strength to keep from getting emotional again. He had on his hard mask, the one I'd seen so often growing up. His lips pursed to keep back words he didn't dare say aloud for fear of losing control of himself.

I finally understood what that mask meant.

When he turned to me, he pulled an envelope out of his pocket. "These are for you. I found them when I was going through some old trunks in the attic, while you were gone. I want you to have them with you."

I took the envelope and opened it. Inside, I found two snapshots. One was from when I was little. I recognized myself at about five years old. I was seated at a picnic table covered with a checkered cloth and plates of food.

Abram was there, looking so much younger and happier.

My mom was there too, standing by the table with a plate in one hand. She was alert and smiling, having looked up for the photo as if someone had just called her name.

I stared at it for a long time, the memory of that day coming back in bits and pieces.

The other photo was even older, taken long before I was born. It showed a handsome man in a suit—Abram Rose. He had his arm around a woman who was seven or eight months pregnant.

Abram pointed to the woman. "That's your grandmother, Moira Rose."

I'd never seen a picture of her. Her features were so familiar, not unlike Mom's, but not quite the same either. She was beautiful with strawberry blonde hair that curled close to her head. She wore a purple dress whose hem rippled on a secret breeze. My eyes lifted back to her face, and my heart skipped a beat. It was Doc Bella. There was no mistaking the steadiness of her gaze and the non-committal smile.

Abram said, "She died during childbirth with your mother."

I opened my mouth to tell him it wasn't so but changed my mind. It wasn't my place to reveal Bella's secret to him, not there, not then. It was too much. I hugged him extra hard. His pain was the same as my pain, and it always had been. I just hadn't realized it. I whispered next to his ear, "Thank you, Grandpa."

◆

When I was a little girl, Grandpa used to take me down to the public pool in the summer. It was always filled with screaming boys and girls. The smell of coconut and chlorine could make me woozy with happiness.

The older kids would climb the long ladder to the high dive, ease out to the edge, then jump off. The crowd's cacophony was punctuated by their regular *kersplooshes*.

The first time I climbed that ladder, the height shocked me. I stood there, clinging to the steel railing at the back of the board, knocked-kneed and terrified. I was in the clouds, above the din.

The people below looked small, their heads bobbing in the water, petals on a puddle. The distance between me and the water seemed unbridgeable.

I lost my nerve and had to back down the ladder to the cruel jeers of the other children.

I never did climb back up, but I never forgot how it felt to stand at the edge, looking out into the open air with no promise that there would be anything but pain—and maybe even death—to catch me.

That's why I'd worked so hard for security, stability—tedium. I'd wanted my feet firmly planted on the ground, so I kept every day the same, more or less. *Tick tock.* The clock had ruled my world. I'd paced myself to the beat of the metronome that droned in my subconscious day after day, night after night.

When you spend your life at the edge of a precipice, you remain ever-vigilant for those unexpected gusts of wind or ground tremors. I knew the day would eventually come when I'd lose my footing and fall—or fly away.

As I stood at the airport window, looking out at the plane parked there, I remembered the high dive, the expanse of emptiness between me and the crystal waters, and the fear that had overtaken me as I realized how far up I had climbed.

I had arrived again at the top of the ladder, and I looked out at empty air. Who knew if there would be anything to catch me?

Then, Jake was at my elbow. "Hey," he said. "How are you doing?" His eyes crinkled with friendship.

·"I'm fine," I said.

"They're boarding the plane. Shall we?"

"Yeah."

Walking down the gangplank to the plane, I stepped out onto the diving board, exposed on all sides.

I found my seat, and Mom sat next to me, while Corona and Jake settled in across the aisle.

The diving board felt unstable. It moved beneath me. I wondered if I could back down the ladder again, or was it too late.

The plane pulled away from the building and taxied down the runway.

I dug in my purse for the straight pin I'd put there.

The plane accelerated, and Corona said, "There's a terabyte of adventure comin' our way! Let the download begin!"

My hands shook. The diving board rattled.

I felt the moment when it sprang, and I was launched upward and outward.

The plane left the ground.

I waited for the explosions or the heart attack, straight pin poised to prick me back to life. I waited to fall, but I didn't.

Eventually, I opened my eyes, and there we were, soaring across the sky, climbing into the atmosphere. I looked out the window and saw clouds *below* us. The moon was a huge sliver in the sky, antique white and gray against a backdrop of twinkling mysteries.

Who said there was no magic in the world?

Not long ago, people would have called me crazy if I'd told them that, one day, man would fly tens of thousands of feet above the ground. I'd have been laughed out of the village back then, maybe even locked up in an institution or stoned to death, and yet there I was.

Flying.

I dropped the pin to the floor and watched the moon slowly slide over the edge of the world.

## THE END

# Appendix

Bella Rosenblum placed the crystal bowl on the oak slab with care. She poured hot water into it from a thermos, pleased when the steam rose into the cold night air. All around her, the sounds of the forest hushed as if in anticipation of what her scrying would reveal.

With a whispered incantation, Bella infused her magick into the steam and water, asserting her will with words of focus and the names of the people whose minds she wanted to enter—whose eyes she wanted to see through.

♦

## "Colin Aubrey"

Colin felt the hag's frustration like a hum along his spine. Her scream, the rip of rending reality that accompanied her attacks, had woken him on more than one occasion. He'd never had the nerve to investigate it.

The hag had come looking for him. It wanted him gone from its world, and if it couldn't get to him, then it would go after anyone else whose discordance attracted it. That meant hunting other patients, people with gifts or curses.

Lately, the hag's attention had turned to Viviane. Maybe it knew that killing her would weaken him. Maybe it was just spiteful.

Colin was remembering his attempt to leave and draw the hag away. How it had failed. He was trying to find another way to keep Viviane safe without confronting the hag directly. *I can't just fly away,* he thought. *If I do, Bella will make sure I never see Viviane again, so long as I live. She can and would do that. I know. Or she might just leave me to deal with all this on my own. Fuck. I won't survive without her.*

*But that cunt of a hag...*

The hag was on the move. Colin felt it shifting at the base of his neck, as if he had a connection to it. He sat up in bed and looked at the clock. It was after 9:30 p.m., and the men's wing had gone quiet. The distant sound of the television in the rec room told Colin that the orderlies were distracted. He got up and crept from his room, driven by a sense of urgency. He saw no other choice but to confront it.

He palmed the secret keycard given to him so he could flee on a moment's notice if he had to. With it, he could move through the Center's passageways, and his instincts directed him to the back stairwell. As he opened the door, he thought, *I know you're here.* He didn't know what he was going to do if he came face to face with it.

The floor was cold on his bare feet, and a chill raised goose bumps on his arms. The stairwell was more emergency exit than anything else. It was undecorated concrete block. Colin went all the way down to the basement, pausing from time to time to listen. It wasn't long before he heard one of the doors open above, then footsteps.

Whoever it was stopped for a moment. In the pause, Colin heard a shuffling sound, soft like a whisper, but it echoed in the stairwell above.

Then a woman called out, "Hello?"

It was Viviane. Colin recognized her voice. *No, Viv, no. Go back.* He listened harder and stayed as still as he could.

Viviane descended a couple more steps, and her shadow appeared on the wall above Colin, stretching long. She stopped again. Her shadow stopped too, but other shadows didn't.

They kept moving.

Colin's scalp crawled.

Viviane said, "Who's there? Look, I don't care who you are or what you're smoking, but you're scaring me, so just say something."

Colin said nothing. He was listening and watching for the hag. He could feel her close, the vibrations in his bones so intense he felt they might liquefy. His legs went weak. *Go away, Viv. Leave!*

The shadows were expanding, moving like a storm front across the wall.

Colin had to get Viviane out of there.

◆

## "Malum Mara"

The stink of magick lingered in the hag's nose. She licked it off her fingers, putting almost her entire hand in her mouth to suck off the residue. Hovering, shivering in a clean corner, she let the sounds of simple humanity wash over her. She could hear them for a dozen yards all around, their voices blending into a babbling brook of white noise that soothed her.

She paused in her licking to watch the choreographed movements of the doctors, nurses, visitors, and patients—and the predictability with which they performed their functions. They were matter *without* magick, and their presence eased her pain and appeased her hunger—for the moment.

She thought of her target and its protector, the mated pair. So close she had come to destroying them, to purging them from her world—*her* world—the world she existed to consume. Instead, she'd toyed with them and found that play could be exhilarating.

Impure with magick, the pathogen had writhed beneath her, and she'd felt the acceleration of her core being, had known hunger unavoidable, and had willed it to lie still. It would've been neutralized and absorbed if it hadn't been for the protector.

The hunt stirred in her legs and excitation spread with crackling energy through her torso and out her extremities. She gave her palm one final lick, then lifted her nose into the air. She couldn't immediately expurgate that protected pathogen, but there were others, others who didn't have anyone watching over them.

With a hum of gratitude and anticipation, she thought of the infected one who had guided her there to the watering hole where she'd found so much delight. Eventually, she'd go back for that one too, she would, and then she'd be free to absorb the pathogen and its protector. For the moment, however, she contented herself with taking advantage of the convergence.

She melted through matter, swimming in Reality, at one with it as the shark is at one with the sea. She crossed space and followed the edge of actuality, never once slipping over the boundary into the forbidden fields, until at last, she arrived back at her nesting place.

She couldn't ignore the vibrations of her prey. They were gathered in this place in large numbers, a herd of them. Slowly, she would pick them off, one by one. And though her most recent attack had failed, she would soon succeed with one of the unprotected, and she'd feed.

Harmonic fluctuations summoned her, and she didn't have to think. Instinct took over. She kept to the high points, up near the ceilings where she wouldn't encounter any resistance. Slipping along gray veins, she made her way to the den of a vibrating female.

It sat there as if it belonged, pretending to be human, and that enraged her. It did *not* belong. She would *not* let it remain. She slid up alongside it and had it in her embrace before it knew what was happening. She enfolded it and touched it in its warmest places, her hands and body soaking up its will, its passion, and its consciousness. She drained it of those things, until nothing remained. Finally, she took its breath.

The rending was music to her ears, the scratch of nails on stone, the scream of sudden death. It was the tearing that allowed the healing, and by removing the foreign object, she created a vacuum. It was the vacuum that screeched in protest, like metal being crushed. The vacuum could not stay, would not stay; and until it was filled, until the warm, sweet flesh of space and time rushed in to fill it, Reality screamed.

♦

## "Nathanatos"

The son of Rebus and Ríoghain sat in the backseat of the limousine, cool air blowing out the vent at him. He let his chin drop forward, and the thick shock of his bangs slid down to veil his eyes. He didn't bother to push them back.

The news had been a mixed blessing. The police had called earlier that day to tell Nathan they found Colin's body. Under any other circumstances, it would have devastated Nathan, but since he was already furious with Colin, he couldn't find it in himself—not yet—to grieve. If anything, he was angrier.

The tinted windows kept the interior dark, and Nathan preferred it that way. The sunlight, his brother's domain, hurt his eyes and raised his temperature uncomfortably. It wouldn't be long before the sun had set, and meanwhile, he waited and listened to the industrial music coming out of the speakers. He had it turned up so loud he could hear the windows rattle with each bass beat. The music enveloped him and gave him the illusion that he was alone, instead of encased in a metal box amidst a hundred thousand Realists, all of whom, he thought, had as much imagination as a rock.

*Now I can go home,* he thought. *But I need to take proof back with me or Father will send me right back, probably with a few new scars for good measure. Lovely. I'll be glad when this is all over.* Nathan hated the duties imposed on him by his station and by his birth. He hated the politics.

Nathan studied his driver, Pest, wishing he himself could be such a simple man with such simple needs. The chauffeur was seated behind the wheel, his tablet in front of him. He scrolled without shame through a series of pictures of aroused women in leather—draped, wrapped, and shackled in chains. Nathan had had to trust Pest, and much to his relief, Pest had proven reliable—perhaps because of his simplicity.

A glint of gold hit the rear window, casting a dancing light inside. Nathan watched it with derision and cool patience. It foreshadowed a time for action. Nathan reached over and turned off the music. He opened the communication channel with the front seat and said, "I go in five minutes."

Pest lifted his head and turned an ear toward the barrier, but he didn't look back. In profile, his face was a high desert landscape of mesas and rock outcroppings. He nodded once.

The other thing Nathan liked about Pest was that he rarely spoke.

Nathan smoothed his eyebrows and straightened his sleeves. He suspected it would be an easy in-and-out, and if successful, he'd be done in this noisy, stinky, filthy world for awhile, maybe forever.

*I'm not amused, Brother,* he thought, observing the humans outside the car as if they were fish in an aquarium. *You just had to go and die, didn't you. That's infuriating on so many levels. I could've stayed home in the luscious— and well-missed—arms of Coriander. But no, you had to go and run away. And of course, Father chose me to chase after his rebel son.*

*What's worse, now that you're dead, it'll be my fault. Father will take all his frustration out on me. Oh, and now I'll be forced to sit the throne and be royal asshole when Father dies. I've spent my entire life avoiding the sycophancy and subterfuge of Gehenna politics. But once again, you've left me holding a bag full of turds and the maggots that live in them. I rue the day Father impregnated my mother. I wish I'd never been born.*

On cue, Pest got out of the car and came back to open Nathan's door for him. Nathan stepped out into twilight and took a deep breath of asphalt and exhaust. Across the parking lot, the Peoria County morgue was soaking up shadows, its windows blackened and deepening.

"Wait here," Nathan told Pest. He didn't look back or wait for acknowledgement. He knew Pest would obey. He strode across the lot to the building.

A woman at the front desk looked up and said, "Hello. Can I help you?"

Nathan stopped, attention trapped by the lobby's two-story mural of riverboats, industry, and farmland. He tore his gaze away from the appalling image and said, "I imagine so. I'm here to identify my brother's body. I'm Nathan Aubrey."

The woman's interest in him doubled. She directed him to a bank of chairs, and from where he waited, he heard the woman say into the phone, "We have a family member here for an identification. Number 6593-3667. It's the brother. Name's Nathan Aubrey. No, Aubrey. That's A.U. B as in boy. R.E.Y." She paused, listening, then said, "Yes. He's on his way down with John."

An escort came out of the back, checked a blue folder, and then called his name.

Nathan followed and focused on not thinking. A general disdain filled him for the people and the colon of a hallway down which they traveled. The escort's right shoe squeaked with every step on the linoleum floor, and Nathan fell into a rhythm with it.

They passed through a section of hall ripe with the scent of rotting flesh, shit, and chemistry. A Normal would never have noticed. Nathan sucked his cheeks in, tugged a handkerchief from his pocket, and pressed the silk to his nose. He stared at the back of the escort's head, with its just-been-fucked tangle and bland roots; he could feel the scowl on his face where the muscles tensed and pulled down the sides of his mouth. He had to remind himself to blink.

The escort took him to a small waiting room with a cozy arrangement of love seat and chair, a coffee table, a water cooler in the corner, and gentle music playing from hidden speakers. "Would you like to sit down?"

"No."

The escort produced a photograph-sized piece of paper from the folder and said, "They've explained to you that your brother was in the water for quite some time, so he may not look exactly as you remember him."

It wasn't phrased as a question, and though no one *had* explained that to Nathan, he nodded in acknowledgement.

The escort placed the photograph face down on the coffee table. Beside it, he set out a printed form and an ink pen. "If it's your brother, then I'll need you to sign this form. Take your time," he said and stepped back to the door, eyes locked on the floor. "Whenever you're ready."

Nathan was more than ready. It was the turning of the tarot card, flipping that photograph over. It spelled out Nathan's fate. A man was lying on a stainless-steel gurney. He was covered to his neck with a white sheet, and his head was supported on a hard, x-shaped headrest.

Even with the combination of bloating and lifeless flesh, Nathan could tell.

A blast of fury made his jaw clench and his eyes go hard.

*It's not Colin,* he thought. *It's not him.* Nathan's work wasn't done. He couldn't go home, and he had nothing to appease his father. It was the ultimate con, and he'd fallen for it.

The realization struck him funny. Laughter overtook him, and he tipped his head back and let it out. The look on the escort's face made him laugh even harder.

The escort came out. "So, it's *not* your brother?"

"Oh no," said Nathan between chortles. "It's him. It's definitely him."

*You're not dead.* Nathan wiped the laugh-tears from his cheeks. *But when I catch up to you—and I will catch up to you—I'm going to kill you DEAD.*

# Thank You from the Author
## WW24052020

If you enjoyed STALKING THE MOON, *please* take a moment to give it a review. Leaving a review is the kindest thing you can do for the authors you love and who love you back.

A peripheral novelette to this book, titled "Charlie Darwin, or the Trine of 1809," is available for free download when you subscribe my email list at WyrdwoodAngel.com/newsletter.

And, in appreciation, here's a sneak preview of the second book in the *Wyrdwood Welcome* trilogy.

◆

## JUMPING THE MOON

### Sneak Preview

I recently learned something important—that when you're on an adventure, your natural inclination is to face forward. Each developing moment brings new information, new sights, sounds, and feelings, so there's no possible way to look back without missing out on something.

As the plane taxied toward the airport—Portland International Airport a.k.a. PDX—I heard someone say that our flight had been "uneventful." On the contrary, it had been so full of events, I hadn't closed my eyes once. I'd never flown before.

My mom sat on my left, Corona at the window, and Jake was across the aisle from us. The flight from Peoria to Chicago had been scary. The plane was small, and we'd hit a lot of turbulence. Then O'Hare was enormous. We all had to stay together, which wasn't easy between Mom's lack of attention and Corona's attention to everything. Jake took charge of Corona, and I kept one hand on Mom.

I'd never seen so many people in one place in my entire life, all different, all living lives that felt—to them—just as solid as mine felt to me. All were going places, talking about things important to them, loving each other, working, thinking, breathing… and yet not once did I see a collision of bodies. It was miraculous.

When we got on the big plane, the flight attendant said, "Hi," and smiled at me. I beamed right back.

We found our seats, stowed our carry-ons, and settled in. Then we flew two thousand miles across the country. I looked out the window and saw clouds below us. *Below us!* There was a time when people would have called me a god for looking down upon the world from such a height. Or they'd have laughed me out of the village—maybe even locked me up in an institution. And yet there I was.

My eyes weren't big enough to take it all in.

We crossed the Rockies, and I saw mountains for the first time in my life.

Corona commented, "I always knew I was short, but I never knew I was so tiny." I couldn't have agreed more.

Why, I wondered, had I never left Illinois? Not even for vacation. I was almost to my thirties, and I'd spent the first third of my life stunted, hemmed in by schedules and duties. That ol' tick-tock of the clock. I'd never known what I was missing.

Everything changed the moment my car went into the lake. My eyes had opened even as I was drowning. That was when Colin Aubrey, my fiancé, was ripped from me, and when the machine that had been my life fell apart. The gears grinded. Springs sprung. And the cuckoo decided to fly away.

To Wyrdwood.

Still looking out the window, Corona asked, "How's Colin going to know where you went? Aren't you worried he won't be able to find you?"

I wove my hands together in my lap, and my pin came to mind. I shoved the thought aside. With more confidence than I felt, I said, "He'll find me. If he shows up at Abram's door, Abram knows to tell him where I am. And I left a letter for him."

"You must miss him."

I nodded. Being separated from Colin was like having a darkness sitting in your peripheral vision. I was always searching for his face in crowds, always on alert for his voice, scanning the skies for his winged silhouette. He was the last thing I thought about at night before sleeping and the first thing when I woke up, usually with alternating emotions of sadness and anger. He'd abandoned me. Twice. Three times if you count the time he dropped me while a thousand feet in the air.

For years, Colin had tried to tell me he could fly, and I just thought it was a delusion caused by his amnesia. To say that he'd surprised the hell out of me when he'd proven he had wings and could fly was the understatement of the century. That was the moment I knew for sure that I was either completely insane or there was much more to the story. I still couldn't think about how majestic he'd looked without a portion of my mind trying to sweep it under a rug.

"He'll show up," said Corona.

I rubbed my hands over my face and said, "I know," but I didn't know at all. I let my hands fall limp onto my lap. "Only thing is, I'm not his first priority, and I don't think he's safe with me."

Corona rested her hand on mine. "His family won't be trying to kill him forever. I hope. You have no idea where he is?"

"None. He went one way, and I'm going to Wyrdwood."

Corona was silent for a moment before asking, "What do you think it'll be like there?"

"I don't know," I admitted with a nervous chuckle.

"We'll be in a brand new place."

"A place called *Wyrd*wood." She emphasized the "weird."

I shrugged. "We'll fit right in."

"True!" She leaned in and lowered her voice. "And peeps there have lived their whole lives without ever once thinking about us, looking at us. Judging us. I'm pretty fucking psyched about that." Her brown eyes shone. "It's a brand new start, Viv. We can be squeaky, fresh out of the box." She did a little wiggle in her seat.

I laughed. "When you put it like that, it does sound kind of exciting."

◆

After a while, the pilot announced that we'd begun our descent into Portland, and we slid down through the clouds. The landscape appeared below us. I realized that this was the layer we lived in.

The suburbs of Portland sprawled across the land, each a maze of streets lined with houses. The area wasn't flat like Chicago. Hills covered with green trees forced mankind's structures to go over and around them. A thick river—the Columbia—snaked through it all. Portland was a vast hive of humans, buildings, and parking lots. Skyscrapers clustered together to one side. Long bridges crossed between land masses. Cars ran along them in solid streams, their headlights glowing.

I watched out the window as we approached the runway, pushing down my fear. The ground rose up to meet us. We were going so fast, and then there was a bump, a bounce, and the roar of the engines. A thrill rose up from my gut and made my chest feel full. My heart. We had landed.

Rain spattered the window, and it felt like a special welcome.

I said, "Hello, Portland."

We took down our carry-ons and followed the crowd off the plane, up another tube, and into PDX. It was smaller than O'Hare and much less chaotic. The people weren't in as much of a hurry. They sat around reading or looking out the giant windows at the planes criss-crossing between land and sky. No one was shouting or even talking loudly.

As soon as I was back on land, I whispered, "Simon?" I'd been doing so whenever I thought about it—ever since my invisible friend had left—checking to see if he was back. He wasn't. Or if he was, he wasn't declaring it. I had neither seen nor heard Simon since leaving Malum Center. He'd been my constant companion ever since I was thirteen. For so long, I'd thought he was a figment of my imagination. He'd been my guardian and guide throughout my toughest years. When I finally learned he was real, he left—or so it seemed. He wouldn't tell me where he was going or why. The silence he'd left in his wake made me feel sad and vulnerable.

Our little group walked through the Portland airport, past shops selling smoked salmon, fleece, and Trail Blazers' basketball souvenirs. Jake had done all this a thousand times before, so we followed him like ducklings to Baggage Claim. He tried to get us to walk instead of riding the moving sidewalk, but he lost that vote. Corona and I each took one of Gisèle's arms and guided her on. Then we streamed along, the breeze in our hair. When we walked too, it felt almost like flying.

Baggage Claim was in the underbelly of the airport. The energy there was different, the crowd impatient and anxious, everyone searching for something or someone. They surrounded large carousels with suitcases going around like a sushi bar. The people checked out each morsel to see if it was what they wanted.

A hole in the wall gave birth to suitcases, the newborns riding the merry-go-round. They all had that well-traveled look. It made me happy to see them claimed and reunited with their owners.

As we waited for our suitcases, a pair of women approached Jake. He greeted them with smiles.

"How was your trip?" asked a tall redhead with strong bones and a voice like melted butter. Something about her sparked my curiosity. She was a striking beauty, despite the ragged scar that cut down one side of her face. Dressed in a peach crocheted sweater, skinny blue jeans, and white sneakers with no socks, she had a cosmopolitan style that screamed self-confidence.

Jake replied, "Good. I'm glad it's almost over though." He launched forward to nab one of the suitcases.

The woman let her gaze drift over the rest of us, evaluating. She caught my eye, and I looked away.

The second woman was older, with black hair caught up in a French twist. A narrow streak of white grew from front-and-center, just above her forehead. Her dark eyes were warm and welcoming as she held her hand out to me. "You must be Viviane," she said. "I'm Rio. Welcome to the Pacific Northwest. We're your ride to Wyrdwood."

I shook her hand. "Thank you. It's nice to be here." I indicated my mother and Corona respectively. "This is Gisèle and Corona." Suddenly, I was feeling shy.

Corona bounced, "Do you work with Jake? Are you from Lost Lambs?"

The redhead took a step toward Jake, helping him move the bags onto a big cart.

Rio answered, "Yes, we are. You're going to love it there. We've got the ocean, the forest, mountains, a river… everything you could possibly want."

It was as if a cork had popped from Corona's mouth, and she started talking a mile a minute. Truth be told, I was grateful. I felt so overwhelmed by everything that I had no words. I don't think I could have made rational small-talk if I'd tried.

A girl with piercings all over her face walked by, as did a man with blue hair and a couple dressed in rags, wearing socks inside sandals. One woman had her blond hair all in knots, dreadlocks. People played with hand-held devices and talked to thin air, an earbud in one ear. I saw a man in a turban and a group of Japanese in suits, and an eagle.

*An eagle.* It flew down from a beam overhead and landed at the redhead's feet.

Corona gasped. *I* gasped. No one else noticed.

The eagle pecked at a nearby man's loose shoestring, pulling it fully undone.

The redhead laughed, deep and rich. "The looks on their faces!" she said.

Jake laughed, too. "Guys, this is Hilda, and that's Hugs, her familiar. She's harmless."

"Who?" Corona asked, "Hilda or Hugs?"

Hilda raised both eyebrows.

Jake said, "Both."

"Don't you believe it," Hilda said under her breath.

Corona asked, "No one but us can see Hugs?"

Jake nodded. "That's right. Hugs is a magickal creature. Normals can't see her."

That brought my overwhelm to a whole new level. I latched onto my mother, the noise and sights of the airport forgotten. I was so engrossed in watching Hilda and her familiar that I walked into someone's luggage and nearly fell. A strong hand captured my upper arm and kept me on my feet. When I looked up, a man with tusks looked down at me. *Not a man.* My insides began to vibrate at a low resonance. His eyes were kind, his smile gentle. He said, "Careful there."

My every instinct was to get away from him, and I nearly stumbled again.

Jake was at my side in a heartbeat. "Thank you," he told the man, helping me himself. "She's new to the Sight."

The tusked man rumbled a sympathetic hum and released me.

I realized I was holding my breath.

Jake put an arm around my shoulders. "You're okay. Let's get to the van."

I nodded, glancing back at the man-not-man. He was watching the carousel for his luggage and had forgotten all about me.

We caught up with the others.

I asked, "What was that?"

Hilda answered me, her tone clipped. "Who. *Who* was that. He's a person, like you and me."

My cheeks grew hot. "I'm sorry. I didn't mean…"

Rio said, "You would probably say he's a nature spirit. They're a race known as Orcneas. They've been around longer than humans."

Jake asked, "Where's Gisèle?"

"What? Mom?" I asked, turning in place to search for her. "Where is she?"

"Shit," Jake said. "Did you guys see where she went?"

"Oh holy crap," cried Corona. "I was watching the Orcneas!"

I took off into the crowd, searching for her.

"Viviane!" Jake called. "Wait!"

But I couldn't wait. Not a second. My heart was hammering. She could have been… But then I spotted her going out the exit doors. I took off running, pushing people out of my way. When I got to the exit, the automatic doors opened too slowly, and I squeezed through the moment the gap was wide enough.

Mom was crossing the sidewalk, moving steadily toward the curb. She stepped right into traffic.

"Mom! Stop!" I flew toward her, bent forward to reach for her. I grabbed a fistful of her sweater and yanked her back just in time. A car of laughing teens went by inches in front of her. I tugged her into my arms. "Mom! Don't do that!"

An instant later, Jake was at my side, guiding us both back to safety.

"Well," said Hilda dryly, "that was unexpected. Note to self: buy leashes."

Rio commented, "Ah, the complexities of family life."

I wanted to glare at them, but for some reason it struck me funny, and I started to laugh. It wasn't the good kind of laugh, but the edge-of-hysteria kind.

Jake stayed by my side, one hand on my shoulder. "Breath with me."

It took me the entire walk to the van before I had myself under control again.

TO BE CONTINUED…

Receive an alert when the next Wyrdwood book is available. Sign up for my mailing list at:
WyrdwoodAngel.com/newsletter

The Wyrdwood Welcome trilogy includes:

**Stalking the Moon** (1)<br>
**Jumping the Moon** (2)<br>
**Hexing the Moon** (3)

All available now.

# About the Author

Angel Leigh McCoy has worn many faces, told many stories, loved many people, and lived many lives. Through it all, writing has been her one constant.

Angel is a spark of creative force behind the epic **Dire Multiverse** (https://diremultiverse.com) and this darkly fanciful **Wyrdwood Project** (WyrdwoodAngel.com).

She's an award-winning video game writer, having worked on "CONTROL," IGN's Game of the Year 2019. Prior to that, she spent ten years weaving intricate tales for millions of *Guild Wars 2* fans. As a writer for White Wolf's *World of Darkness*, she created stories about vampires, changelings, mages, and werewolves.

# Mental Health Resources

**National Suicide Prevention Lifeline**
(https://suicidepreventionlifeline.org/) – speak with a real person (US). (1-800-273-8255)

**Suicide.org**
list of international suicide hotlines in many countries

**Help When You Need It**
(http://helpwhenyouneedit.org/) – a directory of services available all over the US.

**HearingVoices.org**
– a network of people who hear voices and those who love them. (US: [https://www.hearingvoicesusa.org/] or UK: [http://www.hearing-voices.org/])

**National Alliance on Mental Illness**
(https://www.nami.org/Find-Support/NAMI-HelpLine/
Top-HelpLine-Resources) – a directory of helpline resources (US)

**Checkpoint.org**
– an international list of services and help lines. "Wherever you are, whatever you need."

# Stalking the Moon